– a new publishing imprint to bring you the very best in adventure SF. Time travel, galactic empires, alien invasions – all the traditional elements that have made science fiction the most exciting form of literature of the 20th century. In Venture SF, we'll be bringing you novels of action adventure – no short stories, no fantasy, no boredom. If action adventure SF is your type of reading, then Venture SF is for you – every book published by us will be the first appearance in paperback in the UK. We'll be publishing one new book every month – Start collecting them now!

VENTURE SCIENCE FICTION SERIES

We All Died at Breakaway Station by Richard C. Meredith
Come, Hunt an Earthman by Philip E. High
Hammer's Slammers by David Drake
Interstellar Empire by John Brunner
The Starwolf Trilogy by Edmond Hamilton
Starhunt by David Gerrold
Sold – For a Spaceship by Philip E. High
Run, Come See Jerusalem! by Richard C. Meredith
Cross The Stars by David Drake
Chronicles of the Star Kings by Edmond Hamilton

Series editors, Rog Peyton and Rod Milner

Edmond Hamilton

CHRONICLES OF THE STAR KINGS

Two classic novels in one volume

Arrow Books
Venture SF

Arrow Books Limited
62-65 Chandos Place, London WC2N 4NW

An imprint of Century Hutchinson Ltd

London Melbourne Sydney Auckland
Johannesburg and agencies throughout
the world

First published in one volume 1986

Some of the material in *Return to the Stars* originally
appeared in different form in *Amazing Stories* and
Fantastic Science Fiction

Printed and bound in Great Britain by
Anchor Brendon Limited, Tiptree, Essex

ISBN 0 09 947860 9

Book One

THE STAR KINGS

1

JOHN GORDON

When John Gordon first heard the voice inside his mind, he thought that he was going crazy.

It came first at night when he was just falling asleep. Through his drowsing thoughts, it spoke sharp and clear.

"Can you hear me, John Gordon? Can you hear me call?"

Gordon sat up, suddenly wide awake and a little startled. There had been something strange and upsetting about it.

Then he shrugged. The brain played strange tricks when a man was half-asleep and the will relaxed. It couldn't mean anything.

He forgot it until the next night. Then, just as he began to slip into the realm of sleep, that clear mental voice came again.

"Can you hear me? If you can hear me, try to answer my call!"

Again Gordon woke up with a start. And this time he was a little worried. Was there something the matter with his mind? He had always heard it was bad if you started to hear voices.

He had come through the war without a scratch. But maybe those years of flying out in the Pacific had done something to his mind. Maybe he was going to be a delayed psychoneurotic casualty.

"What the devil, I'm getting excited about nothing," Gordon told himself roughly. "It's just because I'm nervous and restless."

Restless? Yes, he was that. He had been, ever since the war ended and he returned to New York.

You could take a young accountant clerk out of a New York insurance office and make him into a war pilot who could handle thirty tons of bomber as easily as he handled his fingers You could do that, for they had done it to Gordon.

But after three years of that, it wasn't so easy to give that pilot a discharge button and a "thank you" and send him back to his office desk. Gordon knew that, too, by bitter experience.

It was queer. All the time he had sweated and risked his

neck out there over the Pacific, he had been thinking how wonderful it would be to get back to his old job and his comfortable little apartment.

He had got back, and they were just the same as before. But he wasn't. The John Gordon who had come back was used to battle, danger and sudden death, but not used to sitting at a desk and adding up figures.

Gordon didn't know what he wanted, but it wasn't an office job in New York. Yet he'd tried to get these ideas out of his mind. He'd fought to get back into the old routine, and the fight had made him more and more restless.

And now this queer calling voice inside his brain! Did that mean that his nervousness was getting the best of him, that he was cracking up?

He thought of going to a psychiatrist, but shied at the idea. It seemed better to fight down this thing himself.

So the next night, Gordon grimly waited for the voice to call and prepared to prove to himself that it was a delusion.

It did not come that night, nor the next. He supposed it was over. Then the third night, it came more strongly than ever.

"John Gordon, listen to me! You are not having delusions! I am another man, speaking to your mind by means of a science I possess."

Gordon lay there in semi-sleep, and that voice seemed wonderfully real to him.

"Please try to answer me, John Gordon! Not with speech, but with thought. The channel is open—you can answer if you try."

Dazedly, Gordon sent an answering thought out into the darkness.

"Who are you?"

The reply came quickly and clearly, with a pulse of eagerness and triumph in it.

"I am Zarth Arn, prince of the Mid-Galactic Empire. I speak to you from two hundred thousand years in your future."

Gordon felt vaguely aghast. That couldn't be true! Yet that voice was so real and distinct in his mind.

"Two hundred thousand years? That's insane, impossible, to speak across a time like that. I'm dreaming."

Zarth Arn's reply came quickly. "I assure you that it is no

dream and that I am as real as you are, even though two thousand centuries separate us."

He went on. "Time cannot be crossed by any material thing. But thought is not material. Thought can cross time. Your own mind travels a little into the past every time that you remember something."

"Even if it's true, why should you call me?" Gordon asked numbly.

"Much has changed in two hundred thousand years," Zarth Arn told him. "Long ago, the human race to whose first era you belong spread out to the other stars of the galaxy. There are great star-kingdoms now, of which the greatest one is the Mid-Galactic Empire.

"I am high in that Empire, and am a scientist and seeker of truth above all else. For years, I and a colleague have been delving into the past by throwing my mind back across the ages, groping and making contact with minds of men whose spirits are attuned to my own.

"With many of those men of the past, I have temporarily exchanged bodies! The mind is a webwork of electrical energy which inhabits the brain. It can be drawn by suitable forces from the brain, and another electric webwork, another mind, installed in its place. My apparatus can accomplish that by sending my whole mind instead of just a thought-message into the past.

"Thus my mind has occupied the body of a man of past ages, while his mind was simultaneously drawn across time to inhabit my body. In that way, I have lived in and explored the history of many different eras of past human history.

"But I have never gone so far back in time as your own remote era. I want to explore your age, John Gordon. Will you help me? Will you consent to a temporary exchange of bodies with me?"

Gordon's first reaction was a panicky refusal. "No! It would be ghastly, insane!"

"There would be no danger," Zarth Arn insisted. "You would merely spend some weeks in my body in this age, and I in yours. And then Vel Quen, my colleague here, would effect a re-exchange.

"Think, John Gordon! Even as it would give me a chance

to explore your long-dead age, so would it give you a chance to see the wonders of my time!

"I know your spirit, restless, eager for the new and unknown. No man of your age has ever been given such a chance to plunge across the great gulf of time into the future. Will you reject it?"

Suddenly Gordon felt caught by the glamor of the idea. It was like a wild bugle-call summoning to adventure hitherto undreamed.

A world and universe two thousand centuries in the future, the glories of a star-conquering civilization—to behold all that with his own eyes?

Was it worth risking life and sanity for? If all this was true, was he not being offered a supreme chance at the adventure for which he had been so restlessly longing?

Yet still he hesitated. "I wouldn't know anything about your world when I awoke in it!" he told Zarth Arn. "Not even the language."

"Vel Quen would be here to teach you everything," the other answered quickly. "Of course, your age would be equally strange to me. For that reason, if you agree, I should want you to prepare thought-spools from which I could learn your language and ways."

"Thought-spools? What are they?" Gordon asked, puzzled.

"They are not yet invented in your age?" said Zarth Arn. "In that case, leave me some children's picture-books and dictionaries for learning your language and some sound-records of how it is spoken."

He continued. "You don't need to decide at once, John Gordon. Tomorrow I'll call you again and you can give me your decision then."

"Tomorrow I'll think that all this has just been a crazy dream!" Gordon exclaimed.

"You must assure yourself that it is no dream," Zarth Arn said earnestly. "I contact your mind when you are partly asleep because then your will is relaxed and the mind is receptive. But it is no dream."

When Gordon awoke in the morning, the whole incredible thing came back to him with a rush.

"*Was* it a dream?" he asked himself wonderingly. "Zarth

Arn said it would seem like one. Of course, a dream-person would say that."

Gordon still could not make up his mind whether or not it had been real, by the time he went to work.

Never had the insurance office looked so utterly drab and stifling as on that long day. Never had the petty routine of his duties seemed so barren and monotonous.

And all through the day, Gordon found himself dreaming wild visions of the splendor and magic wonder of great star-kingdoms two hundred thousand years in the future, of worlds new, strange, luring.

By the end of the day, his decision was reached. If this incredible thing was really true, he was going to do what Zarth Arn asked.

He felt a little foolish as he stopped on his way home and bought children's picture-books, language texts, and phonograph records intended for the teaching of English.

But that night, Gordon went early to bed. Strung to the highest pitch of feverish excitement, he waited for Zarth Arn's call.

It did not come. For Gordon could not even begin to fall asleep. He was too tautly excited even to doze.

For hours, he tossed and turned. It was nearly dawn by the time he fell into a troubled doze.

Then, at once, the clear mental voice of Zarth Arn came into his mind.

"At last I can contact you! Now tell me, John Gordon, what is your decision?"

"I'll do it, Zarth Arn," answered Gordon. "But I must do it at once! For if I spend many more days thinking about the thing, I'll believe myself going crazy over a dream."

"It can be done at once!" was the eager reply. "Vel Quen and I have our apparatus ready. You will inhabit my body for six weeks. At the end of that time, I will be ready for the re-exchange."

Zarth Arn continued rapidly. "You must first make me one promise. Nobody in this age but Vel Quen will know of this mind-exchange. You must tell *no one* here in my time that you are a stranger in my body. To do so might bring disaster on us both."

"I promise," Gordon replied quickly. He added troubledly, "You'll be careful with my body, won't you?"

"You have my word," was the answer of Zarth Arn. "Now relax yourself, so that your mind will offer no resistance to the force that draws it across the time-dimension."

That was easier to say than to do. Relaxing was not what a man felt like doing when his mind was about to be drawn from his body.

But Gordon tried to obey, to sink deeper into the dozing state.

Suddenly he felt a strange, uncanny turning inside his brain. It was not a physical sensation, but it gave a feeling of magnetic power.

Fear such as John Gordon had never before experienced shrieked in his mind as he felt himself rushing into unplumbed darkness.

2

FUTURE UNIVERSE

Consciousness came back slowly to Gordon. He found himself lying on a high table in a room of brilliant sunlight.

For some moments he lay looking up dazedly, feeling a terrible weakness and shakiness. Right over his head, as though just swung back, was a curious apparatus like a silver cap with many wires.

Then a face bent down into his view. It was the wrinkled face of an old, white-haired man. But the excitement he evidently felt made his blue eyes youthfully eager.

He spoke to Gordon in a voice shrill with excitement. But he spoke in a language that was almost entirely unfamiliar.

"I can't understand you," Gordon said helplessly.

The other pointed to himself and spoke again. "Vel Quen," he said.

Vel Quen? Gordon remembered now. Zarth Arn had said that was the name of his scientific colleague in the future.

The future? Then the two scientists *had* effected that incredible exchange of minds and bodies across the abyss of time?

With sudden wild excitement, Gordon tried to sit up. He couldn't do it. He was still too weak, and slipped back.

But he had got a glimpse of his own body as he sat up, and the sight had stunned him.

It wasn't his body. It was not John Gordon's stocky, muscular figure. This was a taller, slimmer body he now inhabited, one dressed in silky white sleeveless shirt and trousers, and sandals.

"Zarth Arn's body!" husked Gordon. "And back in my own time, Zarth Arn is awaking in mine!"

Old Vel Quen apparently recognized the name he spoke. The old scientist nodded quickly.

"Zarth Arn—John Gordon," he said, pointing at him.

The exchange had worked! He had crossed two thousand centuries and was now in another man's body!

It didn't feel any different. Gordon tried moving his hands and feet. Every muscle responded perfectly. Yet his hair still bristled from the ghastly strangeness of it. He had an hysterical nostalgia for his own body.

Vel Quen seemed to understand his feelings. The old man patted his shoulder reassuringly, then offered him a crystal beaker filled with foaming red liquid. Gordon drank it, and began to feel stronger.

The old scientist helped him get up from the table, and steadied him as he stood looking wonderingly around the room.

Brilliant sunlight poured through tall windows that filled all eight sides of the octagonal chamber. The light flashed and glittered off machines and instruments and racks of queer metal spools. Gordon was no scientist, and all this science of the future baffled him.

Vel Quen led him toward a corner in which there was a tall mirror. He stood transfixed the moment he caught a glimpse of himself in the glass.

"So this is what I look like now!" Gordon whispered, staring wildly at his own image.

His figure was now that of a tall, black-haired young man of well over six feet. The face was dark, aquiline and rather handsome, with serious dark eyes. It was altogether different from John Gordon's own square, tanned face.

He saw that he was wearing snug-fitting shirt and trousers. Vel Quen threw a long, silky white cloak around his shoulders. The old scientist himself was similarly attired.

He gestured to Gordon that he must rest. But weak as Gordon felt, he couldn't without first looking out at this unknown world of the far future.

He stumbled to one of the windows. He expected to look forth on wondrous vistas of super-modern cities, marvelous metropoli of the star-conquering civilization. But Gordon was disappointed.

Before him lay a scene of wild, forbidding natural grandeur. This octagonal chamber was the upper floor of a massive little cement tower which was perched on a small plateau at the edge of a sheer precipice.

Stupendous mountain peaks crowned with glittering white snow rose in the bright sunlight. From them and from the tower, dark and awesome defiles dropped for thousands of feet. There was not another building in sight. It looked much like the Himalayas of his own time.

Weakness made John Gordon sway dizzily. Vel Quen hastily led him out of the tower-room and down to a small bedroom on the floor below. He stretched on a soft couch and was almost instantly asleep.

When Gordon awoke, it was another day. Vel Quen came in and greeted him, then checked his pulse and respiration. The old scientist smiled reassuringly, and brought him some food.

There was a thick, sweet, chocolate-colored drink, some fruit, some wafers like dry biscuits. It was all evidently charged with nutritional elements, for Gordon's hunger vanished after the slight meal.

Then Vel Quen began to teach him his language. The old man used a box-like little apparatus which produced realistic stereoscopic images, carefully naming each object or scene he exhibited.

Gordon spent a week in his task, not going outside the tower. He picked up the language with astonishing quickness, partly because of Vel Quen's scientific teaching and partly because it was based on his own English. Two thousand centuries had greatly enlarged and changed its vocabulary, but it was not like a completely alien tongue.

At the end of that week Gordon's strength had fully returned, and by that time he was able to speak the language fluently.

"We are on the planet Earth?" was the first eager question he had put to Vel Quen.

The old scientist nodded. "Yes, this tower is located amid the highest mountains of Earth."

So it was the Himalayas whose snowy peaks rose around the tower, as Gordon had guessed. They looked as wild and lonely and grand as when he had flown over them in war days long ago.

"But aren't there any cities or people left on Earth?" he cried.

"Certainly there are. Zarth Arn chose this lonely spot on the planet, simply so that his secret experiments would not be disturbed.

"From this tower, he has been exploring the past by going back into the bodies of many men in various epochs of human history. Yours is the remotest period of the past that Zarth Arn has yet tried to explore."

It was a little overwhelming to John Gordon to realize that other men had found themselves in his own uncanny present position.

"Those others—they were able to return without trouble to their own bodies and times?"

"Of course—I was here to operate the mind-transmitter, and when the time came I effected the re-exchange just as I will do with you later."

That was reassuring. Gordon was still wildly excited by this unprecedented adventure into a future age, but he hated to think that he might be marooned indefinitely in a stranger's body.

Vel Quen explained to Gordon in detail the amazing scientific method of contacting and exchanging minds across time.

He showed him the operation of the telepathic amplifier that could beam its thought-message back to any selected mind in the past. And then he outlined the operation of the mind-exchange apparatus itself.

"The mind is an electric pattern in the neurones of the brain. The forces of this apparatus detach that pattern and embody it in a network of nonmaterial photons.

"That photon-mind can then be projected along any dimension. And since time is the fourth dimension of matter, the photon-mind can be hurled into past time. The forces operate in a two-way channel, simultaneously detaching and projecting both minds so as to exchange them."

"Did Zarth Arn himself invent this method of exchanging minds?" Gordon asked wonderingly.

"We invented it together," Vel Quen said. "I had already perfected the principle. Zarth Arn, my most devoted scientific pupil, wanted to try it out and he helped me build and test the apparatus.

"It has succeeded beyond our wildest dreams. You see those racks of thought-spools?* In them is the vast mass of information brought back by Zarth Arn from past ages he has explored thus. We've worked secretly because Arn Abbas would forbid his son to take the risk if he knew."

"Arn Abbas?" repeated Gordon questioningly. "Who is he, Vel Quen?"

"Arn Abbas is sovereign of the Mid-Galactic Empire, ruling from its capital world at the sun Canopus. He has two sons. The oldest is his heir, Jhal Arn. The second son is Zarth Arn."

Gordon was astounded. "You mean that Zarth Arn, the man whose body I now inhabit, is son of the greatest ruler in the galaxy?"

The old scientist nodded. "Yes, but Zarth is not interested in power or rule. He is a scientist and scholar, and that is why he leaves the court at Throon to carry on his exploration of the past from this lonely tower on Earth."

Gordon remembered now that Zarth Arn had said he was high in the Empire. But he had had no suspicion of his true exalted position.

---

* *Note:* Thought-spools were a development of the encephalographic records made as early as 1933 by American psychologists, in which the electric thought-fluctuations of the brain were recorded on moving tape. In this improved model, the encephalographic recording was played back through an electric apparatus and produced pulsations which re-created the recorded thoughts in the listener's brain. . . . Ed.

"Vel Quen, what exactly is the Mid-Galactic Empire? Does it take in all the galaxy?"

"No, John Gordon. There are many star-kingdoms in the galaxy, warlike rivals at times. But the Mid-Galactic Empire is the largest of them."

Gordon felt a certain disappointment. "I had thought the future would be one of democracy, and that war would be banished."

"The star-kingdoms are really democracies, for the people rule," Vel Quen explained. "We simply give titles and royal rank to our leaders, the better to hold together the widely separated star-systems and their human and aboriginal races."

Gordon could understand that. "I get it. Like the British democracy in my own day, that kept up the forms of royalty and rank to hold together their realm."

"And war *was* banished on Earth, long ago," Vel Quen went on. "We know that from traditional history. The peace and prosperity that followed were what gave the first great impetus to space-travel.

"But there have been wars between the star-kingdoms because they are so widely separated. We are now trying to bring them together in union and peace, as you unified Earth's nations long ago."

Vel Quen went to the wall and touched a switch beside a bank of lenses. From the lenses was projected a realistic little image of the galaxy, a flat, disk-shaped swarm of shining sparks.

Each of those little sparks represented a star, and their number was dizzying to John Gordon. Nebulae, comets, dark clouds—all were faithfully represented in this galactic map. And the map was divided by zones of colored light into a number of large and small sections.

"Those colored zones represent the boundaries of the great star-kingdoms," Vel Quen explained. "As you see, the green zone of the Mid-Galactic Empire is much the largest and includes the whole north * and middle of the galaxy. Here near its northern border is Sol, the sun of Earth, not far from the wild frontier star-systems of the Marches of Outer Space.

---

* *Note:* Six arbitrarily assigned directions were used as axes of reference in galactic travel—north, east, south, west, zenith and nadir. . . . Ed.

"The little purple zone south of the Empire comprises the Baronies of Hercules, whose great Barons rule the independent star-worlds of Hercules Cluster. Northwest lies Fomalhaut Kingdom, and south of it stretch the kingdoms of Lyra, Cygnus, Polaris and others, most of these being allied to the Empire.

"This big black blot southeast of the Empire is the largest dark cloud in the galaxy, and within it lies the League of Dark Worlds, composed of suns and worlds engulfed in the perpetual dimness of that cloud. The League is the most powerful and jealous rival of the Empire.

"The Empire is dominant and has long sought to induce the star-kingdoms to unite and banish all war in the galaxy. But Shorr Kan and his League have intrigued against Arn Abbas' policy of unification, by fomenting the jealousies of the smaller star-kingdoms."

It was all a little overwhelming for John Gordon, man of the 20th Century. He looked in wonder at that strange map.

Vel Quen added, "I shall teach you how to use the thought-spools and then you can learn that great story."

In the following days while he learned the language, Gordon had thus learned also the history of two thousand centuries.

It was an epic tale that the thought-spools unfolded of man's conquest of the stars. There had been great feats of heroism in exploration, disastrous wrecks in cosmic clouds and nebulae, bitter struggles against stellar aborigines too alien for peaceful contact.

Earth had been too small and remote to govern all the vast ever-growing realm of man. Star-systems established their own governments, and then banded into kingdoms of many stars. From such a beginning had grown the great Mid-Galactic Empire which Arn Abbas now governed.

Vel Quen finally told Gordon, "I know you want to see much of our civilization before you return to your own body and time. First let me show you what Earth looks like now. Stand upon this plate."

He referred to one of two round quartz plates set in the floor, which were part of a curious, complex apparatus.

"This is a telestereo, which projects and receives stereoscopic images that can see and hear," Vel Quen explained. "It operates almost instantaneously over any distance." *

Gordon stood gingerly with him on the quartz plate. The old scientist touched a switch.

Abruptly, Gordon seemed to be in another place. He knew he was still in the tower laboratory, but a seeing, hearing image of himself now stood on a stereo-receiver on a terrace high in a great city.

"This is Nyar, largest city of Earth," said Vel Quen. "Of course, it cannot compare with the metropoli of the great star-worlds."

Gordon gasped. He was looking out over a mammoth city of terraced white pyramids.

Far out beyond it he could glimpse a spaceport, with rows of sunken docks and long, fishlike star-ships in them. There were also a few massive, grim-looking warships with the Empire's comet emblem on them.

But it was the great city itself that held his stunned gaze. Its terraces were flowering green gardens with gay awnings and crowds of pleasure-seeking people.

Vel Quen switched them to other stereo-receivers in Nyar. He had glimpses of the interior of the city, of halls and corridors, of apartments and workshops, of giant underground atomic power plants.

The scene suddenly vanished from John Gordon's fascinated eyes as Vel Quen snapped off the telestereo and darted toward a window.

"There is a ship coming!" he exclaimed. "I can't understand it. No ship ever lands here!"

Gordon heard a droning in the air and glimpsed a long, slim, shining craft dropping out of the sky toward the lonely tower.

Vel Quen looked alarmed. "It's a warship, a phantom-cruiser, but has no emblem on it. There's something wrong about this!'

The shining ship landed with a rush on the plateau a

---

* *Note:* The telestereo operated by sub-spectrum rays many times faster than light, the rays that were the foundation of interstellar travel and civilization. Using the fastest of this famous group of rays, it could communicate almost instantly across the galaxy. . . . Ed.

quarter-mile from the tower. A door in its side instantly slid open.

From it poured a score of gray-uniformed, helmeted men who carried weapons like long, slim-barrelled pistols, and who advanced in a run toward the tower.

"They wear the uniform of Empire soldiers but they should not have come here," Vel Quen said. His wrinkled face was puzzled and worried. "Could it be—"

He broke off, seeming to reach a sudden decision. "I am going to notify the Nyar naval base at once!"

As the old scientist turned from John Gordon toward the telestereo, there came a sudden loud crash below.

"They have blasted in the door!" cried Vel Quen. "Quick, John Gordon, take the—"

Gordon never learned what he meant to tell him. For at that moment, the uniformed men came rushing up the stair into the room.

They were strange-looking men. Their faces were white, a pallid, colorless and unnatural white.

"League soldiers!" cried Vel Quen, the instant he saw them thus close. He whirled to turn on the telestereo.

The leader of the invaders raised his long, slim pistol. A tiny pellet flicked from it and buried itself in Vel Quen's back. It instantly exploded in his body. The old scientist dropped in his tracks.

Until that moment, ignorance and bewilderment had held Gordon motionless. But he felt a hot rage burst along his nerves as he saw Vel Quen fall. He had come to like the old scientist, in these days.

With a fierce exclamation, Gordon plunged forward. One of the uniformed men instantly raised his pistol.

"Don't blast him—it's Zarth Arn himself!" yelled the officer who had shot down Vel Quen. "Grab him!"

Gordon got his fists home on the face of one of them, but that was all. A dozen hands grasped him, his arms were twisted behind his back, and he was held as helpless as a raging child.

The pallid officers spoke swiftly to Gordon. "Prince Zarth, I regret we had to blast your colleague but he was about to call for help and our presence here must not be detected."

The officer continued rapidly. "You yourself will not be

harmed in the slightest. We have been sent to bring you to our leader."

Gordon stared at the man. He felt as though all this was a crazy dream.

But one thing was clear. They didn't doubt he was Zarth Arn. And that was natural, seeing that he *was* Zarth Arn, in body.

"What do you mean?" he demanded furiously of the other. "Who are you?"

"We come from the Cloud!" answered the pallid officer instantly. "Yes, we are from the League and have come to take you to Shorr Kan."

It was still all baffling to John Gordon. Then he remembered some of the things that old Vel Quen had told him.

Shorr Kan was leader of the League of the Dark Worlds which was the greatest foe of the Empire. That meant that these men were enemies of the great star-kingdom to whose ruling house Zarth Arn belonged.

They thought that *he* was Zarth Arn and were kidnapping him! Zarth Arn had never foreseen anything like this happening when he had planned the exchange of bodies!

"I'm not going with you!" Gordon cried! "I'm not leaving Earth!"

"We'll have to take him by force," rasped the officer to his men. "Bring him along."

3

MYSTERY RAIDERS

There was a sudden interruption. Into the tower came running a uniformed soldier, his face livid with excitement.

"The radar officer reports three craft of cruiser size heading in from space toward this quarter of Earth!"

"Empire patrol-cruisers!" yelled the League officer. "Quick, out of here with him!"

But Gordon had seized the moment of their alarm to bunch himself. Now with a violent effort he broke free of their grasp.

He grabbed up a heavy metal tool as the pallid men rushed him and struck savagely with it at their faces.

They were at a disadvantage for they did not want to kill or injure him, while he had no such reluctance. His savage blows dropped two of the soldiers. Then the others seized him again and wrested his makeshift weapon from him.

"Now to the ship with him!" panted the pallid League officer. "And hurry!"

Held by four big League soldiers, Gordon was dragged down the stairs and out of the tower into the biting, frosty air.

They were halfway to the shining ship when he saw the grim black gun-muzzles that projected from its side swinging suddenly to point skyward. Volleys of small shells burst upward from them.

The pallid officer yelled as he looked upward. John Gordon glimpsed three massive, fish-shaped warships diving straight down toward them.

There was an immense explosion. It hit Gordon and his captors like a giant hand and hurled them from their feet.

Half stunned, Gordon heard the deafening drone of great ships swooping toward the ground. By the time he stumbled to his feet, it was all over.

The League ship was a wreck of fused metal. The three cruisers that had destroyed it were landing. Even as they touched the ground, their small guns flicked deadly explosive pellets that picked off the dazed League soldiers who still sought to fight.

Gordon found himself standing, his late captors a heap of torn, blasted corpses less than a hundred feet away. The doors of the cruisers were sliding open, and men in gray helmets and uniforms came running toward Gordon.

"Prince Zarth, you're not hurt?" cried their leader to Gordon.

The man was big and burly, with bristling black hair and a craggy, knobby face whose complexion was faintly copper-red. His black eyes were snapping with cheerful excitement.

"I'm Hull Burrel, captain commanding a Sirius-sector patrol," he told Gordon, saluting. "Our radar spotted an unauthorized vessel approaching Earth, and we followed it to find it at your laboratory here."

He glanced at the dead men. "Cloudmen, by Heaven!

Shorr Kan has dared send men to abduct you! This could be cause for war!"

John Gordon thought swiftly. These excited Empire officers also naturally took him for the son of their ruler.

And he couldn't tell them the truth, couldn't tell them he was John Gordon in Zarth Arn's body! For Zarth Arn had made him promise to tell that to no one, had warned that to do so would mean disaster! He'd have to keep up the strange imposture with these men until rid of them.

"I'm not hurt," Gordon said unsteadily. "But they shot Vel Quen and I'm afraid he's dead."

They hurried with him to the tower. He ran hastily up the stairs and bent over the old scientist.

One look was enough. A gaping hole had been blasted in Vel Quen's body by the explosion of the tiny atomic pellet.

Gordon was appalled. The death of the old scientist meant that he was now completely on his own in this unfamiliar future universe.

Could he ever get back to his own body and time? Vel Quen had thoroughly explained the principle and operation of the mind-projecting apparatus. He might be able to operate it if he could get into telepathic contact with the real Zarth Arn.

Gordon quickly made up his mind. It was vital for him to stay here in the tower with the apparatus which alone could restore him to his own body and time.

"I must report this attack at once to your father, Prince Zarth," the captain named Hull Burrel was saying.

"There is no need," Gordon said quickly. "The danger is over. Keep the whole matter confidential."

He expected his authority as son of the sovereign to over-awe the captain. But Hull Burrel, surprise on his craggy copper face, demurred.

"It would be a breach of duty if I failed to report so serious a matter as a League raid like this!" the captain protested.

He went to the telestereo and touched its switches. In a moment on its receiver-plate appeared the image of a uniformed officer.

"Chief of Fleet Operations speaking from Throon," he said crisply.

"Captain Hull Burrel of the Sirius-sector patrol wishes to

report a matter of the utmost importance to his highness, Arn Abbas," declared the big coppery captain.

The official stared. "Cannot the matter be submitted to Commander Corbulo?"

"It cannot—its importance and urgency are too great," Hull Burrel declared. "I take the responsibility for insisting on this audience."

There was a little wait. Then on the telestereo the image of a different man flashed into being.

He was a massive giant well past middle age, with shaggy, bristling brows over penetrating, hard gray eyes. He wore a brilliantly embroidered cloak over a dark jacket and trousers, and his great, graying head was bare.

"Since when do mere naval captains insist—," he began angrily, and then as his image looked past Hull Burrel he caught sight of John Gordon. "So this concerns you, Zarth? What's wrong?"

Gordon realized that this massive, bleak-eyed man was Arn Abbas, sovereign of the Mid-Galactic Empire and Zarth Arn's father— *his* father.

"It's nothing serious," Gordon began hastily, but Hull Burrel interrupted.

"Your pardon, Prince Zarth, but this *is* serious!" He continued to the emperor. "A League phantom-cruiser clipped in to Earth and made an attempt to kidnap the prince. By chance my patrol was making an unscheduled stop at Sol, and we detected them by radar and followed them here just in time to destroy them.

Arn Abbas uttered an angry roar. "A League warship violating Empire space? And trying to kidnap my son? Curse that devil Shorr Kan for his insolence! He's gone too far this time!"

Hull Burrel added, "We weren't able to take any of the Cloud-men alive but Prince Zarth can give you the details of the attempt."

Gordon wanted above all else to minimize the whole thing and finish the nerve-racking strain of having to keep up this imposture.

"It must have been just a surprise sneak attempt," he said hastily to Arn Abbas. "They won't dare try it again—I'll be in no more danger here."

"No danger? What are you talking about?" rumbled Arn

Abbas angrily. "You know as well as I do why Shorr Kan was trying to get his hands on you, and what he'd have done if he succeeded!"

The massive ruler continued commandingly to Gordon. "You're not going to stay there on Earth any longer, Zarth! I've had enough of your slipping away to that remote old planet for your crazy secret scientific studies. This is what comes of it! We'll take no more such chances! You're going to come here to Throon at once!"

John Gordon's heart sank. To Throon, the royal planet of the sun Canopus which lay nearly halfway across the galaxy? He couldn't go there!

He couldn't carry on this masquerade in Zarth Arn's body at the court itself! And if he left the laboratory here, he'd have no chance of contacting Zarth Arn and re-exchanging their bodies.

"I can't come to Throon now," Gordon protested desperately. "I have to remain here on Earth for a few days more to carry out my researches."

Arn Abbas uttered a bellow of anger. "You do as I say, Zarth! You'll come to Throon and you'll come right now!"

And the emperor swung his angry gaze to Hull Burrel and ordered, "Captain, bring the prince here at once in your cruiser. And if he refuses, bring him here under guard!"

4

MAGIC PLANET

The big cruiser sped through the interstellar spaces at a velocity already hundreds of times that of light. Earth and Sol had hours before receded astern. Ahead of the ship expanded the heart of the galaxy, thick with glittering star-swarms.

John Gordon stood in the wide, many-windowed bridge of the *Caris* with Hull Burrel and two helmsmen, feeling a quaking inward awe as he looked at that incredible vista ahead. The enormous speed of the warship was evidenced by the fact that the stars ahead grew visibly brighter as he watched.

Gordon felt no acceleration, thanks to the dim, blue-glowing stasis of force that cradled everything in the ship. He tried to remember what he had learned about the motive power of these great ships. They were propelled by an energy drive which utilized the famous sub-spectrum rays that were the basis of galactic civilization.*

"It still seems crazy of Shorr Kan to send a League cruiser into our realm on such an errand!" Hull Burrel was saying. "What good would it do him if he did manage to capture you?"

Gordon had wondered about that himself. He couldn't see

---

* *Note:* Gordon's study of the history of two hundred thousand years had shown him how the entire structure of galactic civilization was based upon that epochal discovery of sub-spectrum rays.

The era of space-travel had really dawned in 1945 and '46, with the first release of atomic energy and the discovery that radar could function efficiently in space. By the end of the 20th Century, atomic-powered rockets guided by radar had reached the Moon, Mars and Venus.

Interplanetary exploration and exploitation had increased rapidly. But the vast distances to other stars remained unconquerable until late in the 22nd Century, when three great inventions made interstellar travel possible.

The most important of the three was the discovery of sub-spectrum rays. These were hitherto unsuspected octaves of electromagnetic radiation far below even the gamma and cosmic rays in wavelength, and which had velocities vastly greater than the speed of light.

Of these sub-spectrum rays the most useful were the so-called pressure rays in the Minus-30th octave of the spectrum, which could react against the tenuous cosmic dust of space with a powerful pressure. These pressure rays formed the driving power of star-ships. They were produced in generators powered by atomic turbines, and were jetted from the stern of a ship to drive it thousands of times faster than light.

The second vital invention was that of the mass-control. Einstein's equations had shown that if a ship travelled as fast as light, its mass would expand to infinity. This difficulty was overcome by the mass-control, which "bled" off mass as energy to maintain a constant mass unaltered by velocity. The energy thus obtained was stored in accumulators and fed back automatically whenever speed was reduced.

The final invention concerned the human element. Men's bodies would have been unable ordinarily to withstand those vast accelerations, but this obstacle was conquered by the cradle-stasis. This was a stasis of force which gripped every atom in a ship. The energy-drive jets gave their thrust, not to the ship directly, but to its stasis. Thus everyone and everything in the ship remained unaffected by acceleration. Magnetic apparatus furnished artificial gravity on shipboard, similar to that of the tiny gravitation-equalizers worn by all star-travellers.

the reason for wanting to capture the mere second son of the emperor.

"I suppose," he ventured, "that Shorr Kan figured he could use me as a hostage. I'm glad you got the murderous devils, for killing Vel Quen."

To forestall the strain of further conversation, Gordon turned abruptly. "I think I'd like to rest, captain."

With a quick word of apology, Hull Burrel led the way from the bridge and down by narrow corridors and catwalks through the ship.

Gordon pretended to glance only casually about him, but

The fastest of the sub-spectrum rays, those of the Minus-42nd octave, were so speedy that they made light seem to crawl. These super-speed rays were used in telestereo communication and also in the vital function of radar for the star-ships.

Using these inventions to build star-ships, mankind took at once to interstellar space. Alpha Centauri, Sirius and Altair were quickly visited. Colonies were soon established on suitable star-worlds. For some 10,000 years, Sol and Earth remained the center of government of a growing region of colonized stars.

Until then, there had been no serious conflicts. Aboriginal alien races of intelligence had been found at some star-systems and were helped and educated, but there was found no scientific civilization on any star-world. That had been expected, for if such a race existed it would have visited *us* long before we ourselves had conquered space.

But in the year 12,455, a group of star-systems near Polaris complained that Earth was too remote to appreciate their problems, and they set up an independent kingdom. By 39,000, the kingdoms of Lyra, Cygnus, and the Baronies of the great Hercules Cluster had declared independence.

Criminals and fugitives from the law seeking refuge in the Cloud eventually founded the League of Dark Worlds. By 120,000, the star-kingdoms were many. But the biggest was still the Mid-Galactic Empire, and hosts of star-worlds remained loyal to it. For convenience its government had been shifted in 62,339 from Earth to a world of the great sun Canopus.

The Empire took the lead of the star-kingdoms in the year 129,411 when the galaxy was suddenly invaded by alien and powerful creatures from the Magellanic Clusters outside. And after that invasion was repelled the Empire had steadily grown by exploring and colonizing the wild, unmapped star-systems in the frontier regions called the Marches of Outer Space.

Thus when Gordon found himself in the galaxy of this year 202,115, he found its star-kingdoms already old in traditions and history. Many wars had been fought between them, but the Empire had steadily sought to prevent such sanguine galactic struggles and to unify them in peace. But now the ominous growth of the League of Dark Worlds had reached a point where the safety of the Empire itself was challenged. . . . Ed.

was really devoured by interest in what he saw. There were long, narrow galleries of atomic guns, navigation rooms and radar rooms on this upper deck.

Officers and men whom they met snapped to attention, saluting him with deep respect. These men of the Mid-Gálactic Empire differed in complexion, some of them faintly blue of skin, others reddish, others tawny yellow. He knew it was because they came from different star-systems, and had learned that Hull Burrel himself was an Antarian.

Hull Burrel slid open the door of an austere little room. "My own cabin, Prince Zarth. I beg you'll use it till we reach Throon."

Left alone, John Gordon felt a slight relaxing of the extreme tension under which he had been laboring for hours.

They had left Earth as soon as Vel Quen's burial was over. And every moment of the hours since then had impressed on Gordon the vital necessity of playing a part.

He could not tell the weird truth about himself. Zarth Arn had insisted that to tell anyone would bring disaster on both Gordon and himself. Why was it so dangerous? Gordon couldn't guess, as yet.

But he was sure that he must heed that warning, must let no one suspect that he was the prince only in physical body. Even if he told, they wouldn't believe him! Old Vel Quen had said that Zarth Arn's weird experiments had been wholly secret. Who would credit such a crazy story?

Gordon had determined that his only possible course of action was to play the part of Zarth Arn as best he could at Throon, and return as soon as possible to the tower-laboratory on Earth. Then he could plan a way to re-effect the exchange of minds.

"But it seems that I'm being sucked into some crazy tangle of galactic conflict that'll make it hard to get away," he thought, dismayed.

Lying on the padded bunk, Gordon wondered wearily if any man since time began had ever found himself in such a situation as this.

"There's nothing for it but to bull ahead and play it out as Zarth Arn, if I can," he thought. "If Vel Quen had only lived!"

He felt again a pang of regret for the old scientist. Then, tired and unstrung, he fell asleep.

When Gordon awoke, he unconsciously expected to see the familiar plaster ceiling of his New York apartment overhead. Instead, he looked at a glittering metal ceiling and heard a deep, steady drone.

He realized then it had been no wild dream. He was still in Zath Arn's body, in this big warship that was racing through the galaxy toward a doubtful reception for himself.

A uniformed man who bowed respectfully when he entered brought him food—an unfamiliar red substance that seemed to be synthetic meat, fruit, and the chocolate-like drink he already knew.

Hull Burrel came in then. "We're making almost two hundred parsecs an hour and will reach Canopus in three days, highness." *

Gordon did not venture any reply other than a nod. He realized how fatally easy it would be to make slips of pure ignorance.

That possibility was a weight on his mind in the hours that followed, adding to the already superhuman strain of his imposture.

He had to go through the big cruiser as though such a ship was familiar to him, he had to accept references to a thousand things which Zarth Arn would know, without betraying his ignorance.

He carried it off, he hoped, by wrapping himself in brooding silence. But could he carry it off at Throon?

On the third day, John Gordon entered the spacious bridge to be dazzled by a blinding flare of light that forced a way even through the heavy filter-screens across the windows.

"Canopus at last," remarked Hull Burrel. "We shall dock at Throon in a few hours."

Again, wild bugle-calls of excitement soared in Gordon's mind as he looked through the windows at a tremendous spectacle.

It was *worth* all risk and danger, it was worth that nightmare traverse from body to body across the gulf of time, for a man of the 20th Century to look on such a sight as this!

---

* *Note:* A parsec was the term invented by 20th Century Earth astronomers to measure galactic distances. It equalled a distance of 3.258 light years, or 18,000,000,000,000 miles.

The majesty of Canopus was a thundering impact on his senses. The colossal sun revised all his limited ideas of grandeur. It blazed here in white splendor like a firmament aflame, drenching the warship and all space with a glorious, supernal radiance.

Gordon's senses reeled, as he tried to keep his face impassive. He was only a man of the past and his brain was not used to such a shock of wonder as this.

The drone of the great pressure-ray generators dropped in key as the cruiser swung in around an Earth-sized planet that was one of a dozen worlds circling this monster star.

And this was Throon. This world of green continents and silver seas spinning in opalescent white sunshine was the heart and brain of the Empire that stretched half across the galaxy.

"We'll dock at Throon City, of course," Hull Burrel was saying. "Commander Corbulo has stereoed me to bring you to Arn Abbas at once."

Again, Gordon tensed. "I will be glad to see my father," he ventured.

His father? A man he had never seen, a ruler who governed the titan expanse of suns and worlds behind him, and who was parent of the man in whose physical body Gordon now lived?

Again, Zarth Arn's remembered warning steadied Gordon. Tell no one the truth—no one! Brazen through this incredible imposture somehow, and get back to Earth for the re-exchange as soon as he could—

The silvery seas and green continents of Throon rushed up toward the *Caris* as the warship made planet-fall with massive disregard of preliminary deceleration.

Gordon caught his breath as he looked down. From the edge of a silver ocean rose a lofty range of mountains that flashed and glittered as though of glass. They *were* of glass, he saw a moment later, a towering range formed by extrusion of vast masses of molten silicates from the planet.

And perched on a plateau of these Glass Mountains high above the sea was a fairy, unreal city Its graceful domes and towers were like bubbles of colored glass themselves. Pinnacles and terraces took the light of Canopus and flashed it back in a glory of quivering effulgence. Throon City, this—the core and capital of the Empire.

The big cruiser sank toward a huge spaceport just north of

the fairy city. In its sunken docks and quays brooded scores, hundreds, of the Empire's star-roving warships. Massive, thousand-foot long battleships, heavy cruisers, fast destroyers and slim phantom-cruisers and ponderous, tub-shaped monitors with huge guns—all these craft wore the shining comet-emblem of the Mid-Galactic Empire.

Gordon stepped out of the *Caris* with Hull Burrel and the respectful officers, into sunlight so weirdly white and beautiful that not even the urgency of his situation prevented him looking about in increased wonder.

The brooding bulks of the great battleships loomed up in the docks all around him, their batteries of grim atom-guns silhouetted against the sky. In the distance rose the incredible, shimmering domes and spires of the city.

Hull Burrel's puzzled voice jerked Gordon from his petrification, recalling him to the necessities of the present.

"The car is waiting for us in the tubeway, highness," reminded the Antarian captain.

"Of course," Gordon said hastily, forcing himself to move.

He had to watch the trend of Hull Burrel's direction, so as not to go astray. They made their way between the looming ships, past great mobile cranes, respectfully saluting officers, uniformed men standing at rigid attention.

Every minute John Gordon felt more strongly the hopelessness of what he had set out to do. How could he maintain his impersonation, when everything here was so stunningly new and strange?

"Disaster for both of us if you tell!" That warning of Zarth Arn—the real Zarth Arn—rang through his mind again with a chilling, steadying effect.

"Bull it through!" he told himself. "They can't dream that you're not the prince, no matter what mistakes you make. Watch every moment—"

They reached the opening of a lighted stair that led down beneath the tarmac of the spaceport. Below were round metal tunnels branching off into the darkness. A cylindrical metal car waited.

No sooner had Gordon and Hull Burrel taken their places in its pneumatic-slung chairs, than the car started moving with great speed. Its velocity was so great that to Gordon it seemed barely five minutes before they stopped.

They stepped out into a similar lighted, underground vestibule. But here uniformed guards with slim, rifle-like atom-guns were on duty. They saluted with the weapons to Gordon.

A young officer, saluting likewise, informed Gordon, "Throon rejoices at your return, highness."

"There's no time now for civilities," Hull Burrel broke in impatiently.

Gordon walked with the Antarian captain to an open doorway beyond which lay a corridor with alabaster walls.

The floor of the corridor began to move smoothly as they stepped onto it, almost startling Gordon into an exclamation. As it bore them forward and up long winding ramps, Gordon numbly comprehended that they were already in the lower levels of Arn Abbas' palace.

The very nerve-center of the vast star-empire whose rule swayed suns and worlds across thousands of light-years! He couldn't yet fully grasp and realize it or the coming ordeal.

The moving walk swept them into an antechamber in which another file of guards saluted and stood apart from high bronze doors. Hull Burrel stood back as Gordon went through into the room beyond.

It was a small room wholly without magnificence. Around its walls were many telestereo instruments, and there was a curious low desk with a panel of grids and screens on its face.

Behind the desk a man sat in a metal chair, with two other men standing beside him. All three looked at Gordon as he approached. His heart hammered violently.

The man in the chair was a giant, dominating figure in dull-gold garments. His massive, powerful face, bleak gray eyes and thick black hair graying at the temples gave a leonine impression.

Gordon recognized him as Arn Abbas, ruler of the Empire, Zarth Arn's father. No, *his* father! He had to keep thinking of it that way!

The younger of the two standing men was like Arn Abbas himself, thirty years younger—tall and stalwart but with more friendliness in his face. That would be Jhal Arn, his elder brother, he guessed.

And the third man, grizzled, stocky, square-faced, wearing the uniform of the Empire navy but with golden bars of rank thick on his sleeve—this must be Chan Corbulo, the Commander of the space fleet.

Gordon, his throat tight with tension, stopped in front of the seated man. He nerved himself against those bleak eyes, knowing that he had to speak.

"Father—," he began tightly. Instantly, he was interrupted.

Arn Abbas, glaring at him, uttered an exclamation of wrath.

"Don't call me father! You're not my son!"

5

WEIRD MASQUERADE

Gordon felt a staggering shock. Could Arn Abbas suspect the weird impersonation he was carrying on?

But the next words of the giant ruler a little reassured Gordon, even though they were furious in tone.

"No son of mine would go straying off to the edge of the Empire to play scientific hermit for months, when I need him here! Your cursed science-studies have made you utterly forget your duty."

Gordon breathed a little more easily. "Duty, father?" he repeated.

"Duty to me and to the Empire!" roared Arn Abbas. "You know that I need you here. You know the game that's being played across the galaxy, and what it means to all our star-worlds!"

His big fist pounded his knee. "And see what burying yourself there on Earth nearly brought about! Shorr Kan nearly scooped you up! You know what that would mean?"

"Yes, I know," Gordon nodded. "If Shorr Kan had got hold of me, he could use me as a hostage against you."

Next moment, he realized that he had blundered. Arn Abbas glared at him, and Jhal Arn and Corbulo looked surprised.

"What in the name of all the star-devils are you talking about?" demanded the emperor. "You should know as well as

I why Shorr Kan wanted his hands on you. To get the secret of the Disruptor, of course!"

The Disruptor? What was that? Gordon desperately realized that again his ignorance had betrayed him.

How could he keep going in this mad imposture when he didn't know the vital facts about Zarth Arn's life and background?

Gordon might have blurted out the truth then and there had not remembrance of his promise to Zarth Arn steadied him. He tried to look unruffled.

"Of course—the Disruptor," he said hastily. "That's what I was referring to."

"You certainly did not sound like it!" snapped Arn Abbas. He uttered a fierce exclamation. "By Heaven, at a time when I need sons to help me, I've got one real son and I've got another who's so cursed dreamy-eyed he doesn't even remember the Disruptor!"

The massive ruler leaned forward, anger dissolving momentarily into an earnestness that betrayed his deep anxiety.

"Zarth, you've got to wake up! Do you realize that the Empire stands on the verge of a terrible crisis? Do you realize just what that devil Shorr Kan is planning?

"He's sent ambassadors to the Hercules Barons, to the kingdoms of Polaris and Cygnus, even to Fomalhaut Kingdom. He's doing everything to detach our allies from us. And he's building every new warship and weapon he can, there inside the Cloud."

Grizzled Commander Corbulo nodded grimly. "It's certain vast preparations are going on inside the Cloud. We know that, even though our scanner-beams can't get through the screens that Shorr Kan's scientists have flung around their work."

"It's the dream of his life to crack the Empire and reduce the galaxy to a ruck of small warring kingdoms that the League could devour one by one!" Arn Abbas went on. "Where *we* are trying to unify the galaxy in peace, he wants to split and separate it.

"Only one thing holds Shorr Kan back and that is the Disruptor. He knows we have it, but he doesn't know just what it is or what it can do, any more than anyone else does. And because only you and Jhal and I know the secret of the Disruptor, that arch-devil has tried to get his hands on you!"

Light broke upon John Gordon's mystification. So that was what the Disruptor was—some mysterious weapon whose secret was known only to three men of the Empire's ruling house?

Then Zarth Arn knew that secret. But *he* didn't know it, even though he wore Zarth Arn's body! Yet he had to pretend that he did.

"I never thought of it that way, father," Gordon said hesitatingly. "I know the situation is critical."

"So critical that things may well come to a crisis within weeks!" affirmed Arn Abbas. "It all depends on how many of our allied kingdoms Shorr Kan is able to detach, and whether he will dare to risk the Disruptor."

He added loudly, "And because of that, I forbid you to go back to your hideout on Earth any more, Zarth! You'll stay here and do your duty as the second prince of the Empire should."

Gordon was appalled. "But father, I've got to go back to Earth for at least a short time—"

The massive ruler cut him off. "I told you I forbade it, Zarth! Do you dare to argue with me?"

Gordon felt the crash of all his desperate plans. This was disaster.

If he couldn't go back to Earth and the laboratory there, how could he contact Zarth Arn and re-exchange their bodies?

"I'll hear no more objections!" continued the emperor violently as Gordon started to speak. "Now get out of here! Corbulo and I have things to discuss."

Blindly, helplessly, Gordon turned back toward the door. More strongly than even before, he felt a dismayed consciousness of being utterly trapped and baffled.

Jhal Arn went with him, and when they had reached the ante-chamber the tall elder prince put his hand on Gordon's arm.

"Don't take it too hard, Zarth," he encouraged. "I know how devoted you are to your scientific studies, and what a blow Vel Quen's death must have been to you. But father is right—you are needed here, in this gathering crisis."

Gordon, even in his dismay, had to choose his words. "I want to do my duty. But what help can I give?"

"It's Lianna that father is referring to," Jhal Arn said seriously. "You *have* dodged your duty there, Zarth."

He added, as though anticipating objections from Gordon, "O, I know why—I know all about Murn. But the Fomalhaut Kingdom is vital to the Empire in this crisis. You'll have to go through with it."

Lianna? Murn? The names had no meaning to John Gordon. They were mystery, like everything else in this mad imposture.

"You mean that Lianna—," he began, and left the words hanging in hope of provoking further explanation from Jhal Arn.

But Jhal only nodded. "You've got to do it, Zarth. Father is going to make the announcement at the Feast of Moons tonight."

He clapped Gordon on the back. "Buck up, it's not as bad as all that! You look as though you'd been condemned to death. I'll see you at the Feast."

He turned back into the inner room, leaving Gordon staring blankly after him.

Gordon stood, bewildered and badly worried. What kind of tangled complications was his involuntary impersonation of Zarth Arn getting him into? How long could he hope to carry it through?

Hull Burrel had gone into the inner room when Gordon came out. Now as Gordon stood frozenly, the big Antarian came out too.

"Prince Zarth, I owe you good fortune!" he exclaimed. "I expected to get reprimanded by Commander Corbulo for putting off my regular patrol course to touch at Sol."

"And he didn't reprimand you?" Gordon said mechanically.

"Sure he did—gave me the devil with bells on," Burrel grinned. "But your father said it turned out so lucky in giving me a chance to rescue you, that he's appointed me aide to the Commander himself!"

Gordon congratulated him. But he spoke perfunctorily, for his mind was upon his own desperately puzzling position.

He couldn't just stand here in the ante-room longer. Zarth Arn must have apartments in this great palace, and he'd be expected to go to them. The devil of it was he had no idea where there were!

He couldn't let his ignorance be suspected, though. So he took leave of Hull Burrel and walked confidently out of the ante-room by a different door, as though he knew quite well where he was going.

Gordon found himself in a corridor, on a gliding motowalk. The motowalk took him into a great circular room of shining silver. It was brilliantly illuminated by white sunlight pouring through high crystal windows. Around its walls marched black reliefs depicting a wilderness of dark stars, embers of burned out suns and lifeless worlds.

John Gordon felt dwarfed by the majesty and splendor of this great, somber chamber. He crossed it and entered another vast room, this one with walls that flamed with the glowing splendor of a whirling nebula.

"Where the devil are Zarth Arn's quarters in this place?" he wondered.

He realized his helplessness. He couldn't ask anyone where his own quarters were. Neither could he wander aimlessly through this vast palace without arousing wonder, perhaps suspicion.

A gray-skinned servant, a middle-aged man in the black livery of the palace, was already looking at him wonderingly across this Hall of the Nebula. The man bowed deeply as Gordon strode to him.

Gordon had had an idea. "Come with me to my apartments," he told the servant brusquely. "I have a task for you."

The gray man bowed again. "Yes, highness."

But the man remained there, waiting. Waiting for him to walk ahead, of course!

Gordon made an impatient gesture. "Go ahead! I'll follow."

If the servant found it strange he let none of that feeling appear in his masklike face. He turned and proceeded softly out of the great nebula room by another door.

Gordon followed him into a corridor and onto a motowalk that glided upward like a sliding ramp. Swiftly and quietly the moving walk took them up through splendid, lofty corridors and stairs.

Twice they confronted groups coming downward by the return walk—two brilliantly-jewelled white girls and a laughing, swarthy naval captain in one; two grave gray officials in the other. All of them bowed in deep respect to Gordon.

The motowalk switched off down a shimmery, pearl-walled passageway. A door ahead slid softly open of its own accord.

Gordon followed through it into a high chamber with pure white walls.

The gray servant turned inquiringly toward him. "Yes, highness?"

How to get rid of the man? Gordon cut that problem short by taking the easiest method.

"I find I won't need you after all," he said carelessly "You may go."

The man bowed himself out of the room, and Gordon felt a slight relaxing of his tension. Clumsy, his stratagem—but at least it had got him to the temporary refuge of Zarth Arn's apartments.

He found himself breathing heavily as though from exhausting effort. His hands were shaking. He had not realized the nervous effort his impersonation cost him. He mopped his brow.

"My God! Was any man ever in a position like this before?"

His tired mind refused to grapple with the problem now. To evade it, he walked slowly through the rooms of the suite.

Here was less splendor than he had seen elsewhere in the great palace. Apparently, Zarth Arn had not been of luxurious tastes. The rooms were comparatively austere.

The two living rooms had silken hangings and a few pieces of metal furniture of beautiful design. There was a rack of hundreds of thought-spools and one of the thought-spool "readers." A side room held much scientific apparatus, was in fact a small laboratory.

He glanced into a small bedroom, then went on toward tall windows that opened on a terrace gay with green verdure and flooded by sunlight. Gordon went out onto the terrace, and then froze.

"Throon City! Good Lord, who ever dreamed of a place like *this*!"

The little garden-terrace of his suite was high in the west wall of the huge, oblong palace. It looked out across the city.

City of the great star-empire's glory, gathering in itself an epitome of the splendor and power of that vast realm of many thousand star-worlds! Metropolis of grandeur so great that it stunned and paralyzed the eyes of John Gordon of little Earth!

The enormous white disk of Canopus was sinking toward the horizon, flashing a supernal brilliance across the scene. In that transfiguring radiance, the peaks and scarps of the Glass Mountains here above the sea flung back the sunset in banners and pennons of wild glory.

And outshining even the stupendous glory of the glassy peaks shone the fairy towers of Throon. Domes, minarets, graceful porticoes, these and the great buildings they adorned were of shimmering glass. Mightiest among the structures loomed the gigantic palace on whose high terrace he stood. Surrounded by wondrous gardens, it looked out royally across the great metropolis and the silver ocean beyond.

In the radiant sunset out there over the glittering peaks and heaving ocean there flitted swarms of fliers like shining fireflies. From the spaceport to the north, a half-dozen mighty battleships rose majestically and took off into the darkening sky.

The full grandeur and vastness of this star-empire hammered into Gordon's mind. For this city was the throbbing heart of those vast glooms and linked stars and worlds across which he had come.

"And *I* am supposed to be one of the ruling house of this realm!" he thought, dazed. "I can't keep it up. It's too vast, too overpowering—"

The enormous sun sank as Gordon numbly watched. Violet shadows darkened to velvet night across the metropolis.

Lights came on softly all through the glittering streets of Throon, and on the lower terraces of this giant palace.

Two golden moons climbed into the heavens, and hosts of countless stars broke forth in a glory of unfamiliar constellations that rivalled the soft, throbbing lights of the city.

"Highness, it grows late!"

Gordon turned jerkily, startled. A grave servant, a stocky man with bluish skin, was bowing.

One of Zarth Arn's personal servants, he guessed. He would have to be careful with this man!

"Yes, what of that?" he asked, with an assumption of impatience.

"The Feast of Moons will begin within the hour," reminded the servant. "You should make ready, highness."

Gordon suddenly remembered what Jhal Arn had said of a Feast. A royal banquet, he guessed, to be held this night.

What was it Jhal had said of some announcement that Arn

Abbas was to make? And what had been the talk of "Murn" and "Lianna" and his duty?

Gordon braced himself for the ordeal. A banquet meant exposing himself to the eyes of a host of people—all of whom, no doubt, knew Zarth Arn and would notice his slightest slip. But he had to go.

"Very well, I will dress now," he told the servant.

It was at least a slight help that the blue-skinned servitor procured and laid out his garments for him. The jacket and trousers were of silky black, with a long black cloak to hang from his shoulders.

When he had dressed, the servant pinned on his breast a comet-emblem worked in wonderfully-blazing green jewels. He guessed it to be the insignia of his royal rank in the Empire.

Gordon felt again the sense of unreality as he surveyed his unfamiliar figure, his dark, aquiline face, in a tall mirror.

"I need a drink," he told the servant jerkily. "Something strong."

The blue servant looked at him in faint surprise, for a moment.

"*Saqua,* highness?" he asked, and Gordon nodded.

The brown liquor the man poured out sent a fiery tingle through Gordon's veins.

Some of the shaky strain left his nerves as he drank another goblet of the *saqua.* He felt a return of reckless self-confidence as he left the apartment.

"What the devil!" Gordon thought. "I wanted adventure—and I'm getting it!"

More adventure than he had bargained for, truly! He had never dreamed of such an ordeal as was now ahead of him—of appearing before the nobility of this star-flung Empire as its prince!

All the mammoth, softly-lit palace seemed astir with soft sound and laughter and movement, as streams of brilliantly-garbed men and women moved along its motowalks. Gordon, to whom they bowed respectfully, noted their direction and went forward casually.

The gliding walks took him down through the lofty corridors and halls to a broad vestibule with wonderful golden walls. Here councillors, nobles, men and women high in the Empire, drew aside for him.

Gordon nerved himself, strode toward the high doors whose massive golden leaves were now thrown back. A silk-garbed chamberlain bowed and spoke clearly into the vast hall beyond.

"His highness, Prince Zarth Arn!"

6

THE FEAST OF MOONS

Gordon stopped stock still, shaken by an inward quaking. He stood on a wide dais at the side of a circular hall that was of cathedral loftiness and splendor.

The vast, round room of black marble held rows of tables which themselves glowed with intrinsic light. They bore a bewildering array of glass and metal dishes, and along them sat some hundreds of brilliantly-dressed men and women.

But not all these banqueters were human! Though humans were dominant, just as they were throughout the galaxy, there were also representatives of the Empire's aboriginal races. Despite their conventional garb, those he could see clearly looked grotesquely alien to Gordon—a frog-like, scaly green man with bulging eyes, a beaked, owl-faced winged individual, two black spidery figures with too many arms and legs.

John Gordon's dazed eyes lifted, and for a moment he thought this whole vast room was open to the sky. High overhead curved the black vault of the night heavens, gemmed with thousands of blazing stars and constellations. Into that sky, two golden moons and one of pale silver hue were climbing toward conjunction.

It took a moment for Gordon to realize that that sky was an artificial planetarium-ceiling, so perfect was the imitation. Then he became aware that the eyes of all these folk had turned upon him. On the dais, there was a table with a score of brilliant people, Jhal Arn's tall figure had risen and was beckoning impatiently to him.

Jhal Arn's first words shocked him back to realization of how badly his caution and self-control had slipped.

"What's the matter, Zarth? You look as though you'd never seen the Hall of Stars before!"

"Nerves, I guess," Gordon answered huskily. "I think I need another drink."

Jhal Arn burst into laughter. "So you've been fortifying yourself for tonight? Come, Zarth, it isn't that bad."

Gordon numbly slid into the seat to which Jhal Arn had led him, one separated by two empty chairs from the places where Jhal sat with his lovely wife and little son.

He found grizzled Commander Corbulo on his other side. Across the table sat a thin, nervous-eyed and aging man who he soon learned was Orth Bodmer, Chief Councillor of the Empire.

Corbulo, a stern figure in his plain uniform, bowed to Gordon as did the other people along this raised table.

"You're looking pale and downcast, Zarth," rumbled the grizzled space-admiral. "That's what you get, skulking in laboratories on Earth. Space is the place for a young man like you."

"I begin to think you're right," muttered Gordon. "I wish to Heaven I was there now."

Corbulo grunted. "So that's it? Tonight's announcement, eh? Well, it's necessary. The help of the Fomalhaut Kingdom will be vital to us if Shorr Kan attacks."

What the devil were they talking about, John Gordon wondered bitterly? The names "Murn" and "Lianna" that Jhal Arn had mentioned, this reference to Fomalhaut star-kingdom again—what did they portend?

Gordon found a servant bending obsequiously over his shoulder, and told the man, *"Saqua,* first."

The brown liquor spun his brain a little, this time. He was aware, as he drank another goblet, that Corbulo was looking at him in stern disapproval, and that Jhal Arn was grinning.

The brilliant scene before him, the shining tables, the splendid human and unhuman throng, and the wonderful sky-ceiling of stars and climbing moons, held Gordon fascinated. So this was the Feast of Moons?

Music that rippled in long, haunting harmonies of muted strings and woodwinds was background to the gay, buzzing chatter along the glittering tables. Then the music stopped and horns flared a loud silver challenge.

All rose to their feet. Seeing Jhal Arn rising, Gordon hastily followed his example.

"His highness, Arn Abbas, sovereign of the Mid-Galactic Empire, Suzerain of the Lesser Kingdoms, Governor of the stars and worlds of the Marches of Outer Space!

"Her highness, the Princess Lianna, ruler of the Kingdom of Fomalhaut!"

The clear, loud announcements gave John Gordon a shock of astonishment even before the giant, regal figure of Arn Abbas strode onto the dais, with a girl upon his arm.

So "Lianna" was a girl, a princess—ruler of the little western star-kingdom of Fomalhaut? But what had she to do with him?

Arn Abbas, magnificent in a blue-black cloak upon which blazed the glorious jewels of the royal comet-emblem, stopped and turned his bleak eyes angrily on Gordon.

"Zarth, are you forgetting protocol?" he snapped. "Come here!"

Gordon stumbled forward. He got only a swift impression of the girl beside the emperor.

She was tall, though she did not look so beside Arn Abbas' giant height. As tall as himself, her slim, rounded figure perfectly outlined by her long, shimmering white gown, she held her ash-golden head proudly high.

Pride, beauty, consciousness of authority—these were what Gordon read in the chiselled white face, the faintly scornful red mouth, the cool, clear gray eyes that rested gravely on him.

Arn Abbas took Gordon's hand in one of his, and Lianna's in the other. The towering sovereign raised his voice.

"Nobles and captains of the Empire and our allied star-kingdoms, I announce to you the coming marriage of my second son, Zarth Arn, and the Princess Lianna of Fomalhaut!"

Marriage? Marriage to this proudly beautiful star-kingdom princess? Gordon felt as though hit by a thunderbolt. So *that* was what Jhal Arn and Corbulo had been referring to? But good God, he couldn't go through with this! He wasn't Zarth Arn—

"Take her hand, you fool!" snarled the emperor. "Have you lost your wits?"

Numbly, John Gordon managed to grasp the girl's slim, ring-laden fingers.

Arn Abbas, satisfied, stalked forward to take his seat at the table. Gordon remained frozen.

Lianna gave him a sweet, set smile, but her voice was impatient as she said in an undertone, "Conduct me to our place, so that the others can sit down."

Gordon became aware that the whole host in the Hall of Stars remained standing, looking at himself and the girl.

He stumbled forward with her, clumsily handed her into her chair, and sat down beside her. There was the rustle of the hosts re-seating themselves, and the rippling music sounded forth again.

Lianna was looking at him with fine brows arched a little, her eyes clouded by impatience and resentment.

"Your attitude toward me will create gossip. You look positively appalled!"

Gordon nerved himself. He had to keep up his imposture for the time being. Zarth Arn was apparently being used as a political pawn, was being shoved into this marriage and had agreed to it.

He had to play the real Zarth's part, for now. He'd find some way of getting back to Earth to exchange places with the real Zarth Arn, before the marriage.

He drained his *saqua* goblet again, and leaned toward Lianna with a sudden recklessness.

She expected him to be an ardent fiance, to be Zarth Arn. All right, blast it, he would be! It was no fault of his if there was deception in it. He hadn't asked to play this role!!

"Lianna, they're so busy admiring you that they don't even look at me," he told her.

Lianna's clear eyes became puzzled in expression. "I never saw you like this before, Zarth."

Gordon laughed. "Why, then, there's a new Zarth Arn—Zarth Arn is a different man, now!"

Truth enough in that assertion, as only he knew! But the girl looked more perplexed, her fine brows drawing together in a little frown.

The feast went on, in a glow of warmth and color and buzzing voices. And the *saqua* Gordon had drunk swept away his last trace of apprehension and nervousness.

Adventure? He'd wanted it and he'd gotten it, adventure such as no man of his time had ever dreamed. If death itself were the end of all this, would he not still be gainer? Wasn't it worth risking life to sit here in the Hall of Stars at Throon, with the lords of the great star-kingdoms and a princess of far-off suns at his side?

Others beside himself had drunk deeply. The handsome, flushed young man who sat beyond Corbulo and whom Gordon had learned obliquely was Sath Shamar, ruler of the allied kingdom of Polaris, crashed his goblet down to punctuate a declaration.

"Let them come, the sooner the better!" he was exclaiming to Corbulo. "It's time Shorr Kan was taught a lesson."

Commander Corbulo looked at him sourly. "That's true, highness. Just how many first-line battleships will Polaris contribute to our fleet, if it comes to teaching him that lesson?"

Sath Shamar looked a little dashed. "Only a few hundred, I fear. But they'll make up for it in fighting ability."

Arn Abbas had been listening, for the emperor's rumbling voice sounded from his throne-like seat on Gordon's right.

"The men of Polaris will prove their fidelity to the Empire, no fear," declared Arn Abbas. "Aye, and those of Fomalhaut Kingdom, and of Cygnus and Lyra and our other allies."

Sath Shamar flushedly added, "Let the Hercules Barons but do their part and we've nothing to fear from the Cloud."

Gordon saw all eyes turn to two men further along the table. One was a cold-eyed oldster, the other a tall, rangy man of thirty. Both wore on their cloaks the flaring sun-cluster emblem of Hercules Cluster.

The oldster answered. "The Confederacy of the Barons will fulfill all its pledges. But we have made no formal pledge in this matter."

Arn Abbas' massive face darkened a little at that cool declaration. But Orth Bodmer, the thin-faced chief Councillor, spoke quickly and soothingly to the cold-eyed Baron.

"All men know the proud independence of the great Barons, Zu Rizal. And all know you'd never acquiesce in an evil tyranny's victory."

Arn Abbas, a few moments later, leaned to speak frowningly to Gordon.

"Shorr Kan has been tampering with the Barons! I'm going to find out tonight from Zu Rizal just where they stand."

Finally Arn Abbas arose, and the feasters all rose with him.

The whole company began to stream out of the Hall of Stars into the adjoining halls.

Courtiers and nobles made way for Gordon and Lianna as they went through the throng. The girl smiled and spoke to many, her perfect composure bespeaking a long training in the regal manner.

Gordon nodded carelessly in answer to the congratulations and greetings. He knew he was probably making many blunders, but he didn't care by now. For the first time since leaving Earth, he felt perfectly carefree as that warm glow inside him deepened.

That *saqua* was a cursed good drink! Too bad he couldn't take some of it back with him to his own time. But nothing material could go across time. That was a shame—

He found himself with Lianna on the threshold of a great hall whose fairy-like green illumination came from the flaming comets that crept across its ceiling "sky." Hundreds were dancing here to dreamy, waltz-like music from an unseen source.

Gordon was astounded by the dream-like, floating movements of the immeasurably graceful dance. The dancers seemed to hover half-suspended in the air each step. Then he realized that the room was conditioned somehow by anti-gravity apparatus to reduce their weight.

Lianna looked up at him doubtfully, as he himself realized crestfallenly that he couldn't perform a step of these floating dances.

"Let's not dance," Lianna said, to his relief. "You're such a poor dancer as I remember it, that I'd rather go out in the gardens."

Of course—the retiring, studious real Zarth Arn would be that! Well, so much the better.

"I greatly prefer the gardens," Gordon laughed. "For believe it or not, I'm an even poorer dancer than I was before."

Lianna looked up at him perplexedly as they strolled down a lofty silver corridor. "You drank a great deal at the Feast. I never saw you touch *saqua* before."

Gordon shrugged. "The fact is that I never drank it before tonight."

He uttered a low exclamation when they emerged into the gardens. He had not expected such a scene of unreal beauty as this.

These were gardens of glowing light, of luminous color! Trees and shrubs bore masses of blossoms that glowed burning red, cool green, turquoise blue, and every shade between. The soft breeze that brought heavy perfume from them shook them gaily like a forest of shining flame-flowers, transcendently lovely.

Later, Gordon was to learn that these luminous flowers were cultivated on several highly radioactive worlds of the star Achernar, and were brought here and planted in beds of similarly radioactive soil. But now, suddenly coming on them, they were stunning.

Behind him, the massive terraces of the gigantic oblong palace shouldered the stars. Glowing lights flung boldly in step on climbing step against the sky! And the three clustered moons above poured down their mingled radiance to add a final unreal touch.

"Beautiful, beyond words," Gordon murmered, enthralled by the scene.

Lianna nodded. "Of all your world of Throon, I love these gardens the best. But there are wild, unpeopled worlds far in our Fomalhaut Kingdom that are even more lovely."

Her eyes kindled and for the first time he saw emotion conquer the regal composure of her lovely little face.

"Lonely, unpeopled worlds that are like planets of living color, drenched by the wonderful auroras of strange suns! I shall take you to see them when we visit Fomalhaut, Zarth."

She was looking up at him, her ash-gold hair shining like a crown in the soft light.

She expected him to make love to her, Gordon thought. He was—or at least, she thought he was—her fiance, the man she had chosen to marry. He'd have to keep up his imposture, even now.

Gordon put his arm around her and bent to her lips. Lianna's slim body was pliant and warm inside the shimmering white gown, and her half-parted lips were dizzyingly sweet.

"I'm a cursed liar!" Gordon thought, dismayed. "I'm kissing her because I *want* to, not to keep up my role!"

He abruptly stepped back. Lianna looked up at him with sheer amazement on her face.

"Zarth, what made you do that?"

Gordon tried to laugh, though that thrillingly sweet contact still seemed trembling through his nerves.

"Is it so remarkable for me to kiss you?" he countered.

"Of course it is—you never did before!" Lianna exclaimed. "You know as well as I that our marriage is purely a political pretense!"

Truth crashed into Gordon's mind like a blast of icy cold, sweeping the fumes of *saqua* from his brain.

He had made an abysmal slip in his imposture! He should have guessed that Lianna didn't *want* to marry Zarth Arn any more than he wanted to marry her—that it was purely a political marriage and they but two pawns in the great game of galactic diplomacy.

He had to cover up this blunder as best he could, and quickly! The girl was looking up at him with that expression of utter mystification still on her face.

"I can't understand you doing this when you and I made agreement to be mere friends."

Gordon desperately voiced the only explanation possible, one perilously close to the truth.

"Lianna, you're so beautiful I couldn't help it. Is it so strange I should fall in love with you, despite our agreement?"

Lianna's face hardened and her voice had scorn in it. "You in love with *me?* You forget that I know all about Murn."

"Murn?" The name rang vaguely familiar in Gordon's ears. Jhal Arn had mentioned "Murn."

Once more Gordon felt himself baffled by his ignorance of vital facts. He was cold sober now, and badly worried.

"I—I guess maybe I just had too much *saqua* at the Feast, after all," he muttered.

Lianna's amazement and anger had faded, and she seemed to be studying him with a curiously intent interest.

He felt relief when they were interrupted by a gay throng streaming out into the gardens. In the hours that followed, the presence of others made Gordon's role a little easier to play.

He was conscious of Lianna's gray eyes often resting on him, with that wondering look. When the gathering broke up and he accompanied her to the door of her apartments, Gordon was uneasily aware of her curious, speculative gaze as he bade her good night.

He mopped his brow as he went on the gliding motowalk

to his own chambers. What a night! He had had about as much as one man could bear!

Gordon found his rooms softly lit, but the blue servant was not in evidence. He tiredly opened the door of his bedroom. There was a quick rush of little bare feet. He froze at sight of the girl running toward him, one he had never seen before.

She seemed of almost childish youthfulness, with her dark hair falling to her bare shoulders and her soft, beautiful little face and dark-blue eyes shining with gladness. A child? It was no child's rounded figure that gleamed whitely through the filmy robe she wore!

Gordon stood, stupefied by this final staggering surprise in an evening of surprises, as the girl ran and threw soft bare arms around his neck.

"Zarth Arn!" she cried. "At last you've come! I've been waiting so long!"

7

STAR-PRINCESS

John Gordon for the second time that night held in his arms a girl who thought he was the real Zarth Arn. But the dark-haired, lovely young girl who had thrown her arms around him was far different from the proud Princess Lianna.

Warm lips pressed his own in eager passionate kisses, as he stood bewildered. The dark hair that brushed his face was soft and perfumed. For a moment, impulse made Gordon draw her lithe figure closer.

Then he pushed her back a little. The beautiful little face that looked up at him was soft and appealing.

"You never told me that you had come back to Throon!" she accused. "I didn't know until I saw you at the Feast!"

Gordon stumbled for an answer. "I didn't have time. I—"

This final surprise of the day had staggered him badly. Who was this lovely young girl? One with whom the real Zarth Arn had been conducting an intrigue?

She was smiling up at him fondly, her little hands still resting on his shoulders.

"It's all right, Zarth. I came up right after the Feast and I've been waiting for you."

She snuggled closer. "How long will you be staying on Throon? At least, we'll have these few nights together."

Gordon was appalled. He had thought his fantastic imposture difficult before. But *this*—!

A name suddenly bobbed into his thoughts, a name that both Jhal Arn and Lianna had mentioned as though he knew it well. The name of "Murn." Was it the name of this girl?

He thought it might be. To find out, he spoke to her diffidently.

"Murn—"

The girl raised her dark head from his shoulder to look at him inquiringly.

"Yes, Zarth?"

So this was Murn? It was this girl of whom Lianna had mockingly reminded him. So that Lianna knew of his intrigue?

Well, the name was something, anyway. Gordon was trying to grope his way through the complexities of the situation. He sat down, and Murn promptly nestled in his lap.

"Murn, listen—you shouldn't be here," he began huskily. "Suppose you were seen coming to my apartment?"

Murn looked at him with astonishment in her dark blue eyes. "What difference does that make, when I'm your wife?"

His wife? Gordon, for the twentieth time that day, was smitten breathless by the sudden, complete destruction of his pre-conceived ideas.

How in Heaven's name could he keep up the part of Zarth Arn when he didn't know the most elementary facts about the man? Why hadn't Zarth Arn or Vel Quen told him these things?

Then Gordon remembered. They hadn't told him because it wasn't supposed to be necessary. It had never been dreamed that Gordon, in Zarth Arn's body, would leave Earth and come to Throon. That raid of Shorr Kan's emissaries had upset all the plan, and had introduced these appalling complications.

Murn, her dark head snuggled under his chin, was continuing in a plaintive voice.

"Even though I'm only your morganatic wife, surely there's nothing wrong about my being here?"

So that was it! A morganatic, an unofficial, wife! That custom of old had survived to the days of these star-kings!

For a moment, John Gordon felt a hot anger against the man whose body he inhabited. Zarth Arn, secretly married to this child whom he could not acknowledge publicly and at the same time preparing for a state marriage with Lianna—it was a nasty business!

Or was it? Gordon's anger faded. The marriage with Lianna was purely a political device to assure the loyalty of the Fomalhaut Kingdom. Zarth had understood that, and so did Lianna. She knew all about Murn, and apparently had not resented. Under those circumstances, was Zarth Arn not justified in secretly finding happiness with this girl he loved?

Gordon suddenly woke again to the fact that Murn did not doubt for a moment that he was her loved husband—and that she had every idea of spending the night here with him!

He lifted her from his lap and rose to his feet, looking down at her uncertainly.

"Murn, listen, you must not spend tonight here," he told her. "You will have to avoid my apartment for these next few weeks."

Murn's lovely face became pale and stricken. "Zarth, what are you saying?"

Gordon racked his brain for an excuse. "Now don't cry, please. It isn't that I don't love you any more."

Murn's dark blue eyes had filled with tears. "It's Lianna! You've fallen in love with her. I saw how you paid attention to her at the Feast!"

The pain in her white face made it seem more child-like than ever. Gordon cursed the necessities of the situation. He was deeply hurting this girl.

He took her face between his hands. "Murn, you must believe me when I tell you this. Zarth Arn loves you as much as ever—his feelings have not changed."

Murn's eyes searched his face, and the intense earnestness in it and in his voice seemed to convince her. The pain left her face.

"But if that's so, Zarth, then why—"

Gordon had thought of an excuse, by now. "It's because

of the marriage with Lianna, but *not* because I love the princess," he said.

"You know, Murn, that the marriage is designed to assure the support of the Fomalhaut Kingdom in the coming struggle with the Cloud."

Murn nodded her dark head, her eyes still perplexed. "Yes, you explained that to me before. But I still don't see why it should come between us. You said it wouldn't, that you and Lianna had agreed to regard it as a mere form."

"Yes, but right now we must be careful," Gordon said quickly. "There are spies of Shorr Kan here at Throon. If they discovered I have a secret morganatic wife, they could publish the fact and wreck the marriage."

Murn's soft face became understanding. "Now I see. But Zarth, aren't we going to see each other at all?"

"Only in public, for a few weeks," Gordon told her. "Soon I shall leave Throon again for a little while. And I promise you that when I come back it will all be the same between us as before."

And that was truth, Gordon fervently hoped! For if he could get to Earth and effect the re-exchange of bodies, it would be the *real* Zarth Arn who would come back to Throon.

Murn seemed relieved in mind but still a little rueful, as she threw on a black silk cloak and prepared to leave.

She raised herself on tiptoe to press warm lips lovingly to his. "Good night, Zarth."

He returned the kiss, not with passion but with a queer tenderness. He could understand how Zarth Arn had fallen in love with this exquisite, childlike girl.

Murn's eyes became a little wider, faintly puzzled, as she looked up at him after that kiss.

"You are somehow different, Zarth," she murmured. "I don't know how—"

The subtle instinct of a woman in love had given her vague warning of the incredible change in him, Gordon knew. He drew a long breath of relief when she had gone

Gordon stretched himself on the bed in the little sleeping-room, but found his muscles still tense as steel cords. Not until he had lain many minutes staring at the glowing moonlight that streamed into the dark room, did his nerves relax a little.

One paramount necessity cried aloud in Gordon's mind.

He had to get out of this crazy imposture at the earliest possible moment! He couldn't much longer carry on his weird impersonation of one of the focal figures in the approaching crisis of the great star-kingdoms. Yet how? How was he to get back to Earth to re-exchange bodies with Zarth Arn?

Gordon awoke next morning to glimmering white dawn and found the blue Vegan servant standing beside his bed.

"The princess Lianna asks you to breakfast with her, highness," the servant informed.

Gordon felt quick surprise and worry. Why had Lianna sent this invitation? Could she suspect something? No, impossible. And yet—

He bathed in a little glass room where, he found by pushing buttons at hazard, he could cause soapy, salty or perfumed waters of any temperatures to swirl up neck-high around him.

The Vegan had a silken white suit and cloak ready for him. He dressed quickly, and then went through the palace to Lianna's apartments.

These were suites of fairy-like pastel-walled rooms beyond which one of the broad, flower-hung terraces looked out over Throon. Boyish in blue slacks and jacket, Lianna greeted him on the terrace.

"I have had breakfast laid here," she told him. "You are just in time to hear the sunrise music."

Gordon was astonished to detect a faint shyness in Lianna's gaze as she served him iced, red-pulped fruits and winy purple beverage. She did not now seem the regally proud princess of the night before.

And what was the sunrise music? He supposed that was another of the things he should know but didn't.

"Listen, it is beginning now!" Lianna said suddenly.

High around the city Throon loomed the crystal peaks of the Glass Mountains, lofty in the sunrise. Down from those glorious distant peaks now shivered pure, thrillingly sweet notes of sound.

Storm of music broke louder and louder from the glittering peaks! Wild, angelic arpeggios of crystalline notes rang out like all the bells of heaven. Tempests of tiny tinklings like pizzicati of fairy strings was background to the ringing chords.

Gordon realized now that he was hearing the sounds given forth by the sudden expansion of the glassy peaks as Canopus' rays warmed them. He heard the crystal music reach its ringing crescendo as the big white sun rose higher. Then it died away in a long, quivering note.

Gordon exhaled a long breath. "That was the most wonderful thing I've ever heard."

Lianna looked at him, surprised. "But you've heard it many times before."

He realized he had made another slip. They had walked to the rail of the terrace, and Lianna was looking up at him intently.

She suddenly asked a question that startled him. "Why did you send Murn away last night?"

"How did you know about that?" he exclaimed.

Lianna laughed softly. "You should know there are no secrets in this palace. I've no doubt it is buzzing right now with the news that we breakfasted together."

Was that so? Gordon thought in dismay. In that case, he might have some explaining to do to Murn when next they met.

"Did you and she quarrel?" Lianna persisted. Then she flushed slightly and added, "Of course, it's really none of my affair."

"Lianna, it is your affair," Gordon said impulsively. "I only wish—"

He stopped. He could not go on, to say that he only wished he could tell her the truth.

He did wish that with all his heart and soul, at this moment. Murn was adorable, but it was Lianna whom he would never forget.

Lianna looked up at him with puzzled gray eyes. "I don't understand you as well as I thought I did, Zarth."

She was silent for a moment, and then suddenly spoke a little breathlessly.

"Zarth, I can't fence with people. I have to speak straight out. Tell me—did you really mean it when you kissed me last night?"

Gordon's heart jumped, and the answer sprang from his lips. "Lianna, I did!"

Her gray eyes looked up at him gravely, wondering. "It seemed strange yet I felt you did. Yet I still can hardly believe—"

She suddenly, with the imperiousness that betrayed regal training, put her hands on his shoulders. It was open invitation to kiss her again.

Not if the whole palace had crumbled about them could Gordon have resisted doing so. And again, the feel of her slim, electrically alive figure in his arms, the touch of sweet, breathless lips, shook him.

"Zarth, you've changed!" Lianna whispered, wonderingly, unconsciously repeating Murn. "I almost believe that you love me—"

"Lianna, I do!" burst from Gordon. "I have, from the first moment I saw you!"

Her eyes softened, clung brilliantly to his. "Then you want our marriage to be a real one? You would divorce Murn?"

Gordon came to himself with a crashing shock. Good God, what was he doing?

He couldn't compromise the real Zarth, who loved Murn with all his heart.

8

THE SPY FROM THE CLOUD

Gordon was temporarily delivered from his impasse of bewilderment by a providential interruption. It came from a chamberlain who hesitantly emerged onto the terrace.

"Highness, your father requests you and the Princess Lianna to come to the tower-suite," he told Gordon, bowing.

Gordon seized upon the chance to evade further discussion. He said awkwardly, "We had better go at once, Lianna. It may be important."

Lianna remained looking at him with steady gaze, as though expecting him to say more. But he didn't.

He *couldn't*! He couldn't tell her that he loved her, only to have the real Zarth Arn come back and deny it!

She was silent as they followed the chamberlain by gliding ramps up to the highest tower of the palace. Here were rooms whose glass walls looked out over all the shimmering towers of Throon and the stupendous encircling panorama of glassy peaks and sea.

Arn Abbas was restlessly pacing the room, a giant, dominating figure. The thin-faced Chief Councillor, Orth Bodmer, was speaking to him, and Jhal Arn was also present.

"Zarth, this matter concerns you and Lianna both," Arn Abbas greeted them.

He explained curtly. "The crisis between us and the League is deepening. Shorr Kan has called all League star-ships home to the Cloud. And now I'm afraid the Hercules Barons are wavering toward him."

Gordon quickly recalled the luke-warm attitude of Zu Rizal and the other Hercules Baron the night before.

Arn Abbas' massive face was dark. "I sounded Zu Rizal last night after the Feast. He said the Barons couldn't commit themselves to full alliance with the Empire. They're worried by persistent rumors to the effect that Shorr Kan has some powerful new weapon.

"I believe, though, that Zu Ruzal doesn't represent the feelings of all the Barons. They may be doubtful but they don't want to see the Cloud conquer. I think they can be brought into full alliance with the Empire. And I'm going to send you to accomplish that, Zarth."

"Send *me*?" Gordon exclaimed, startled. "But I couldn't carry out a mission like that!"

"Who could carry it out better, highness?" Orth Bodmer said earnestly to him. "As the emperor's own son, your prestige would make you a potent ambassador."

"We're not going to argue about it—you're going whether you like it or not!" snapped Arn Abbas.

Gordon was swept off his feet. He to act as ambassador to the great star-lords of Hercules Cluster? How could he?

Then he saw a chance in this. Once in space on that mission, he might manage to touch at Earth and would then be able to re-exchange bodies with the real Zarth Arn! If he could do that—

"This means," Arn Abbas was saying, "that your marriage to Lianna must take place sooner than we planned. You must leave for Hercules in a week. I shall announce that your marriage to Lianna will be solemnized five days from now."

Gordon felt as though he had suddenly stepped through a trapdoor into an abyss.

He had assumed that this marriage lay so far in the future he didn't need to worry about it! Now his assumption was wrecked!

He desperately voiced protest. "But is it necessary for us to hold the marriage before I go to Hercules as an ambassador?"

"Of course it is!" declared Arn Abbas. "It's vital to hold the western star-kingdoms to us. And as husband of the princess of Fomalhaut Kingdom, you'll carry more weight with the Barons."

Lianna looked at Gordon with that curiously steady gaze and said, "Perhaps Prince Zarth has some objection?"

"Objection? What the devil objection could he have?" demanded Arn Abbas.

Gordon realized that open resistance would do him no good. He had to stall for time, as he had been doing since he was first flung into this involuntary impersonation.

He'd surely find a way somehow to dodge this nightmare complication. But he'd have to have time to think.

He said lamely, "Of course it's all right with me if Lianna approves."

"Then it's settled," said Arn Abbas. "It's short notice but the star-kings can get here in time for the ceremony. Bodmer and I will frame the announcement now."

That was a dismissal, and they left the room. Gordon was glad that Jhal Arn came with them, for the last thing he wanted at this moment was to face Lianna's clear, questioning eyes.

The next few days seemed utterly unreal to Gordon. All the palace, all the city Throon, hummed with activity of preparations. Hosts of servants were busy, and each day swift star-ships arrived with guests from the more distant parts of the Empire and the allied kingdoms.

Gordon was at least relieved that he hardly saw Lianna in this hectic time except at the magnificent feasts that celebrated the coming event. Nor had he seen Murn, except at a distance. But time was running out and he had not found any way out of this fantastic impasse.

He couldn't tell them the truth about himself. That would

break his solemn promise to Zarth Arn. But then what was he to do? He racked his brain, but on the eve of the appointed day he still had found no solution.

That night in the Hall of Stars was held the great reception for the royal and noble guests who had come from far across the galaxy for the wedding. The scene was one of staggering splendor.

Gordon and Lianna stood on the raised reception-dais, with Arn Abbas' giant figure on one side of them and Jhal Arn and his beautiful wife Zora on the other. Behind them were Commander Corbulo and Orth Bodmer and the other highest officials of the Empire.

The brilliant throng whom chamberlains announced as they streamed toward the dais, the majestic magnificence of the Hall of Stars, the televisor screens through which he knew half the galaxy was watching—all this numbed John Gordon.

He felt more and more like a man in a strange and impossible dream. Surely he would wake up at any moment and find himself back in his own 20th Century world?

"The King of the Cygnus Suns!" rang the chamberlain's measured announcements. "The King of Lyra!"

They streamed before Gordon in a blurred succession of faces and voices. He recognized but few of them—the cold-eyed Zu Rizal of the Hercules Barons, young Sath Shamar of Polaris, one or two others.

"The King-Regent of Cassiopeia! The Counts of the Marches of Outer Space!"

Lesser luminaries and officials of the Empire continued the procession to the dais. Among these last came a bronzed naval captain who offered Gordon a thought-spool as he bowed.

"A small petition from my squadron to your highness on this happy occasion," the officer murmured. "We hope that you will listen to it."

Gordon nodded. "I will, captain—"

He was suddenly interrupted by Commander Corbulo. The grizzled naval chief had been staring at the bronzed officer's insignia and he suddenly pushed forward.

"No officer of that squadron should be nearer here than Vega right now!" snapped Corbulo. "What is your name and division-number?"

The bronzed captain looked suddenly gray and haggard. He recoiled, his hand darting into his jacket.

"That man's a spy, perhaps an assassin!" yelled Corbulo. "Blast him!"

The detected spy already had a short, stubby atom-pistol flashing in his hand.

Gordon swept Lianna swiftly behind him. He whirled back then toward the other.

But, at Corbulo's shouted command, from secret apertures high in the walls of the Hall of Stars had flicked down swift atom-pellets that tore into the spy's body and instantly exploded. The man fell to the floor, a torn, blackened corpse.

Screams rent the air, as the crowd recoiled in sudden panic. Gordon was as stunned as everyone else in the Hall by what had happened.

But Arn Abbas' rumbling roar rose quickly to dominate the scene. "There is nothing to fear! The man is dead, thanks to Corbulo's vigilance and our guards inside the walls!"

The big ruler shot orders. "Take the body into another room. Zarth, you and Jhal come along. Corbulo, have that thought-spool ray-searched, it may be dangerous. Lianna, will you reassure our guests?"

Gordon went with the giant emperor into another, smaller room where the blasted body of the spy was quickly carried.

Jhal Arn bent over the body, ripped away the scorched jacket. The mangled torso was not bronze in color like the face. It was a curiously pallid white.

"A Cloud-man! A League spy, as I thought!" snapped Arn Abbas. "One of Shorr Kan's agents in clever disguise!"

Jhal Arn looked puzzled. "Why did he come here? He wasn't primarily trying to assassinate any of us—he didn't draw his weapon until he was detected."

"The thought-spool he was trying to give Zarth may tell us something," muttered the ruler. "Here's Corbulo."

Commander Corbulo had the thought-spool in his hand. "It's been thoroughly ray-examined and is a simple thought-spool and nothing more," he reported.

"It's cursed strange!" rumbled Arn Abbas, his face dark. "Here, put the spool in this reader and we'll listen to it."

The thought-spool was inserted in the reading-mechanism on the desk. Arn Abbas flicked the switch.

The spool started unwinding. Gordon felt the impact of its recorded, amplified thought-pulsations beating into his mind as into the minds of the others.

A clear, resonant voice seemed speaking in his mind as he listened.

"Shorr Kan to the Prince Zarth Arn: It is unfortunate that the arrangements we agreed on for bringing you to the Cloud were thwarted by the chance interference of an Empire patrol. I regret this as much as you do. But rest assured that I will make new arrangements at once for getting you here in safety and secrecy.

"The terms upon which we agreed still stand. As soon as you join forces with me and impart to us the secret of the Disruptor, we of the Cloud will be able to attack the Empire without fear of defeat and you will be publicly recognized as my co-equal in ruling the entire galaxy. Make no move that might arouse suspicion, but wait until my trusted agents are able to bring you safely to me."

9

IN THE PALACE PRISON

To Gordon, at first, that thought-message did not make sense. A message from Shorr Kan to him, to Zarth Arn?

Then as the significance of it sank in, he felt a shock of bewilderment and dismay. And his dismay deepened as he encountered the raging eyes of Arn Abbas.

"By Heaven, my own son a traitor to the Empire!" cried the ruler. "My own son intriguing secretly to betray us to the Cloud!"

Gordon found his voice. "This message is a lie! I never made any arrangements with Shorr Kan, nor had any discussions with him!"

"Then why would he send you such a secret message as this!" roared the emperor.

Gordon caught desperately at the only explanation that suggested itself to him.

"Shorr Kan must have sent this message hoping it would be discovered and make trouble! There can be no other reason."

Jhal Arn, whose handsome face was deeply troubled, spoke quickly.

"Father, that sounds possible enough. It's impossible to believe that Zarth could be a traitor."

"Bah, it's too thin!" raged Arn Abbas. "Shorr Kan is too clever to devise such a harebrained plan that would gain him so little. Why, his spy was only detected at all by the mere chance of Corbulo noticing his naval insignia."

His massive face darkened. "Zarth, if you *have* been secretly plotting with the Cloud, the fact that you're my son won't save you!"

"I swear I haven't!" Gordon cried. "I didn't arrange with those League raiders to come to Earth for me. And why in the world should I betray the Empire?"

"You're my second son," Arn Abbas reminded grimly. "You may have secretly envied Jhal the succession, all the time you pretended to be absorbed in your scientific studies. Such things have happened!"

If his position had seemed nightmare to John Gordon before, it seemed doubly nightmare now.

"This thing is going to be sifted to the bottom!" roared Arn Abbas. "In the meantime, you'll remain locked up in the palace prison!"

Jhal Arn protested. "You can't send Zarth down there!"

Commander Corbulo supported the protest. "At least for appearance's sake, confine Prince Zarth to his own quarters."

Arn Abbas glared at them. "Have you two lost your wits? Don't you realize that if Zarth *is* a traitor, he represents mortal danger to the Empire?

"He knows the secret of the Disruptor, that only Jhal and I beside him know! Let Shorr Kan get that secret, and the Cloud will strike like lightning! Do you want to take a chance of that?"

"But the wedding tomorrow, the guests—," Jhal began.

"Announce that Prince Zarth was suddenly taken ill," snapped the ruler. "Corbulo, you take him down to the prison. And you're responsible for him with your life!"

Gordon's thoughts were whirling wildly. Suppose he told

them the truth, the *real* truth? Suppose he told them that he was only Zarth Arn in physical body and was really John Gordon of the 20th Century? Surely Zarth Arn couldn't blame him for breaking his pledge of secrecy *now*?

But would they believe if he told? He knew that they wouldn't. No one would believe that incredible story. Zarth Arn had kept his method of mind-exchange secret, and no one even dreamed of its possibility. They'd think he was merely trying a desperate, wild lie to save himself.

Gordon's shoulders sagged. He made no further protest but dully went with Commander Corbulo out of the room.

On the corridor motowalk that bore them downward to the lower levels of the palace, Corbulo spoke to him bluntly.

"Zarth, I don't believe a word of all this talk of treachery on your part. I have to lock you up, but you can depend on me to do everything I can to clear you."

The unexpected support from the veteran officer pulled Gordon a little out of his stunned despair.

"Corbulo, I swear the whole thing is some kind of frame-up! Surely my father can't believe I'd really betray the Empire?"

"You know as well as I what a violent temper Arn Abbas has," said the Commander. "But as soon as he cools off, I'll make him listen to reason."

Deep down beneath the great palace they came to a massive metal door. Corbulo flashed a tiny beam from a heavy ring on his finger, into a needle-hole in the door. It slid aside and revealed a square, bare little metal room.

"This is a cell of your father's secret prison, Zarth. I never thought I'd be locking you in here. But don't worry—we'll do our best to change Arn Abbas' mind."

Gordon gripped his hand gratefully, and entered the room. The massive door slid shut.

The room had only a cot with a thin pad for furniture. There were two taps in the wall, one for water and the other for nutritional fluid. Walls, floor and ceiling were of solid metal.

Gordon sat down heavily. At first, he felt a little cheered by Corbulo's assurance of support. But then his hope faded. Even if Corbulo and Jhal believed in him, how could they prove his innocence?

And, the thought forced into his mind, what if he really

was guilty of treachery? What if Zarth Arn, the real Zarth Arn, had in the past been intriguing with Shorr Kan?

Gordon shook his head. "No, I can't believe that! Zarth Arn was a scientific enthusiast, not a schemer. And if he'd been plotting with the Cloud, he'd not have exchanged minds with me."

But if Zarth Arn had been innocent of intrigue, why had Shorr Kan sent him that message referring to their past discussions?

Gordon gave it up. "I'm just out of my depth. I should have known that my ignorance would get me into some disaster if I tried to play Zarth's part!"

He thought miserably of Lianna. They'd have to tell her what had happened, even if they kept it concealed from everyone else.

Would she too think him a traitor? That possibility stung Gordon to despair.

He was for a time in a fever of self-torment, but finally a despairing apathy succeeded it. After hours, he slept.

Gordon estimated it was evening of the next day when he awoke. The door opening had aroused him. He stood up, and then stared incredulously at the two figures entering.

One was Corbulo's stocky form. But the other, the slimmer figure in dark jacket and slacks—

"Lianna!" Gordon exclaimed. "What are you doing down here?"

She came toward him, her face pale but her gray eyes alight as she put her small hands on his shoulders. Her words came in a rush.

"Zarth, they told me all about your father's accusation. Arn Abbas must be mad!"

His eyes hungrily searched her face. "You don't believe I'm a traitor, Lianna?"

"I *know* you are not!" she exclaimed. "I told Arn Abbas so, but he was too angry to listen to me."

Gordon felt a wave of sharp emotion. "Lianna, I think it was what you might believe that tortured me most!"

Corbulo came forward, his grizzled face grave. "You must talk quickly, princess! We must be out of here with Zarth Arn in twenty minutes, to keep my schedule."

"Out of here with *me*?" Gordon repeated. "You mean you're going to let me leave here?"

Corbulo nodded curtly. "Yes, Zarth, I made up my mind and told the princess this evening. I'm going to help you escape from Throon."

Gordon warmed to this hard-faced Commander. "Corbulo, I appreciate your faith in me. But it would look like running away."

"Zarth, you have to go!" Corbulo told him earnestly. "I thought I could bring your father around. But unfortunately, in your apartments were discovered other incriminating messages to you from Shorr Kan!"

Gordon was stupefied. "Then they're fakes, planted there on purpose to incriminate me!"

"I believe that, but they've deepened your father's raging belief in your guilt," Corbulo declared. "I fear that in his present anger, he may order you executed as a traitor!"

The Commander added, "I'm not going to let him do that and then regret it later when you're proved innocent. So you must get away from Throon until I can prove your innocence!"

Lianna added eagerly, "We have it all planned, Zarth. Corbulo has a light naval cruiser with trusted officers waiting at the spaceport. That ship will take us up to my Fomalhaut Kingdom. We'll be safe there until Corbulo and your brother can prove you're not guilty."

Gordon was more deeply astonished. "You say— *we*? Lianna, you'd go with me, a fugitive? Why?"

For answer, firm, warm arms went around his neck and soft lips pressed his in quivering, sweet contact.

Her voice was a husky whisper. "That is why, Zarth."

Gordon's mind whirled. "You mean that you love me? Lianna, is it true?"

"I have, since the night of the Feast of Moons when you kissed me," she whispered. "Until then, I had liked you but that was all. But since then, you've been somehow different."

Gordon's arms tightened around her "Then it's the different Zarth Arn, the new Zarth Arn, you love?"

She looked up at him steadily. "I have just told you so."

There deep in the secret prison beneath the great palace of Throon, Gordon felt a wild, soaring joy that blotted from his mind all consciousness of the deadly web of peril and intrigue in which he was caught.

It was he himself, even though in a stranger's physical body, who had won Lianna's love! Though she might never know it, it was not Zarth Arn she loved but John Gordon!

10

FLIGHT INTO THE VOID

The secret of his identity trembled on Gordon's lips. He wanted with all his soul to tell Lianna that he was Zarth Arn only in physical body, that he was really John Gordon of the past.

He couldn't do it, he had to keep his pledge to Zarth Arn. And after all, what good would it do to tell her when he had to leave her eventually and go back to his own time?

Could any self-devised torment be more damnable? To be forced to separate himself by half a universe and two thousand centuries of time from the only girl he had ever really loved?

Gordon spoke huskily. "Lianna, you must not go with me. It's too dangerous."

She looked up quickly with brilliant eyes. "Does a daughter of star-kings fear danger? No, Zarth, we go together!"

She added, "Don't you see, your father won't be able to send after you by force when you're with me in my little Fomalhaut Kingdom. The Empire needs allies too much to estrange my people thus."

Gordon's mind raced. Here might be his chance to get to Earth! Once away from Throon, he might by some pretext get Corbulo's men to take them first to Earth and the laboratory there.

There, he could manage to re-effect the mind-exchange with the real Zarth Arn without letting Lianna know what he was doing. And the real Zarth, on returning, could surely prove his innocence.

Corbulo interrupted by coming up to them. His hard face was deeply worried.

"We cannot wait longer here! The corridors will be clear now, and it is our only chance to go."

Disregarding Gordon's protests against her accompanying him, Lianna seized his wrist and tugged him forward.

Corbulo had opened the massive sliding door. The corridors outside were softly lighted, silent, deserted.

"We go to a little-used branch of the tubeway," Corbulo told them hastily. "One of my most trusted officers is waiting there."

They hurried along the corridors, deep beneath the mighty palace of Throon. Not a sound came from the mammoth structure over their heads. These secret passages were sound-proofed.

Nor did they meet anyone. But as they emerged into a wider corridor, Corbulo led the way with caution. Finally they stepped into a small room that was a vestibule to one of the tubeways. A car was waiting in the tube, and a man in naval uniform waited beside it.

"This is Thern Eldred, captain of the cruiser that will take you to Fomalhaut Kingdom," Corbulo said quickly. "You can trust him absolutely."

Thern Eldred was a tall Sirian, the faintly greenish hue of his face gave evidence. He looked a hard-bitten, rangy veteran of space, but his curt face lighted as he bowed deeply to Gordon and Lianna.

"Prince Zarth, Princess—I am honored by this trust! The Commander has explained everything to me. You can rely on me and my men to get you to any part of the galaxy!"

Gordon hesitated, troubled. "It still seems like running away."

Corbulo swore a spaceman's oath. "Zarth, it's your only chance! With you gone, I'll have time to dig out evidence of your innocence and bring your father around. Stay here, and he's likely to have you shot as a traitor."

Gordon might have stayed despite that danger had it not been for the potent factor which was wholly unknown to these others—the fact that this was his only chance to get to Earth and make contact with the real Zarth Arn.

He gripped Corbulo's hand. And Lianna softly told the bluff Commander, "You're risking much for us. I shall never forget."

They stepped into the car. Thern Eldred hastily followed them in and touched a lever. The car started racing headlong through the darkness.

Thern Eldred glanced tensely at his watch. "Everything has been scheduled to the minute, highness," he told Gordon. "My cruiser, the *Markab,* is waiting in a secluded dock at the spaceport. Ostensibly we take off to join the Sagittarius patrol."

"You're risking your neck for us too, captain," Gordon said earnestly.

The Sirian smiled. "Commander Corbulo has been like a father to me. I could not refuse the trust when he asked me and my men."

The car slowed and halted beside another little vestibule in which two naval officers armed with atom-pistols were waiting.

They saluted sharply as Gordon and Lianna stepped out. Thern Eldred quickly followed and led the way up a gliding ramp.

"Now muffle your cloaks about your faces until we get aboard the *Markab,*" he told them. "After that, you need fear nothing."

They emerged onto a corner of the spaceport. It was night, two golden moons strung across the blazing starry sky, casting down a warm light in which the massive ships, cranes and machines glinted dully.

Towering from the docks, dwarfing all else, loomed the black bulks of the mighty first-line battleships. As they followed Thern Eldred along the side of one, Gordon glimpsed the portentous muzzles of its heavy atom-gun batteries silhouetted against the stars.

The Sirian made a signal and held them suddenly back, as a troop of noisy sailors swaggered past. Standing there in the dark, Gordon felt the pressure of Lianna's fingers on his hand. Her face, in the dim light, smiled at him undauntedly.

Then Thern Eldred motioned them on. "We must hurry!" he sweated. "We're behind schedule—"

The black, fishlike mass of the *Markab* rose before them in the golden moonlight. Lights glittered from small portholes, and there was a steady throbbing of power from the stern of the light cruiser.

They followed the Sirian and his two officers up a narrow

gangway toward a waiting open door in the side of the ship. But suddenly, the silence was violently broken.

Annunciators about the spaceport screamed a loud siren alarm. Then a man's hoarse, excited voice shouted from the speakers.

"General alarm to all naval personnel!" yelled that wild voice. "Arn Abbas has just been assassinated!"

Gordon froze, wildly clutching Lianna's hand as they stopped there on the gangway.

The voice was shouting on. "Apprehend Prince Zarth Arn wherever he is encountered! He is to be arrested immediately!"

"Good God!" cried Gordon. "Arn Abbas murdered—and they think I escaped and did it!"

The whole great spaceport was waking to the alarm, the voice shouting its wild message over and over from a hundred annunciators. Bells were ringing, men yelling and running.

Far southward, over the distant towers of the city Throon, gleaming fliers were rushing up in the night sky and racing wildly across the heavens in half a dozen different directions.

Thern Eldred tried to urge the frozen Gordon and Lianna up the gangway. "You must hurry, highness!" cried the Sirian. "Your only chance is to get away at once!"

"Run away and let them think I murdered Arn Abbas?" cried Gordon. "No! We're going back to the palace at once!"

Lianna, her face pale, swiftly supported him. "You must return. Arn Abbas' murder will shake the whole Empire!"

Gordon had turned with her to start back down the gangway. But Thern Eldred, his green face wearing a hard, taut expression, suddenly whipped out and extended a little glass weapon.

It was a short glass rod on whose end was mounted a glass crescent that had two metal tips. He darted it toward Gordon's face.

"Zarth, it's a paralyzer! Look out!" cried Lianna, who recognized the menace of the weapon where Gordon did not.*

The tips of the glass crescent touched Gordon's chin.

---

* *Note:* A paralyzer was a weapon designed to stun an opponent when at close quarters. It did so by releasing a brief high-voltage electroshock that travelled through the nerves to the brain.

Lightning seemed to crash through his brain with a paralyzing shock.

He felt himself falling, every muscle frozen, consciousness leaving him. He had a dim sensation of Lianna's voice, of her staggering against him.

There was only darkness in Gordon's mind then. In that darkness he seemed to float for ages before finally light began to dawn.

He became aware that his body was tingling painfully with returning life. He was lying on a hard, flat surface. There was a steady, loud droning sound in his ears.

Gordon painfully opened his eyes. He lay on a bunk in a little metal cabin, a tiny lighted room with little furniture.

Lianna, her face colorless and her eyes closed, lay in another bunk. There was a little porthole window from which he saw a sky of blazing stars. Then Gordon recognized the droning sound as the throb of a star-ship's powerful atomic turbines and drive-generators.

"Good God, we're in space!" he thought. "Thern Eldred stunned us and brought us—"

They were in the *Markab,* and from the high drone of its drive the light cruiser was hurtling through the galactic void at its utmost speed.

Lianna was stirring. Gordon stumbled to his feet and went to her side. He chafed her wrists and face till her eyes opened.

The girl instantly became aware of their situation, with her first glance. Remembrance came back to her.

"Your father murdered!" she cried to Gordon. "And they think you did it, back at Throon!"

Gordon nodded sickly. "We've got to go back. We've got to make Thern Eldred take us back."

Gordon stumbled to the door of the cabin. It would not slide open when he tried it. They were locked in.

Lianna's voice turned him around. The girl was at the porthole, looking out. She turned a very pale face.

"Zarth, come here!"

He went to her side. Their cabin was near the bows of the cruiser, and the curve of the wall allowed them to look almost straight forward into the vault of stars into which the *Markab* was racing.

"They're not taking us toward Fomalhaut Kingdom!" Lianna exclaimed. "Thern Eldred has betrayed us!"

Gordon stared into the blazing jungle of stars that spread across the sky ahead.

"What's the meaning of this? Where is Thern Eldred taking us?" Gordon asked.

"Look to the west of Orion Nebula, in the distance ahead of us!" Lianna exclaimed.

Gordon looked as she pointed through the round window.* He saw, far away in the starry wilderness ahead of their racing ship, a black little blot in the heavens. A dark, brooding blotch that seemed to have devoured a section of the starry firmament.

He knew instantly what it was. The Cloud! The distant, mysterious realm of semi-darkness within which lay the stars and planets of that League of the Dark Worlds of which Shorr Kan was master, and that was hatching war and conquest for the rest of the galaxy.

"They're taking us to the Cloud!" Lianna cried. "Zarth, this is Shorr Kan's plot!"

11

GALACTIC PLOT

The truth flashed over Gordon's mind. All that had happened to him since he had taken up the impersonation of Zarth Arn had been instigated by the cunning scheming of that master plotter who ruled the Cloud.

Shorr Kan's plots had reached out to involve him in gathering conflict between the giant galactic confederations, through many secret agents. And one of those agents of the powerful master of the Dark Worlds must be Thern Eldred!

"By Heaven, I see it now!" Gordon exclaimed, to the stunned girl. "Thern Eldred is working for the Cloud, and has betrayed Commander Corbulo!"

* *Note:* The "windows" of a star-ship were not simple windows, but vision-screens operating by sub-spectrum rays far faster than light. So that even when a ship was moving faster than the rays of light, these windows gave a true picture of surrounding space.

"But why should they do this, Zarth? Why implicate you in the murder of your own father?"

"To compromise me hopelessly so that I can't return to Throon!" gritted Gordon.

Lianna had paled slightly. She looked up at him steadily, though.

"What is going to happen to us in the Cloud, Zarth?" she asked.

Gordon felt an agony of apprehension for her. It was his fault that she was in this deadly danger. She had been trying to help him, and had incurred this peril.

"Lianna, I knew you shouldn't have come with me! If anything happens to you—"

He stopped and swung around, as the door slid open. Thern Eldred stood there.

At sight of the tall Sirian standing and regarding them with a cynical smile on his pale green face, Gordon started forward in an access of hot rage.

Thern Eldred quickly drew one of the little glass weapons from his jacket.

"Please note this paralyzer in my hand," he advised dryly. "Unless you want to spend more time unconscious, you'll restrain yourself."

"You traitor!" raged Gordon. "You've betrayed your uniform, your Empire!"

Thern Eldred nodded calmly. "I've been one of Shorr Kan's most trusted agents for years. I expect to receive his warmest commendations when we reach Thallarna."

"Thallarna? The mysterious capital of the League?" said Lianna. "Then we are going to the Cloud?"

The Sirian nodded again. "We'll reach it in four days. Luckily, knowing the patrol-schedules of the Empire fleet as I do, I am able to follow a course that will prevent unpleasant encounters."

"Then Arn Abbas was murdered by you League spies!" Gordon accused harshly. "You *knew* it was going to happen! That's why you were in such a hurry to get us away!"

The Sirian smiled coolly. "Of course. I was working on a schedule of split-seconds. It had to look as though you had murdered your father and then fled. We just pulled it off."

Gordon raged. "By heaven, you're not to the Cloud yet!

Corbulo knows I didn't commit that murder! He'll put two and two together and be out to track you down!"

Thern Eldred stared at him, then threw back his head in a roar of laughter. He laughed until he had to wipe his eyes.

"Your pardon, Prince Zarth, but that's the funniest thing you've said yet!" he chuckled. "Corbulo after me? Why, haven't you guessed yet that Corbulo himself planned this whole thing?"

"You're mad!" Gordon exclaimed. "Corbulo is the most trusted official in the Empire!"

Thern Eldred nodded. "Yes, but *only* an official, only Commander of the fleet. And he has ambitions beyond that post, has had them a long time. For the last few years, he and a score of others of us officers have been working secretly for Shorr Kan."

The Sirian's eyes gleamed. "Shorr Kan has promised that when the Empire is shattered, we shall each of us have a star-kingdom of our own to rule. And Corbulo is to have the biggest."

Gordon's angry incredulity somehow faded a little, before the ring of truth in the Sirian's voice.

Horrified, Gordon realized that it might be true! Chan Corbulo, Commander of the Empire's great navy, might be a secret traitor for all he knew.

Evidence pointing that way rose swiftly in Gordon's mind. Why else had Corbulo broken his duty and helped him to escape? Why, at the very moment when Arn Abbas' assassination was imminent?

Thern Eldred read something of what passed in Gordon's mind, from his face. And the Sirian laughed again.

"You begin to realize now what a dupe you've been. Why, it was Corbulo himself who shot down Arn Abbas last night! And Corbulo will swear that he saw it done by *you*, Zarth Arn!"

Lianna was pale, incredulous. "But why? Why implicate Zarth?"

"Because," smiled the Sirian, "it's the most effective way to split the Empire and leave it wide open to the Cloud's attack. And there's another reason that Shorr Kan will explain to you."

The malice and triumph in Thern Eldred's eyes detonated the rage that gathered in John Gordon's mind.

He plunged forward, heedless of Thern Eldred's warning shout. He managed by a swift contortion of his body to avoid the glass paralyzer that the other jabbed at him. His fist smashed into the Sirian's face.

Thern Eldred, as he sprawled backward, had Gordon atop him like a leaping panther. But the Sirian had managed to cling to his weapon. And before Gordon could carry out his intention of wrestling it away, Thern Eldred desperately jabbed up with it again.

The crescent at the end of the glass rod touched Gordon's neck. A freezing shock smote like lightning through his body. He felt his senses darken swiftly.

When Gordon for a second time came back to consciousness, he was again lying in one of the bunks. This time, the freezing ache in his body was more painful. And this time, Lianna was sitting beside him and looking down at him with anxious gray eyes.

Her eyes lighted as he opened his own. "Zarth, you've been unconscious more than a day! I was beginning to worry."

"I'm—all right," he muttered. He tried to sit up, but her little hands quickly forced him back down onto the pad.

"Don't, Zarth—you must rest until your nerves recover from the electroshock."

He glanced at the porthole window. The vista of blazing stars outside seemed unchanged. He could glimpse the black blot of the Cloud, looking only a little larger in the distant forest of suns.

Lianna followed his glance. "We are travelling at tremendous speed but it will still require a few days before we reach the Cloud. In that time, we may encounter an Empire patrol."

Gordon groaned. "Lianna, there's no hope for that. This is itself an Empire cruiser and could pass any patrol. And if Corbulo is really leader of this treachery, he'd have his patrols arranged so that this ship could pass unseen."

"I've thought and thought about it and I still can hardly believe it," Lianna said. "Corbulo a traitor! It seems fantastic! And yet—"

Gordon himself no longer doubted. The evidence was too overwhelming.

"Men will betray any trust when ambition drives them, and Corbulo is ambitious," he muttered. Then, as deeper realization came to him, "Good God, this means that if the League does attack the Empire, the Commander of the Empire forces will sabotage their defense!"

He rose painfully from the bunk despite Lianna's protestations.

"If we could only get word back to Throon somehow! That would at least put Jhal Arn on his guard!"

Lianna shook her ash-golden head a little sadly. "I fear there's no chance of that, once we're prisoners in the Cloud. Shorr Kan is not likely to let us go."

It all spun in John Gordon's mind in a bewildering chaos of known and unknown factors, in the hours that followed.

A few things, though, stood out clearly. They all, everyone in this universe, thought that he was Zarth Arn. And thus it was believed that he knew the secret of the Disruptor, that mysterious scientific weapon known only to Arn Abbas and his two sons.

That was why Corbulo had risked the plot that was sending him and Lianna now as prisoners to the Cloud! Once Shorr Kan had that secret, mysterious weapon, he would have nothing to fear from the Empire whose fleet was commanded by his own man. He would attack them at once!

The *Markab* droned on and on. When the ship bells signalled evening of the arbitrary "day," the aspect of the starry firmament had changed. Orion Nebula flamed now in all its titan glory far in the east.

Straight ahead, far in the distance against the remotest suns of the galaxy, brooded the black blot of the Cloud. It was visibly larger than before, and its gigantic dimensions were now becoming more clearly apparent.

Neither Thern Eldred nor any of his officers or men entered the cabin. There was no opportunity for a second attack. And after searching vainly through the room, Gordon conceded defeatedly that there was nothing in it that might facilitate escape.

Sick anxiety for Lianna's safety deepened in him. He reproached himself again for letting her accompany him on this flight.

But she did not seem afraid as she looked up at him. "Zarth, at least we're together for a little while. It may be all of happiness we'll get."

Gordon found his arms instinctively starting to go around her, his hand touching her shining hair. But he forced himself to step back.

"Lianna, you'd better get some sleep," he said uncomfortably.

Lianna, looked at him with a wondering little smile. "Why, Zarth, what's the matter?"

Gordon had never in his life wanted anything so much as to reach forth to her. But to do so would be the blackest treachery.

Treachery to Zarth Arn, who had trusted his body, his life, to Gordon's pledge! Yes, and treachery to Lianna herself.

For if he were able to reach the Earth laboratory, it would be the real Zarth Arn who would come back to her—Zarth Arn, who loved Murn and not Lianna.

"That won't ever happen!" whispered a subtle, tempting voice in Gordon's mind. "You and she will never escape from the Cloud. Take what happiness you can, while you can!"

Gordon desperately fought down that insinuating voice. He spoke huskily to the puzzled girl.

"Lianna, you and I will have to forget all talk of love."

She seemed stricken by amazement, unbelief. "But Zarth, at Throon that morning you told me you loved me!"

Gordon nodded miserably. "I know. I wish to God I hadn't. It was wrong."

Little clouds began to gather in Lianna's gray eyes. She was white to the lips.

"You mean that you are still in love with Murn, after all?"

Gordon forced the answer to that out of strained, desperate resolve. He spoke what he knew was the exact truth.

"Zarth Arn does still love Murn. You have to know that, Lianna."

The incredulity in Lianna's white face gave way to a hurt that went deep in her gray eyes.

Gordon had expected stormy resentment, wrath, bitter reproach. He had steeled himself against them. But he had not expected this deep, voiceless hurt, and it was too much for him.

"To the devil with my promise!" he told himself fiercely.

"Zarth Arn wouldn't hold me to it if he knew that situation—he couldn't!"

And Gordon stepped forward and grasped the girl's hand. "Lianna, I'm going to tell you the whole truth! Zarth Arn doesn't love you—but *I* do!"

He rushed on. "I'm not Zarth Arn. I'm an entirely different man, in Zarth Arn's body. I know it sounds incredible, but—"

His voice trailed off. For he read in Lianna's face her quick disbelief and scorn.

"Let us at least have no more lies, Zarth!" she flared.

"I tell you, it's true!" he persisted. "This is Zarth Arn's physical body, yes. But I am a different man!"

He knew from the expression on her face that his attempt had failed. He knew that she did not believe and never would believe.

How could he expect her to believe it? If positions had been reversed, would he have credited such a wild assertion? He knew he wouldn't.

No one in this universe would credit it, now Vel Quen was dead. For only Vel Quen had known about Zarth Arn's fantastic experiments.

Lianna was looking at him, her eyes now calm and level and without a trace of emotion in her face.

"There is no need for you to explain your actions by wild stories of dual personality, Zarth. I understand clearly enough. You were simply doing what you conceived to be your duty to the Empire. You feared lest I might refuse the marriage at the last moment, so you pretended love for me to make sure of me and of Fomalhaut's support."

"Lianna, I swear it isn't so!" Gordon groaned. "But if you won't trust me to speak truth—"

She ignored his interruption. "You need not have done it, Zarth. I had no thought of refusing the marriage, since I knew how much depended on my kingdom supporting the Empire.

"But there's no further need for stratagems. I will keep my promise and so will my kingdom. I will marry you, but our marriage will be only a political formality as we first agreed."

John Gordon started to protest, then stopped. After all, the course she proposed was the only one he could take.

If the real Zarth Arn returned, his marriage with Lianna could not be anything more than political pretense.

"All right, Lianna," Gordon said heavily. "I repeat, that I never lied to you. But it all doesn't make much difference now, anyway."

He gestured, as he spoke, toward the porthole. Out there in the star-blazing void ahead of the rushing cruiser, the monster blot of the Cloud was looming ever bigger and closer.

Lianna nodded quietly. "We do not have much chance of escaping Shorr Kan's clutches. But if a chance does present itself, you will find me your ally. Our personal emotions mean little compared to the urgent necessity of getting back with a warning to the Empire."

Gordon saw less and less chance of that, in the hours that followed. For now the *Markab,* its velocity at great heights, was rushing ever nearer the Cloud.

That "night" when the ship lights dimmed, he lay in his bunk thinking bitterly that of all men in history he had had the most ironic joke played upon him.

The girl across the cabin loved him, and he loved her. And yet soon a gulf of space and time incredible might forever separate them, and she would always believe him faithless.

12

IN THE COSMIC CLOUD

Next "morning" they woke to find that the cloud was colossal now ahead. Its vast blotch loomed across half the firmament, a roiling gloom that reached out angry, ragged arms of shadow like an octopus whose dark tentacles clutched at the whole galaxy.

And the *Markab* now was being companioned through space by four massive black battleships with the black disk of the League of Dark Worlds marked on their bows. They were so close, and maintained so exactly the same speed, they could be clearly seen.

"We might have known that Shorr Kan would send an escort," Lianna murmured. She glanced at Gordon. "He thinks that he has the secret of the Disruptor almost in his hands, in your person."

"Lianna, set your mind at rest on one thing," Gordon told her. "He'll never get that secret from me."

"I know you are not traitor to the Empire," she said somberly. "But the League scientists are said to be masters of strange tortures. They may force it from you."

Gordon laughed shortly. "They won't. Shorr Kan is going to find that he had made one bad miscalculation."

Nearer and nearer the five ships flew toward the Cloud. All the universe ahead was now a black, swirling gloom.

Then, keeping to their tight formation, the squadron plunged into the Cloud.

Darkness swept around the ship. Not a total darkness but a gloomy, shadowy haze that seemed smothering after the blazing glory of open space.

Gordon perceived that the cosmic dust that composed the Cloud was not as dense as he had thought. Its huge extent made it appear an impenetrable darkness from outside. But once inside it, they seemed racing through a vast, unbroken haze.

There were stars in here, suns that were visible only a few parsecs away. They shone wanly through the haze, like smothered bale-fires, uncanny witch-stars.

The *Markab* and its escort passed comparatively close to some of these star-systems. Gordon glimpsed planets circling in the feeble glow of the smothered suns, worlds shadowed by perpetual twilight.

Homing on secret radar beams, the ships plunged on and on through the Cloud. Yet it was not until next day that deceleration began.

"We must be pretty nearly there," Gordon said grimly to the girl.

Lianna nodded, and pointed ahead through the window. Far ahead in the shadowy haze burned a dull red, smoldering sun.

"Thallarna," she murmured. "The capital of the League of Dark Worlds, and the citadel of Shorr Kan."

Gordon's nerves stretched taut as the following hours of rapid deceleration brought them closer to their destination.

Meteor-hail rattled off the ships. They twisted and changed course frequently. The shrilling of meteor-alarms could be heard each few minutes, as jagged boulders rushed upon them and then vanished in the automatic trip-blast of atomic energy from the ship.

Angry green luminescence that had once been called nebulium edged these stormy, denser regions. But each time they emerged into thinner haze, the sullen red sun of Thallarna glowed bigger ahead.

"The star-system of Thallarna was not idly chosen for their capital," Lianna said. "Invaders would have a perilous time threading through these stormy mazes to it."

Gordon felt the sinister aspect of the red sun as the ships swung toward it. Old, smoldering, sullen crimson, it glowed here in the heart of the vast and gloomy Cloud like an evil, watching eye.

And the single planet that circled it, the planet Thallarna itself, was equally somber. Strange white plains and white forests of fungoid appearance covered much of it. An inky ocean dashed its ebon waves, eerily reflecting the bloody light of the red sun.

The warships sank through the atmosphere toward a titan city. It was black and massive, its gigantic, blocklike buildings gathered in harshly geometrical symmetry.

Lianna exclaimed and pointed to the huge rows of docks outside the city. Gordon's incredulous eyes beheld a vast beehive of activity, thousands of grim warships docked in long rows, a great activity of cranes and conveyors and men.

"Shorr Kan's fleet makes ready, indeed!" she said. "And this is only one of their naval bases here. The League is far stronger than we dreamed!"

Gordon fought a chilling apprehension. "But Jhal Arn will be calling together all the Empire's forces, too. And he has the Disruptor. If Corbulo can only be prevented from further treachery!"

The ships separated, the four escort battleships remaining above while the *Markab* sank toward a colossal, cubical black pile.

The cruiser landed in a big court. They glimpsed soldiers running toward it—Cloud-men, pallid-faced men in dark uniforms.

It was some minutes before the door of their own cabin opened. Thern Eldred stood in it with two alert League officers.

"We have arrived and I learn that Shorr Kan wishes to see

you at once," the Sirian traitor told Gordon. "I beg you to make no resistance, which would be wholly futile and foolish."

Gordon had had two experiences with the glass paralyzers to convince him of that. He stood, with Lianna's hand on his, and nodded curtly.

"All right. The sooner we get this over with, the better."

They walked out of the ship, their gravitation-equalizers * preventing them from feeling any difference in gravity. The air was freezing and the depressing quality was increased by the murky gloom that was thickening as the red sun set.

Cold, gloomy, shadowed forever by the haze, this world at the heart of the Cloud struck Gordon as a fitting place for the hatching of a plot to rend the galaxy.

"This is Durk Undis, a high officer of the League," the Sirian was saying, "The Prince Zarth Arn and the Princess Lianna, Durk."

Durk Undis, the League officer, was a young man. But though he was not unhandsome, his pallid face and deep eyes had a look of fanaticism in them.

He bowed to Gordon and the girl, and gestured toward a doorway.

"Our Commander is waiting," he said clippedly.

Gordon saw the gleam of triumph in his eye, and in the faces of the other rigid Cloud-men they passed.

He knew they must be exultant, at this capture of one of the Empire's royal family and the striking down of mighty Arn Abbas.

"This ramp, please," Durk Undis said, as they entered the building. He could not help adding proudly to Gordon, "You are doubtless surprised at our capital? We have no useless luxuries here."

Spartan simplicity, an austere bareness, reigned in the gloomy halls of the great building. Here there was none indeed of the luxury and splendor of the great palace at Throon. Uniforms were everywhere. This was the center of a military empire.

---

* *Note:* The gravitation-equalizers were marvelously compact projectors worn in a tiny belt-case by everyone, in this star-travelling age. They automatically gave the body a positive or negative magnetic-gravitational charge that made weight the same no matter how large or small a world was visited.

They came to a massive door guarded by a file of stalwart, uniformed Cloud-men armed with atom-guns. These stepped aside, and the door opened.

Durk Undis and the Sirian walked on either side of Gordon and Lianna into a forbidding room.

It was even more austere than the rest of the place. A single desk with its row of visors and screens, a hard, uncushioned chair, a window looking out on the black massiveness of Thallarna—these were all.

The man behind the desk rose. He was tall, broad-shouldered, about forty years of age. His black hair was close-clipped, his strong, pallid face sternly set, and his black eyes harsh and keen.

"Shorr Kan, Commander of the League of the Dark Worlds!" intoned Durk Undis, with fanatic intensity. And then, "These are the prisoners, sir!"

Shorr Kan's stern gaze fastened on Gordon's face, and then briefly on Lianna's.

He spoke in clipped tones to the Sirian. "You have done well, Thern Eldred. You and Chan Corbulo have proved your devotion to the great cause of the League, and you will not find it ungrateful."

He went on, "You had better take your cruiser back at once to the Empire and rejoin your fleet lest suspicion fall on you."

Thern Eldred nodded quickly. "That will be wisest, sir. I shall be ready to execute any orders you send through Corbulo."

Shorr Kan added, "You can go too, Durk. I shall question our two unwilling guests now."

Durk Undis looked worried. "Leave them here with you alone, sir? It is true they have no weapons, but—"

Shorr Kan turned a stern face on the young fanatic. "Do you think I stand in any danger from this flabby Empire princeling? And even if there were danger, do you think I would shrink from it if it was required by our cause?"

His voice deepened. "Will not millions of men soon hazard their lives for that cause, and gladly? Should one of us shrink from any peril when upon our unswerving devotion depends the success of all we have planned?

"And we *will* succeed!" rang his voice. "We shall take by force our rightful heritage in the galaxy, from the greedy

Empire that thought to condemn us to perpetual banishment in these dark worlds! In that great common enterprise, do you believe I think of risks?"

Durk Undis bowed, almost worshipfully, and the Sirian imitated the action. They withdrew from the room.

Gordon had felt an astonishment, at Shorr Kan's thundering rhetoric. But now he was further astonished.

For as the door closed, Shorr Kan's stern face and towering figure relaxed. The League commander lounged back in his chair and looked up at Gordon and Lianna with a grin on his dark face.

"How did you like my little speech, Zarth Arn?" he asked. "I know it must sound pretty silly, but they love that kind of nonsense."

Gordon could only stare, so amazed was he by the sudden and utter transformation in the personality of Shorr Kan.

"Then you don't believe in any of that stuff yourself?" he demanded.

Shorr Kan laughed. "Do I look like a complete fool? Only crazy fanatics would swallow it. But fanatics are the mainspring of any enterprise like this, and I have to be the biggest fanatic of all when I'm talking to them."

He motioned to chairs. "Sit down. I'd offer you a drink but I don't dare to keep the stuff around here. It might be found and that would destroy the wonderful legend of Shorr Kan's austere life, his devotion to duty, his ceaseless toil for the people of the League."

He looked at them with calmly cynical, keen black eyes for a moment.

"I know a good bit about you, Zarth Arn. I've made it my business to find out. And I know that while you're a scientific enthusiast rather than a practical man, you're a highly intelligent person. I'm also aware that your fiancée, the Princess Lianna, is not a fool.

"Very well, that makes things a lot easier. I can talk to intelligent people. It's these idiots who let their emotions rule them who have to be handled with high-sounding nonsense about destiny, and duty, and their sacred mission."

Gordon, his first shock of surprise over, began to understand this ruler whose name shadowed the whole galaxy.

Utterly intelligent, and yet at the same time utterly cynical, ruthless, keen and cold as a sword-blade, was Shorr Kan.

Gordon felt a strange sense of inferiority in strength and shrewdness to this arch-plotter. And that very feeling made his hatred more bitter.

"You expect me to discuss things calmly with you, after having me brought here by force and branded to the galaxy as a parricide?"

Shorr Kan shrugged. "I admit that that's unpleasant for you. But I had to have you here. You'd have been here days ago, if the men I sent to seize you at your Earth laboratory hadn't failed."

He shook his dark head ruefully. "It just shows how chance can upset the cleverest plans. They should have had no trouble bringing you from Earth. Corbulo had given us a complete schedule of the Empire patrols in that sector, so they could be avoided. And then that cursed Antarian captain had to make an unscheduled visit to Sol!"

The cloud-leader concluded. "So I had to get you here some other way, Prince Zarth. And the best way was to send you an incriminating thought-message that would get you into trouble. Corbulo, of course, had orders to "discover" my messenger, and then later to assist your flight from Throon so his killing of Arn Abbas would be blamed on you!"

Gordon seized on one point in that explanation. "Then it's true that Chan Corbulo is working for you?"

Shorr Kan grinned. "I'll wager that was a bad shock to you, wasn't it? Corbulo is pretty cunning. He's mad for power, for a star-kingdom of his own to rule. But he's always concealed that under the bluff, honest spaceman pose that made the whole Empire admire him."

He added, "It may assuage your disillusion to learn that only Corbulo and a score of other officials and officers in the Empire are traitors. But they're enough to wreck the Empire fleet's chances when it comes to the showdown."

Gordon leaned forward tensely. "And just when is that showdown going to come?"

13

MASTER OF THE CLOUD

Shorr Kan lounged back in his chair before he answered. "Zarth Arn, that depends to some extent on whether or not you're willing to cooperate with me."

Lianna spoke scornfully. "By 'cooperate' you mean, betray the Empire."

The League commander was not ruffled. "That's one way of putting it. I'd prefer to define it as simply to become realistic."

He leaned forward and his strong, mobile face was in deep earnest as he continued.

"I'll put my cards on the table, Zarth. The League of Dark Worlds has secretly built up its fleet here stronger than the Empire navy. We have every weapon of war you have, and a brand new weapon that will play the devil with your fleet when we use it."

"What kind of a weapon? Sounds like a bluff to me," commented Gordon.

Shorr Kan grinned. "You can't fish information out of me. But I will tell you that it's a weapon that can strike down enemy warships from *inside* them."

He added, "With that new weapon, with our powerful fleet, and above all with your Commander Corbulo secretly in our pay, your Empire fleet won't have a chance when we attack! We'd have attacked before now if it hadn't been for one thing. And that's the Disruptor.

"Corbulo couldn't tell us about the Disruptor, since only the royal house of the Empire are allowed to know about it. And while the traditions of its awful power may be exaggerated, we know that they are not baseless. For your ancestor Brenn Bir did with the Disruptor somehow completely annihilate the alien Magellanians who invaded the galaxy two thousand years ago."

Shorr Kan's face tightened. "You know the secret of that

mysterious weapon or power, Zarth. And I want it from you!"

John Gordon had expected no less. But he continued to fence. "I suppose," he said ironically, "that you're going to offer me a star-kingdom if I give you the secret of the Disruptor?"

"More than that," Shorr Kan said levelly. "I'm offering you the sovereignty of the whole galaxy!"

Gordon was astonished by the audacity of this man. There was something breathtaking about him.

"We agreed to talk intelligently," Gordon snapped. "Do you suppose me stupid enough to believe that after you conquered the Empire and power over the whole galaxy, you'd give it to me?"

Shorr Kan smiled. "I said nothing about giving you the *power*. I spoke of giving you rule. They are different things."

He explained rapidly. "Once the Disruptor secret is mine, I can shatter the Empire and dominate the galaxy. But half the galaxy would still hate me as a usurper, an alien. There would be endless revolts and unrest.

"So, once I've got my hand on everything, I'd put forward Zarth Arn, legitimate son of the late Arn Abbas, as new sovereign of the galaxy! I, Shorr Kan, would merely be your trusted advisor. It would be a peaceful federation of the whole galaxy, I'd announce."

He grinned again. "See how much simpler it would make things for me? A legitimate emperor, no revolts, no unrest. You and Lianna would be the rulers, and enjoy every luxury and respect. I don't care for the pomp and outward show of power, and would be quite content to wield the real power from behind the throne."

"And if I decided to use my position as nominal ruler to turn the tables on you?" Gordon asked curiously.

Shorr Kan laughed. "You wouldn't, Zarth. The core of the armed forces would be loyal Cloud-men I could trust."

He stood up "What do you say? Remember that right now you're a fugitive from the Empire, sought for the murder of your own father All that can be cleared up, the charge can be disproved, and you can live the greatest sovereign in history. Isn't it intelligent to do so?"

Gordon shrugged. "Your proposal is certainly clever. But I'm afraid you've wasted your time. The stumbling-block is that under no circumstances will you get the Disruptor secret from me."

He expected a burst of rage from the League ruler. But Shorr Kan merely looked disappointed.

"I was hoping you'd be clearheaded enough to discount all this nonsense about patriotism and loyalties, and use a little sense."

Lianna flashed, "Of course you cannot understand loyalty and honor, when you have none yourself!"

Shorr Kan looked at her frowningly, though still apparently without anger.

"No, I don't have any," he agreed. "What, after all, are loyalty, honor, patriotism, all those admirable qualities? Just ideas that people happen to think are praiseworthy, and therefore will die for. I'm a realist. I refuse to injure myself for any mere idea."

He turned again to Gordon. "Let's not talk any more about it right now. You're tired, your nerves are taut, you're in no shape to make a decision. Get a good night's rest, and think it over tomorrow—and use your brains, not your emotions. You'll surely see that I'm right."

He added, more slowly, "I could tell you that if you persist in refusing to cooperate, there's a highly unpleasant alternative. But I don't want to threaten you, Zarth! I want you to come in with me, not from any love of me or the League, but simply because you're smart enough to recognize your own interests."

Gordon for the first time glimpsed the steel within the velvet glove, as he saw the glint in Shorr Kan's black eyes.

The League commander had pressed a signal-button as he spoke. The door opened and Durk Undis entered.

"Give Prince Zarth and his fiancée the best possible quarters," Shorr Kan told the younger Cloud-man. "They must be strictly guarded, but let the guard be unobtrusive. Any disrespect to them will be severely punished."

Durk Undis bowed and stood waiting. Gordon took Lianna's arm and silently left the room

All the way through the corridors and ramps of the gloomy building, Gordon felt that unsettling sense of having met a man who was far stronger than he in shrewdness and cunning, and who might be able to handle him like putty.

This huge citadel of the League of Dark Worlds was a dreary place, by night. The lights that glowed at intervals along its corridors could not dispel the insidious haze that wrapped this world.

The apartment to which they were conducted was far from luxurious. The square, white-walled rooms were strictly utilitarian in design and furniture, with transparent sections of wall looking out over the somber city Thallarna.

Durk Undis bowed stiffly to them. "You will find nutrition-dispensers and all else needful. Let me warn you not to try venturing out of these rooms. Every exit is strictly guarded."

When the League officer had gone, John Gordon turned and looked at Lianna, who stood by the window.

Something in the brave erectness of her little figure choked him with tenderness. He went to her side.

"Lianna, if I could assure *your* safety by giving up the secret of the Disruptor, I would," he said huskily.

She turned quickly. "You must not give it up! Without it, Shorr Kan still hesitates to move. And while he hesitates, there is a chance that Corbulo's treachery may be discovered."

"There's little chance of our exposing him, I'm afraid," Gordon said. "There's no possibility of escape from here."

Lianna's slim shoulders sagged a little. "No, I realize that," she murmured. "Even if by some miracle we could escape this building and seize a ship, we could never find our way out through the mazes of the Cloud."

The Cloud! It was the sky here, dark, heavy and menacing, showing no star as its ebon folds enwrapped this grim city.

That dark sky gave Gordon a feeling of claustrophobia, a sense of all the trillions of miles of shadowy gloom that encompassed him and shut him from the star-bright spaces of the galaxy outside.

Thallarna was not sleeping. Out there in the severely straight streets streamed many heavy vehicles. Fliers came and went in swarms. Thunderous reverberations droned dimly to them from the distant docks where squadrons of heavy warships were constantly coming and going.

Gordon took the couch in the living-room of their austere apartment, without expectation of being able to sleep. But his tired body relaxed in almost drugged slumber in a short time.

Dawn awoke him—a sickly, shadowy dawn that only

slowly revealed the outlines of the room. He found Lianna sitting on the edge of his couch, looking down at him with curious intentness.

She flushed slightly. "I wondered if you were awake. I have our breakfast ready. It is not bad, the nutritional fluid. Though it's likely to become monotonous."

"I doubt if we will be here long enough to grow tired of it," Gordon said grimly.

She looked at him. "You think that Shorr Kan will insist on your giving him the Disruptor secret today?"

"I'm afraid so," he said. "If that secret is all that is holding back his attack, he'll want it as soon as possible."

Through the hours of the gloomy day, as the red sun swept with somber slowness across the shadowy sky, they expected Shorr Kan's summons.

But it was not until night had returned that Durk Undis and four armed soldiers entered the apartment.

The young fanatic Cloud-man again bowed stiffly. "The commander will see you now, Prince Zarth. Alone," he added quickly, as Lianna stepped forward with Gordon.

Lianna's eyes flashed. "I go where Zarth goes!"

"I regret that I must carry out my orders," said Durk Undis coldly. "Will you come now, Prince Zarth?"

Lianna apparently realized the hopelessness of further resistance. She stood back.

Gordon hesitated, then let impulse sweep him and strode back to her. He took her face between his hands and kissed her.

"Don't worry, Lianna," he said, and turned away.

His heart beat painfully as he followed Durk Undis through the corridors. He was certain that he had seen Lianna for the last time.

Maybe better this way! he thought. Maybe better to forget her in death than to go back to his own time and be forever haunted by memory of love irrevocably lost!

Gordon's desperate thoughts received a check when he followed his guards into a room. It was not the austere study of the previous day.

This was a laboratory. There was a table, above which hung a massive metal cone connected by cables to a complicated apparatus of banked, vacuum tubes and moving tapes. Here were two thin, nervous-looking Cloud-men—and Shorr Kan.

Shorr Kan dismissed Durk Undis and the guards, and quickly greeted Gordon.

"You've slept, rested? That's good. Now tell me what you've decided."

Gordon shrugged. "There was no decision to make. I can't give you the secret of the Disruptor."

Shorr Kan's strong face changed slightly in expression, and he spoke after a pause.

"I see. I might have expected it. Old mental habits, old traditions—even intelligence can't conquer them, sometimes."

His eyes narrowed slightly. "Now listen, Zarth. I told you yesterday that there was an unpleasant alternative if you refused. I didn't go into details because I wanted to gain your willing cooperation.

"But now you force me to be explicit. So let me assure you first of one thing. I am going to have the Disruptor secret from you, whether you give it willingly or not."

"Torture, then?" sneered Gordon. "That is what I expected."

Shorr Kan made a disgusted gesture. "Faugh, I don't use torture. It's clumsy and undependable, and alienates even your own followers. No, I have quite another method in mind."

He gestured to the older of the two nervous-looking men nearby. "Land Allar, there, is one of our finest psycho-scientists. Some years ago he devised a certain apparatus which I've been forced to utilize several times."

"It's a brain-scanner. It literally reads the brain, by scanning the neurones, plotting the synaptic connections, and translating that physical set-up into the knowledge, memories and information possessed by that particular brain. With it, before this night is over, I can have the Disruptor secret right out of your brain."

"That," said John Gordon steadily, "is a rather unclever bluff."

Shorr Kan shook his dark head. "I assure you it is not. I can prove it to you if you want me to. Otherwise, you must take my word that the scanner *will* take everything from your brain."

He went on, "The trouble is that the impact of the scanning ray on the brain for hour after hour in time breaks down the synaptic connections it scans. The subject emerges from the process a mindless idiot. That is what will happen to you if we use it on you."

The hair bristled on Gordon's neck. He had not a doubt now that Shorr Kan was speaking the truth. If nothing else, the pale, sick faces of the two scientists proved his assertion.

Weird, fantastic, nightmarishly horrible—yet wholly possible to this latterday science! An instrument that mechanically read the mind, and in reading wrecked it!

"I don't want to use it on you, I repeat," Shorr Kan was saying earnestly. "For as I told you, you'd be extremely valuable to me as a puppet emperor after the galaxy is conquered. But if you persist in refusing to tell that secret, I simply have no choice."

John Gordon felt an insane desire to laugh. This was all too ironic.

"You've got everything so nicely calculated," he told Shorr Kan. "But again, you find yourself defeated by pure chance."

"Just what do you mean?" asked the League ruler, with dangerous softness.

"I mean that I can't tell you the secret of the Disruptor because I don't know it!"

Shorr Kan looked impatient. "That is a rather childish evasion. Everyone knows that as son of the emperor you would be told all about the Disruptor."

Gordon nodded. "Quite true. But I happen not to be the emperor's son. I'm a different man entirely."

Shorr Kan shrugged. "We are gaining nothing by all this. Go ahead."

The last words were addressed to the two scientists. At that moment Gordon savagely leaped for Shorr Kan's throat!

He never reached it. One of the scientists had a glass paralyzer ready, and swiftly jabbed it at the back of his neck.

Gordon sank, shocked and stunned. Only dimly, he felt them lifting him onto the metal table. Through his dimming vision, Shorr Kan's hard face and cool black eyes looked down.

"Your last chance, Zarth! Make but a signal and you can still avoid this fate."

Gordon felt the hopelessness of it all, even as his raging anger made him glare up at the League commander.

The paralyzer touched him again. This shock was like a

physical blow. He just sensed the two scientists busy with the massive metal cone above his head, and then darkness claimed him.

14

DARK-WORLD MENACE

Gordon came slowly to awareness of a throbbing headache. All the devil's triphammers seemed to be pounding inside his skull, and he felt a sickening nausea.

A cool glass was held to his lips, and a voice spoke insistently in his ear.

"Drink this!"

Gordon managed to gulp down a pungent liquid. Presently his nausea lessened and his head began to ache less violently.

He lay for a little time before he finally ventured to open his eyes. He still lay on the table, but the mental cone and the complicated apparatus were not now in sight.

Over him was bending the anxious face of one of the two Cloud scientists. Then the strong features and brilliant black eyes of Shorr Kan came down in his field of vision.

"Can you sit up?" asked the scientist. "It will help you recover faster."

The man's arm around his shoulders enabled Gordon weakly to slide off the table and into a chair.

Shorr Kan came and stood in front of him, looking down at him with a queer wonder and interest in his expression.

He asked, "How do you feel now, John Gordon?"

Gordon started. He stared back up at the League commander.

"Then you know?" he husked.

"Why else do you think we halted the brain-scanning?" Shorr Kan retorted. "If it weren't for that, you'd be a complete mental wreck by now."

He shook his head wonderingly. "By Heaven, it was incredible! But the brain-scanner can't lie. And when the first minutes of its reading drew out the fact that you were John

Gordon's mind in Zarth Arn's body, and that you did *not* know the Disruptor secret, I stopped the scanning."

Shorr Kan added ruefully. "And I thought I had that secret finally in my grasp! The pains I've taken to fish Zarth Arn into my net, and all for nothing! But who'd dream of a thing like this, who'd guess that a man of the ancient past was inside Zarth's body?"

Shorr Kan knew! John Gordon tried to rally his dazed faculties to deal with this startling new factor in the situation.

For the first time, someone in this future universe was cognizant of the weird imposture he had carried out! Just what would that mean to him?

Shorr Kan was striding to and fro. "John Gordon of ancient Earth, of an age two hundred thousand years in the past, here inside the brain and body of the second prince of the Empire! It still doesn't make sense!"

Gordon answered weakly. "Didn't your scanner tell you how it happened?"

The League commander nodded. "Yes, the outlines of the story were clear after a few minutes' scanning, for the whole fact of your imposture was uppermost in your mind."

He uttered a soft curse. "That young fool Zarth Arn! Trading bodies with another man across time! Letting his crazy scientific curiosity about the past take him ages away, at the very moment his Empire is in danger."

He fastened his gaze again on Gordon. "Why in the devil's name didn't you tell me?"

"I tried to tell you, and got nowhere with it," Gordon reminded him.

Shorr Kan nodded. "That's right, you did. And I didn't believe. Who the devil *would* believe a thing like this, without the brain-scanner's proof of it?"

He paced to and fro, biting his lip. "Gordon, you've upset all my careful plans. I was sure that with you I had the Disruptor secret."

John Gordon's mind was working swiftly now as his strength slowly returned. The discovery of his true identity changed his whole situation.

It might give him a remote chance of escape! A chance to get away with Lianna and warn the Empire of Corbulo's treachery and the imminent danger! Gordon thought he dimly saw a way.

He spoke a little sullenly to Shorr Kan. "You're the first one to discover the truth about me. I deceived all the others—Arn Abbas, Jhal Arn, Princess Lianna. They didn't dream the truth."

Shorr Kan's eyes narrowed a little. "Gordon, that sounds as though you *liked* being prince of the Empire?"

Gordon laughed mirthlessly. "Who wouldn't? Back in my own time I was a nobody, a poor ex-soldier. Then, after Zarth Arn proposed that strange exchange of bodies across time, I found myself one of the royal family of the greatest star-kingdom in the universe! Who wouldn't like that change?"

"But you had promised to go back to Earth and re-exchange bodies with Zarth Arn, according to what the scanner revealed," pointed out Shorr Kan. "You'd have had to give up all your temporary splendor."

Gordon looked up at him, with what he hoped was a cynical expression.

"What the devil?" he said contemptuously to Shorr Kan. "Do you really think I'd have kept that promise?"

The League commander stared at him intently. "You mean that you were planning to deceive the real Zarth Arn, and keep his body and identity?"

"I hope you're not going to get righteous with me!" flared Gordon. "It's what you would have done yourself in my place, and you know it!

"Here I was, set for life as one of the great men of this universe, about to marry the most beautiful girl I've ever seen. No one could possibly ever doubt my identity. All I had to do was simply forget my promise to Zarth Arn. What would *you* have done?"

Shorr Kan burst into laughter. "John Gordon, you're an adventurer after my own heart! By Heaven, I see that they bred bold men back in those ancient times on Earth!"

He clapped Gordon on the shoulder, his good spirits seeming partly restored.

"Don't get downhearted because I know the truth about you, Gordon. No one else knows it, except these scientists who'll never speak. You might still be able to live out your life as Prince Zarth Arn."

Gordon pretended to catch eagerly at the bait. "You mean—you wouldn't give me away?"

"That's what I mean. You and I ought to be able to help each other," Shorr Kan nodded.

Gordon sensed that the high-powered brain behind those keen black eyes was working rapidly.

He realized that trying to fool this utterly intelligent and ruthless plotter was the hardest task he had ever essayed. But unless he succeeded, Lianna's life and the Empire's safety were forfeit.

Shorr Kan helped him to his feet. "You come with me and we'll talk it over. Feel like walking yet?"

When they emerged from the laboratory, Durk Undis stared at Gordon as though he saw a man risen from the dead.

The fanatic young Cloud-man had not expected him to emerge from that room living and sane, Gordon knew.

Shorr Kan grinned. "It's all right, Durk. Prince Zarth is cooperating with me. We shall go to my apartments."

"Then you already have the Disruptor secret, sir?" burst out the young fanatic eagerly.

Shorr Kan's quick frown checked him. "Are you questioning me?" snapped the commander.

As they walked on, John Gordon's mind was busy with this byplay. It encouraged him in the belief that his dim scheme might be made to work.

But he would have to go carefully, carefully! Shorr Kan was the last man in the universe to be easily deceived. Gordon sweated with realization that he walked a sword-edge over an abyss.

Shorr Kan's apartments were as austere as the bare office in which Gordon had first seen him. There were a few hard chairs, bare floors, and in another room an uncomfortable-looking cot.

Durk Undis had remained outside the door. As Gordon looked around, Shorr Kan's smile returned.

"Miserable hole for the master of the Cloud to live in, isn't it?" he said. "But it all helps to impress my devoted followers. You see, I've worked them up to attack the Empire by stressing the poverty of our worlds, the hardness of our lives. I daren't live soft myself."

He motioned Gordon to a chair, and then sat down and looked at him intently.

"It's still cursed hard to believe," he declared. "Talking here to a man of the remotest past! What was it like, that age of yours when men hadn't even left the little Earth?"

Gordon shrugged. "It wasn't so much different, at bottom. There was war and conflict, over and over. Men don't change much."

The League commander nodded emphatically. "The mob remains always stupid. A few million men fighting on your old planet, or ten thousand star-worlds ranged against each other in this universe—it's the same thing at bottom."

He continued swiftly. "Gordon, I like you. You're intelligent, daring and courageous. Since you *are* intelligent, you understand that I wouldn't let a mere passing liking influence me, powerfully. I think we can help each other."

He leaned forward. "You're not Zarth Arn. But no one in the universe knows that, but me. So, to the galaxy, you are Zarth Arn. And as such, I can use you as I hoped to use the real Zarth, to act as puppet ruler after the Cloud has conquered the galaxy."

John Gordon had hoped for this. But he pretended startled astonishment.

"You mean, you'd make me the nominal ruler of the galaxy?"

"Why not?" retorted the other. "As Zarth Arn, one of the Empire's royal blood, you'd still serve to quiet rebellion after the Empire is conquered. Of course, I'd wield the real power, as I said."

He added frankly, "From one viewpoint you're better for my purpose than the real Zarth Arn. He might have had scruples, might have given me trouble. But you have no loyalties in this universe, and I can depend on you to stick with me from pure self-interest."

Gordon felt a brief flash of triumph. That was exactly what he had wanted Shorr Kan to think—that he, John Gordon, was merely an ambitious, unscrupulous adventurer from the past.

"You'd have everything you could desire!" Shorr Kan was continuing. "Outwardly, you'd be the ruler of the whole galaxy. The Princess Lianna for your wife, power and wealth and luxury beyond your dreams!"

Gordon pretended a stunned, rapt wonder at the prospect. "I, the emperor of the galaxy? I, John Gordon?"

And then suddenly, without warning, the plan he was

precariously trying to carry through slipped away from Gordon's mind and the voice of the tempter whispered in his ear.

He could do this thing, if he wanted to! He could be at least nominally the supreme sovereign of the entire galaxy with all its thousand on thousands of mighty suns and circling worlds! He, John Gordon of New York, could rule a universe with Lianna at his side!

All he had to do was to join with Shorr Kan and attach his loyalty to the Cloud. And why shouldn't he do that? What tie bound him to the Empire? Why shouldn't he strike out for himself, for such power and splendor as no man in all human history had ever dreamed of attaining?

15

MYSTERY OF THE GALAXY

John Gordon fought a temptation whose unexpectedness added to its strength. He was appalled to realize that he wanted with nearly all his soul to seize this unprecedented opportunity.

It wasn't the pomp and power of galactic rule that tempted him. He had never been ambitious for power, and anyway it would be Shorr Kan who had the real power. It was the thought of Lianna that swayed him. He'd be with her always then, living by her side—

Living a lie! Pretending to be another man, haunted for the rest of his life by memory of how he had betrayed Zarth Arn's trust and wrecked the Empire! He couldn't do it! A man had his code to live by, and Gordon knew he could never break his pledge.

Shorr Kan was watching him keenly. "You seem stunned by the prospect, Gordon. It's a tremendous opportunity for you, all right."

Gordon rallied his wits. "I was thinking that there are lots of difficulties. There's the Disruptor secret, for instance."

Shorr Kan nodded thoughtfully. "That's our biggest difficulty. And I was so sure that once I had Zarth Arn, I'd have it!"

He shrugged. "But that can't be helped. We shall have to

make our attack on the Empire without it, and rely on Corbulo to see that Jhal Arn never gets a chance to use the Disruptor."

"You mean—assassinate Jhal Arn as he did Arn Abbas?" questioned Gordon.

The Cloud-man nodded. "Corbulo was to do that anyway on the eve of our attack. He'll be appointed one of the regents for Jhal's child. Then it'll be even easier for him to sabotage the Empire's defense."

Gordon realized that Shorr Kan's failure to gain the Disruptor secret was not going to stave off the League's impending attack!

"Those are *your* problems," Gordon said bluntly. "It's my own prospects I was thinking of. You're to make me puppet emperor when the galaxy is conquered. But if we don't have that Disruptor secret, maybe your own League forces won't accept me."

Shorr Kan frowned. "Why should they refuse to accept you on that account?"

"They, like everyone else, think I'm Zarth Arn and believe I know the Disruptor secret," Gordon pointed out. "They'll ask, 'If Zarth Arn is now on our side, why doesn't he give us that secret?' "

The Cloud-man swore. "I hadn't thought of that difficulty. Curse the Disruptor, anyway! Its existence hampers us at every turn!"

"What *is* the Disruptor, really?" Gordon asked. "I've had to pretend I know all about it, but I haven't any idea what it is."

"No one has!" Shorr Kan replied. "Yet it's been a terrible tradition in the galaxy for the last two thousand years.

"Two thousand years ago the alien, unhuman Magellanians invaded the galaxy. They seized several star-systems and prepared to expand their conquests. But Brenn Bir, one of the great scientist-kings of the Empire, struck out against them with some fearful power or weapon. Tradition says he destroyed not only the Magellanians but also the star-systems they infested, and nearly destroyed the galaxy itself!

"Just what Brenn Bir used, no one now knows. It's been called the Disruptor, but that tells nothing. The secret of it, known only to the Empire's royal house, has never been used since. But memory of it haunts the galaxy, and has maintained the Empire's prestige ever since."

"No wonder you've tried to get hold of it before attacking the Empire," said Gordon. "But there's still a way we can get that secret!"

Shorr Kan stared. "How? Jhal Arn is the only remaining one who knows about it, and we've no chance of capturing him."

"There's one other man who knows the secret," Gordon reminded swiftly. "The real Zarth Arn!"

"But the real Zarth's mind is back in that remote past age in your body—," Shorr Kan began. Then he stopped, eyeing Gordon narrowly. "You've something in mind. What?"

Gordon was tense as he unfolded the scheme on which his dim, precarious plan of escape depended.

"Suppose we can make the real Zarth tell us that secret, across time?" he proposed boldly. "There in Zarth's laboratory on Earth are the psycho-mechanisms by which I could speak to him across time. I learned the method from Vel Quen, and I could reach him.

"Suppose I tell him—'Shorr Kan's men hold me prisoner and won't release me unless I tell the Disruptor secret, which I don't know. I won't be permitted to re-exchange minds with you until they have the secret.'

"Suppose I tell the real Zarth *that?* What do you think he'll do? He doesn't want to be marooned back there in my own world and age, in my own body, for the rest of his life. This is his universe, he's got a morganatic wife here he dearly loves, he'd sacrifice anything to get back here. He'll tell us that secret, across time!"

Shorr Kan looked at him in wondering admiration. "By Heaven, Gordon, I believe it would work! We *could* just get the Disruptor secret that way!"

He stopped and asked suddenly, "Then when you had forced that secret out of Zarth, you'd re-exchange minds with him?"

Gordon laughed. "Do I look like a complete fool? Of course I won't. I'll simply break the contract then and let Zarth Arn live the rest of his life back in my own time and body while I keep on playing *his* part."

Shorr Kan threw back his head in a burst of laughter. "Gordon, I repeat, you're a man after my own heart!"

He began to pace to and fro as seemed his habit when thinking rapidly.

"The main difficulty will be to get you to Earth to make that contact with the real Zarth," he declared. "Empire patrols are thick all along the frontier, and the main Empire fleet is maneuvering near the Pleiades. And Corbulo can't order that whole region cleared, without arousing suspicion."

Shorr Kan paused, then continued. "The only kind of League ship that has any chance of reaching Earth through all that is a phantom-cruiser. Phantoms are able to slip through tight places, where even a battle-squadron couldn't fight a way."

Gordon, who had only the mistiest notion of what kind of a warship was mentioned, looked puzzled. "A phantom? What's that?"

"I forgot for a moment that you're really a stranger in this age," Shorr Kan said. "A phantom-cruiser is a small cruiser with armament of a few very heavy atom-guns. It can become totally invisible in space."

He explained, "It does that by projecting a sphere of force around itself that refracts perfectly all light and radar rays. So no ship can detect it. But to hold that concealing sphere of force requires terrific power, so a phantom is only good for twenty or thirty hours travel 'dark'."

John Gordon nodded understandingly. "I get it. And it looks like the best chance to reach Earth, all right."

"Durk Undis will go with you with a full crew of trusted men," Shorr Kan continued.

That was bad news to Gordon. That fanatic young Cloud-man hated him, he knew.

"But if Durk Undis learns that I'm not really Zarth Arn—," he began to object.

"He won't," Shorr Kan interrupted. "He'll simply know that he's to take you to your laboratory on earth for a brief time, and that he's to bring you back safely."

Gordon eyed the Cloud-man. "It sounds as though he's to be a guard. You don't entirely trust me?"

"What the devil made you think I did?" Shorr Kan retorted cheerfully. "I trust no man entirely. I do trust to men following their self-interest, and that's why I feel I can rely on you. But just to make sure—Durk Undis and a crew of picked men go with you."

Again, Gordon chilled to a realization that he was playing his desperate game against a man so shrewd and skilled in intrigue that it seemed almost hopeless he could succeed.

He nodded coolly, however. "That's fair enough. But I might also say that I don't entirely trust *you,* Shorr Kan. And for that reason, I don't go on this mission unless Lianna goes with me."

Shorr Kan looked genuinely surprised for a moment. "The Fomalhaut girl? Your fiancee?"

Then an ironic smile flickered in his eyes. "So that's your weak point, Gordon—that girl?"

"I love her and I'm not going to leave her here for you to tamper with," Gordon asserted sullenly.

Shorr Kan snorted. "If you knew me better, you'd know that one woman means no more to me than another. Do you think I'd risk my plans for a pretty face? But if you're jealous, you can take her with you."

He added, "How are you going to explain it all to her, though? You can't very well tell her the truth about our deal."

Gordon had thought of that already. He said slowly, "I'll make up a story that you're going to let us go if I bring you certain valuable scientific secrets from my Earth laboratory."

Shorr Kan nodded understandingly. "That will be your best course."

He added rapidly, "I'll give orders at once to have our best phantom-cruiser prepared. You ought to be able to start tomorrow night."

Gordon stood up. "I'll be glad to get some rest. I feel as though I'd been through a grinder."

Shorr Kan laughed. "Man, that's nothing to what the brain-scanner would have made of you if it had run longer than a few minutes. What a twist of fate! Instead of a mindless idiot, you're to be nominal emperor of the galaxy!"

He added, his face setting for just a moment to a steely hardness, "But never forget that your power is only nominal and that it is *I* who will give the orders."

Gordon met his searching gaze steadily. "I might forget it if I thought I'd gain by that. But I'm pretty sure I wouldn't. I'm pretty sure that once I'm ruler, I'll fall if you fall. So you will be able to rely on me—or on my self-interest."

The Cloud-man chuckled. "You're right. Didn't I say I always like to deal with intelligent people? We'll get along."

He pressed a button. When Durk Undis quickly entered the room, he told him:

"Escort Prince Zarth back to his quarters and then return here for orders."

All the way back through the corridors, Gordon's thoughts were feverish. Relaxation from the intolerable strain of playing his part left him trembling.

So far, his precarious scheme for escape was succeeding. He had gambled on Shorr Kan's ruthless, cynical personality reacting in a certain way, and had won.

But he well knew that this success was only the beginning. Ahead loomed far greater difficulties which he had not yet found the least way of solving.

He'd have to go ahead, even though his scheme was suicidal in riskiness! There was no other way.

When he entered the somber apartment, Lianna sprang from a chair and ran toward him. She grasped his arm.

"Zarth, you're all right?" she cried, her gray eyes shining. "I was afraid—"

She loved him, still. Gordon knew it from her face, and again he felt that wild, hopeless rapture.

He had to fight his impulse to take her into his arms. Something of what he felt must have showed in his face, for Lianna flushed and stepped back a little.

"Lianna, I'm all right though a little shaky," Gordon told her, sinking into a chair. "I had a taste of Cloud science and it wasn't pleasant."

"They tortured you? They made you tell the Disruptor secret?"

He shook his head. "I didn't tell that secret. And I'm not going to. I convinced Shorr Kan he couldn't get it from me."

Gordon went on, telling her as much of the truth as he could. "I made that devil believe that I would have to go to my Earth laboratory to get that secret for him. And he's sending us, to get it. We'll leave in a phantom-cruiser tomorrow night."

Lianna's eyes flashed. "You're going to outwit him? You have some plan?"

"I wish I did," groaned Gordon. "This is as far as my plan goes. It will get us out of the Cloud, that's all. Then it's up to me. Somehow, I'll have to find a way for us to escape that ship and get a warning of Corbulo's treachery to Jhal Arn."

He added wearily, "The only way I can think of is somehow to sabotage the phantom-cruiser so it'll be captured by Empire warships. But how to do that, I don't know. That young fanatic Durk Undis is going with a picked crew to guard us, and it won't be easy."

Faith and courage shone in Lianna's eyes. "You'll find a way somehow, Zarth. I know you will."

Her faith could not overcome the chill realization in Gordon's mind that his hare-brained scheme was almost impossible.

He might be dooming both Lianna and himself by trying it. But they were doomed anyway unless he betrayed the real Zarth Arn and the Empire, and the momentary temptation to do that had left Gordon forever.

He slept heavily, well into the next day. It was dusk when Shorr Kan and Durk Undis finally came.

"Durk Undis has all his orders, and the phantom is ready," Shorr Kan told Gordon. "You should get to Earth in five days, and be back here in eleven."

His face lit. "Then I'll announce to the galaxy that we have the Disruptor secret and that Zarth Arn has joined us, and will give Corbulo the secret signal and launch the League's attack!"

Two hours later, from the huge Thallarna spaceport, the slim, shining phantom-cruiser on which Gordon and Lianna had embarked rose from its dock and plunged headlong out through the Cloud.

16

SABOTAGE IN SPACE

When Gordon and Lianna had entered the *Dendra,* the phantom-cruiser that was to bear them on the mission, they were led to the mid-deck corridor by Durk Undis.

The fanatic young Cloud-man bowed stiffly to them and

gestured toward the door of a small suite of two tiny cabins.

"These cabins will be your quarters. You will remain in them until we reach Earth."

"We will *not* remain in them!" Gordon flared. "The princess Lianna is already suffering from the confinement of the voyage here. We'll not stay cooped up in those tiny rooms for days more."

Durk Undis' lean face hardened. "The commander gave orders that you were to be strictly guarded."

"Did Shorr Kan say we were to be prisoned in two tiny rooms every minute?" Gordon demanded. He saw the slight uncertainty in Durk Undis' face, and pressed his attack. "Unless we have a chance to get a little exercise, we'll refuse to carry out this whole plan."

The fanatic Cloud-man hesitated. Gordon had guessed rightly that Durk Undis did not want to go back to his superior and report the mission aborted by such a slight difficulty.

Finally, Durk Undis said grudgingly, "Very well, you will be permitted to walk in this corridor twice each day. But you will not be allowed in it any other time, or when we're running 'dark.' "

The concession was not as much as Gordon had wanted but he guessed that it was the most he could obtain. So, with anger still assumed, he followed Lianna into the cabin-suite and heard the lock click after them.

As the *Dendra* rose from Thallarna and started arrowing out at high speed through the gloomy hazes of the Cloud, Lianna looked inquiringly at Gordon.

"The confinement does not really bother me, Zarth. You have some plan?"

"No more than the plan I already mentioned, of somehow drawing the attention of an Empire patrol to this ship so that it'll be discovered and captured," he admitted.

He added determinedly, "I don't know yet how it can be done but there must be a way."

Lianna looked doubtful. "This phantom undoubtedly has super-sensitive radar equipment, and will be able to spot ordinary patrols long before they spot us. It will dark-out till we're past them."

The steady drone of big drive-generators building up velocity became an unwavering background, in the following hours.

The *Dendra* plunged through hails of tiny meteor-particles, through dust-currents that made it pitch and toss roughly. It often changed direction as it threaded its way out through the Cloud.

It was the middle of the following day before they emerged from the gloomy haze into the vast, clear vault of star-gemmed space. At once, the phantom-cruiser picked up still greater speed.

Gordon and Lianna looked from the window at the brilliant galactic spectacle ahead. To their astonishment, the distant spark of Canopus lay out of sight far on their left. Ahead of the *Dendra* glittered a vault of strange stars in which Orion Nebula glowed in flaming glory.

"We're not heading straight back into the Empire," Lianna said. "They're going to avoid the most guarded Empire frontier by swinging up west of Orion Nebula and on past the Marches of Outer Space to curve in toward Sol."

"Going the long way around to sneak into the Empire by the back way!" Gordon muttered. "It's probably the way that Cloud ship came that tried to kidnap me from Earth."

His faint hopes sank. "There's less chance of an Empire patrol catching us, if we're going through a little-travelled region."

Lianna nodded. "We are not likely to meet more than a few patrol cruisers, and Durk Undis can slip past them under dark-out."

Discouragedly, Gordon stared out at the brilliant scene. His gaze shifted to the direction in which he knew Canopus must lie.

Lianna caught the direction of his gaze and looked up at him questioningly. "You are thinking of Murn?"

It startled Gordon. He had almost forgotten the dark, lovely girl whom the real Zarth Arn loved.

"Murn? No! I was thinking of that black traitor Corbulo, spinning his plots back there on Throon and just waiting his chance to murder Jhal Arn and wreck the Empire's defenses."

"That is the greatest danger," Lianna agreed soberly. "If they could only be warned of Corbulo's treachery, the League's plan of attack could still be foiled."

"And we're the only ones who can warn them," Gordon muttered.

Yet on the third day after this, he had to confess to himself that it seemed more than ever an impossibility.

The *Dendra* was by now well inside the boundaries of the Empire, beating northward on a course that would take it just west of the gigantic, glowing Orion Nebula.

Once beyond the great Nebula, they would fly northwestward along the little-travelled edges of the Marches of Outer Space. Few Empire warships would be in the region bordering that wild frontier of unexplored star-systems. And Sol and its planet Earth would be nearby, then.

Twice during these three days, an alarm bell had rung through the *Dendra* as its radar operators detected Empire warships nearby. Each time, in their cabins, Gordon and Lianna had seen the whole vault of space outside the window suddenly blacked out.

Gordon had exclaimed in astonishment when it first happened. "What's wrong? All space has gone dark!"

Lianna looked at him in surprise. "They've turned on the dark-out of our ship. You surely remember that when a phantom-cruiser runs dark, those inside it can see nothing of outside space?"

"Oh, of course," Gordon said hastily. "It's been so long since I've been in one of these craft that I'd forgotten."

He understood now what was happening. The new, loud whine that permeated the cruiser was the sound of the dark-out generators that were flinging an aura of potent force around the ship.

That aura slightly refracted every ray of light or radar beam that struck it, so that the phantom-cruiser could neither be seen or ranged by radar. Of necessity, that deflection of all outside light left the cruiser moving in utter darkness.

Gordon heard the dark-out generators down in the lower deck whining for nearly an hour. They apparently required almost all the power of the ship, the drive-machinery merely purring and the ship moving almost on inertia.

The thing happened again the following morning, when the *Dendra* was drawing up closer to the west borders of Orion Nebula. That glowing mass now stretched billions of miles across the firmament beside them.

Gordon saw many hot stars inside the Nebula. He recalled

that it was their electron-barrage that excited the hazy dust of the Nebula to its brilliant glow.

That "evening," he and Lianna were walking in the long corridor under the close scrutiny of an armed Cloud-man when the alarm bell again rang sharp warning through the ship.

The Cloud-man instantly stepped forward. "Dark-out! Return to your cabins immediately!"

Gordon had hoped for a chance like this and resolved to seize it. They might never have another.

As the familiar whine of the dark-out came on, as he and Lianna moved toward their cabins, he leaned to whisper to her.

"Act faint and collapse just as we enter the cabin!"

Lianna gave not a sign of hearing him, except that her fingers quickly pressed his hand.

The Cloud-officer was a half-dozen paces behind them, his hand resting on the butt of his atom-pistol.

Lianna, at the door of the cabin, tottered weakly and pressed her heart.

"Zarth, I feel ill!" she whispered huskily, then began to sag to the floor.

Gordon caught her, held her. "She's fainted! I knew this confinement would be too much for her!"

He turned angrily toward the startled Cloud-man. "Help me get her into the cabin!" Gordon snapped.

The officer was anxious to get them out of the corridor. His orders had been that they were immediately to be reconfined whenever a dark-out began.

Zeal to obey his orders betrayed him. The Cloud-man stepped forward and stooped to help pick up Lianna and carry her inside.

As he did so, Gordon acted! He callously let Lianna fall to the floor, and snatched at the butt of the Cloud-man's atom-gun.

So swift was his movement that he had the gun out of its holster before the other realized it. The Cloud-man began to straighten and his mouth opened to yell an alarm.

Gordon smashed the barrel of the heavy atom-pistol against the man's temple below his helmet. The officer's face relaxed blankly, and he slumped like a bag of rags.

"Quick, Lianna!" sweated Gordon. "Into the cabin with him!"

Lianna was already on her feet. In an instant, they had dragged the limp form into the little room and shut the door.

Gordon stooped over the man. The skull was shattered. "Dead," he said swiftly. "Lianna, this is my chance!"

He was beginning to strip off the dead man's jacket. She flew to his side. "Zarth, what are you going to do?"

"There must be at least one Empire patrol cruiser nearby," Gordon rasped. "If I can sabotage the *Dendra's* dark-out equipment, the patrol will spot us and capture the ship."

"More likely they'll blow it to fragments!" Lianna warned.

His eyes held hers. "I know that, too. But I'm willing to take the chance if you are."

Her gray eyes flashed. "I'm willing, Zarth. The future of the whole galaxy hangs in the balance."

"You stay here," he ordered. "I'll put on this fellow's uniform and helmet and it may give me a little better chance."

In a few minutes, Gordon had struggled into the dead man's black uniform. He jammed on the helmet, then holstered the atom-gun and slid out into the corridor.

The dark-out was still on, the *Dendra* cautiously groping its way through self-induced blackness. Gordon started aft.

He had already, during these past days, located the sound of the dark-out generators as coming from aft on the lower deck. He hastened in the direction of that loud whine.

There was no one in the corridor. During dark-out, every man and officer was at action stations.

Gordon reached the end of the corridor. He hurried down a narrow companionway to the lower deck. Here doors were open, and he glanced into the big drive-generator rooms. Officers stood at flight-panels, men watched the gauges of the big, purring energy-drive.

An officer glanced up surprisedly as Gordon quickly passed the door. But his helmet and uniform seemed to reassure the Cloud-man.

"Of course!" Gordon thought. "The guard I killed would be just returning to his station from locking us up!"

He was now closer to the loud whine of the dark-out generators. They were just forward of the main drive-machinery rooms, and the door of the dark-out room was also open.

Gordon drew his atom-pistol and stepped into the doorway. He looked into a big room whose generators were emitting that loud whine. One whole side of it was a bank of giant vacuum tubes that pulsed with white radiance.

There were two officers and four men in the room. An officer at the switch-panel beyond the tubes turned to speak to a man, and glimpsed Gordon's taut face in the doorway.

"Zarth Arn!" yelled the officer, grabbing for his gun. "Look out!"

Gordon triggered his pistol. It was the first time he had used one of these weapons and his ignorance betrayed him.

He was aiming at the vacuum tubes across the room but the gun kicked high in his hand. The exploding pellet blasted the ceiling. He flung himself down in a crouch as a pellet from the officer's pistol flicked across the room. It struck the door-frame above his head, flaring instantly.

"General alarm!" the officer was yelling. "Get—"

Gordon triggered again at that moment. This time he held his weapon down. The atomic pellets from his pistol exploded amid the bank of giant tubes.

Electric fire mushroomed out into the dark-out room! Two men and an officer screamed as raging violet flames enveloped them.

The officer with the gun swung around, appalled. Gordon swiftly shot him. He shot then at the nearest big generator.

His pellet only fused its metal shield. But the giant vacuum tubes were still popping, the whole room an inferno. The two men left there staggered in the violet fires, screaming and falling.

Gordon had recoiled into the corridor. He yelled exultantly as he saw the blackness outside the window suddenly replaced by a vault of brilliant stars.

"Our dark-out has failed!" yelled a voice on one of the upper decks.

Bells shrilled madly. Gordon heard a rush of feet as Cloud-men started pouring down from an upper deck toward the dark-out room.

17

WRECKED IN THE NEBULA

Gordon glimpsed a dozen League soldiers bursting into the farther end of this lower-deck corridor. He knew that his game was up, but he turned his atom-pistol savagely loose upon them.

The pellets flew down the passage and exploded. The little flares of force blasted down half the Cloud-men there. But the others raced forward with wolfish shouts. And his pistol went dead in his hand, its loads exhausted.

Then it happened! The whole fabric of the *Dendra* rocked violently and there was a crash of riving plates and girders. All space outside the ship seemed illuminated by a brilliant flare.

"That Empire cruiser has spotted us and is shelling us!" yelled a wild voice. "We're hit!"

Continued rending crash of parting struts and plates was accompanied by the shrill singing of escaping air. Then came the quick *slam-slam* of automatic bulkheads closing.

The corridor in which Gordon stood was suddenly divided by the automatic doors closing! He was cut off from the men at its end.

"Battle-stations! Space-suits on!" rang Durk Undis' sharp voice from the annunciators throughout the ship. "We're crippled and have to fight it out with that Empire cruiser!"

Bells were ringing, alarms buzzing. Then came the swift shudder of recoil from big atom-guns broadsiding. Far away in space, out there in the vast blackness, Gordon glimpsed points of light suddenly flaring and vanishing.

A duel in space, this! His sudden sabotage of the darkout concealment had exposed the *Dendra* to the Empire cruiser which it had been trying to evade. That cruiser had instantly opened fire.

"Lianna!" Gordon thought wildly. "If she's been hurt—"

He turned and scrambled up the companionway to the mid-deck.

Lianna came running to meet him in the corridor there. Her face was pale but unafraid.

"There are space-suits in the locker here!" she exclaimed. "Quick, Zarth! The ship may be hit again any moment!"

The girl had kept her head enough to find one of the lockers of space-suits placed at strategic locations throughout the ship.

In their cabin, she and Gordon hastily struggled into the suits. They were of stiffened metallic fabric, with spherical glassite helmets whose oxygenators started automatically when they were closed.

Lianna spoke, and he heard her voice normally by means of the short-range audio apparatus built into each suit.

She cried to him, "That Empire cruiser is going to shell this ship to fragments now that it can't go dark!"

Gordon was dazed by the strangeness of the scene from the windows. The *Dendra,* maneuvering at high speed to baffle the radar of the other ship, was loosing its heavy atom-shells continuously.*

Far in space, tiny pinpoints of light flared and vanished swiftly. So tremendous was the distance at which this duel was being conducted, that the gigantic flares of the exploding atom-shells were thus reduced in size.

Space again burst into blinding light about them as the Empire cruiser's shells ranged close. The *Dendra* rocked on its beam-ends from the soundless explosions of force.

Gordon and Lianna were hurled to the floor by the violent shocks. He was aware that the drone of the drive-generators had fallen to a ragged whine. More automatic bulkheads were slamming shut.

"Drive-rooms half wrecked!" came a shout through his space-suit audiophone. "Only two generators going!"

"Keep them running!" rang Durk Undis' fierce order. "We'll disable that Empire ship with our new weapon, in a few moments!"

Their new weapon? Gordon swiftly recalled how Shorr

---

* *Note:* The shells of the big atom-guns used in space battle were self-propelled by jetting the sub-spectrum pressure rays that hurled them many times faster than light.

Kan had affirmed that the League had a potent new weapon of offense that could strike down any ship.

"Lianna, they've got their hands too full to bother with us right now!" Gordon exclaimed. "This is our chance to get away! If we can get off in one of the spaceboats, we can reach that Empire ship!"

Lianna did not hesitate. "I am willing to try it, Zarth!"

"Then come on!" he exclaimed.

The *Dendra* was still rocking wildly, and he steadied Lianna as he led the way hastily down the corridor.

The space-suited gunners in the gun-galleries they passed were too engrossed in the desperate battle to glimpse them.

They reached the hatch in whose wall was a closed valve leading to one of the space life-boats attached to the hull. Gordon fumbled frantically for a moment with the valve.

"Lianna, I don't know how to open this! Can you do it?"

She swiftly grasped the catches, pulled at them. But there was no response.

"Zarth, the automatic trips have locked! That means that the space-boat is wrecked and unusable!"

Gordon refused to let despair conquer him: "There are other space-boats! On the other side—"

The *Dendra* was still rocking wildly, its parting girders cracking and screeching. Shells were still exploding blindingly outside.

But at that moment they heard a fiercely exultant cry from Durk Undis.

"Our weapon has disabled them! Now give them full broadsides!"

Almost instantly came a thin cheer. "We got them!"

Through the porthole beside the hatch, Gordon glimpsed far out there in the void a sudden flare like that of a new nova. It was no pinpoint of light this time, but a blazing star that swiftly flared and vanished.

"They've destroyed the Empire cruiser somehow!" cried Lianna.

Gordon's heart sank. "But we can still get away if we can get to one of the other space-boats!"

They turned to retrace their way. As they did so, two dishevelled Cloud officers burst into the cross-corridor.

"Get them!" yelled one. They started to draw their atom-pistols from the holsters of their space-suits.

Gordon charged desperately, the heel of the staggering ship hurling him into the two men. He rolled with them on the corridor floor, fiercely trying to wrest a weapon from one.

Then more voices rang loud about him. He felt himself seized by many hands that tore him loose from his antagonists. Hauled to his feet, panting and breathless, Gordon found a half-dozen Cloud-men holding Lianna and himself.

Durk Undis' fierce, flushed face was recognizable inside the glassite helmet of the foremost man.

"You traitor!" he hissed at Gordon. "I *told* Shorr Kan no spawn of the Empire could be depended on!"

"Kill them both now!" urged one of the raging Cloud-men. "It was Zarth Arn who sabotaged the dark-out and got us into this fix!"

"No, they don't die yet!" snapped Durk Undis. "Shorr Kan will deal with them when we get back to the Cloud."

"*If* we get back to the Cloud," corrected the other officer bitterly. "The *Dendra* is crippled, its last two generators will barely run, the space-boats are wrecked. We couldn't make it halfway back."

Durk Undis stiffened. "Then we'll have to hide out until Shorr Kan can send a relief ship for us. We'll call him by secret wave and report what has happened."

"Hide out where?" cried another Cloud-officer. "This is Empire space! That patrol-cruiser undoubtedly got off a flash report before we finished it. This whole sector will be searched by Empire squadrons within twenty-four hours!"

Durk Undis bared his teeth. "I know. We'll have to get out of here. And there's only one place to go."

He pointed through a porthole to a brilliant coppery star that shone hotly just a little inside the glowing haze of huge Orion Nebula.

"That copper sun has a planet marked uninhabited on the charts. We can wait there for help. The cursed Empire cruisers won't look long for us if we jettison wreckage to make it appear we were destroyed."

"But the charts showed that that sun and its planet are the center of a dust-whorl! We can't go there!" objected another Cloud-man.

"The whorl will drift is in, and a high-powered relief ship will be able to come in and get back out," Durk Undis insisted. "Head for it with all the speed you can get out of the generators. Don't draw power yet to message Thallarna. We can do that after we're safe on that world."

He added, pointing to Gordon and Lianna, "And tie these two up and keep a man with drawn gun over them every minute, Linn Kyle!"

Gordon and Lianna were hauled into one of the metal cabins whose walls were badly bulged by the damage of battle. They were dumped into two recoil-chairs mounted on rotating pedestals.

Plastic fetters were snapped to hold their arms and legs to the frame of the chairs. The officer Linn Kyle then left them, with a big Cloud-soldier with drawn atom-pistol remaining guard over them.

Gordon managed to rotate his chair by jerks of his body until he faced Lianna.

"Lianna, I thought we had a chance but I've just made things worse," he said huskily.

Her face was unafraid as she smiled at him through her glassite helmet.

"You had to try it, Zarth. And at least you've thwarted Shorr Kan's scheme."

Gordon knew better. He realized sinkingly that his attempt to get the *Dendra* captured by Empire forces had been a complete failure.

Whatever was the new, potent weapon the Cloud-men had used, it had been too much for the Empire cruiser. He had succeeded only in proving to the Cloud-men and Shorr Kan that he was their enemy.

He'd never have a chance now to warn Throon of Corbulo's treachery and the impending attack! He and Lianna would be dragged back to the Cloud and to Shorr Kan's retribution.

"By God, not that!" Gordon swore to himself. "I'll make them kill us before I let Lianna be taken back there!"

The *Dendra* throbbed on for hours, limping on its last two generators. Then it cut off power and drifted. Soon the ship was entering the strange glow of the gigantic nebula.

At intervals came ominous cracklings and creakings from many parts of the ship. When a guard came to relieve their watch-dog, Gordon learned from the brief talk of the two Cloud-men that only eighteen men remained alive of the officers and crew.

The staggering ship began some hours later to buck and lurch in the grip of strong currents. Gordon realized they must be entering the great dust-whorl in the nebula, to which Linn Kyle had referred.

More and more violent grew the bucking until the *Dendra* seemed shaking itself apart. Then came a loud crash, and a singing sound that lasted for minutes.

"The air has all leaked out from the ship now," Lianna murmured. "Without our space-suits, we'd all be dead."

Death seemed close to John Gordon, in any case. The crippled ship was now in the full grip of the mighty nebula dust-current that was bearing it on toward a crash on the star-world ahead.

Hours passed. The *Dendra* was now using the scant power of its two remaining generators again, to keep from being drawn into the coppery sun they were nearing.

Gordon and Lianna could get only occasional glimpses of their destination, through the porthole. They glimpsed a planet revolving around that copper-colored star—a yellow, tawny world.

Durk Undis' voice rang in a final order. "Strap in for crash-landing!"

The guard who watched Gordon and Lianna strapped himself into a recoil-chair beside them. Air began to scream through the wreck.

Gordon had a flashing glimpse of weird ocher forests rushing upward. The generators roared loud in a brief deceleration effort. Then came a crash that hurled Gordon into momentary darkness.

18

MONSTER MEN

Gordon came to himself, dazed and shaken, to find that it was Lianna's anxious voice that had aroused him.

The girl was leaning toward him from the chair in which she was bound. Her face was worried.

"Zarth, I thought for a moment you were really hurt! Your recoil-chair almost broke loose completely."

"I'm all right," Gordon managed to answer. His eyes swung to take in the scene. "We've landed, all right!"

The *Dendra* was no longer a ship. It was now a twisted, wrecked mass of metal whose voyaging was forever ended.

Walls had bulged like paper, metal girders and struts had been shorn away like cardboard, by the impact of the crash. Hot coppery sunlight streamed through a gaping rent in the cabin wall. Through that opening, Gordon could glimpse the scene outside.

The wreck lay amid towering ocher jungles of strange trees whose broad leaves grew directly from their smooth yellow trunks. Trees and brush and strange shrubs of yellow-and-black flowers had been crushed by the fall of the wreck. Golden spore-dust drifted in the metallic sunlight, and strange webbed-winged birds or creatures flew through the ocher wilderness.

To Gordon's ears came the ragged hum of atomic turbines and generators, close to them in the wreck.

"Durk Undis' men have been working to start the two generators," Lianna said. "They were not badly damaged, it seems."

"Then they're going to send a call back to the Cloud," Gordon muttered. "And Shorr Kan will send another ship here!"

The officer Linn Kyle came into their cabin, no longer wearing a space-suit.

"You can take the suits off the prisoners," Linn Kyle told their guard. "Keep them fettered in the chairs, though."

Gordon was relieved to get rid of the heavy suit and helmet. He found the air breathable but laden with strange, spicy scents.

Just across the corridor from their prison was the stereo room. They heard a transmitter there soon begin its high-pitched whine. Then the taut voice of Durk Undis reached them.

"Calling headquarters at Thallarna! *Dendra* calling!"

Lianna asked, "Won't their call arouse attention? If it's heard by Empire warships, it will."

Gordon had no hope of that. "No, Durk Undis mentioned a secret wave they would use. No doubt that means they can call Thallarna without being overheard."

For minutes, the calls continued. Then they heard Durk Undis order the transmitter turned off.

"We'll try again," they heard him say. "We've got to keep trying until we reach headquarters."

Gordon hitched his recoil-chair around by imperceptible jerks of his body. He could now look across the shattered corridor into the stereo-room, whose door sagged from its frame.

In there, two hours later, he saw Durk Undis and his operator again try to reach Thallarna with a call. As the generators astern began humming, the operator closed the switches of his transmitter and then carefully centered a series of vernier dials on his panel.

"Be careful to keep exactly on the wave," Durk Undis cautioned. "If the cursed Empire ships get even a whisper of our call, they'll run a direction-fix on it and be here to hunt us."

Then, again, began the series of calls. And this time, Durk Undis succeeded in obtaining a response.

"*Dendra* calling, Captain Durk Undis speaking!" he exclaimed eagerly into the transmitter. "I can't go stereo, for lack of power. But here's my identification."

He uttered a series of numbers, evidently a prearranged identification code. Then he rapidly gave the space coordinates of the planet inside the nebula where the wreck lay, and reported the battle and its sequel.

Shorr Kan's ringing voice came from the receiver of the apparatus.

"So Zarth Arn tried to sabotage the mission? I didn't think he was such a fool! I'll send another phantom-cruiser for you at once. Maintain silence until it arrives, for the Empire fleet mustn't suspect you're in their realm."

"I assume that we will not now be continuing the mission to Earth?" said Durk Undis.

"Of course not!" snapped Shorr Kan. "You'll bring Zarth Arn and the girl back to the Cloud. Above all, he mustn't get away to carry any news to Throon!"

Gordon's heart chilled, as he heard. Lianna looked mutely at him.

Durk Undis and the other Cloud-men were jubilant. Gordon heard the fanatic young captain give his orders.

"We'll maintain sentries around the wreck. We don't know what kind of creatures are in these jungles. Linn Kyle, you command the first watch."

Night swept upon the ocher jungles as the coppery sun sank. The dank breath of the forest became stronger.

The night was like one of wondrously glowing moonlight, for the flaring nebula sky dripped strange radiance upon the brooding jungles and the wreck.

Out of the nebula-illuminated jungle there came a little later the echo of a distant cry. It was a throaty, bestial call, but with a creepy human quality in its tones.

Gordon heard Durk Undis' sharp voice. "That must be a beast of some size! Keep your eyes open."

Lianna shivered slightly. "They tell strange tales of some of these lost worlds in the nebula. Few ships ever dare to enter these dust-whorls."

"Ships are going to enter this one, if I can bring it about," muttered Gordon. "We're not going back to the Cloud!"

He had discovered something that gave him a faint hope. The recoil-chair in which he was fettered had suffered like the rest of the wreck from the shock of the crash-landing. The metal frame of the chair was slightly cracked along the arm to which his wrist was fettered.

The crack was a slight one, not affecting the strength of the chair. But it presented a slightly raised and ragged edge. Against this roughened edge, Gordon began secretly rubbing the plastic fetter on his wrist.

Gordon realized the improbability of this small abrasion

severing the plastic. But it was at least a possibility, and he kept it up by imperceptible movements until his muscles ached.

Toward morning, they were awakened from doze by a repetition of the weird, throaty call in the distant forests. The next day, and the next, passed as the Cloud-men waited. But on the third night, horror burst upon them.

Soon after nightfall that night, a yell from one of the Cloud-men sentries was followed by the crash of an atom-pistol.

"What is it?" cried Durk Undis.

"Creatures that looked like men—but they melted, when I fired at them!" cried another voice. "They disappeared like magic!"

"There's another! And more of them!" cried a third Cloud-man. "See!"

Guns went off, the explosion of their atomic pellets rocking the night. Durk Undis yelled orders.

Lianna had swung her chair around on its pedestal, toward the porthole. She cried out.

"Zarth! Look!"

Gordon managed to hitch his chair around also. He stared at the unbelievable sight outside the porthole.

Out there, manlike creatures in scores were pouring out of the jungle toward the wreck. They looked like tall, rubbery human men. Their eyes were blazing as they charged.

Durk Undis and his men were using their atom-pistols. The blinding flare of the atomic pellets darkened the soft nebula-glow.

But wherever those pellets blasted the strange invaders, the rubbery men simply melted. Their bodies melted down into viscous jelly that flowed back over the ground in slow retreat.

"They're coming from the other side too!" yelled the warning of Linn Kyle.

Durk Undis' voice rang imperatively. "Pistols won't hold them off long! Linn, take two men and start the ship's generators. Hook a jet-cable to them and we can spray these creatures with pressure-rays!"

Lianna's eyes were distended by horror, as they witnessed the rubbery horde seize two of the Cloud-men and bear them back into the jungles.

"Zarth, they are monsters! Not men, yet not beasts—"

Gordon saw that the fight was going badly. The rubbery

horde had pressed Dick Undis' men back close against the wreck.

It seemed that the weird attackers could not be harmed. For those who were hit simply melted to jelly and flowed away.

The generators in the wreck began humming loudly. Then Linn Kyle and his two men emerged dragging a heavy cable. At the end of this they had hastily attached one of the pressure-ray jet projectors that ordinarily propelled the ship.

"Use it, quickly!" shouted Durk Undis. "The brutes are too much for us!"

"Stand clear!" yelled Linn Kyle.

He switched on the heavy ray-projector he held. Blinding beams of force leaped from it and cut through the rubbery horde. The ground instantly became a horrible stream of creeping, flowing jelly.

The monstrous attackers sullenly retreated. And the viscous slime upon the ground retreated also toward the shelter of the jungle.

There came then a raging chorus of unhuman, throaty shouts from out in the ocher forest.

"Quick, rig other jet-projectors!" Durk Ungis ordered. "It's all that will keep them off. We need one on each side of the wreck."

"What in the name of all devils *are* the things?" cried Linn Kyle, his voice shrill with horror.

"There's no time for speculating on that!" rapped the other. "Get those projectors ready."

Gordon and Lianna witnessed another attack, a half-hour later. But this time, four jets of pressure-rays met the rubbery horde. Then the attacks desisted.

"They've gone!" sweated a Cloud-man. "But they carried off two of us!"

As the generators were turned off, Gordon heard a new sound from the distance.

"Lianna, hear that?"

It was a pulsing, throbbing sound like the deep beat of distant drums. It came from far westward in the nebula-lit jungle.

Then, breaking into the throbbing drumbeat, there came a faint, agonized series of human screams. There swelled up a triumphant chorus of throaty shouts, then silence.

"The two Cloud-men who were captured," Gordon said sickly. "God knows what happened to them out there."

Lianna was pale. "Zarth, this is a world of horror. No wonder the Empire has left it uncolonized."

The menace to themselves seemed doubled, to Gordon. Almost, to assure Lianna's safety from the nightmare terrors of this planet, he would have gone willingly back to the Cloud.

But his determination returned. They'd get away, but not to go back to the hands of Shorr Kan if he could help it!

He forced himself to continue the slow, squirming movements that rubbed his plastic fetter against the rough crack in the chair-frame. Finally in weariness he slept, to awaken hours after dawn.

In the coppery sunlight, the ocher jungles were deceptively peaceful looking. But captives and captors alike knew now what weird horror brooded out in those golden glades.

Gordon, through the long day, continued to squirm and hitch to increase the abrasion on the fetter. He desisted only when the eyes of their guard were upon him.

Lianna whispered hopefully, "Do you think you can get free?"

"By tonight I should be able to wear it through," he murmured.

"But then? What good will it do? We can't flee out there into the jungle!"

"No, but we can call help," Gordon muttered. "I've thought of a way."

Night came, and Durk Undis gave his men sharp orders. "Two men on each of those jet-projectors, ready to repel the creatures if they come! We'll keep the generators running continuously."

That was welcome news, to Gordon. It made more possible the precarious scheme he had evolved.

He felt that by now the tough plastic must be abraded halfway through. But it still felt too strong to break.

The generators had begun humming. And the worried Cloud-men had not long to wait for the attack they dreaded. Once more from the nebula-illumined jungles came the weird, throaty shouts.

"Be ready the minute they appear!" called Durk Undis.

With a chorus of throaty cries, the rubbery horde rolled

in a fierce wave out of the jungle. Instantly the jet projectors released beams of the powerful pressure-rays upon them.

"It's holding them back! Keep it up!" Durk Undis cried.

"But they don't *die*!" cried another man. "They melt down and flow away!"

Gordon realized this was his opportunity. The Cloud-men were all engaged out there in defending the wreck, and the generators were running.

He expanded his muscles in an effort to break his fetter. But he had misjudged its strength. The tough plastic held.

Again he tried, straining wildly. This time the fetter snapped. Hastily, he unfastened the other fetters.

He got to his feet and quickly freed Lianna. Then he hurried across the corridor toward the stereo-room just oposite.

"Watch and warn me if any of the Cloud-men come back in here!" he told the girl. "I'm going to try to start the transmitter."

"But do you know enough about it to send out a call?" asked Lianna.

"No, but if I can start it up, *any* untuned wave will direct instant attention to this planet," Gordon explained swiftly.

He fumbled in the dimness of the room for the switches he had observed the operator use to start the transmitter.

Gordon closed them. The transmitter remained dead. There was no whine of power, no glow of big tubes. A baffled feeling grew in him as he realized the failure of his plan.

19

WORLD OF HORROR

Gordon forced himself to remain calm despite the wild din of struggle outside the wreck. He went over the switches he had seen the operator use to start the transmitter.

He had missed one! As he closed it, the motor-generators in the stereo-room broke into loud life, and the big vacuum tubes began glowing.

"The generators must be failing! Our jets are losing power!" came a cry from one of the Cloud-men outside the wreck.

"Zarth, you're drawing so much power from the two generators that it's cutting their ray-jets!" warned Lianna. "They'll be in here to find out what's wrong!"

"I only need a moment!" Gordon sweated, bending tensely over the bank of vernier dials.

It was impossible, he knew, for him to try sending any coherent message. He knew almost nothing about this complicated apparatus of future science.

But if he could send out any kind of untuned signal, the very fact of such a signal coming from a supposedly uninhabited planet would surely arouse the suspicion of the Empire cruisers searching out there.

Gordon spun the verniers at random. The equipment sputtered, hummed and faltered, beneath his ignorant handling.

"The brutes are getting through!" Durk Undis' voice yelled. "Linn, get in there and see what's wrong with the generators!"

The battle outside was closer, fiercer. Lianna uttered a cry of warning.

Gordon whirled around. Linn Kyle stood, wild and dishevelled, in the door of the stereo-room.

The Cloud-man uttered an oath and grabbed out his atom-pistol. "By God, I might have known—"

Gordon dived for him, tackled him and brought him to the floor with a crash. They struggled furiously.

Through the increasing din, Gordon heard Lianna's horror-laden scream. And he glimpsed weird figures pouring into the room from astern and seizing the terrified girl.

The rubbery attackers! The spawn of this crazy nebula world had broken through Durk Undis' weakened defenses and were inside the wreck!

"Lianna!" Gordon yelled hoarsely, as he saw the girl borne swiftly from her feet by clutching hands.

The blank faces, the ghastly eyes of the rubbery aliens were close to him as he tore free from Linn Kyle and tried to rise.

He couldn't! The rubbery bodies were piling on him and on the Cloud-man. Arms that felt like tentacles grasped and lifted them. Linn Kyle's wild shot hit one and it melted to crawling jelly, but the others seized the Cloud-man.

Crash of atom-pistols thundered through the corridors of the wreck. Durk Undis' high voice rang over the wild uproar.

"Drive them out of the ship and hold the doors until we can get the ray-jets going again!"

Gordon heard Linn Kyle's yell choked off in his throat as he himself and the Cloud-man were swung swiftly up off their feet. The rubbery horde was retreating out of the shattered stern of the wreck, and were taking the two and Lianna with them.

Gordon fought to free himself of the clutching rubbery arms, and couldn't. He realized with horror that his weakening of the Cloud-men's defense to send his desperate call had exposed Lianna and himself to a more ghastly peril.

"Durk, they have us!" screeched Linn Kyle. Through the crash of guns and yells, Gordon heard the other's startled cry.

But they were out of the wreck now, and their captors were bounding with them through the towering jungle. The whole rubbery horde was retreating into the nebula-lit forest as Durk Undis and his remaining men got their ray-jets in action again.

Gordon's senses swam. These hideous captors hurtled through the jungle with him like preternaturally agile apes. Lianna and Linn Kyle were borne along as swiftly. Down from the flaming nebula sky dripped a glowing radiance that silvered the unearthly forest.

The pace of their strange captors quickened, after some minutes of travel through the jungle. Now rock slopes began to lift from the thick forest.

The weird horde swept with them into a deep stony gorge. It was a place more awesome than the jungle. For its rock cliffs gleamed with a faint light that was no reflection of the nebula sky, but was intrinsic.

"Radioactive, those cliffs," Gordon thought numbly. "Maybe it explains these unholy freaks—"

Speculation was swept from his mind by the hideous clamor that arose. There were hordes of the rubbery creatures here in the gorge. They greeted the captives with throaty, deafening cries.

Gordon found himself held tightly beside Lianna. The girl's face was deathly white.

"Lianna, you're not hurt?"

"Zarth, no! But what are they going to do to us?"

"My God, I don't know!" he husked. "They had some reason for taking us alive."

The quasi-human horde had seized on Linn Kyle! They were stripping all clothing off the Cloud-man's body.

Throaty clamor like the applause of an infernal audience rose loudly as Linn Kyle was now borne forward. Rubbery creatures squatting on the ground beat it with their limbs in a drumming rhythm.

Linn Kyle, struggling wildly, was carried quickly on down the gorge. Then as the horde parted to permit his passage, Gordon glimpsed where they were bearing the Cloud-man.

At the center of the gorge, ringed by faintly glowing radioactive rocks, lay a sunken pool twenty yards across. But it was not a pool of water, but of *life!*

A great, twitching, crawling mass of jelly-like life, heaving and sucking beneath the light of the flaring nebula-sky.

"What is it?" cried Lianna. "It looks living!"

The final horror assaulted Gordon's reeling mind. For now he saw the things around the edges of the pool.

Little jelly-like things like miniature human bodies budded out of that mass of viscous life! Some were attached to the main mass by mere threads. One broke free in that moment and came walking uncertainly up the bank.

"God in Heaven!" he whispered. "These creatures come from the pool of life. They're *born* from it!"

Linn Kyle's screams ripped the din of throaty shouts and drumming rhythm. The rubbery creatures who held the Cloud-man tossed his naked body into the viscous pool!

The Cloud-man screamed again, horribly. Gordon turned aside his gaze, retching.

When he looked again, Linn Kyle's body was engulfed by the viscous jelly that swirled hungrily over it. In a few moments the Cloud-man was gone, absorbed into the pool of life.

"Lianna, don't look!" Gordon cried hoarsely.

He made a mad attempt to free himself. He might as well have been a child in the grasp of those rubbery arms.

But his attempt drew attention to himself. The creatures began to tear away his clothing. He heard Lianna's smothered cry.

Crash of atom-pistols thundered through the infernal din of

drumming and shouting! Pellets exploded in blinding fire amid the swarming horde. Rubbery creatures staggered, fell, melted into jelly that promptly flowed back toward the pool!

"Durk Undis!" yelled Gordon. He had glimpsed the young Cloud-captain's narrow face and blazing eyes, forcing through the horde at the head of his men.

"Get Zarth Arn and the girl, quick!" yelled Durk Undis to his men. "Then back to the wreck!"

Gordon almost admired the ruthless young fanatic, at that moment. Durk Undis had been ordered by Shorr Kan to bring Gordon back to the Cloud, and he'd carry out that order or die trying.

The monstrous horde swirled in crazy uproar, momentarily stunned by the unexpected attack. Gordon wrenched free from the two creatures who still held him. He reached Lianna's side.

It was a crazy chaos of whirling, quasi-human figures and exploding atom-pellets, of Durk Undis' yells and the throaty uproar of the horde.

As the bewildered horde fell back for a moment, Durk Undis and his men blasted the last creatures still around Lianna and Gordon. Next moment, with Gordon and the half-senseless girl in their midst, the Cloud-men hastily retreated back out of the gorge.

"They're coming after us!" yelled one of the men beside Gordon.

Gordon perceived that the ghastly horde had recovered presence of mind. With a hideous throaty clamor, the unhuman mob crashed into the jungle in pursuit.

They made half the distance back to the wreck of the *Dendra,* before the jungle ahead of them swarmed also with the creatures.

"They're all around us—have cut us off!" Durk Undis exclaimed. "Try to fight through!"

It was hopeless and he knew it, and Gordon knew it. A dozen atom-pistols couldn't hold off that mindless horde for long.

Gordon stood with Lianna behind him, using a clubbed branch he tore from a fallen tree as a bludgeon against the swarming, rubbery attackers. With it, he could at least kill Lianna before they dragged her back to that ghastly pool of life!

The whole nightmare fight was suddenly shadowed by a big black mass dropping down on them from the flaming nebula sky!

"It's a ship!" screamed one of the Cloud-men; "One of *our* ships!"

A phantom-cruiser with the black, blotlike insignia of the Cloud on its bows thundered down upon them with krypton searchlights flaring to light the whole scene.

The rubbery horde retreated in sudden panic. As the cruiser crushed to a landing in the jungle close by, Cloud-soldiers with atom-guns sprang from it.

Gordon, raising Lianna's half-senseless form from the ground, found Durk Undis covering him with an atom-pistol. The newcomers were hastily approaching.

"Holl Vonn!" Durk Undis greeted the stocky, crop-haired Cloud-captain who was foremost. "You got here just in time!"

"So it seems!" exclaimed Holl Vonn, staring horrifiedly at the viscous living jelly still creeping away from the scene of battle. "What in God's name were those things that were attacking you?"

"They're creatures of this crazy planet," Durk Undis panted. "I think they were human once—human colonists who mutated under radioactive influence. They've got a strange new reproduction-cycle, being born from a pool of life and going back to it when hurt to be born again."

He continued swiftly. "That can be told later. The thing now is to get away from here at once. There must already be Empire squadrons searching the whole area west of the nebula."

Holl Vonn nodded quickly. "Shorr Kan said to bring Zarth Arn and Lianna back to the Cloud at once. We'd better run eastward through the nebula and then beat back southward along the Rim."

Gordon had revived Lianna. She was looking wonderingly at the towering ship and the armed Cloud-men.

"Zarth, what happened? Does this mean—"

"It means that we're going back to the Cloud, to Shorr Kan," he said hoarsely.

Durk Undis motioned curtly to the new Cloud-ship. "Into the *Meric*, both of you."

Holl Vonn suddenly stiffened. "Listen—by heaven!"

His square face was suddenly livid as he pointed wildly upward.

Four massive shapes were rushing down on them from the nebula-sky! Not phantoms these, but big cruisers with heavy batteries of atom-guns along their sides with the flaring comet-emblem of the Mid-Galactic Empire on their bows.

"An Empire squadron!" yelled Holl Vonn wildly. "We're trapped here! They've already spotted us!"

Gordon felt sudden wild hope. His desperate expedient had succeeded, had brought one of the searching Empire squadrons to this world!

20

DOOM OFF THE PLEIADES

Durk Undis uttered a raging exclamation as the Empire cruisers swooped from the sky.

"To the ship! We'll cut our way back through them to space!"

"We've not a chance!" cried Holl Vonn, his face deathly as he started to run toward his ship. "They've caught us flat!"

Durk Undis froze for a second, then whipped out his atom-pistol again. He whirled around toward Gordon and Lianna.

The young fanatic's eyes were flaming. "Then we'll finish Zarth Arn and Lianna right here! Shorr Kan's orders—no matter what happens to us, these two must not get back to Throon!"

Gordon lunged at him as he spoke! In the few seconds since the Empire cruisers had appeared, Gordon had realized that in this desperate emergency the Cloud-man would kill himself and Lianna rather than let them escape.

He had bunched himself an instant before Durk Undis swung around with the weapon. He hit the Cloud-man like a human projectile. Durk Undis was hurled violently backward.

Holl Vonn was running into his ship, shouting orders. As

Durk Undis sprawled, Gordon seized Lianna's hand and darted with her into the concealment of the nebula-lit jungle.

"If we can keep out of it for a few moments, we're saved!" he told her. "Those Empire ships will come down here to search."

"Holl Vonn is charging them!" cried Lianna, pointing upward.

Thunderous roar of generators screaming with power broke upon the air as the long, slim mass of Holl Vonn's phantom, the *Meric,* hurtled up into the glowing sky.

Gordon saw then that whatever else the men of the Cloud might be, they were not cowards. Knowing himself trapped, knowing instant destruction was the penalty for being caught here in Empire space after the destruction of an Empire ship, Holl Vonn came out fighting!

Atom-guns of the *Meric* volleyed exploding shells at the swooping Empire ships. The nebula sky seemed to burst into blinding brilliance with the explosions.

It was magnificent but hopeless, that charge of one phantom against four heavy cruisers. The great batteries of the cruisers seemed literally to smother the *Meric* in atom-shells.

Blossoming flowers of atomic fire unfolded and momentarily concealed the Cloud ship. Then it was revealed as a fusing, fiery wreck that hurtled headlong across the sky to crash in the distant jungle.

"Zarth, look out!" screamed Lianna at that instant, and pushed Gordon aside.

An atomic pellet flicked close past his face and exploded in a nearby thicket!

Durk Undis, his face deadly, was close by and was raising his weapon to fire again. Lianna had desperately grasped his arm.

Gordon realized then the tenacity of the young Cloud-captain, who had remained and followed to kill Lianna and himself.

"By Heaven, I'll finish it now!" Durk Undis was exclaiming, hurling Lianna violently away from him with a sweep of his arm.

Gordon, charging, reached him at that moment. The Cloud-man uttered a sound of sudden agony as Gordon fiercely twisted his arm.

The atom-pistol dropped from his fingers. Eyes blazing, he kneed Gordon in the stomach and smashed hard fists into his face.

Gordon hardly felt the blows, in his overpowering passion. He rocked forward and fell with the Cloud-man as they grappled.

Braced with his back against the trunk of a towering golden tree, Durk Undis got his hands on Gordon's throat and squeezed.

Gordon felt a roaring in his ears, and a sudden blackness swept over him. His groping hands grabbed the Cloud-man's bristling black hair. He hammered Durk Undis' head violently back against the tree.

He was so deep in that roaring blackness that it was only after many minutes that Lianna's voice penetrated his ears.

"Zarth, it's over! He's dead!"

Gordon, gulping air into starved lungs, felt his senses clearing. He found himself still gripping Durk Undis' hair.

The whole back of the Cloud-man's skull was a bloody mess where he had hammered it again and again against the tree-trunk.

He staggered up to his feet, sick, almost retching. Lianna sprang to his side as he swayed.

"Lianna, I didn't see him. If you hadn't cried out and rushed him, he'd have killed me."

A stern new voice rang suddenly from close by. Gordon staggered around to face that direction.

Gray-uniformed Empire soldiers with raised atom-guns were forcing through the soft-lit jungle toward them. One of the Empire cruisers had landed nearby, while the others still hovered overhead.

The man who spoke was a hard-eyed, handsome young Empire captain who stared wonderingly at Gordon's dishevelled figure and Lianna.

"You two don't look like Cloud-people! But you were with them—"

He stopped suddenly and took a step forward. His eyes peered at Gordon's bruised, bloody face.

"Prince Zarth Arn!" he cried, stupefied. Then his eyes flamed hatred and passion. "By Heaven, we've caught you!

And with Cloud-men! You joined *them* when you fled from Throon!"

A quiver of passion ran through all the Empire soldiers who had gathered. Gordon saw mortal hatred in their eyes.

The young captain stiffened. "I am Captain Dar Carrul of the Empire navy and I arrest you for the assassination of the late emperor and for treason!"

Gordon, dazed as he was, found his voice at that. "I didn't murder Arn Abbas! And I didn't join the Cloud—I was held prisoner by these Cloud-men and only just escaped before you came!"

He pointed at the corpse of Durk Undis. "*He* tried to kill me before letting me escape! And what brought you to this planet searching? An untuned signal-wave from here, wasn't it?"

Dar Carrul looked startled. "How did you know that? Yes, it is true that our operators detected such a signal coming from this uninhabited world, when we were searching space west of the nebula."

"Zarth sent that signal!" Lianna told him. "He used that method to attract Empire ships here!"

Dar Carrul looked a little bewildered. "But everyone knows you killed your father! Commander Corbulo saw you do it! And you fled from Throon—"

"I didn't flee, I was carried off," Gordon declared. He cried earnestly, "All I ask is to be taken to Throon to tell my story!"

Dar Carrul seemed more and more perplexed by the unexpected turn of the situation.

"You will certainly be taken to Throon for trial," he told Gordon. "But it is not for a mere squadron captain to handle such a grave matter as this one. I will take you under guard to our main squadron and report for instructions."

"Let me talk at once by stereo to my brother, to Jhal Arn!" pleaded Gordon tautly.

Dar Carrul's face tightened. "You are a proclaimed fugitive, charged with the gravest of crimes against the Empire. I cannot allow you to send messages. You must wait until I receive instructions."

He made a gesture, and a dozen soldiers with drawn atom-guns stepped forward around Gordon and Lianna.

"I must ask you to enter our ship at once," the young captain said clippedly.

Ten minutes later, the cruiser took off from the nebula-world of horror. With the other three Empire cruisers, it raced out westward through the vast glow of Orion Nebula.

In the cabin in which they two had been placed under guard, Gordon paced furiously to and fro.

"If they only let me tell Jhal Arn of the danger, of Corbulo's treachery!" he rasped. "If that has to wait till we're taken to Throon, it might be too late!"

Lianna looked worried. "Even when we get to Throon, it may not be easy to convince Jhal Arn of your innocence, Zarth."

Gordon's taut anger was chilled by that. "But they've got to believe me! They surely won't credit Corbulo's lies when I tell them the truth?"

"I hope not," Lianna murmured. She added with a flash of pride, "I will corroborate your story. And I am still princess of Fomalhaut Kingdom!"

Hours seemed to drag as the cruisers hurtled headlong out of Orion Nebula, and on westward through open space.

Lianna slept exhaustedly after a time. But Gordon could not sleep. His very nerve seemed taut as he sensed the approaching climax of the gigantic galactic game in which he had been but a pawn.

He *must* convince Jhal Arn of the truth of his story! And he must do so quickly, for as soon as Shorr Kan learned that he had escaped to tell the truth, the master of the Cloud would act swiftly.

Gordon's head ached. Where would it all end? Was there any real chance of his clearing up this great tangle and getting to Earth for the re-exchange of bodies with the real Zarth Arn?

Finally the cruisers decelerated. Orion Nebula was now a glow in the starry heavens far behind them. Close ahead lay the shining clusters of suns of the Pleiades. And near the Pleiades' famous beacon-group there stretched a far-flung echelon of tiny sparks.

The sparks were ships! Warships of the Mid-Galactic Empire's great navy cruising here off the Pleiades, one of the many mighty squadrons watching and warding the Empire's boundaries!

Lianna had awakened. She looked out with him as the cruiser slowly moved past gigantic battleships, columns of grim cruisers, slim phantoms and destroyers and scouts.

"This is one of the main battle-fleets of the Empire," she murmured.

"Why are we being kept here, instead of letting us give our warning?" sweated Gordon.

Their cruiser drew up alongside a giant battleship, the hulls grating together. They heard a rattle of machinery.

Then the cabin door opened and young Dar Carrul entered. "I have received orders to transfer you at once to our flagship, the *Ethne*."

"But let us talk first by stereo to Throon, to the Emperor!" Gordon cried. "Man, what we have to tell may save the whole Empire from disaster!"

Dar Carrul shook his head curtly. "My orders are that you are to send no messages but are to be transferred immediately. I presume that the *Ethne* will take you at once to Throon."

Gordon stood, sick with disappointment and hope delayed. Lianna plucked his arm.

"It won't take long for that battleship to reach Throon, and then you'll be able to tell," she encouraged.

The two went with guards around them down through the cruiser to a hatchway. From it a short tubular gangway had been run to the battleship.

They went through it under guard of soldiers from the battleship. Once inside the bigger ship, the gangway was cast off and the airlock closed.

Gordon looked around the vestibule chamber at officers and guards. He saw the hatred in their faces as they looked at him. They too thought him assassin of his father, traitor to the Empire!

"I demand to see the captain of this battleship immediately," he rasped, to the lieutenant of guards.

"He is coming now," answered the lieutenant icily, as a tramp of feet came from a corridor.

Gordon swung toward the newcomers, with on his lips a fiery request to be permitted to call Throon. He never uttered it.

For he was looking at a stocky, uniformed figure, a man whose grizzled, square face and bleak eyes he knew only too well.

"Corbulo!" he cried.

Commander Corbulo's bleak eyes did not waver as his harsh voice lashed out at Gordon.

"Yes, traitor, it is I. So you two have been caught at last?"

"You call me traitor!" Gordon choked. "You yourself the greatest traitor in all history—"

Chan Corbulo turned coldly toward the tall, swarthy Arcturian captain who had entered with him and was glaring at Gordon.

"Captain Marlann, there is no need to take this assassin and his accomplice to Throon for trial. I *saw* them murder Arn Abbas! As Commander of the Empire fleet, I adjudge them guilty by space-law and order them executed immediately!"

21

MUTINY IN THE VOID

Gordon's mind rocked to disastrous realization. As he stared frozenly into Chan Corbulo's grim triumphant face, he understood what had happened.

As Commander of the Empire navy, Corbulo had received the report of the capture of Gordon and Lianna. The archtraitor had known that he must not let Gordon return to Throon with what he knew. So he had swiftly come here and ordered the two captives brought aboard his own flagship to do away with them before they could tell what they knew.

Gordon looked wildly around the circle of officers. "You've got to believe me! I'm no traitor! It was Corbulo himself who murdered my father and who is betraying the Empire to Shorr Kan!"

He saw hard, cold unbelief and bitter hatred in the officers' faces. Then Gordon recognized one familar face.

It was the craggy red face of Hull Burrel, the Antarian

captain who had saved him from the Cloud-raiders on Earth. He remembered now that for that, Hull Burrel had been promoted aide to the Commander.

"Hull Burrel, you surely believe me!" Gordon appealed. "You know that Shorr Kan tried to have me kidnapped before."

The big Antarian scowled. "I thought then he did. I didn't know then you were secretly in league with him, that all that was just pretense."

"I tell you, it wasn't pretense!" Gordon cried. "You've all let Corbulo pull the wool over your eyes."

Lianna, her gray eyes blazing in her white face, added, "Zarth speaks the truth! Corbulo is the traitor!"

Chan Corbulo made a brusque gesture. "We've had enough of these wild lies. Captain Marlann, see that they are locked out into space at once. It's the most merciful manner of execution."

The guards stepped forward. And then, as Gordon felt the bitterness of despair, he glimpsed the satisfied smirk in Corbulo's eyes and it stung him to a final desperate effort.

"You're letting Corbulo make fools of you all!" he raged. "Why is he so set on executing us instantly, instead of taking us to Throon for trial! Because he wants to silence us! We know too much!"

At last, Gordon perceived that he had made a little impression on the officers. Hull Burrel and others looked a little doubtful.

The Antarian glanced questioningly at Corbulo. "Commander, I beg you will pardon me if I'm overstepping my position. But perhaps it would be more regular to take them to Throon for trial."

Val Marlann, the swarthy Arcturian captain of this battleship, supported Hull Burrel. "Zarth Arn is one of the royal family, after all. And the princess Lianna is a ruler in her own right."

Lianna said swiftly, "This execution means that Fomalhaut Kingdom will break its alliance with the Empire, remember!"

Chan Corbulo's square face stiffened in anger. He had been confident that Gordon and Lianna were on the brink of death, and this slight hitch irritated him.

His irritation made Corbulo do the wrong thing. He tried to ride roughshod over the objections just advanced.

"There is no need to take black traitors and assassins to Throon!" he snapped. "We will execute them at once. Obey my orders!"

Gordon seized on that opportunity to make a flaming appeal to the gathered officers.

"You see? Corbulo will never let us go to Throon to tell what we know! Has he even reported our capture to the Emperor?"

Hull Burrel, with gathering trouble on his craggy face, looked at a young Earth-man officer.

"You are communication-officer, Verlin. Has any report of Zarth Arn's capture been made to the Emperor!"

Corbulo exploded in rage. "Burrel, how dare you question my conduct? By God, I'll break you for this!"

The young Earthman, Verlin, looked uncertainly at the raging Commander. Then he hesitantly answered Hull Burrel's question.

"No report of any kind has been made to Throon. The Commander ordered me to make no mention of the capture yet."

Gordon's voice crackled. "Doesn't that at least make you doubt?" he cried to the frowning officers. "Why should Corbulo keep my capture secret from my brother? It's because he knows Jhal Arn would order us brought to Throon for judgment, and he doesn't want that!"

And Gordon added passionately, "We do not ask for any pardon, for any clemency. If I'm guilty, I deserve execution. All I ask is to be taken to Throon for trial. If Corbulo persists in refusing that, it can only be because he is the traitor I say he is!"

Faces changed expression. And Gordon knew that he had finally awakened deep doubt in their minds.

"You're throwing away the Empire fleet if you let this traitor command it!" he pressed. "He's in league with Shorr Kan. Unless you let me go to Throon to prove that, the fleet and Empire are doomed!"

Hull Burrel looked around his fellow officers, and then at Chan Corbulo. "Commander, we mean no disrespect. But Zarth

Arn's demand for a trial is reasonable. He should be taken to Throon."

A low chorus of supporting voices came from the other officers. Deep ingrained as was their discipline, deeper still was the doubt and the fear for the Empire that Gordon had awakened.

Corbulo's face flared dull red with fury. "Burrel, you're under arrest! By God, you'll take the spacewalk with these two for your insubordination! Guards, seize him!"

Tall, swarthy Captain Val Marlann stepped forward and intervened.

"Wait, guards! Comander Corbulo, you are supreme officer of the Empire fleet but I am captain of the *Ethne*. And I agree with Burrel that we cannot summarily execute these prisoners."

"Marlann, you're captain of the *Ethne* no longer!" raged Corbulo. "I hereby remove you and take personal command of this ship."

Val Marlann stiffened in open defiance as he rasped an answer.

"Commander, if I'm wrong I'm willing to take the consequences. But by God, something about all this does smell to Heaven! We're going to Throon and find out what it is!"

Gordon heard the mutter of agreement from the other officers. And Chan Corbulo heard it also.

The baffled rage on his grizzled face deepened, and he uttered a curse.

"Very well, then—to Throon! And when I get through with you at the courts-martial there, you'll wish you'd remembered your discipline. Insubordination in high space! Just wait!"

And Corbulo turned angrily and shouldered out of the room, going forward along a corridor.

Burrel and the other officers looked soberly at each other. Then Val Marlann spoke grimly to Gordon.

"Prince Zarth, you'll get the trial at Throon you asked for. And if you've not told the truth, it's our necks."

"It must be the truth!" Hull Burrel declared. "I never could understand why Zarth Arn should murder his own father! And why would Corbulo be so wild to execute them if the commander had nothing to hide?"

At that moment, from the annunciators throughout the ship, broke a loud voice.

"Commander Corbulo, to all hands! Mutiny has broken out on the *Ethne*! Captain Val Marlann and his chief officers, my aide Hull Burrel, and Prince Zarth and Princess Lianna are the ringleaders! All loyal men arm and seize the mutineers!"

Hull Burrel's blue eyes flashed an arctic light. "He's raising the ship against us! Val, get to the annunciators and call off the men! You can convince them!"

The officers plunged for the corridors leading up into the interior of the mighty battleship.

Gordon cried, "Lianna, wait here! There may be fighting!"

Then, as he ran with Hull Burrel and the others through the corridors, they heard a growing uproar somewhere ahead.

The great battleship was suddenly in chaos, alarm bells ringing, voices yelling from the annunciators, feet pounding through the corridors.

The spacemen who had rushed to obey the supreme commander's order were now bewildered by a clash of authority. Some, who tried to obey and arrest Val Marlann and his officers, were instantly attacked by those of their own comrades who remained loyal to the ship's captain.

In most of the ship, the crew had not had time to arm. Improvised metal clubs and fists took the place of atom-pistols. Battle joined and raged swiftly in crewrooms, in gun-galleries, in corridors.

Gordon and Hull Burrel found themselves with Val Marlann in the midst of a seething, battling mob in the main mid-deck corridor.

"I've got to get through to an annunciator switchboard!" cried Val Marlann. "Help me crash through them!"

Gordon and the big Antarian, with Verlin, the young communication officer, joined him and plunged into the crazy fight.

They got through, but left big Hull Burrel battling a knot of spacemen back in the mob.

Val Marlann yelled into the annunciator switchboard. "Captain Marlann to all hands! Cease fighting! The announcement of mutiny was a fake, a trick! Obey me!"

Verlin grabbed Gordon's arm as a distant whine of power reached their ears over the din.

"That's the stereo-transmitter going!" the young communication officer cried to Gordon. "Corbulo must be calling for help from the other ships of the fleet!"

"We've got to stop that!" Gordon cried. "Lead the way!"

They raced forward along a corridor, then cross-ship and up a companionway to the top deck.

Val Marlann's orders thundering from the annunciators seemed to be rapidly quieting the uproar in the ship. Its crew knew his voice better than any other. Long habit brought them to obey.

Verlin and Gordon plunged into a big, crowded stereo-room whose tubes and motor-generators were humming. Two bewildered-looking technicians were at the patrol panel.

Chan Corbulo, an atom-pistol gripped in his hand, stood on the transmitter-plate speaking loudly and rapidly.

"—command all nearby battleships to send boarding parties aboard the *Ethne* at once to restore order! You will arrest—"

Corbulo, from the tail of his eye, saw the two men burst into the room. He swung swiftly around and triggered his pistol.

The pellet that flew from it was aimed at Gordon. But Verlin, plunging ahead, took it full in his breast.

Gordon tripped headlong over the falling body of the young Earthman. That stumble made Corbulo's quick second shot flick just over Gordon's head.

As he fell, Gordon had hurled himself forward. He tackled Corbulo's knees and brought him crashing to the floor.

The two technicians ran forward and hauled Gordon off the Commander. But their grip on him relaxed when they glimpsed his face.

"Good God, it's Prince Zarth Arn!" one of them cried.

Instinctive respect for the ruling house of the Empire confused the two men. Gordon wrenched free from them and grabbed for the pistol in Verlin's holster.

Corbulo had regained his feet. on the other side of the room. He was again raising his weapon.

"*You'll* never go to Throon!" he roared. "By—"

Gordon shot, from where he crouched on the floor. The atomic pellet, loosed more by guess than by aim, hit Corbulo's neck and exploded. It flung him backwards as though a giant hand had hit him.

Val Marlann and Hull Burrel came bursting into the stereo-room with other officers. The whole great ship seemed suddenly quiet.

Marlann bent over Corbulo's blasted body. "Dead!"

Hull Burrel, panting, his face flaming, told Gordon grimly, "We've killed our Commander. God help us if your story is not true, Prince Zarth!"

"It's true—and Corbulo was only one of a score of traitors in Shorr Kan's hire," Gordon husked, shaken with reaction. "I'll prove it all at Throon."

The image of a dark, towering Centaurian battleship captain suddenly appeared on the receiver-plate of the stereo.

"Vice-Commander Ron Giron calling from the *Shaar!* What the devil is going on aboard the *Ethne*? We're coming alongside to board you as Commander Corbulo ordered."

"No one will board this ship!" Val Marlann answered swiftly. "We're going at once to Throon."

"What does this mean?" roared the vice-commander. "Let me speak to Commander Corbulo himself!"

"You can't—he's dead," clipped Hull Burrel. "He was betraying the fleet to the Cloud. At Throon, we'll prove that."

"It *is* mutiny, then?" cried Ron Giron. "You'll stand by for boarding parties and consider yourselves under arrest, or we'll open fire!"

"If you fire on the *Ethne,* you'll destroy the Empire's only chance to foil Shorr Kan's plot!" cried Val Marlann. "We've staked our lives on the truth of what Prince Zarth Arn has told us, and we're taking him to Throon."

John Gordon himself stepped forward to make an appeal to the glaring vice-commander.

"Commander Giron, they're telling you the truth! Give us this chance to save the Empire from disaster!"

Giron hesitated. "This is all insane! Corbulo dead and accused of treachery, Zarth Arn returned—"

He seemed to reach decision. "It's beyond me but they can sift it at Throon. To make sure that you go there, four battleships will escort the *Ethne*. They'll have orders to blast you if you try to go anywhere but Throon!"

"That's all we ask!" Gordon cried. "One more word of warning! A League attack may come at any time now. I know it is coming, and soon."

Commander Giron's towering figure stiffened. "The devil

you say! But we've already taken all possible dispositions. I'll call the Emperor and report all this to him."

The image disappeared. Through the portholes, they saw four big battleships move up and take positions on either side of the *Ethne*.

"We start for Throon at once," Val Marlann said swiftly. "I'll give the orders."

As the officer hurried out, and annunciators and bells started buzzing through the ship, Gordon asked a question.

"Am I to consider myself still a prisoner?"

"Blazes, no!" Hull Burrel exclaimed. "If you've told us the truth, there's no reason to keep you a prisoner. If you haven't told the truth, then we're due for court-martial and execution anyway!"

Gordon found Lianna in the corridor, hurrying in search of him. He told her rapidly what had happened.

"Corbulo dead? One great danger removed!" she exclaimed. "But Zarth, now our lives and the Empire's fate depend on whether we can prove to your brother that our story is true!"

At that moment the mighty *Ethne* began to move ponderously through the void, as its great turbines roared loud.

In a few minutes, the big battleship and its four grim escorts were hurtling headlong across the starry spaces toward Throon.

22

GALACTIC CRISIS

Huge, glaring white Canopus flared in the star-sown heavens in blinding splendor, as the five great battleships rushed toward it at rapidly decreasing speed.

Once again, John Gordon looked from a ship's bridge at the glorious capital sun of the Empire and its green, lovely world. But how much had happened since first he had come to Throon!

"We dock at Throon City in two hours," Hull Burrel was saying. And he added grimly, "There'll be a reception committee waiting for us. Your brother has been advised of our coming."

"All I ask is a chance to prove my story to Jhal," declared Gordon, "I'm sure I can convince him."

But, inwardly, he had a sickening feeling that he was *not* entirely sure. It all depended on one man, and on whether Gordon had correctly judged that man's reactions.

All the hours and days of the headlong homeward flight across the Empire, Gordon had been tortured by that haunting doubt. He had slept but little, had scarcely eaten, consumed by growing tension.

He *must* convince Jhal Arn! Once that was done, once the last traitor was rooted out, then the Empire would be ready to meet the Cloud's attack. His, John Gordon's, duty would be fulfilled and he could return to Earth for his re-exchange of bodies with the real Zarth Arn. And the real Zarth could come back to help defend the Empire.

But Gordon felt an agony of spirit every time he thought of that re-exchange of bodies. For on that day when he returned to his own time, he would be leaving Lianna forever.

Lianna came into the wide bridge as he thought of her. She stood beside him with her slim fingers clasping his hand encouragingly as they looked ahead.

"Your brother will believe you, Zarth—I know he will."

"Not without proof," Gordon muttered. "And only one man can prove my story. Everything hinges on whether or not he has heard of Corbulo's death and my return, and has fled."

That tormenting uncertainty deepened in him as the five big battleships swung down toward Throon City.

It was night in the capital. Under the light of two hurtling moons glimmered the fairylike glass mountains and the silver sea. The shimmering towers of the city rose boldly in the soft glow, a pattern of lacy light.

The ships landed ponderously in docks of the naval spaceport. Gordon and Lianna, with Hull Burrel and Captain Val Marlann, emerged from the *Ethne* to be met by a solid mass of armed guards.

Two officers walked toward them, and with them came Orth Bodmer, the Chief Councillor. Bodmer's thin face was lined with deep worry as he confronted Gordon.

"Highness, this is a sorry homecoming!" he faltered. "God send you can prove your innocence!"

"Jhal Arn has kept our return and what happened out there off the Pleiades, a secret?" Gordon asked quickly.

Orth Bodmer nodded. "His Highness is waiting for you now. We are to go at once to the palace by tubeway. I must warn you that these guards have orders to kill instantly if any of you attempt resistance."

They were swiftly searched for weapons, and then led toward the tubeway. Guards entered the cars with them. They had seen no one else, the whole spaceport having been cleared and barred off.

It seemed a dream to John Gordon as they whirled through the tubeway. Too much had happened to him, in too short a time. The mind couldn't stand it. But Lianna's warm clasp of his hand remained a link with reality, nerving him for this ordeal.

In the great palace of Throon, they went up through emptied corridors to the study in which Gordon had first confronted Arn Abbas.

Jhal Arn sat now behind the desk, his handsome face a worn mask. His eyes were utterly cold and expressionless as they swept over Gordon and Lianna and the two space-captains.

"Have the guards remain outside, Bodmer," he ordered the Councillor in a toneless voice.

Orth Bodmer hesitated. "The prisoners have no weapons. Yet perhaps—"

"Do as I order," rasped Jhal Arn. "I have weapons here. There's no fear of my brother being able to murder *me*."

The nervous Chief Councillor and the guards went out and closed the door.

Gordon was feeling a hot resentment that burned away all that numb feeling of unreality.

He strode a step forward. "Is this the kind of justice you're going to deal the Empire?" he blazed at Jhal Arn. "The kind of justice that condemns a man before he's heard?"

"Heard? Man, you were *seen*, murdering our father!" cried Jhal Arn, rising. "Corbulo saw you, and now you've killed Corbulo too!"

"Jhal Arn, it is not so!" cried Lianna. "You must listen to Zarth!"

Jhal Arn turned somber eyes on her. "Lianna, I have no blame for you. You love Zarth and let him lead you into this. But as for him, the studious, scholarly brother I once loved, the brother who was plotting all the time for power, who struck our father down—"

"Will you listen?" cried Gordon furiously. "You stand there mouthing accusations without giving me a chance to answer them!"

"I have heard your answers already," rasped Jhal Arn. "Vice-Commander Giron told me when he reported your coming that you were accusing Corbulo of treachery to cover up your own black crimes."

"I can prove that if you'll just give me a chance!" Gordon declared.

"What proof can you advance?" retorted the other. "What proof, that will outweigh the damning evidence of your flight, of Corbulo's testimony, of Shorr Kan's secret messages to you?"

Gordon knew that he had come to the crux of the situation, the crisis upon which he would stand or fall.

He talked hoarsely, telling of Corbulo's treacherous assistance in helping Lianna and him escape, of how that escape had been timed exactly with the assassination of Arn Abbas.

"It was to make it look as though I'd committed the murder and fled!" Gordon emphasized. "Corbulo himself struck down our father and then said he'd seen me do it, knowing I wasn't there to deny the charge!"

He narrated swiftly how the Sirian traitor captain had taken him and Lianna to the Cloud, and briefly summarized the way in which he had induced Shorr Kan, by pretending to join him, to allow him to go to Earth. He did not, could not, tell how his ruse had hinged on the fact that he was really not Zarth Arn at all. He couldn't tell that.

Gordon finished his swift story, and saw that the black cloud of bitter disbelief still rested on Jhal Arn's face.

"The story is too fantastic! And it has nothing to prove it but your word and the word of this girl who's in love with you. You said you could prove your tale!"

"I can prove it, if I'm given a chance," Gordon said earnestly.

He continued swiftly. "Jhal, Corbulo was not the only

traitor in high position in the Empire. Shorr Kan himself told me there were a score of such traitors, though he didn't name them.

"But one traitor I know to be such is Thern Eldred, the Sirian naval captain who took us to the Cloud! He can prove it all, if I can make him talk!"

Jhal Arn frowned at Gordon for a moment. Then he touched a stud and spoke into a panel on the desk.

"Naval Headquarters? The Emperor speaking. There is a captain in our forces named Thern Eldred, a Sirian. Find out if he's on Throon. If he is, send him here immediately under guard."

Gordon grew tense as they waited. If the Sirian were away in space, if he had somehow heard of events and had fled—

Then a sharp voice finally came from the panel. "Thern Eldred has been found here. His cruiser has just returned from patrol. He is being sent to you now."

A half-hour later the door opened and Thern Eldred stepped inside. The Sirian had a wondering look on his hard-bitten greenish face. Then his eyes fell on Gordon and Lianna.

"Zarth Arn!" he exclaimed, startled, recoiling. His hand went to his belt, but he had been disarmed.

"Surprised to see us?" Gordon rasped. "You thought we were still in the Cloud where you left us, didn't you?"

Thern Eldred had instantly recovered his self-possession. He looked at Gordon with assumed perplexity.

"I don't understand what you mean, about the Cloud!"

Jhal Arn spoke curtly. "Zarth claims that you took him and Lianna by force to Thallarna. He accuses you of being a traitor to the Empire, of plotting with Shorr Kan."

The Sirian's face stiffened in admirably assumed anger.

"It's a lie! Why, I haven't seen Prince Zarth Arn and the princess since the Feast of Moons!"

Jhal Arn looked harshly at Gordon "You said you could prove your claim, Zarth So far, it's only your word against his."

Lianna broke in passionately. "Is my word nothing, then? Is a Princess of Fomalhaut to be believed a liar?"

Again, Jhal Arn looked at her somberly. "Lianna, I know

you would lie for Zarth Arn, if for nothing else in the universe."

Gordon had expected the Sirian's denial. And he was counting on his estimate of this man's character, to get the truth out of him.

He stepped forward to confront the man. He kept his passionate anger restrained, and spoke deliberately.

"Thern Eldred, the game is up. Corbulo is dead, the whole plot with Shorr Kan is about to be exposed. You haven't a chance to keep your guilt hidden, and when it's exposed it'll mean execution for you."

As the Sirian started to protest, Gordon continued swiftly, "I know what you're thinking! You think that if you stick to your denials you can face me down, that that's your only chance now to save your skin. But it won't work, Thern Eldred!

"The reason it won't work is because your cruiser, the *Markab*, had a full crew in it when it took us to the Cloud. I know those officers and men had been bribed to support you, that they'll deny ever going to the Cloud. They'll deny it, at first. But when pressure is put on them, there's bound to be at least one weak one among them who'll confess to save himself!"

Now, for the first time, Gordon saw doubt creep into the Sirian's eyes. Yet Thern Eldred angrily shook his head.

"You're still talking nonsense, Prince Zarth! If you want to question my men in the *Markab*, go ahead. Their testimony will show that you're not telling the truth."

Gordon pressed his attack, his voice ringing now. "Thern Eldred, you can't bluff it out! You know one of them will talk! And when he does, it's execution for you.

"There's only one way you can save yourself. That's to turn evidence against the other officials and officers in this plot with you, the others who have been working for Shorr Kan. Give us their names, and you'll be allowed to go scot-free out of the Empire!"

Jhal Arn sternly interrupted. "I'll sanction no such terms! If this man is a traitor, he'll suffer the penalty."

Gordon turned passionately to him. "Jhal, listen! He deserves death for his treachery. But which is most important—

that he be punished, or that the Empire be saved from disaster?"

The argument swayed Jhal Arn. He frowned silently for a moment, and then spoke slowly.

"Very well, I'll agree to let him go free if he does make any such confession and names his confederates."

Gordon swung back to the Sirian. "Your last chance, Thern Eldred! You can save yourself now, or never!"

He saw the indecision in Thern Eldred's eyes. He was staking everything on the fact that this Sirian was a ruthless realist, ambitious, selfish, with no real loyalty to anyone but himself.

And Gordon's gamble won. Confronted by the imminence of discovery, presented with a loophole by which he might save his own skin, Thern Eldred's defiant denials broke down.

He spoke huskily. "I have the Emperor's word that I am to go scot-free, remember?"

"Then you *were* in a plot?" raged Jhal Arn. "But I'll keep my word. You'll go free if you name your confederates, as soon as we have seized them and verified what you tell."

Thern Eldred was ghastly pale but tried to smile. "I know when I'm in a trap, and I'm cursed if I'll get myself killed just for loyalty to Shorr Kan. He wouldn't do it for me!"

He went on, to Jhal Arn. "Prince Zarth has told the truth. Chan Corbulo was leader of the little clique of officials who planned to betray the Empire to the Cloud. Corbulo killed Arn Abbas, and had me carry off Zarth and Lianna so they'd be blamed. Everything the prince has said is true."

Gordon felt his eyes blur, his shoulders sag, as those words brought shaky relief from his intolerable strain of many days.

He felt Lianna's warm arms around him, heard her eager voice as big Hull Burrel and Val Marlann excitedly slapped his back.

"Zarth, I knew you'd clear yourself!"

Jhal Arn, face pale as death, came toward Gordon. His voice was hoarse when he spoke.

"Zarth, can you ever pardon me? My God, how was I to know? I'll never forgive myself!"

"Jhal, it's all right," Gordon stumbled. "What else were you to think when it was so cunningly planned?"

"The whole Empire shall soon know the truth," Jhal Arn

exclaimed. He swung to Thern Eldred. "First, the names of the other traitors."

Thern Eldred went to the desk and wrote for minutes. He silently handed the sheet to Jhal Arn, who then summoned guards forward.

"You'll be confined until this information is verified," he told the Sirian sternly. "Then I'll keep my promise. You shall go free—but the tale of your treachery will follow you to the remotest stars!"

Jhal Arn turned his eyes to the list of names, when the guards had taken the Sirian out. He cried out, stunned, "Good God, look!"

Gordon saw. The first name on the list was "Orth Bodmer, Chief Councillor of the Empire."

"Bodmer a traitor? It's impossible!" Jhal Arn cried. "Thern Eldred has merely accused him because of some grudge."

Gordon frowned. "Perhaps. But Corbulo was as trusted as Orth Bodmer, remember!"

Jhal Arn's lips tightened. He spoke sharply into a panel on the desk. "Tell Councillor Bodmer to come in at once."

The answer was quick. "Councillor Bodmer left the anteroom some time ago. We do not know where he went."

"Find him and bring him here at once!" ordered Jhal Arn.

"He fled when he saw Thern Eldred brought in here to be questioned!" cried Gordon. "Jhal, he *knew* the Sirian would expose him!"

Jhal Arn sank into a chair. "Bodmer a traitor! Yet it must be so. And look at these other names. Byrn Ridim, Korrel Kane, Jon Rollory—all trusted officials."

The guard-captain reported. "Highness, we can't find Orth Bodmer anywhere in the palace! He wasn't seen to leave, but isn't to be found!"

"Send out a general order for his arrest," snapped Jhal Arn. He handed the list of names to the guard-captain. "And arrest all these men instantly. But do so without arousing attention."

He looked haggardly at Gordon and Lianna. "All this treachery has already shaken the Empire! And the southern star-kingdoms are wavering! Their envoys have requested urgent audience with me tonight, and I fear they mean to throw off their alliance with the Empire!"

23

THE SECRET OF THE EMPIRE

Gordon suddenly noticed that Lianna's slim figure was sagging with weariness. He uttered an exclamation of self-reproach.

"Lianna, you must be half dead after all you've been through!"

Lianna tried to smile. "I'll admit that I won't be sorry to rest."

"Captain Burrel will see you to your apartments, Lianna," said Jhal Arn. "I want Zarth to be here with me when the star-kingdom envoys come, to impress on them that our royal house is again united."

He added to Hull Burrel and Val Marlann, "You two and all your men are completely cleared of the mutiny charge, of course. I'm your debtor for life for helping to expose Corbulo and save my brother."

When they had escorted Lianna out, Gordon sank tiredly into a chair. He was still feeling reaction after the long strain.

"Zarth, I'd rather let you rest too but you know how vital it is to hold the star-kingdoms when this crisis is deepening," Jhal said. "Curse that black devil, Shorr Kan!"

A servant brought *saqua* and the fiery liquor cleared Gordon's numbed mind and brought strength back into his weary body.

Presently a chamberlain opened the door of the room, bowing low.

"The ambassadors of the Kingdoms of Polaris, of Cygnus, of Perseus and of Cassiopeia, and of the Baronies of Hercules Cluster!"

The envoys, in full dress uniforms, stopped in amazement when they saw Gordon standing beside Jhal Arn.

"Prince Zarth!" exclaimed the chubby Hercules envoy. "But we thought—"

"My brother has been completely cleared and the real

traitors have been apprehended," Jhal informed them. "It will be publicly announced within the hour."

His eyes ran over their faces. "Gentlemen, for what purpose have you requested this audience?"

The chubby Hercules ambassador looked at the grave, aged envoy from Polaris Kingdom. "Tu Shal, you are our spokesman."

Tu Shal's lined old face was deeply troubled as he stepped forward and spoke.

"Highness, Shorr Kan has secretly just offered all our kingdoms treaty of friendship with the League of Dark Worlds! He declares that if we cling to our alliance with the Empire, we are doomed."

The Hercules ambassador added, "He has made the same offer to us Barons, warning us not to join the Empire."

Jhal Arn looked swiftly at Gordon. "So Shorr Kan is now sending ultimatums? That means he is almost ready to strike."

"We none of us have any love for Shorr Kan's tyranny," Tu Shal was saying. "We prefer to hold to the Empire that stands for peace and union. But it is said that the Cloud has prepared such tremendous armaments and has such revolutionary new weapons that they'll carry all before them if war comes."

Jhal Arn's eyes flashed. "Do you dream he can conquer the Empire when we have the Disruptor to use in case of necessity?"

"That's just it, highness!" said Tu Shal. "It's being said that the Disruptor was never used but once long ago, and that it proved so dangerous then that you would not dare to use it again!"

He added, "I fear that our kingdoms will desert their allegiance to the Empire unless you prove that that is a lie. Unless you prove to us that you do dare to use the Disruptor!"

Jhal Arn looked steadily at the envoys as he answered. And his solemn words seemed to Gordon to bring the whisper of something alien and supernally terrible into the little room.

"Tu Shal, the Disruptor is an awful power. I will not disguise that it is dangerous to unchain that power in the galaxy. But it was done once when the Magellanians invaded, long ago.

"And it will be done again, if necessary! My father is dead, but Zarth and I can unloose that power. And we *will* unloose it and rive the galaxy before we let Shorr Kan fasten tyranny on the free worlds!"

Tu Shal seemed more deeply troubled than before. "But highness, our kingdoms demand that we *see* the Disruptor demonstrated before they will believe!"

Jhal's face grew somber. "I had hoped that never would the Disruptor have to be taken from its safekeeping and loosed again. But it may be that it would be best to do as you ask."

His eyes flashed. "Yes, it may be that when Shorr Kan learns that we can still wield that power and hears what it can do, he will think twice before precipitating galactic war!"

"Then you will demonstrate it for us?" asked the Hercules envoy, his round face awed.

"There's a region of deserted dark-stars fifty parsecs west of Argol," Jhal Arn told them. "Two days from now, we'll unchain the power of the Disruptor there for you to see."

Tu Shal's troubled face cleared a little. "If you do that, our kingdoms will utterly reject the overtures of the Cloud!"

"And I can guarantee that the Barons of the Cluster will declare for the Empire!" added the chubby envoy from Hercules.

When they had gone, Jhal Arn looked with haggard face at Gordon. "It was the only way I could hold them, Zarth! If I'd refused, they'd have been panicked into submitting to Shorr Kan."

Gordon asked him wonderingly, "You're really going to unloose the Disruptor to convince them?"

The other was sweating. "I don't want to, God knows! You know Brenn Bir's warning as well as I do! You know what nearly happened when *he* used it on the Magellanians two thousand years ago!"

He stiffened. "But I'll run even that risk, rather than let the Cloud launch a war to enslave the galaxy!"

Gordon felt a deeper sense of wonder and perplexity, mixed with cold apprehension.

What was it, really, the age-old secret power which even Jhal Arn who was its master could not mention without fear?

Jhal Arn continued urgently. "Zarth, we'll go down now to the Chamber of the Disruptor. It's been long since either of us was there, and we must make sure everything is ready for that demonstration."

Gordon for the moment recoiled. He, a stranger, couldn't pry into this most guarded secret in the galaxy!

Then he suddenly realized that it made little difference if he did see the thing. He wasn't scientist enough to understand it. And in any case, he'd be going back soon to his own time, his own body.

He'd have to find a chance to slip away to Earth in the next day or so, without letting Jhal Arn know. He could order a ship to take him there.

Once again, at that thought, came the heartbreaking realization that he was on the verge of parting forever from Lianna.

"Come, Zarth!" Jhal was saying impatiently. "I know you must be tired, but there's little time left."

They went out through the ante-room, Jhal Arn waving back the guards who sprang to accompany them.

Gordon accompanied him down sliding ramps and through corridors and down again, until he knew they must be deeper beneath the great palace of Throon than even the prison where he had been confined.

They entered a spiral stair that dropped downward into a hall hollowed from the solid rock of the planet. From this hall, a long, rock-hewn corridor led away. It was lighted by a throbbing white radiance emitted by luminous plates in its walls.

As Gordon walked down this radiant corridor with Jhal Arn, he felt an astonishment he could hardly conceal. He had expected great masses of guards, mighty doors with massive bolts, all kinds of cunning devices to guard the most titanic power in the galaxy.

Instead, there seemed nothing whatever to guard it! Neither on the stair nor in this brilliant corridor was there anyone. And when Jhal Arn opened the door at the corridor end, it was not even locked!

Jhal Arn looked through the open door with Gordon from the threshold.

"'There it is, the same as ever," he said with a strong tinge of awe in his voice.

The room was a small, round one hollowed also from solid rock and also lighted by throbbing white radiance from wall-plates.

Gordon perceived at the center of the room the group of objects at which Jhal Arn was gazing with such awe.

The Disruptor! The weapon so terrible that its power had only once been unloosed in two thousand years!

"But what *is* it?" Gordon wondered dazedly, as he stared.

There were twelve big conical objects of dull gray metal, each a dozen feet long. The apex of each cone was a cluster of tiny crystal spheres. Heavy, vari-colored cables led from the base of the cones.

What complexities of unimaginable science lay inside the cones, he could not even guess. Beside heavy brackets for mounting them, the only other object here was a bulky cubical cabinet on whose face were mounted a bank of luminous gauges and six rheostat switches.

"It draws such tremendous power that it will have to be mounted on a battleship, of course," Jhal Arn was saying thoughtfully. "What about the *Ethne* you came in? Wouldn't its turbines provide enough power?"

Gordon floundered. "I suppose so. I'm afraid I'll have to leave all that to you."

Jhal Arn looked astounded. "But Zarth, you're the scientist of the family. You know more about the Disruptor than I do."

Gordon hastily denied that. "I'm afraid I don't know. You see, it's been so long that I've forgotten a lot about it."

Jhal Arn looked incredulous. "Forgotten about the Disruptor? You must be joking! That's one thing we don't forget! Why it's drilled into our minds beyond forgetfulness on the day when we're first brought down here to have the Wave tuned to our bodies!"

The Wave? What was that? Gordon felt completely at sea in his ignorance.

He advanced a hasty explanation. "Jhal, I told you that Shorr Kan used a brain-scanning device to try to learn the Disruptor secret from me. He couldn't—but in my deliberate effort to forget it so he couldn't, I seem really to have lost a lot of the details."

Jhal Arn seemed satisfied by the explanation. "So that's it! Mental shock, of course. But of course you still remember the main nature of the secret. Nobody *could* forget that."

"Of course, I haven't forgotten that," Gordon was forced to prevaricate hastily.

Jhal drew him forward. "Here, it will all come back to you. These brackets are for mounting the force-cones on a ship's prow. The colored cables hook to the similarly colored binding-posts on the control panel, and the transformer leads go right back to drive-generators."

He pointed at the gauges. "They give the exact coordinates in space of the area to be affected. The output of the cones has to balance exactly, of course. The rheostats do that—"

As he went on, John Gordon began dimly to perceive that the cones were designed to project force into a selected area of space.

But what kind of force? What did they *do* to the area or object on which they acted, that was so awful? He dared not ask that.

Jhal Arn was concluding his explanation. "—so the target area must be at least ten parsecs from the ship you work from, or you'll get the backlash. Don't you remember it all now, Zarth?"

Gordon nodded hurriedly. "Of course. But I'm glad just the same that it will be your job to use it."

Jhal looked more haggard. "God knows I don't want to! It has rested here all these centuries without being used. And the warning of Brenn Bir still is true."

He pointed up, as he spoke, to an inscription on the opposite wall. Gordon read it now for the first time.

"To my descendants who will hold the secret of the Disruptor that I, Brenn Bir, discovered: Heed my warning! Never use the Disruptor for petty personal power! Use it only if the freedom of the galaxy is menaced!

"This power you hold could destroy the galaxy. It is a demon so titanic that once unchained, it might not be chained again. Take not that awful risk unless the life and liberty of all men are at stake!"

Jhal Arn's voice was solemn. "Zarth, when you and I were boys and were first brought down here by our father to have the Wave tuned to us, we little dreamed that a time might come when we would think of using that which has lain here for so long."

His voice rang deeper. "But the life and liberty of all men *are* at stake, if Shorr Kan seeks to conquer the galaxy! If all else fails, we must take the risk!"

Gordon felt shaken by the implications of that warning. It was like a voice of the dead, speaking heavily in this silent room.

Jhal turned and led the way out of the room. He closed the door and again Gordon wondered. No lock, not bolts, no guard!

They went down the long radiant corridor and emerged from it into the softer yellow light of the well of the spiral stair.

"We'll mount the equipment on the *Ethne* tomorrow morning," Jhal Arn was saying. "When we show the star-kingdom envoys—"

"You will never show them anything, Jhal Arn!"

Out from beneath the spiral stair had sprung a dishevelled man who held an atom-pistol levelled on Gordon and Jhal Arn.

"Orth Bodmer!" cried Gordon. "You were hiding in the palace all the time!"

Orth Bodmer's thin face was colorless, deadly, twitching in a pallid smile.

"Yes, Zarth," he grated. "I knew the game was up when I saw Thern Eldred brought in. I couldn't get out of the palace without being swiftly traced and apprehended, so I hid in the deeper corridors."

His smile was ghastly now. "I hid, until as I had hoped you came down here to the Chamber of the Disruptor, Jhal Arn! I've been waiting for you!"

Jhal's eyes flashed. "Just what do you expect to gain by this?"

"It is simple," rasped Bodmer. "I know my life is forfeit. Well, so is your life unless you spare mine!"

He stepped closer, and Gordon read the madness of fear in his burning eyes.

"You do not break your word when it is given, highness. Promise me that I shall be pardoned, and I will not kill you now!"

Gordon saw that panic had driven this rabbity, nervous traitor to insane resolve

"Jhal, do it!" he cried. "He's not worth risking your life for!"

Jhal Arn's face was dull red with fury. "I have let one traitor go free, but no more!"

Instantly, before Gordon could voice the cry of appeal on his lips, Orth Bodmer's atom-pistol crashed.

The pellet tore into Jhal Arn's shoulder and exploded there as Gordon plunged forward at the maddened traitor.

"You murdering lunatic!" cried Gordon fiercely, seizing the other's gun-wrist and grappling with him.

For a moment, the thin Councillor seemed to have superhuman strength. They swayed, stumbled, and then reeled together from the hall into the brilliant white radiance of the long corridor.

Then Orth Bodmer screamed! He screamed like a soul in torment, and Gordon felt the man's body relax horribly in his grasp.

"The Wave!" screeched Bodmer, staggering in the throbbing radiance.

Even as the man screamed, Gordon saw his whole body and face horribly blacken and wither. It was a shrivelled, lifeless body that sank to the floor.

So ghastly and mysterious was that sudden death, that for a moment Gordon was dazed. Then he suddenly understood.

The throbbing radiance in the corridor and in the Chamber of the Disruptor was the Wave that Jhal Arn had spoken of! It was not light but a terrible, destroying force—a force so tuned to individual human bodily vibrations that it blasted every human being except the chosen holders of the Disruptor secret.

No wonder that no locks or bolts or guards were needed to protect the Disruptor! No man could approach it without being destroyed, except Jhal Arn and Gordon himself. No, not John Gordon but Zarth Arn—it was Zarth Arn's physical body that the Wave was tuned to spare!

Gordon stumbled out of that terrible radiance back into the hall. He bent over the prone form of Jhal Arn.

"Jhal! For God's sake—"

Jhal Arn had a terrible, blackened wound in his shoulder and side But he was still breathing, still alive

Gordon sprang to the stair and shouted upward. "Guards! The Emperor has been hurt!"

Guards, officers, officials, came pouring down quickly. Jhal Arn by then was stirring feebly His eyes opened.

"Bodmer—guilty of this attack on me!" he muttered to them. "Is Zarth all right?"

"I'm here. He didn't hit me, and he's dead now," Gordon husked.

An hour later, he waited in an outer room of the royal apartments high in the palace. Lianna was there, striving to comfort Jhal Arn's weeping wife.

A physician came hurriedly from the inner room to which Jhal Arn had been taken.

"The emperor will live!" he announced. "But he is terribly wounded, and it will take many weeks for him to recover."

He added worriedly, "He insists on Prince Zarth Arn coming in."

Gordon uncertainly entered the big, luxurious bedroom. The two women followed. He stooped over the bed in which Jhal Arn lay.

Jhal Arn whispered an order. "Bring a stereo-transmitting set. And order it switched through for a broadcast to the whole Empire."

"Jhal, you mustn't try it!" Gordon protested. "You can make announcements of my being cleared in another way than that."

"It's not only that that I have to announce," Jhal whispered. "Zarth, don't you realize what it means for me to be stricken down at the very moment when Shorr Kan's plans are reaching their crisis?"

The stereo transmitter was hastily brought in. Its viewer-disk swung to include Jhal Arn's bed, and Gordon and Lianna and Zora.

Jhal Arn painfully raised his head on the pillow, his white face looking into the disk.

"People of the Empire!" he said hoarsely. "The same traitorous assassins who murdered my father have tried to murder me, but have failed. I shall in time be well again.

"Chan Corbulo and Orth Bodmer—*they* were the ringleaders of the group! My brother Zarth Arn has been proved completely innocent and now resumes his royal rank.

"And since I am thus stricken down, I appoint my brother Zarth Arn as regent to rule in my place until I recover. No matter what events burst upon us, give your allegiance to Zarth Arn as leader of our Empire!"

24

STORM OVER THROON

Gordon uttered an involuntary exclamation of dismayed amazement.

"Jhal, no! I can't wield the rule of the Empire, even for a short time!"

Jhal Arn had already made a feeble gesture of dismissal to the technicians. They had quickly switched off the stereo apparatus as he finished speaking, and were now withdrawing.

At Gordon's protest, Jhal Arn turned his deathly-white face and answered in an earnest whisper.

"Zarth, you must act for me. In this moment of crisis when the Cloud darkens across the galaxy, the Empire cannot be left without a leader."

Zora, his wife, seconded the appeal to Gordon. "You're of the royal house. You alone can command allegiance now."

Gordon's mind whirled. What was he to do? Refuse and finally reveal to them the unguessed truth of his identity and his involuntary imposture?

He couldn't do that now! It *would* leave the Empire without a head, would leave all its people and its allies confused and bewildered, would make them imminent prey for the attack of the Cloud.

But on the other hand, how could he carry out the role when he was still so ignorant of this universe? And how then could he get away to Earth to contact the real Zarth Arn across time?

"You have been proclaimed regent to the Empire and it is impossible to retract that now," said Jhal Arn, in a weak whisper.

Gordon's heart sank It *was* impossible to retract that proclamation without throwing the Empire into even deeper confusion.

There was only one course open to him. He would have to occupy the regency until he could slip away to Earth as he'd planned. When they had re-exchanged bodies, the real Zarth could come back to be regent.

"I'll do my best, then," Gordon faltered. "But if I blunder—"

"You won't," Jhal Arn whispered. "I trust everything in your hands, Zarth."

He sank back on his pillow, a spasm of pain crossing his white face. Hastily, Zora called the physicians.

The physicians waved them all from the room. "The emperor must not exert himself further or we will not answer for the consequences."

In the splendid outer rooms, Gordon found Lianna at his side. He looked at her shakenly.

"Lianna, how can *I* lead the Empire and hold the star kings' allegiance, as Jhal would have done?"

"Why can't you?" she flashed. "Aren't you son of Arn Abbas, of the mightiest line of rulers in the galaxy?"

He wanted to cry to her that he was not, that he was only John Gordon of ancient Earth, utterly unfit for such vast responsibility.

He couldn't. He was still caught in the web that had bound him since first—how long ago it seemed!—he had for adventure's sake entered his pact across time with Zarth Arn. He still had to play out the role until he could regain his own identity.

Lianna imperiously waved aside the chamberlains and officials who already were swarming around him.

"Prince Zarth is exhausted! You will have to wait until morning."

Gordon indeed felt drunk with exhaustion, his feet stumbling as he went with Lianna up through the palace to his own old apartment.

She left him there. "Try to sleep, Zarth. You'll have the whole weight of the Empire on you tomorrow."

Gordon had thought he could not possibly sleep, but he was no sooner in bed than drugged slumber overcame him.

He awoke the next morning to find Hull Burrel beside him. The big Antarian looked at him a little uncertainly.

"Princess Lianna suggested that I act as your aide, highness."

Gordon felt relieved. He needed someone he could trust, and he had a strong liking for this big, bluff captain.

"Hull, that's the best idea yet. You know I've never been

trained for rule. There's so much that I ought to know, and don't."

The Antarian shook his head. "I hate to tell you, but things are piling up fast for you to decide. The envoys of the southern star-kingdoms ask another audience. Vice-Commander Giron has called twice in the last hour from the fleet, to talk to you."

Gordon tried to think, as he quickly dressed. "Hull, is Giron a good officer?"

"One of the best," the Antarian said promptly. "A hard disciplinarian but a fine strategist."

"Then," Gordon said, "we'll leave him in command of the fleet. I'll talk to him shortly."

He had to nerve himself for the ordeal of walking down with his new aide through the palace, of replying to bows, of playing this part of regent-ruler.

He found Tu Shal and the other star-kingdom envoys awaiting him in the little study that was the nerve-center of Empire government.

"Prince Zarth, all our kingdoms regret the dastardly attack on your brother," said the Polarian. "But this will not prevent your demonstrating the Disruptor for us as your brother agreed?"

Gordon was appalled. In the whirl of the night's events, he had almost forgotten that promise.

He tried to evade the question. "My brother is badly stricken, as you know. He is unable to carry out his promise."

The Hercules envoy said quickly, "But *you* know how to wield the Disruptor, Prince Zarth. You could carry out the demonstration."

That was the devil of it, Gordon thought dismayedly. He didn't know the details of the Disruptor! He had learned something from Jhal Arn of how the apparatus was operated, but he still hadn't any idea of just what that mysterious, terrible force could do.

"I have heavy duties as regent of the Empire while my brother is helpless, and I may have to postpone that demonstration for a little while," he told them.

Tu Shal's face grew grave. "Highness, you must not! I tell you that failure to give us this reassurance would strengthen the arguments of those who claim the Disruptor is too dangerous to use. It would turn the wavering parties in our kingdoms toward deserting the Empire!"

Gordon felt trapped. He couldn't let the Empire's vital allies desert. Yet how could he wield the Disruptor?

He might be able to learn more from Jhal Arn about it, he thought desperately. Enough so that he could try to wield the Disruptor in at least this demanstration?

He made his voice stern, determined. "The demonstration will be made at the first possible moment. This is all I can say."

It did not satisfy the worried envoys, he could see. They looked furtively at each other.

"I will report that to the Barons," said the chubby envoy of Hercules Cluster. The others bowed also, and left.

Hull Burrel gave him no time to reflect on the pressure that this new complication put upon him.

"Vice-Commander Giron on the stereo now, highness. Shall I put him through?"

When, a moment later, the image of the Empire naval commander appeared on the stereo-plate, Gordon saw that the towering Centaurian veteran was deeply perturbed.

"Prince Zarth, I wish first to know if I am to remain in command of the fleet or if a new commander is being sent out?"

"You're appointed full Commander, subject only to review by my brother when he resumes his duties," Gordon said promptly.

Giron showed no elation. "I thank you, highness. But if I am to command the fleet, the situation has reached the point where I must have political information on which to base my strategic plans."

"What do you mean? What is the situation to which you refer?" Gordon asked.

"Our long-range radar has detected very heavy fleet-movements inside the Cloud!" was the sharp answer. "At least four powerful armadas have left their bases in there and are cruising just inside the northern borders of the Cloud."

Giron added, "This suggests strongly that the League of Dark Worlds is planning a surprise attack on us in at least two different directions. In view of that possibility, it is imperative that I make my own fleet dispositions quickly."

He flashed on the familiar stereo-map of the galaxy's great swarm of stars, with its zones of colored light that represented the Mid-Galactic Empire and the star-kingdoms.

"I've got my main forces strung in three divisions on a line here between Rigel and Orion Nebula, each division self-sufficient in battleships, cruisers, phantoms and so on. The Fomalhaut contingent is incorporated in our first division.

"This is our prearranged defense plan, but it counts on the Hercules Barons' and the Polaris Kingdom's fleets resisting any attempt to invade through their realms. It also counts on the Lyra, Cygnus and Cassiopeia fleets joining us immediately when we flash the "ready" signal. But are they going to fulfill their engagements? I must know if the allied Kingdoms are going to stand with us, before I make my dispositions."

Gordon realized the tremendous gravity of the problem that faced Commander Giron far away in that southern void.

"Then you have already sent the 'ready' signal to the allied Kingdoms?" he asked.

"I took that responsibility two hours ago, in view of the alarming League fleet movements inside the Cloud," was Giron's curt answer. "So far, I have had no reply from the star-kingdoms."

Gordon sensed the crucial nature of the moment. "Give me twenty-four more hours, Commander," he asked desperately. "I'll try in that time to get positive commitments from the Barons and the Kingdoms."

"In the meantime, our position here is vulnerable," rasped the Commander. "I suggest that until we are certain of the Kingdoms' allegiance, we should shift our main forces westward toward Rigel to be in position to counter any stroke through Hercules and Polaris."

Gordon nodded quickly. "I leave that decision entirely in your hands. I'll contact you the moment that I have positive news."

Hull Barrel looked at him soberly, as the image of the Commander saluted and vanished.

"Prince Zarth, you'll not get the Kingdoms to stand by their alliance unless you prove to them we can wield the Disruptor!"

"I know," Gordon muttered. He came to a decision. "I'm going to see if my brother can talk to me."

He realized now that as the Antarian had said, only a clear demonstration of the Disruptor would hold the wavering Kingdoms.

Could *he* dare try to wield that mysterious force? He knew something of its operations from what Jhal Arn had explained, but that something was not enough. If he could only learn more!

The physicians were worried and discouraging when he went to Jhal Arn's apartments.

"Prince Zarth, he's under drugs and is not able to talk to anyone! It would strain his strength—"

"I must see him!" Gordon insisted. "The situation demands it."

He finally had his way but they warned him, "A few minutes is all we can allow, or we must reject all responsibility for whatever may happen."

Jhal Arn opened drugged, hazed eyes when Gordon bent over him. It took him moments to realize what Gordon was saying.

"Jhal, you must try to understand and answer me!" Gordon begged. "I've got to know more about the operation of the Disruptor! You know I told you how Shorr Kan's brain-scanner made me forget."

Jhal Arn's voice was a drowsy murmur. "Strange, it made you forget like that. I thought none of us would ever forget, the way every detail was drilled into us when we were boys."

His whisper trailed weakly, sleepily. "You'll remember it all when you have to, Zarth. The force-cones to be mounted on your ship's prow in a fifty-foot circle, the cables to the transformer follow to the binding-posts of the same color, the power-leads to the generators."

His murmur became so faint that Gordon had to bend his head close. "Get an exact radar fix on the center of your target area. Balance the directional thrust of the cones by the gauges. Only switch in the release when all six directional thrusts are balanced—"

His voice dribbled slowly away, weaker and weaker until it was inaudible. Gordon desperately tried to arouse him.

"Jhal, don't go out on me! I've got to know more than that!"

But Jhal Arn had subsided into a drugged slumber from which he could not be awakened.

Gordon ran it all over in his mind. He knew a little more than he had before.

The procedure of operating the Disruptor was clear. But that wasn't enough. It was like giving a savage of his own time a pistol and telling him how to pull the trigger. The savage might hold the pistol's muzzle in his own face as he pulled that trigger!

"But I've got to pretend at least that I'm going to demonstrate the thing," Gordon thought tensely. "That may hold the envoys of the Kingdoms until I can learn more from Jhal Arn."

He went down with Hull Burrel to that deep-buried level of the palace in which lay the Chamber of the Disruptor.

The Antarian could not enter that corridor of deadly force that was tuned to blast every living being but Jhal Arn and himself. Gordon went in alone, and brought back the brackets for mounting the force-cones.

Hull Burrel looked even at these simple brackets in awe, as they took them up through the palace.

By tubeway, he and Hull Burrel sped to the naval spaceport outside Throon. Val Marlann and his men were waiting by the great, grim bulk of the *Ethne*.

Gordon handed over the brackets. "These are to be mounted on the prow of the *Ethne* so that they will form a circle exactly fifty feet in diameter. You'll also make provision for a heavy power connection to the main drive-generators."

Val Marlann's swarthy face stiffened. "You're going to use the Disruptor from the *Ethne,* highness?" he exclaimed excitedly.

Gordon nodded. "Have your technicians start installing these brackets immediately."

He used the ship's stereo to call Tu Shal, the envoy of Polaris Kingdom.

"As you can see, Tu Shal, we are preparing to make the demonstration of the Disruptor. It will take place as soon as possible," Gordon told the ambassador, with assumed confidence.

Tu Shal's troubled face did not lighten. "It should be quickly, highness! Every capital in the galaxy is badly disturbed by rumors of the movements of Cloud fleets!"

Gordon felt almost hopeless, as he sped back to the palace. He couldn't stall like this much longer. And with Jhal Arn still comatose, he couldn't learn more about the Disruptor now.

As night fell, thunder grumbled over the great palace of Throon from an electric storm moving in from the sea. When Gordon went wearily up to his apartments, he glimpsed violet flares of lightning outside its windows, eerily illuminating the looming Glass Mountains.

Lianna was waiting for him there. She greeted him anxiously.

"Zarth, terrifying rumors of impending League attack are being whispered through the palace. It is to be war?"

"Shorr Kan may only be bluffing," he said numbly. "If only things hold off, until—"

He had almost said, until he could get to Earth and re-exchange bodies so the real Zarth could return to bear this fearful responsibility.

"Until Jhal recovers?" Lianna said, misunderstanding. Her face softened. "Zarth, I know the terrible strain all this is to you. But you're proving that you're Arn Abbas' son!"

He wanted to take her into his arms, to bury his face against her cheek. Some of that must have showed in his face, for Lianna's eyes widened a little.

"Zarth!" cried an eager feminine voice.

He and Lianna both turned sharply. Gordon immediately recognized the lovely, dark-haired girl who had entered his rooms.

"Murn!" he exclaimed.

He had almost forgotten this girl who was the real Zarth Arn's secret wife, and whom the real Zarth loved.

Amazement, then incredulity, crossed her face as she looked at Lianna. "Princess Lianna here! I did not dream—"

Lianna said quietly, "There need be no pretense between us three. I know quite well that Zarth Arn loves you, Murn."

Murn colored. She said uncertainly, "I would not have come if I had known—"

"You have more right here than I have," Lianna said calmly. "I shall go."

Gordon made a movement to detain her, but she was already leaving the room.

Murn came toward him and looked up at him anxiously with soft, dark eyes.

"Zarth, before you left Throon you said you would be different when you returned, that all would be with us as before."

"Murn, you will only have to wait a little longer," he told her. "Then all will be as before, I promise you."

"I stil' cannot understand," she murmured troubledly. "But I'm happy you're cleared of that awful crime, that you've returned."

She looked at him again with that queer shyness as she left. He knew that Murn still sensed a strangeness about him.

Gordon lay in his bed, and in his mind Lianna, Murn, Jhal Arn and the Disruptor all spun chaotically before he finally slept.

He had slept but two hours when an excited voice awoke him. The storm had broken in full fury upon Throon. Blinding lightning danced continuously over the city, and thunder was bellowing deafeningly.

Hull Burrel was shaking him, and the Antarian's craggy face was dark and taut with excitement.

"The devil's to pay, highness!" he cried. "The Cloud's fleets have come out and crossed our frontier! There's already hard cruiser-fighting beyond Rigel, ships are snuffing out by the scores, and Giron reports that two League fleets are heading toward Hercules!"

25

THE STAR KINGS DECIDE

Galactic war! The war the galaxy had dreaded, the long-feared struggle to the death between the Empire and the Cloud!

And it had come at this disastrous moment when he, John Gordon of ancient Earth, bore the responsibility of leading the Empire's defense!

Gordon sprang from bed. "League fleets heading toward Hercules? Are the Barons ready to resist?"

"They may not resist at all!" cried Hull Burrel. "Shorr Kan is stereo-casting to them and to all the Kingdoms, warning them that resistance would be useless because the Empire is going to fail!"

"He's telling them that Jhal Arn is too near death to wield the Disruptor, and that *you* can't use it because you don't know its secret!"

As though the words were a flash illumining an abyss, Gordon suddenly realized that that was why Shorr Kan had finally struck.

Shorr Kan knew that he, John Gordon, was a masquerader inside Zarth Arn's physical body. He knew that Gordon had no knowledge of the Disruptor such as the real Zarth had.

Knowing that, the moment he had heard of Jhal Arn being stricken down, Shorr Kan had launched the League's long-planned attack. He counted on the fact that there was no one now to use the Disruptor against him. He should have realized that was what Shorr Kan would do!

Hull Burrel was shouting on, as Gordon dressed with frantic haste. "That devil is talking by stereo to the star kings right now! You've got to hold them to the Empire!"

Officials, naval officers, excited messengers were already crowding into the room and clamoring wildly for Gordon's attention.

Hull Burrel roughly cleared them from the way as he and Gordon hastened out and raced down through the palace to the study that was the nerve-center of the Mid-Galactic Empire.

All the palace, all Throon, was waking this fateful night! Voices shouted, lights were flashing on, great warships taking off for space could be heard rushing across the storm-swept sky.

In the study, Gordon was momentarily stunned by the many telestereos that blazed with light and movement. Two of them gave view from the bridges of cruisers in the thick of the frontier fighting, shaking to thundering guns and rushing through space ablaze with atom-shells.

But then Gordon's eyes flew toward the stereo on which the dark, dominating image of Shorr Kan stood speaking. His black head bare, his eyes flashing confidently, the Cloud-man was broadcasting.

"—so I repeat, Barons and rulers of the star-kingdoms, that the Cloud's war is not directed against you! Our quarrel is only with the Empire, which has too long sought to dominate the whole galaxy under the guise of working for peaceful federation. We in the League of Dark Worlds have finally struck out against that selfish aggrandizement.

"Our League offers friendship to your Kingdoms! You need not join this struggle and be dragged down to destruction with the Empire. All we ask is that you let our fleets pass through your realms without resistance. And you shall be full, equal members in the real democratic federation of the galaxy which we shall establish when we have conquered.

"For we shall conquer! The Empire will fall. Its forces cannot stand against our mighty new fleets and weapons. Nor can their long-vaunted Disruptor save them now, for they have no one to use it. Jhal Arn, who knows it, lies stricken down —and Zarth Arn does not know how to use it!"

Shorr Kan's voice rang loud with supreme confidence as he emphasized his final declaration.

"Zarth Arn does not know that because he is not really Zarth Arn at all—he is an impostor masquerading as Zarth Arn! I have absolute proof of that! Would I have challenged the Disruptor's menace if I had not? The Empire cannot use that secret, and thus the Empire is doomed. Star kings and Barons, do not join a doomed cause and wreck your own realms!"

Shorr Kan's image faded from the stereo as he concluded that ringing declaration.

"Good God, he must have gone crazy!" gasped Hull Burrel to Gordon. "To claim that you're not really yourself!"

"Prince Zarth!" rang an officer's excited call across the room. "Commander Giron calling—urgent!"

Still stunned by Shorr Kan's audacious stroke to neutralize the Kingdoms, Gordon stumbled hastily to that other stereo.

In its view, Commander Ron Giron and his officers stood on a battleship's bridge, bent over their radar screens. The towering Centaurian veteran turned toward Gordon.

"Highness, what about the star-kingdoms?" he rasped. "We've radar reports that two of the big League fleets that came out of the Cloud are now speeding west toward Hercules and Polaris. Are the Barons and the Kingdoms going to submit to them or resist? We must know that!"

"We'll know that for certain just as soon as I can contact the Kingdoms' envoys," Gordon said desperately. "What is your situation?"

Giron made a curt gesture. "Only our cruiser-screens are fighting so far. Some Cloud phantoms slipped through them and are sniping at our main fleet here back of Rigel, but that's not serious yet.

"What *is* serious is that I daren't commit my main forces on this southern front if the League is going to flank me through Hercules! If the Barons and the Kingdoms are not going to join us, I'll have to fall far back westward to cover Canopus from that flank thrust."

Gordon, staggered by the moment of awful responsibility, tried to steady his whirling thoughts.

"Avoid commitment of your main forces as long as possible, Giron," he begged. "I'm still hoping to hold the Kingdoms to us."

"If they fail us now, we're in a bad fix!" Giron said grimly. "The League has twice as many ships as we figured! They'll cut around in short order to attack Canopus."

Gordon swung back to Hull Burrel. "Get the ambassadors of the star kings, at once! Bring them here!"

Burrel raced out of the room. But almost at once, he returned.

"The ambassadors are already here! They just arrived!"

Tu Shal and the other envoys of the star-kingdoms crowded into the room a moment later, pale, excited and tense.

Gordon wasted no time on protocol. "You've heard that two of Shorr Kan's fleets are heading for Hercules and Polaris?"

Tu Shal, pallid to the lips, nodded. "The news was brought to us instantly We have heard Shorr Kan's broadcast—"

Gordon interrupted harshly "I demand to know if the Barons are going to resist his invasion or allow him free passage! And I demand to know if the Kingdoms are going to honor their engagements of alliance with the Empire, or surrender to Shorr Kan's threats!"

The deathly-white Lyra ambassador answered. "Our Kingdoms will honor their engagements if the Empire will honor its pledge! When we pledged alliance, it was because the Empire promised to use the Disruptor if necessary to protect us."

"Have I not told you that the Disruptor will be used?" flashed Gordon.

"You promised that but you evaded demonstrating it!" cried the Polaris envoy. "Why should you do that if you know the secret? Suppose that Shorr Kan is right and that you *are* an impostor—then we'd be throwing our realms away in a useless fight!"

Hull Burrel, carried away by anger, uttered a roar. "Do you believe for a moment Shorr Kan's fantastic lie that Prince Zarth is an impostor?"

"Is it a lie?" demanded Tu Shal, gazing fixedly at Gordon's face. "Shorr Kan must know *something* to assure him the Disruptor won't be used, or he'd never have risked this attack!"

"Curse it, you can see for yourself that he's Zarth Arn, can't you?" raged the Antarian captain.

"Scientific cunning can enable one man to masquerade in the disguise of another!" snapped the Hercules envoy.

Gordon, desperate in the face of this final terrible stumbling-block, seized upon an idea that crossed his mind.

"Hull, be still!" he ordered. "Tu Shal and you others, listen to me. If I prove to you that I *am* Zarth Arn and that I can and will use the Disruptor, will your Kingdoms stand by the Empire?"

"Polaris Kingdom will!" exclaimed that envoy instantly. "Prove that and I'll flash instant word to our capital."

Others chimed in swiftly, with the same assurance. And the Hercules ambassador added, "We Barons of the Cluster want to resist the Cloud, if it's not hopeless. Prove that it isn't, and we'll fight!"

"I can prove in five minutes that I am the real Zarth Arn!" rasped Gordon. "Follow me! Hull, you come too!"

Bewilderedly, they hastened after Gordon as he went out of the room and down through the corridors and ramps of the palace.

They came thus down the spiral stair to the hall from which extended that corridor of throbbing deadly white radiance that led to the Chamber of the Disruptor.

Gordon turned to the bewildered envoys. "You all must know what that corridor is?"

Tu Shal answered. "All the galaxy has heard of it. It leads to the Chamber of the Disruptor."

"Can any man go through that corridor to the Disruptor unless he is one of the royal family entrusted with it?" Gordon pressed.

The envoys began to understand now. "No!" exclaimed the Polarian. "Everyone knows that only the heirs of the Empire's rulers can enter the Wave that is tuned to destroy anyone except them."

"Then watch!" Gordon cried, and stepped into the radiant corridor.

He strode down it into the Chamber of the Disruptor. He grasped one of the big gray metal forcecones. Upon the wheeled platform on which it rested, he wheeled that cone back out of the chamber and the corridor.

"Now do you believe that I'm an impostor?" he demanded.

"By Heaven, no!" cried Tu Shal. "No one but the real Zarth Arn could have entered that corridor and lived!"

"Then you are Zarth Arn, and you *do* know how to use the Disruptor!" another cried.

Gordon saw that he had convinced them. They had thought it possible that he might be another man disguised as Zarth Arn. And they knew now that that could not be so.

What they had not even dreamed, what even Shorr Kan had not told lest it meet utter disbelief, was that he was Zarth Arn in physical body but another man in mind!

Gordon pointed to the big force-cone. "That is part of the Disruptor apparatus. The rest of it I'll bring out, to be mounted at once on the battleship *Ethne*. And then that ship goes with me out to use the Disruptor's awful power and crush the League's attack!"

Gordon had decided, had in these minutes of strain made his fateful choice.

He *would* try to use the Disruptor! He knew its operation from Jhal Arn's explanations, even if its purpose and power were still a dread mystery to him. He would risk catastrophe to use it.

For it was his own strange imposture, involuntary though it had been, that had brought the Empire to this brink of disaster. It was his responsibility, his duty to the real Zarth Arn, to attempt this.

Tu Shal's aging face flamed. "Prince Zarth, if you intend thus to keep the Empire's pledge, we will keep our pledge! Polaris Kingdom will fight with the Empire against the Cloud!"

"And Lyra! And we Barons!" rang the eager, excited voices. "We'll flash word to our capitals that you're going out with the Disruptor to join the struggle!"

"Send that word at once, then!" Gordon told them. "Have your Kingdoms place their fleets under Commander Giron's orders!"

And as the excited ambassadors hurried back up the stairs to send their messages, Gordon turned to Hull Burrel.

"Call the *Ethne*'s technicians here with a squad of guards, Hull. I'll bring out the apparatus of the Disruptor and it can be taken at once to the *Ethne*."

Back and forth into the silent, radiant Chamber, Gordon now hastened, bringing out one by one the big, mysterious cones. He had to do this himself—no one else except Jhal Arn could enter there.

By the time he wheeled out the bulky cubical transformer, Hull Burrel was back with Captain Val Marlann and his technicians.

Working hastily, but handling the apparatus with a gingerness that betrayed their dread, the men loaded the equipment into tubeway cars.

A half-hour later they stood in the naval spaceport beneath the shadow of the mighty *Ethne*. It and two other battleships were the only major units left here, the others already on their way to join the epochal struggle.

Under the flare of lightning and crash of thunder and rain, the technicians labored to bolt the big force-cones to the brackets already in place around the prow of the battleship. The tips of the cones pointed forward, and their cables were brought back through the hull into the navigation-room behind the bridge.

Gordon had had the cubical transformer with its control-panel set up here. He directed the hooking of the colored cables to the panel as Jhal Arn had explained. The massive power-leads were hastily run back and attached to the mighty drive-generators of the ship.

"Ready for take-off in ten minutes!" Val Marlann reported, his face gleaming with sweat.

Gordon was shaking with strain. "One last check of the cones. There's time for it."

He raced out into the storm, peering up at the huge, overhanging prow of the warship. The twelve cones fastened up there seemed tiny, puny.

Impossible to think that this little apparatus could produce any such vast effect as men expected! And yet—

"Take-off, two minutes!" yelled Hull Burrel from the gangway, over the din of alarm bells and shouts of hurrying men.

Gordon turned. And as he did so, through the confusion a slim figure ran toward him.

"Lianna!" he cried. "Good God, why—"

She came into his arms. Her face was white, tear-wet, as she raised it to him.

"Zarth, I had to come before you left! If you didn't come back, I wanted you to know—I still love you! I always will, even though I know it's Murn you love!"

Gordon groaned, as he held her in his arms with his cheek against her tear-wet face.

"Lianna! Lianna! I can't promise for the future, you may find all things changed between us in the future, but I tell you now that it is you I love!"

A wave of final, bitter heartbreak seemed to surge up in him at this last moment of wild farewell.

For it was farewell forever, Gordon knew! Even if he survived the battle, it must not be he but the real Zarth Arn who would come back to Throon. And if he didn't survive—

"Prince Zarth!" yelled Hull Burrel's hoarse voice in his ear. "It is time!"

Gordon, as he tore away, had a swift vision of Lianna's white face and shining eyes that he would never forget. For he knew that it was his last.

And then Hull Burrel was dragging him bodily up the gangway, doors were grinding shut, great turbines thundering, bells ringing sharp signals down the corridors.

"Take off" warned the annunciators shrilly, and with a

crash of splitting air the *Ethne* zoomed for the storm-swept heavens.

Upward it roared, and with it raced the other two battleships, bolting like metal things of thought up across the star-sown sky.

"Giron's calling!" Hull Burrel was shouting in his ear as they stumbled forward along the corridors. "Heavy fighting now near Rigel! And the League's eastern fleets are forcing through!"

In the navigation-room where Gordon had set up the Disruptor apparatus, Commander Giron's grim image flashed from a telestereo.

Over the Commander's shoulder Gordon glimpsed a bridge-room window that looked out on a space literally alive with an inferno of bursting atom-shells, of exploding ships.

Giron's voice was cool but swift. "We've joined fleet action with the League's two eastern forces. And we're suffering prohibitive losses. The enemy has some new weapon that seems to strike down our ships from within—we can't understand it."

Gordon started. "The new weapon that Shorr Kan boasted to me about! How does it operate?"

"We don't know!" was the answer. "Ships suddenly drift out of action all around us, and don't answer our calls."

Giron added, "The Barons report their fleet is moving out east of the Cluster to oppose the Cloud's two fleets coming toward them. The fleets of Lyra, Polaris and the other allied Kingdoms are already coming down full speed from the north-west to join my command."

The Comander concluded grimly, "But this new weapon of the League, whatever it is, is decimating us! I'm withdrawing west but they're hammering us hard, and their phantoms keep getting through. I feel it my duty to warn that we can't fight long in the face of such losses."

Gordon told him, "We're coming out with the Disruptor and we're going to use it! But it'll take many hours for us to reach the scene."

He tried to think, before he gave orders. He remembered what Jhal Arn had said, that the target area of the Disruptor's force must be as limited as possible.

"Giron, to utilize the Disruptor it is imperative that the

League's fleets be maneuvered together. Can you somehow do that?"

Giron rasped answer. "The only chance I have of doing that is to retreat slightly southwestward from this branch of the attack, as though I meant to go to the aid of the Barons. That might draw the Cloud's two attacking forces together."

"Then try it!" Gordon urged. "Fall back southwestward and give me an approximate position for rendezvous with you."

"Just west of Deneb should be the approximate position by the time you get here," Giron answered. "God knows how much of our fleet will be left then if this new Cloud weapon keeps striking us down!"

Giron switched off, but in other telestereos unfolded the battle that was going on all along the line near distant Rigel.

Beside the ships that perished in the inferno of atom-shells and the stabbing attack of stealthy phantom-cruisers, the radar screen showed many Empire ships suddenly drifting out of action.

"What in the devil's name has the Cloud got that can disable our warships like that?" sweated Hull Burrel.

"Whatever it is, it's smashing in Giron's wings fast," muttered Val Marlann tensely. "His withdrawal may become a rout!"

Gordon turned from the dazing, bewildering stereos that showed the battle, and glanced haggardly through the bridge windows.

The *Ethne* was already hurtling at increasing velocity past the smaller Argo suns, speeding southward toward the Armageddon of the galaxy.

Gordon felt overwhelmed by dread, a panicky reaction. He had no place in this titanic conflict of future ages! He had been mad to make the impulsive decision to try to use the Disruptor!

He use the Disruptor? How could he, when he knew so little of it? How dared he unchain the ghastly power which its own discoverer had warned could rive and destroy the galaxy itself?

26

BATTLE BETWEEN THE STARS

Throbbing, droning, quivering in every girder to the thrust of its mighty drive-jet, the *Ethne* and its two companion ships raced southward across the starry spaces of the galaxy.

For hour on hour, the three great battleships had rushed at their highest speed toward the fateful rendezvous near the distant spark of Deneb, toward which the Empire forces were retreating.

"The Barons are fighting!" Hull Burrel cried to Gordon from the telestereo into which he was peering with flaming eyes. "God, look at the battle off the Cluster!"

"They should be drawing back by now toward the Deneb region as Giron's forces are doing!" Gordon exclaimed.

He was stunned by the telestereo scene. Transmitted from one of the Cluster ships in the thick of that great battle, it presented an almost incomprehensible vista of mad conflict.

To the eye, there was little design or purpose in the struggle. The star-decked vault of space near the gigantic ball of suns of Hercules Cluster seemed pricked with tiny flares. Tiny flares, shining forth swiftly and as swiftly vanishing! And each of those flares was the bursting of an atomic broadside far in space!

Gordon could not completely visualize that awful battle. This warfare of the far future was too strange for him to supply from experience the whole meaning of that dance of brilliant death-flares between the stars. This warfare, in which ships far, far apart groped for each other with radar beams and fired their mighty atom-guns by instant mechanical computation, seemed alien and unearthly to him.

The pattern of the battle he witnessed began slowly to emerge. The will-o'-the-wisp dance of flares was moving slowly back toward the titanic sun-swarm of the Cluster. The battle-line was crackling and sparkling north and northwest of the great sun-cluster now.

"They're pulling back, as Giron ordered!" Hull Burrel exclaimed. "Good God, half the Barons' fleet must be destroyed by now."

Val Marlann, captain of the *Ethne,* was like a caged tiger as he paced back and forth between the stereos.

"Look at what's happening to Giron's main fleet retreating from Rigel!" he said hoarsely. "They're hammering it like mad now. Our losses must be tremendous!"

The stereo at which he glared showed Gordon the similar, bigger whirl of death-flares withdrawing westward from Rigel.

He thought numbly that it was as well he couldn't visualize this awful Armageddon of the galaxy as the others could. It might well shake his nerve disastrously, and he had to keep cool now.

"How long before we'll rendezvous with Giron's fleet and the Barons'?" he cried to Val Marlann.

"Twelve hours, at least," said the other tautly. "And God knows if there'll be any of the Barons' ships left to join up."

"Curse Shorr Kan and his fanatics!" swore Hull, his craggy face crimson with passion. "All these years, they've been building ships and devising new weapons for this war of conquest!"

Gordon went back across the room, to the control-board of the Disruptor apparatus. For the hundredth time since leaving Throon, he rehearsed the method of releasing the mysterious force.

"But what does that force *do* when I release it?" he wondered again, tensely. "Does it act as a giant beam of lethal waves, or a zone of annihilation for solid matter?"

Vain speculation! It could hardly be those things. Brenn Bir would not have left solemn warning that it could destroy the galaxy, if it were!

Hours of awful strain passed as the *Ethne*'s little squadron drew nearer the scene of the titan struggle. Every hour had seen the position of the Empire's forces growing worse.

Giron, retreating southwestward to join the battered Hercules fleet still fighting off the Cluster, had been joined finally by the Lyra, Polaris and Cygnus fleets near the Ursa Nebula.

The Empire commander had turned on the pursuing League

armada and had fought savagely there for two hours, a staggering rearguard action that had involved both forces in the glowing Nebula.

Then Gordon heard Giron ordering the action broken off. The order, in secret scrambler-code like all naval messages, came from their own stereos.

"Captain Sandrell, Lyra Division—pull out of the Nebula! The enemy is forcing a column between you and the Cygnus Division!"

The Lyra commander's desperate answer flashed. "Their phantoms have piled up the head of our column. But I'll—"

The message was abruptly interrupted, the stereo going dark. Gordon heard Giron vainly calling Sandrell, with no response.

"It's what happens over and over!" raged Hull Burrel. "An Empire ship reports phantoms near, and then suddenly its report breaks off and the ship drifts silent and disabled!"

"Shorr Kan's new weapon!" gritted Val Marlann: "If we only had an idea what it is!"

Gordon suddenly remembered what Shorr Kan had told him, when he had boasted of that weapon in Thallarna.

"—it's a weapon that can strike down enemy warships from inside them!"

Gordon repeated that to the others and cried, "Maybe I'm crazy but it seems to me the only way they could strike down a ship from inside is by getting a force-beam of some kind in on the ship's own stereo beams! Every ship that has been stricken has been stereo-ing at the time!"

"Hull, it could be!" cried Val Marlann. "If they can tap onto our stereos and use them as carrier-beams right into our own ships—"

He sprang to the stereo and hastily called Giron and told him their suspicion.

"If you use squirt transmission on our scrambler code it may baffle their new weapon!" Val Marlann concluded. "They won't be able to get a tap on our beams in time. And keep damper-equipment in your stereo-rooms in case they do get through."

Giron nodded understandingly. "We'll try it. I'll order all our ships to use only momentary transmission, and assemble messages from the squirts on recorders."

Val Marlann ordered men with "dampers," the generators

of blanketing electric fields that could smother dangerous radiation, to stand by near their own stereos.

Already, the Empire ships were obeying the order and were "squirting" their messages in bursts of a few seconds each.

"It's helping—far fewer of our ships are being disabled now!" Giron reported. "But we've been badly battered and the Baron's fleet is just a remnant. Shall we fall back south into the Cluster?"

"No!" Gordon cried. "We daren't use the Disruptor inside the Cluster. You must hold them near Deneb."

"We'll try," Giron said grimly. "But unless you get here in the next four hours, there'll not be many of us left to hold."

"Four hours?" sweated Val Marlann. "I don't know if we can! The *Ethne*'s turbines are running on overload now!"

As the *Ethne*'s small squadron rushed on southward toward the white beacon of Deneb, the great battle east of the star was reeling back toward it.

Death-dance of flaring, falling star-ships moved steadily westward through the galaxy spaces! Up from the south, the battered remnants of the Barons' valiant fleet was coming to join with the Empire and Kingdoms' fleets for the final struggle.

Armageddon of the galaxy, in truth! For now the triumphant two main forces of the Cloud were joining together in the east and rushing forward in their final overwhelming attack.

Gordon saw in the telestereo and radar screens this climactic struggle which the *Ethne* had almost reached.

"A half hour more—we might make it, we might!" muttered Val Marlann through stiff lips.

The watch officer at the main radar screen suddenly yelled. "Phantoms on our port side!"

Things happened then with rapidity that bewildered John Gordon. Even as he glimpsed the Cloud phantom-cruisers suddenly unmasking in the radar screen, there was a titan flare in space to their left.

"One of our escort gone!" cried Hull Burrel. "*Ah!*"

The guns of the *Ethne,* triggered by mechanical computers swifter than any human mind could be, were going off thunderously.

Space around them flashed blinding bright with the explosion of heavy atom-shells which barely missed them. Two distant flares burgeoned up and died, an instant later.

"We got two of them!" Hull cried. "The rest have darked out and they won't dare come out of dark-out again."

Giron's voice came from the stereo, the "squirt" transmission being pieced together by recorders to make a normal message.

"Prince Zarth, the League armada is flanking us and within the hour they'll cut us to pieces!"

Gordon cried answer. "You've got to hold on a little longer, until—"

At that instant, in the stereo-image, Giron vanished and was replaced by pallid, black-uniformed men who raised heavy rod-shaped weapons in quick aim.

"Cloud-men! Those League phantoms have tapped our beam and are using Shorr Kan's new weapon!" screeched Burrel.

A bolt of ragged blue lightning shot from the rod-like weapon of the foremost Cloud-man in the stereo. That flash of force shot over Gordon's head and tore through the metal wall.

Invasion of the ship by stereo-images! Images that could destroy them, by that blue bolt that used the stereo-beam as carrier!

It lasted but a few seconds, then the "squirt" switch functioned and the Cloud-men images and their weapons disappeared.

"So that's how they do it!" cried Burrel. "No wonder they got half our ships with it before we found out about it!"

"Turn on those dampers, quick!" ordered Val Marlann. "We're likely to get another burst from the stereo any moment!"

Gordon felt the hair on his neck bristling as the *Ethne* rushed now into the zone of battle itself. An awful moment was approaching.

Giron had the Empire and Kingdom ships massed in a short defensive line with its left flank pinned on Deneb's great, glaring white mass. The heavier columns of the League fleets were pressing it in a crackling fire of flaring ships, seeking to roll up the right flank.

Space seemed an inferno of dying ships, of flames dancing

between the stars, as the *Ethne* fought forward to the front of the battle. Its own guns were thundering at the Cloud phantoms that were hanging to it steadily, repeatedly emerging from dark-out to attack.

"Giron, we're here!" Gordon called. "Now spread your line out thinner and withdraw at full speed."

"If we do that, the League fleets will bunch together and tear through our thinner line like paper!" protested Giron.

"That's just what I want, to bunch the League ships as much as possible!" Gordon replied. "Quick, we'll—"

Again, the stereo-image of Giron suddenly was replaced by a Cloud-man with the rod-shaped weapon.

The weapon loosed a blue bolt—but the bolt died, smothered by the fields of the "dampers." Then the "squirt" switch functioned again to cut the stereo.

"The way they've cut our communications would be enough alone to decide the battle!" groaned Hull Burrel.

In the radar screen, Gordon tensely watched the maneuver that was now rapidly taking place in space before them.

Giron's columns were falling back westward swiftly, turning to run and spreading out thinly as they did so.

"Here comes the League fleet!" cried Val Marlann.

Gordon too saw them in the screen, the massed specks that were thousands of League warships less than twelve parsecs away.

They were coming on in pursuit but they were not bunching as he had hoped. They merely held a somewhat shorter and thicker line than before.

He knew that he'd have to act, anyway. He couldn't let them get closer before unloosing the Disruptor, remembering Jhal Arn's caution.

"Hold the *Ethne* here and point it exactly at the center of the League battle-line," Gordon ordered hoarsely.

Giron's fleet was now behind them, as the *Ethne* remained facing the oncoming League armada.

Gordon was at the control-panel of the Disruptor transformer. He threw in the six switches of the bank, turning each rheostat four notches.

The gauge-needles began to creep across the dials. The generators of the mighty battleship roared louder and louder as the mysterious apparatus sucked unimaginable amperage from them.

Was that power being stored somehow in the force-cones on the prow? And what had Jhal Arn told him? Gordon tried to remember.

"—the six directional gauges must exactly balance if the thrust is not to create disaster!"

The gauges did *not* balance. He frantically touched this rheostat, then that one. The needles were creeping up toward the red critical marks, but some were too fast, too fast!

Gordon felt beads of sweat on his face, felt stiff with superhuman strain as the others watched him. He couldn't do this! He dared not loose this thing in blind ignorance!

"Their columns are coming fast—eight parsecs away now!" Val Marlann warned tightly.

Three, then four of the needles, were on the red. But the others were short. Gordon hastily notched up their rheostats.

They were all above the red mark now but did not exactly match. The *Ethne* was shaking wildly from the thunder of its straining turbines. The air seemed electric with an awful tension.

The needles matched! Each was in the red zone on the gauge, each at the same figure—

"Now!" cried Gordon hoarsely, and threw shut the main release-switch.

27

THE DISRUPTOR

Pale, ghostly beams stabbed out from the prow of the *Ethne* toward the dim region of space ahead. Those pallid rays seemed almost to creep slowly forward, fanning out as they did so.

Gordon, Hull Burrel and Val Marlann crouched at the window frozen and incapable of movement as they looked ahead. And there seemed no change.

Then the massed specks in the radar screen that marked

the position of the Cloud fleet's advancing line seemed to waver slightly. A flicker seemed to run through that area.

"Nothing's happening!" Burrel groaned. "Nothing! The thing must be—"

A point of blackness had appeared far ahead. It grew and grew, pulsing and throbbing.

And swiftly it was a great, growing blot of blackness, not the blackness of mere absence of light but such living, quivering blackness as no living man had ever seen.

On the radar screen, the area that included half the Cloud fleet's advancing battle-line had been swallowed by darkness! For there was a black blot on the screen too, a blot from which radar-rays recoiled.

"God in Heaven!" cried Val Marlann, shaking. "The Disruptor is destroying space itself in that area!"

The awful, the unimaginable answer to the riddle of the Disruptor's dread power flashed through Gordon's quaking mind at last!

He still did not understand, he would never understand, the scientific method of it. But the effect of it burst upon him. The Disruptor was a force that annihilated, not matter, but space!

The space-time continuum of our cosmos was four-dimensional, a four-dimensioned globe floating in the extra-dimensional abyss. The thrust of the Disruptor's awful beams destroyed a growing section of that sphere by thrusting it out of the cosmos!

It flashed across Gordon's appalled mind in a second. He was suddenly afraid! He convulsively ripped open the release-switch of the thing. Then as the next second ticked, the universe seemed to go mad.

Titan hands seemed to bat the *Ethne* through space with raving power. They glimpsed stars and space gone crazy, the huge glaring white mass of Deneb heaving wildly through the void, comets and dark-stars and meteor-drift of the void streaming insanely in the sky.

Gordon, hurled against a wall, quaked in his soul as the universe seemed to rise in mad vengeance against the puny men who had dared to lay desecrating hands on the warp and woof of eternal space.

Gordon came back to dull awareness many minutes later.

The *Ethne* was whirling and tossing on furious etheric storms, but the starry vault of space seemed to have quieted from its insane convulsion.

Val Marlann, blood streaming from a great bruise on his temple, was clinging to a stanchion and shouting orders into the annunciator.

He turned a ghastly white face. "The turbines are holding and the disturbances are quieting. That convulsion nearly threw our ships into Deneb, and quaked the stars in this whole part of the galaxy!"

"The back-lash reaction!" Gordon choked. "It was that—the surrounding space collapsing upon the hole in space the Disruptor made."

Hull Burrel hung over the radar screen.

"Only half the Cloud ships were destroyed in the convulsion!"

Gordon shuddered. "I can't use the Disruptor again! I won't!"

"You won't have to!" Burrel said eagerly. "The remainder of their fleet is fleeing back in panic toward the Cloud!"

They were not to be blamed, Gordon thought sickly. To have space itself go mad and collapse around one—he would never have dared unloose that force if he had known.

"I know now why Brenn Bir warned never to use the Disruptor lightly!" he said hoarsely. "Pray God it never will be used at all again."

Calls came from the stereo thick and fast, stunned inquiries from Giron's ships.

"What happened?" cried the shaken Commander over and over.

Hull Burrel had not lost sight of their goal, of what they must do.

"The League fleet's in full flight toward the Cloud, or what's left of them are!" he told the Commander exultantly. "If we follow we can smash them once and for all!"

Giron too fired at the opportunity. "I'll order the pursuit at once."

Back across the galactic spaces toward the shelter of the Cloud, the remnants of the League fleet were streaming. And after them, hour by hour, sped the *Ethne* and the Empire's battered fleet.

"They're finished, if we can smash Shorr Kan's rule and destroy their remaining ships!" Burrel exulted.

"You don't think Shorr Kan was with their fleet?" Gordon asked.

"He's too foxy for that—he'd be running things from Thallarna, never fear!" Val Marlann declared.

Gordon agreed, after a moment's thought. He knew Shorr Kan was no coward, but he'd have been directing his vast assault from his headquarters inside the Cloud.

The League of Dark Worlds' ships disappeared into the shelter of the Cloud long hours later. Soon afterward, the Empire fleet drew up just outside that vast, hazy gloom.

"If we go in after them, we might run into ambushes," Giron declared. "The place is rotten with navigational perils that we know nothing about."

Gordon proposed, "We'll demand their surrender, give them an ultimatum."

"Shorr Kan will not surrender!" Hull Burrel warned.

But Gordon had them beam a stereo-cast into the Cloud toward Thallarna, and spoke by it.

"To the Government of the League of Dark Worlds! We offer you a chance to surrender. Give up and disarm under our directions and we promise that no one will suffer except those criminals who led you into this aggression.

"But refuse, and we'll turn loose the Disruptor upon the whole Cloud! We'll blot this place forever from the galaxy!"

Val Marlann looked at him, appalled. "You'd do that? But good God—"

"I wouldn't *dare* do that!" Gordon answered. "I'll never turn loose the Disruptor again. But they've felt its power and may be bluffed by it."

There came no answer to their stereo-message. Again, after an hour, he repeated it.

Again, no answer. Then finally, after another wait, Giron's stern voice came.

"It seems that we'll have to go in there, Prince Zarth."

"No, wait," cried Hull Burrel. "A message is coming through from Thallarna!"

In the stereo had appeared a group of wild-looking Cloud-men, some of them wounded, in a room of Shorr Kan's palace.

"We agree to your terms, Prince Zarth!" their spokesman said hoarsely. "Our ships will be docked and disarmed immediately. You will be able to enter in a few hours."

"It could be a trick!" Val Marlann rasped. "It would give Shorr Kan time to lay traps for us."

The Cloud-man in the stereo shook his head. "Shorr Kan's disastrous tyranny is overthrown. When he refused to surrender, we rose in rebellion against him. I can prove that by letting you see him. He is dying."

The telestereo switched its scene abruptly to another room of the palace. There before them in image sat Shorr Kan.

He sat in the chair in his austere little room from which he had directed his mighty attempt to conquer the galaxy. Armed Cloud-men were around him. His face was marble-white and there was a blasted, blackened wound in his side.

His dulling eyes looked at them out of the stereo, and then cleared for a moment as they rested on Gordon. And then Shorr Kan grinned weakly.

"You win," he told Gordon. "I never thought you'd dare loose the Disruptor. Fool's luck, that you didn't destroy yourself with it—"

He choked, then went on. "Devil of a way for me to end up, isn't it? But I'm not complaining. I had one life and I used it to the limit. You're the same way at bottom, that's why I liked you."

Shorr Kan's dark head sagged, his voice trailed to a whisper. "Maybe I'm a throwback to your world, Gordon? Born out of my time? Maybe—"

He was dead with the words, they knew by the way his strong figure slumped forward across the desk.

"What was he talking about to you, Prince Zarth?" asked Hull Burrel puzzledly. "I couldn't understand it."

Gordon felt a queer, sharp emotion. Life was unpredictable. There was no reason why he should have *liked* Shorr Kan. But he knew now that he had.

Val Marlann and the other officers of the *Ethne* were exultant.

"It's victory! We've wiped out the menace of the League forever!"

The ship was in uproar. And they knew that that wild exultation of relief was spreading through their whole fleet.

Two hours later, Giron began moving his occupation forces inside the Cloud, on radar beams projected from Thallarna. Half his ships would remain on guard outside, in case of treachery.

"But there's no doubt now that they've actually surrendered," he told Gordon. "The advance ships I sent in there report that every League warship is already docked and being disarmed."

He added feelingly, "I'll leave an escort of warships for the *Ethne*. I know you'll be wanting to return to Throon now."

Gordon told him, "We don't need any escort. Val Marlann, you can start at once."

The *Ethne* set out on the long journey back across the galaxy toward Canopus. But after a half-hour, Gordon gave new orders.

"Head for Sol, not Canopus. Our destination is Earth."

Hull Burrel, amazed, protested. "But Prince Zarth, all Throon will be waiting for you to return! The whole Empire, everyone, will be mad with joy by this time, waiting to welcome you!"

Gordon shook his head dully. "I am not going to Throon now. Take me to Earth."

They looked at him puzzledly, wonderingly. But Val Marlann gave the order and the ship changed its course slightly and headed for the far-distant yellow spark of Sol.

For hours, as the *Ethne* flew on toward the north, Gordon remained sitting and staring broodingly from the windows, sunk in a strange, tired daze.

He was going back at last to Earth, to his own time and his own world, to his own body. Only now at last could he keep his pledge to Zarth Arn.

He looked out at the supernally brilliant stars of the galaxy. Far, far in the west now lay Canopus' glittering beacon. He thought of Throon, of the rejoicing millions there.

"All that is over for me now," he told himself dully. "Over forever."

He thought of Lianna, and that blind wave of heartbreak rose again in his mind. That, too, was over for him forever.

Hull Burrel came and told him. "The whole Empire, the whole galaxy, is ringing with your praises, Prince Zarth! Must you go to Earth now when they are waiting for you?"

"Yes, I must," Gordon insisted, and the big Antarian perplexedly left him.

He dozed, and woke, and dozed again. Time seemed scarcely now to have any meaning. How many days was it before the familiar yellow disk of Sol loomed bright ahead of the ship?

Down toward green old Earth slanted the *Ethne,* toward the sunlit eastern hemisphere.

"You'll land at my laboratory in the mountains—Hull knows the place," said Gordon.

The tower there in the ageless, frosty Himalayas looked the same as when he had left it—how long ago it seemed! The *Ethne* landed softly on the little plateau.

Gordon faced his puzzled friends. "I am going into my laboratory for a short time, and I want only Hull Burrel to go with me."

He hesitated, then added, "Will you shake hands? You're the best friends and comrades a man ever had."

"Prince Zarth, that sounds like a farewell!" burst Val Marlann worriedly. "What are you going to do in there?"

"Nothing is going to happen to me, I promise you," Gordon said with a little smile. "I will be coming back out to the ship in a few hours or so."

They gripped his hand. They stood silently looking after him as he and Hull Burrel stepped out into the frosty, biting air.

In the tower, Gordon led the way up to the glass-walled laboratory where rested the strange instruments of mental science that had been devised by the real Zarth Arn and old Vel Quen.

Gordon went over in his mind what the old scientist had told him about the operation of the telepathic amplifier and the mind-transmitter. He checked the instruments as carefully as he could.

Hull Burrel watched wonderingly, worriedly. Finally, Gordon turned to him.

"Hull, I'll need your help later. I want you to do as I ask even if you don't understand. Will you?"

"You know I'll obey any order you give!" said the big Antarian. "But I can't help feeling worried."

"There's no cause to—in a few hours you'll be on your

way to Throon again and I'll be with you," Gordon said. "Now wait."

He put the headpiece of the telepathic amplifier on his head. He made sure it was tuned again to Zarth Arn's individual mental frequency as Vel Quen had instructed. Then he turned on the apparatus.

Gordon *thought.* He concentrated his mind to hurl a thought-message amplified by the apparatus, back across the abyss of dimensional time to the one mind to which it was tuned.

"Zarth Arn! Zarth Arn! Can you hear me?"

No answering thought came into his mind. Again and again he repeated the thought-call, but without response.

Wonder and worry began to grip Gordon. He tried again an hour later, but with no more success. Hull Burrel watched puzzledly.

Then, after four hours had passed, he desperately made still another attempt.

"Zarth Arn, can you hear me? It is John Gordon calling!"

And this time, faint and far across the unimaginable abyss of time, a thin thought-answer came into his mind.

"John Gordon! Good God, for days I've been waiting and wondering what was wrong! Why is it that you yourself are calling instead of Vel Quen?"

"Vel Quen is dead!" Gordon answered in swift thought. "He was killed by League soldiers soon after I came across to this time."

He explained hurriedly. "There has been galactic war here between the Cloud and the Empire, Zarth. I was swept into it, couldn't get back to Earth to call you for the exchange. I had to assume your identity, to tell no one as I promised. One man did learn of my imposture but he's dead and no one else here knows."

"Gordon!" Zarth Arn's thought was feverish with excitement. "You've been true to your pledge, then? You could have stayed there in my body and position, but didn't!"

Gordon told him, "Zarth, I think I can arrange the operation of the mind-transmitter to re-exchange our bodies, from what Vel Quen explained to me. Tell me if this is the way."

He ran over the details of the mind-transmitter operation in his thoughts. Zarth Arn's thought answered quickly, corroborating most of it, correcting him at places.

"That will do it—I'm ready for the exchange," Zarth Arn told him finally. "But who will operate the transmitter for you if Vel Quen is dead?"

"I have a friend here, Hull Burrel," answered Gordon. "He does not know the nature of what we are doing, but I can instruct him how to turn on the transmitter."

He ceased concentrating, and turned to the worried Antarian who had stood watching him.

"Hull, it is now that I need your help," Gordon said. He showed the switches of the mind-transmitter. "When I give the signal, you must close these switches in the following order."

Hull Burrel listened closely, then nodded understandingly. "I can do that. But what's it going to *do* to you?"

"I can't tell you that, Hull. But it's not going to harm me. I promise you that."

He wrung the Antarian's hand in a hard grip. Then he readjusted the headpiece and again sent his thought across the abyss.

"Ready, Zarth? If you are, I'll give Hull the signal."

"I'm ready," came Zarth Arn's answer. "And Gordon, before we say farewell—my thanks for all you have done for me, for your loyalty to your pledge!"

Gordon raised his hand in the signal. He heard Hull closing the switches. The transmitter hummed, and Gordon felt his mind hurled into bellowing blackness . . .

28

STAR-ROVER'S RETURN

Gordon awoke slowly. His head was aching, and he had an unnerving feeling of *strangeness*. He stirred, and then opened his eyes.

He was lying in a familiar room, a familiar bed. This was his little New York apartment, a dark room that now seemed small and crowded.

Shakily, he snapped on a lamp and stumbled out of bed. He faced the tall mirror across the room.

He was John Gordon again! John Gordon's strong, stocky figure and tanned face looked back at him instead of the aquiline features and tall form of Zarth Arn.

He stumbled to the window and looked out on the starlit buildings and blinking lights of New York. How small, cramped, ancient, the city looked now, when his mind was still full of the mighty splendors of Throon.

Tears blurred his eyes as he looked up at the starry sky. Orion Nebula was but a misty star pendant from that constellation-giant's belt. Ursa Minor reared toward the pole. Low above the roof-tops blinked the white eye of Deneb.

He could not even see Canopus, down below the horizon. But his thoughts flashed out to it, across the abysses of time and space to the fairy towers of Throon.

"Lianna! Lianna!" he whispered, tears running down his face.

Slowly, as the night hours passed, Gordon nerved himself for the ordeal that the rest of his life must be.

Irrevocable gulfs of time and space separated him forever from the one girl he had ever loved. He could not forget, he would never forget. But he must live his life as it remained to him.

He went, the next morning, to the big insurance company that employed him. He remembered, as he entered, how he had left it weeks before, afire with the thrill of possible adventure.

The manager who was Gordon's superior met him with surprise on his face.

"Gordon, you feel well enough now to come back to work? I'm glad of it!"

Gordon gathered quickly that Zarth Arn, in his body, had feigned sickness to account for his inability to do Gordon's work.

"I'm all right now," Gordon said. "And I'd like to get back to work."

Work was all that kept Gordon from despair, in the next days. He plunged into it as one might into drugs or drink. It kept him, for a little of the time, from remembering.

But at night, he remembered. He lay sleepless, looking out his window at the bright stars that to his mind's eyes were always mighty suns. And always, Lianna's face drifted before his eyes.

His superior commended him warmly, after a few days. "Gordon, I was afraid your illness might have slowed you down, but you keep on like this and you'll be an assistant manager some day."

Gordon could have shouted with bitter laughter, the suggestion seemed so fantastic. *He* might be an assistant manager? He, who as prince of the Empire's royal house had feasted with the star kings at Throon? He, who had captained the hosts of the Kingdoms in the last great fight off Deneb? He, who had unloosed destruction on the Cloud, and had riven space itself?

But he did not laugh. He said quietly, "That would be a fine position for me, sir."

And then, on a night weeks later, he heard once more a voice calling in his half-sleeping mind!

"Gordon! John Gordon!"

He knew, at once. He knew whose mind called to him. He would have known, even beyond death.

"Lianna!"

"Yes, John Gordon, it is I!"

"But how could you call—how could you even know—"

"Zarth Arn told me," she interrupted eagerly. "He told me the whole story, when he came back to Throon. Told me how it was you, in his body, whom I really loved!

"He wept when he told me of it, John Gordon! For he could hardly speak, when he learned all that you had done and had sacrificed for the Empire."

"Lianna—Lianna—" His mind yearned wildly across the unthinkable depths. "Then at least we can say goodbye."

"No, wait!" came her silvery mental cry. "It need not be goodbye! Zarth Arn believes that even as minds can be drawn across time, so can physical bodies, if he can perfect his apparatus.

"He is working on it now. If he succeeds, will you come to me—you yourself, John Gordon?"

Hope blazed in him, like the kindling of a new flame from ashes. His answer was a throbbing thought.

"Lianna, I'd come if it were only for an hour of life with you!"

"Then wait for our call, John Gordon! It cannot be long until Zarth Arn succeeds, and then our call will come!"

A blaring auto-horn—and Gordon awoke, the eager vibrations of that faraway thought fading from his brain.

He sat up, trembling. Had it been a dream? *Had* it?

"No!" he said hoarsely. "It was real. I know that it was real."

He went to the window, and looked out across the lights of New York at the great blaze of the galaxy across the sky.

Worlds of the star kings, far away across the deeps of infinity and eternity—he would go back to them! Back to them, and to that daughter of star kings whose love had called him from out of space and time.

Book Two

RETURN TO THE STARS

– 1 –

The receptionist opened the inner door. "Will you go right in, Mr. Gordon?"

Gordon said, "Thank you." The door closed softly behind him, and at the same time a man rose from behind a small desk and came toward him. He was a tall man, surprisingly young, with a brisk, friendly, energetic air about him. "Mr. Gordon?" he said, and held out his hand. "I'm Dr. Keogh."

Gordon shook hands and allowed himself to be guided to a chair beside the desk. He sat, looking around the room, looking everywhere but at Keogh, suddenly acutely embarrassed.

Keogh said quietly, "Have you ever consulted a psychiatrist before?"

Gordon shook his head. "I never . . . uh . . . felt the need."

"All of us have problems at some time in our lives," said Keogh. "This is nothing to be ashamed of. The important thing is to realize that a problem does exist. Then, and only then, is it possible to do something about it." He smiled. "You see, you've already taken the vital forward step. From here on it should be much easier. Now then." He studied Gordon's card which he had filled in at what seemed unnecessary length. "You're in the insurance business."

"Yes."

"Judging from your position with the firm, you must be quite successful."

"I've worked hard these last few years," Gordon said, in an odd voice.

"Do you like your work?"

"Not particularly."

Keogh was silent a moment or two, frowning at the card. Gordon fought down an overwhelming impulse to run for the door. He knew that he would only have to come back again. He could not carry this question alone any longer. He had to know.

"I see that you're unmarried," Keogh said. "Like to tell me why?"

"That's part of the reason I came here. There was a girl. . . ." He broke off, then said with sudden fierce determination, "I want to find out whether I've been having delusions."

"What kind of delusions?" asked Keogh gently.

'At the time," said Gordon, "I wasn't in any doubt. It was all real. More real, more *alive*, than anything that had ever happened to me before. But now . . . now I don't know." He looked at Keogh, his eyes full of pain. "I'll be honest with you. I don't want to lose this dream . . . if it was a dream. It's more precious to me than any reality. But I know that if . . . if I . . . oh, hell!" He got up and moved around the room, aimlessly, his broad stocky shoulders hunched and his hands balled into fists. He looked like a man about to jump off a cliff, and Keogh knew that he was just that. He sat quietly, waiting.

Gordon said, "I thought that I went to the stars. Not now, but in the future. Two hundred thousand years in the future. I'll give it to you all in one lump, Doctor, and then you can call for the strait-jacket. I believed that my mind was drawn across time, into the body of another man, and for a while . . . keeping my own identity, you understand, my own memories as John Gordon of twentieth-century Earth . . . for a while I lived in the body of Zarth Arn, a prince of the Mid-Galactic Empire. I went to the stars. . . ."

His voice trailed away. He stood by the window, looking out at falling rain and the roofs and walls and chimneys of West Sixty-fourth Street. The sky was a drab blankness fouled with soot.

"I heard the sunrise music," Gordon said, "that the crystal peaks make above Throon when Canopus comes to warm them. I feasted with the star-kings in the Hall of Stars. And at the end, I led the fleets of the Empire against our enemies, the men from the League of Dark Worlds. I saw the ships die like swarming fireflies off the shores of the Hercules Cluster. . . ."

He did not turn to see how Keogh was taking all this. He had started and he would not stop, and in his voice there was pride and longing and the anguish of loss.

"I've shot the Orion Nebula. I've been into the Cloud, where the drowned suns burn in a haze of darkness. I've killed men, Doctor. And in that last battle, I—"

He stopped and shook his head, turning abruptly away from the window.

"Never mind that now. But there was more. A lot more. A whole universe, a language, names, people, costumes, places, details. Could I have imagined all that?"

He looked at Keogh. Desperately.

Keogh said, "Were you happy in that universe?"

Gordon thought about that, his square, honest face creased in a careful frown. "Most of the time I was frightened. Things were . . ." He made a gesture vaguely indicating great troubles. "I was in constant danger. But . . . yes, I guess I was happy there."

Keogh nodded. "You mentioned a girl?"

Now Gordon turned again to the window. "Her name was Lianna. She was a princess of Fomalhaut Kingdom. She and Zarth Arn were betrothed . . . a matter of state, you understand, and it wasn't supposed to be anything more. Zarth Arn already had a morganatic wife, but I,

Gordon, in Zarth Arn's body—I fell in love with Lianna."

"Did she return your feeling?"

"Yes, it was the end of the world for me when I had to leave her and come back here to my own world, my own time. . . . And here's what makes it so difficult, Doctor. I'd given up hope of ever seeing her again, and then it seemed to me that she spoke to me one night, telepathically, across time, and told me that Zarth Arn believed he could find a way to bring me through physically, in my own body. . . ." His voice trailed off again and his shoulders sagged. "How insane that dream sounds when I tell it. But it made this dreary life worth living for a long while, just the hope, knowing that some day I might go back. And of course nothing ever happened. And now I don't know whether anything ever did happen, really."

He walked back to the chair and sat down, feeling strangely exhausted and empty.

"I've never told this to anyone before. Now that I have, it's like . . . it's as though I'd killed something, or killed part of myself. But I can't go on living between two worlds. If that world of the future was hallucination, and this one is reality, the *only* reality, then I've got to accept it."

He sat, brooding. Now it was Keogh's turn to rise and move about. He turned to glance at Gordon a time or two, as though he were having difficulty finding a point of attack. Then he made up his mind.

"Well," he said briskly, "let us look at the available evidence." He glanced at some scribbled notes on his desk. "You say that your mind was drawn across time, into the body of another man."

"That's right. Zarth Arn was a scientist as well as a noble. He had perfected the method and the equipment. The exchange was effected from his laboratory."

"Very well. Now what happened to your own body,

here in the present day on Earth, while your mind was absent from it?"

Gordon looked at him. "I said exchange. That was the purpose of the whole thing. Zarth Arn wanted to explore the past. He had done this many times before. Only in my case, things got fouled up."

"Then this . . . uh . . . Zarth Arn actually inhabited your body?"

"Yes."

"Went to your place of employment, did your work?"

"Well, no. When I came back, my boss said he was happy to see me recovered from my illness. Apparently Zarth Arn had given that excuse. I don't suppose he wanted to run the risk of making some irreparable blunder. I did not have the same choice."

Keogh said. "I congratulate you on your very logical mind, Mr. Gordon. But there is no proof at all, no physical proof, that this exchange of minds actually took place?"

"No," said Gordon. "Not a bit. How could there be? But what did you mean about my logical mind?"

"You have covered all the loopholes so carefully." Keogh smiled. "It's a gorgeous fantasy, Mr. Gordon. Few men are gifted with that much imagination." He added seriously, "I understand what strength of mind it must have taken to bring you here. I think we are going to have a very good relationship, Mr. Gordon, because I think you already realize subconsciously that your dreams of star-kingdoms and nebulae and beautiful princesses were only the attempt of your mind to escape from a world that you found unbearably humdrum and dull. Dreary, I think was your word. Now, this will take work, and time, and possibly there will be some painful moments, but I don't think you have anything at all to worry about. The fact that you've had no recurrence of the dream for a long period of time is a healthy sign. I shall want to see you twice weekly, if possible."

"I can manage it."

"Good. Miss Finlay will make the appointments for you. Oh, and here is my private number." He handed Gordon a card. "If you should at any time have a recurrence, please call me, no matter how late it is."

He shook Gordon's hand warmly, and a few minutes later Gordon found himself on the street, walking in the rain and feeling nothing but an utter desolation. He knew that Keogh was right, that he must be right. He knew that he had indeed almost resigned himself to that fact and only needed someone to supply the final push. Yet somehow the act of putting it all into words had the cruelty of a surgeon's knife, performing a necessary and humane operation but without anaesthesia.

And it had all seemed, and did still seem, so real. . . .

Brutally he thrust out of his mind and heart the sound of Lianna's voice, the beautiful picture of her face, the memory of her lips.

In his office, Keogh was talking rapidly into his dictation machine, getting down all of what Gordon had told him while it was fresh, and shaking his head in wonder. *This* case was going to be, literally, one for the books.

Twice a week thereafter Gordon visited Keogh, answering his questions, telling more and more of his dream, and under Keogh's skillful guidance learning to look at it objectively. He came to understand the underlying motivations . . . boredom with a job that did not offer him sufficient challenge, desire for fame and aggrandizement, desire for power, desire to punish the world for its frustrations and its failure to appreciate him. On this last point, Keogh had been enormously impressed, not to say startled, by Gordon's description of the Disruptor, a weapon of incredible power which, as Zarth Arn, he had wielded in the great battle against the League.

"You annihilated part of *space*?" Keogh asked, and shook his head. "You do have powerful desires. How fortunate that you took this one out in dreaming."

Lianna was most easily explained of all. She was the dream-girl, the unattainable, and by transferring his feelings to her as he was relieved of the necessity of seeking out or competing for the actual young women by whom he was surrounded. Keogh pointed out to him that he was afraid of women. Gordon had felt that he was merely bored by them, but he supposed Keogh knew his subconscious better than he did. So he did not dispute him.

And steadily, week by week, the dream faded.

Keogh was personally delighted by the whole case. He liked Gordon, who had proved to be an uniquely cooperative patient. And he had acquired a mass of material that was going to keep in learned papers and outstanding lectures for a long time to come.

At last, on one soft May afternoon when the sun shone gently down from a cloud-flecked sky, Keogh said to Gordon, "We have made tremendous progress. I'm very pleased. And I'm going to let you try your wings alone for a while. Come back in three weeks and tell me how you're doing."

They had a drink together to celebrate and later on Gordon bought himself a lavish dinner and took in a show, telling himself all the while how happy he was. When he walked home to his apartment late that night the stars were glowing above the city lights. He studiously avoided looking at them.

He went to bed.

At forty-three minutes past two o'clock Keogh's phone rang, rousing him from sleep. He answered it, and was instantly wide awake. "Gordon! What is it?"

Gordon's voice was wild and shaken. "It's come again. Zarth Arn. He spoke to me. He said—he said he was ready now to bring me through. He said Lianna was waiting. Doctor—*Doctor!* . . .

The voice broke off. "Gordon!" Keogh shouted, but

there was no answer. "Hold on," he said to the humming wire. "Don't panic. I'll be right over."

He was there in fifteen minutes. The door of Gordon's apartment was locked but he roused the manager, who unlocked it grudgingly after examining his credentials. The apartment was empty and quiet. The phone swung from its cord as though it had been dropped in the midst of conversation. Absently Keogh replaced it.

He stood for a little time, thoughtful. He had no doubt of what had happened. Gordon had not been able to stand the loss of his glittering delusion, his dream so Gordon had run away, from his analyst, from reality. He would be back, of course, but then all that work must be done again. . . . Keogh sighed and shook his head, and went out.

-11-

Consciousness returned to Gordon very slowly. He had at first only a confused memory of fear, terror, gut-wrenching, mind-shattering panic that was somehow combined with the sensation of falling right off the world into a state of not-being. He thought that he could hear himself yelling, and he wondered wildly why Keogh did not hear and come to save him. Then he heard other voices, familiar, unfamiliar, far away. A liquid slid coolly down his throat and exploded into white fire in his stomach. He opened his eyes. There was a blank wash of light out of which images emerged gradually. Large forms, walls and windows and furniture. Small forms, close at hand, bending over him.

Faces.

Two faces. One was just a face, male, intent, anxious. The other was his own face . . . .

No. Now wait a minute. His own face was square and blue-eyed and brown-haired, and this face above him was dark-eyed and aquiline, so it could not possibly be his own. And yet . . .

"Gordon. Gordon!" the face was saying.

The other face said, "One moment, Highness." Gordon felt his head raised. A hand holding a glass appeared out of the mist. Gordon drank automatically. Again there was the explosion of white fire inside him, very pleasant and invigorating. The mist began to clear.

He looked up into the dark handsome face, and after a moment he said, "Zarth Arn."

Strong hands gripped him. "Thank God. I was beginning to be afraid. No, don't try to get up yet. Lie still. You were in shock for a long time, and no wonder, with the atoms of your body driven right through the time-dimension. But it's done now. After all these years of work, finally, success!" Zarth Arn smiled. "Did you think I had forgotten you?"

"I thought. . . ." said Gordon, and closed his eyes. Keogh. Keogh, he thought, I need you. Am I truly mad and dreaming? Or is this real?"

Real, as I knew all along, as I never stopped knowing in spite of all your careful logic!

Real.

He struggled to sit up, and they let him. He looked around the laboratory room. It was just the same as the first time he had seen it, except that some new and very elaborate equipment had been installed, a panel of incomprehensible controls at one side and in the center a tall structure like a glass coffin set on end and suspended between two power grids that were like nothing in Gordon's experience. Enormously fat cables snaked out of the room, presumably to a generator somewhere beyond.

The room was octagonal, with tall windows in each side. Through them poured the clear and brilliant sunlight of high altitudes, and through them Gordon could see the mighty peaks of the Himalayas. Old Earth was still here, outside.

He looked down at his hands, at his familiar body. He felt the solidity of the padded table on which he sat, the texture of the sheets, the movement of air across his naked back. He reached out and took hold of Zarth Arn. Bone and muscle, flesh and blood, warm and alive.

Gordon said, "Where is Lianna?"

"Waiting." His nod indicated that she was close by, in

another room. "She wanted to be in here with us, but we thought it better not. As soon as you feel strong enough . . ."

Gordon's heart was pounding. Reality or dream, sanity or madness, what did it matter? He was alive again, and Lianna was waiting. He stood up and laughed as Zarth Arn and the other man caught him and shored up his buckling knees. "It was a long time," he said to Zarth Arn. "I got a little confused. But it's all right now. Whatever this is, I'll settle for it. How about another helping of that hellfire, and some clothes?"

Zarth Arn looked at the other man. "What about it, Lex Vel? Gordon, this is Vel Quen's son. He's taken his father's place with me. If it hadn't been for him I couldn't have solved the insoluble problems that have been driving us both mad ever since you returned to your own time."

"Why be modest?" Lex Vel said. "It's true." He shook Gordon's hand, grinning. "And the answer is no, not yet. Rest awhile and then we'll talk about clothes."

Gordon lay down again, reluctantly. Zarth Arn said, "You'll find quite a welcome at Throon when you get there, Gordon. My brother Jhal is one of the few who know the whole story and he understands what you did for us. We can never repay you, really, but don't think that we've forgotten."

Lying there, Gordon remembered the day when Jhal Arn, ruler of the Empire in the place of his murdered father, had been himself struck down by a would-be assassin, leaving the vast burden of Empire diplomacy and defense upon his, Gordon's, totally inadequate shoulders. By the grace of heaven and sheer fool luck he had bulled it through.

He smiled and said, "Thanks," and then unexpectedly he slept for a while.

When he woke the sunlight was dimmer, the shadows of the high peaks longer. He felt fresh and rested. Zarth

Arn was not there but Lex Vel ran a check on him, nodded, and pointed to some clothing draped over a chair. Gordon rose and dressed, feeling shaky at first but rapidly recovering his strength. The suit was of the silky fabric he remembered, sleeveless shirt and trousers in a warm shade of copper, with a cloak of the same material. He stood before a mirror to adjust the cloak, and he had never seen his own self before in this attire, which had looked natural and right on Zarth Arn but which made him smile now and feel as though he were dressed for a costume ball.

And then it hit him like a thunderbolt.

Lianna had never seen him. She had fallen in love with him as Zarth Arn, a different Zarth Arn to be sure, and she had understood later that the personality she loved belonged to John Gordon of Earth. But would she still love him when confronted with his physical actuality? Or would she be disappointed, would she find him plain and dull-looking, perhaps even repulsive.

Gordon turned to Lex Vel. He said desperate, "I really do need some more of that stimulant. . . ."

Lex Vel glanced at his face and brought him a glass immediately. Gordon drank it down, as Zarth Arn came in and then hurried toward them.

"What is it?"

"I don't know," said Lex Vel. "He seemed all right, and then all at once . . ."

Zarth Arn said gently, "Perhaps I can guess. It's Lianna, isn't it?"

Gordon nodded. "I suddenly realized that she'll be seeing me for the first time . . . a total stranger."

"She's somewhat prepared. Remember, I've been able to describe you to her, and she's asked me to do so at least ten thousand times." He put his hand on Gordon's shoulder. "It may take her awhile to get used to the change, Gordon, but be patient and never doubt how she feels about you. She has spent far too much time here, away from her kingdom. Many times when she should have been at home attending to affairs of state, she was here instead, waiting for the day when we could say we were ready to try." Zarth Arn shook his head, his eyes serious. "She has ignored repeated messages from Fomalhaut, and of course she wouldn't listen to me. Now that you're here and safe, I'm hoping she'll listen to you. Tell her, Gordon. Tell her she must go home."

"Is there trouble?"

"There's always trouble when the head of state isn't attending to business," said Zarth Arn. "How much or how serious it is I don't know because she hasn't told me. But the messages from Fomalhaut were coded URGENT at first. Now they're IMPERATIVE. You will tell her?"

"Of course," said Gordon, rather glad at the moment that he had something besides himself to worry about.

"Good," said Zath Arn, and took him by the arm. "Take heart, friend. Remember, I've described you. She's not expecting an Apollo."

He looked at Gordon in such a way that Gordon had to grin briefly. "My friend," he said, "thanks a lot."

Zarth Arn laughed and led him out. But Gordon still felt afraid.

She was waiting for him in a small room that faced the sunset. Beyond the window the snow peaks caught the light and flamed a glorious hot gold, and below them the gorges were filled with purple shadow. Zarth Arn left Gordon at the doorway, and the two were alone. It was quiet there. She turned from the window to look at him and he stood where he was, afraid to move, afraid to speak. She was as lovely as he remembered, tall and slim and graceful, with her ash-blonde hair and her clear gray eyes. And now finally Gordon knew once and for all that this was true and no dream, because no man could imagine what he was feeling in his heart.

"Lianna," he whispered. And again, "Lianna . . ."

"You are John Gordon." She came toward him, her eyes

searching his face as though for some tiny scrap of familiarity by which she might know him. He wanted to take her in his arms, to hold her and touch her and kiss her with all the stored-up hunger of the lonely years, but he did not dare. He could only stand rigid and miserable while she came closer, searching, and then she stopped. Her gaze dropped and she turned away a little, her red mouth uncertain.

Gordon said, "Is it so much of a shock?"

"Zarth Arn told very truly how you would look."

"And you find me . . ."

"No," she said quickly, and turned to meet his gaze again. "Please don't think that." She smiled, rather tremulously. "If I were meeting you for the first time . . . I mean, *really* for the first time, I would think you a most attractive man." She shook her head. "I mean, I *do* find you attractive. It isn't that at all. It's just that I will have to learn to know you all over again. That is," she added, her eyes very steady on his, "if you still feel toward me as you did."

"I do," he said. "I do," and he put his hands on her shoulders. She did not draw away, but neither did she yield toward him. She only smiled uncertainly and repeated Zarth Arn's words to him. "Be patient with me."

He took his hands away and said, "I will," trying to keep all trace of bitterness out of his voice. He went over to the window. The flaming peaks had darkened and the snowfields were turning to pure blue, as the first stars pricked the sky. He felt as cold and empty and forlorn as the wind that scoured those snows.

"Zarth Arn tells me that you have trouble at home."

She brushed it aside. "Nothing of importance. He wants you to tell me to go home, doesn't he?"

"Yes."

"And I will, tomorrow, on one condition." She was close beside him again, the last of the daylight showing her face pale and clear as a cameo in the dusk. "You must come with me."

He looked at her and touched his arm. "I've hurt you," she said softly. "And I didn't mean to, I didn't want to. Can you forgive me?"

"Of course, Lianna."

"Then come with me. A little time, John Gordon—that's all I need."

"All right," he said. "I'll come." I'll come, he thought fiercely, and if I have to woo and win you all over again, I'll do it so good and damn well that you'll forget there was ever a time when I looked like somebody else.

-III-

The royal star-cruiser with the White Sun of Fomalhaut glittering on her bows lifted from the starport, beyond which lay the greatest city of latterday Earth. It was a city of wide space and lifting beauty. Flared and fluted pylons towered at the intersections of the grid of roadways. Down through the yellow sunshine flocked the local Terran flyers, skimming like birds to roost on the pylons' landing pads. It was not like the cities that Gordon remembered.

The starship left all this behind and plunged back into her true element, the glooming tideless seas of space that run so deep between the island suns. The yellow spark of Sol, and the old green planet from which the human race had spread through a universe, dropped back into obscurity. Now once more the ranked stars shone before Gordon, in all their naked splendor. No wonder, he thought, that he had been smothered by the cramped horizons of twentieth-century Earth, after having once seen this magnificence.

Across the broad loom of the galaxy, the nations of the star-kings were marked in many-colored fire, crimson and gold and emerald green, blue and violet and diamond white . . . the kingdoms of Lyra, Cygnus, Cassiopeia, Polaris, and the capital of the great Mid-Galactic Empire at Canopus. The Hercules Cluster blazed with its baronies of swarming suns. To the south, as the cruiser beat westward toward Fomalhaut, the Orion Nebula sprawled its coiling radiance across the firmament. Far northward lay the black blot of the Cloud, where drowned Thallarna lay now in peace.

Once, as the cruiser altered course to skirt a dangerous bank of stellar drift, Gordon caught sight of the Magellanic Clouds, the as yet unknown and unexplored star-clouds lying like offshore islands in the inter-galactic gulf. He remembered that there had once been an invasion of the alien Magellanians into the ten-young Empire, an invasion crushed for all time by an ancestor of Zarth Arn's who had for the first time used that terrible secret weapon of the Empire, the thing called the Disruptor.

Gordon thought of Keogh and his detailed psychological explanation of what he had called "the Disruptor fantasy." He smiled, shaking his head. A pity Keogh was not here with him. Keogh could explain the cruiser as a womb symbol, and he could explain Lianna as the unattainable dream-girl, and Gordon's romance with her wish fulfillment. But he wondered just how Keogh would explain Korkhann, Lianna's Minister of Nonhuman Affairs.

His first meeting with Korkhann, which took place the night before take-off, had been a shock to Gordon. He had known that there were nonhuman citizens in the kingdoms of the stars, and he had even seen a few of them, briefly and more or less distantly, but this was the first time he had actually encountered one face to face.

Korkhann was a native of Krens, a star-system on the far borders of Fomalhaut Kingdom. From it, Korkhann said, one might look out across the vast wilderness of the Marches of Outer Space, as though perched precariously on the last thin edge of civilization.

"The counts of the Marches," Zarth Arn had explained to Gordon, "are allied to the Empire, as you remember. But they're a wild lot, and apparently determined to remain that way. They say their oath of fealty did not include opening their borders to Empire ships, and they refuse to do so. My brother often feels that we might be better off to have the counts as enemies rather than friends."

"Their time will come," Korkhann said. "Just now, my immediate problems are closer to home." And he had bent his severe yellow gaze upon Lianna, who reached out and placed her hand affectionately on his sleek gray plumes.

"I have been a trial to you," she said, and turned to Gordon. "Korkhann came here with me and he has been in touch with Fomalhaut almost constantly by sterocommunicator, doing his best to deal with affairs at long distance."

And Korkhann turned his round unwinking eyes and his beaked nose to Gordon and said in his harsh whistling voice, "I'm glad you have been safely delivered here at last, John Gordon, while Her Highness still has a kingdom to go back to."

Lianna had made light of that, and Gordon had been still distracted by this sudden confrontation with a five-foot-high creature who walked erect, clothed in pride and his own beautiful feathers, who spoke the English-derived language of the Empire, and who gestured gracefully with the long clawed fingers that terminated his flightless wings. But now, on the voyage, Gordon remembered.

They were alone, the three of them, in the cruiser's small but lavishly fitted lounge, and Gordon had been looking forward to the hour when Korkhann would finish his impossibly complicated chess game with Lianna and retire to his own cabin. He sat pretending to scan a tape from the cruiser's library, covertly watching Lianna as she bent her head over the board, thinking how beautiful she was and then glancing at Korkhann and trying to stifle the inner qualm of revulsion he had been fighting ever since that first meeting. And suddenly he said, "Korkhann . . ."

The long slim head turned, making the neck-plumage shift and shine in the lamplight. "Yes?"

"Korkhann, what did you mean when you said you were glad I had come while Lianna still had a kingdom to go back to?"

Lianna said impatiently, "There's no need to go into all that now. Korkhann is a loyal friend and a devoted minister, but he worries too . . ."

"Highness," said Korkhann gently. "We have never had even small falsehoods between us, and this would be a bad time to begin. You worry just as much as I do about Narath Teyn, but because of another matter you have set aside that worry, and in order to salve your conscience you must deny that there is anything to worry about."

Gordon thought, 'He sounds exactly like Keogh.' And he waited for the explosion.

Lianna's mouth set and her eyes were stormy. She rose, looking imperious in a way that Gordon remembered, but Korkhann continued to sit and bear her angry gaze quietly. Abruptly she turned away.

"You make me furious," she said, "so what you say is probably true. Very well, then. Tell him."

"Who," asked Gordon, "is Narath Teyn?"

"Lianna's cousin," Korkhann said. "He is also the presumptive heir to the crown of Fomalhaut."

"But I thought Lianna . . ."

"Is the legal and undoubted ruler. Yes. But there must always be a next in succession. How much do you know about the kingdom, John Gordon?"

He indicated the tape. "I've been studying, but I haven't had time to learn too much." He frowned at Korkhann. "I could wonder why this would concern the Minister of Nonhuman Affairs."

Korkhann nodded and rose from the forgotten chess

game. "I can show you." He dimmed the lights and touched a wall stud. A panel slid back, revealing a three-dimensional map of Fomalhaut Kingdom, a spatter of tiny suns in the simulated blackness of space, dominated by the white star that gives the area its name.

"There are many nonhuman races in the galaxy," Korkhann said. "Some are intelligent and civilized, some are brutish, some are making the change from the one to the other, some probably never will. In the early days there were some unfortunate confrontations, not without reason on both sides. You find me repellent. . . ."

Gordon started, and was aware that Lianna had turned to look at him. He felt his face turn hot, and he said with unnecessary sharpness, "Whatever gave you that idea?"

"Forgive me," Korkhann said. "You have been most studiously polite, and I don't wish to insult you, especially as I understand that yours is a purely instinctive reaction."

"Korkhann is a telepath," said Lianna. She added, "Quite a lot of the nonhumans are, so if what he says is true, John Gordon, you had better conquer that instinct."

"You see," said Korkhann, "well over half the worlds of our kingdom are nonhuman." His quick clawed fingers pointed them out—the tiny solar-systems with their motelike planets. "On the other hand, the uninhabited worlds that were colonized by your people, here and here. . . ." Again the long finger flicked. "These are the planets with the heavy populations, so that humans outnumbered nonhumans by about two-thirds. You know that the princess rules with the aid of a council, which is divided into two chambers, with representation in one based upon planetary units, and in the other on population. . . ."

Gordon was beginning to get part of the picture. "So one chamber of the council would always be dominated by one group."

"Exactly," Korkhann said. "Therefore, the opinion of the ruler is often the deciding one. You can see that because of this, the sympathies of the ruler are of more than ordinary importance in Fomalhaut Kingdom."

"There was never any real difficulty until about two years ago," Lianna said. "Then a campaign began to make the nonhumans believe that the humans were their enemies, that I in particular hated them and was hatching all sorts of plots. Complete nonsense, but among nonhumans as well as among humans there are always those who will listen."

"Gradually," Korkhann said, "a pattern emerged. A certain group among the nonhuman populations aspires to take over the rule of Fomalhaut Kingdom, and as a first step they must replace Lianna with a ruler more to their liking."

"Narath Teyn?"

"Yes," said Korkhann, "and I will answer your unspoken question also, John Gordon. No, Lianna, it is a fair question and I wish to answer it." The bright yellow eyes met Gordon's squarely. "You wonder why I support the human cause against my own kind. The answer is quite simple. It is because in this case the human cause is the just one. The group behind Narath Teyn talk very eloquently of justice, but they think only of power. And somewhere in all this there is something hidden, an evil which I do not understand but which frightens me nevertheless."

He shrugged, rippling the gray shoulder-plumes. "Beyond all that, Narath Teyn is . . ."

He stopped as someone rapped sharply on the door.

Lianna said, "Enter."

A junior officer entered and stood at rigid attention. "Highness," he said, "Captain Harn Horva respectfully requests your presence on the bridge, at once." His eyes flicked to Korkhann. "You too, sir, if you please."

Gordon felt the small shock of alarm in the air.

Only an emergency of considerable importance would bring such a request from the captain. Lianna nodded.

"Of course," she said, and turned to Gordon. "Come with us."

The young officer led the way. They followed him down narrow gleaming corridors and up a steep companionway to the ship's control-center, still archaically called "the bridge."

Aft was a long curving bulkhead filled with the massed panels of the computer banks, the guidance systems, the controls that governed velocity, mass, and the accumulator banks. Here under the steel floorplates the throbbing of the generators was as close and intimate as the pulsing of one's own blood. Forward a series of screens gave visual and radar images of space along a 180-degree perimeter, and at one side was the stereo-communicator. As they entered the bridge Gordon was aware of the complete silence, broken only by the electronic purlings and hummings of the equipment. The technicians all appeared to be holding their breath, their attention fixed half on their instruments and half on the taut little group around the radar screens, the captain, first and second officers, and radar men.

Harn Horva, a tall vigorous gray-haired man with very keen eyes and a strong jaw, turned to greet them. "Highness," he said. "I'm sorry to disturb you, but it is necessary."

To Gordon's untutored eye the screens showed nothing but a meaningless speckle of blips. He turned his attention instead to the visual screens.

The cruiser was approaching an area of cosmic drift. Gordon saw it first as a sort of tenuous dark cloud occluding the stars beyond it. Then as he looked he began to see its individual components, bits and pieces of interstellar wrack gleaming faintly in the light of far-off suns. Rocks as big as worlds, rocks as small as houses, and every size in-between, embedded in a tattered stream of dust that stretched for a parsec or two across the void. It was still a long way off. The cruiser would pass it on her port beam, with distance to spare. Nothing else showed. He could not understand what the excitement was about.

Harn Horva was busy explaining to Lianna.

"Our regular radar is picking up only the normal blips associated with drift. But the hot-spot scanners are getting some high-energy emissions that are not all typical of drift." His face was grim, his voice driving on to a harsh conclusion. "I'm afraid we'll have to assume that there are ships lying up in there, using the drift as a screen."

"Ambush?" asked Lianna, her own voice perfectly steady. And Gordon's heart jumped and began to pound. "I don't see how that could be possible, Captain. I know that you've been following the tactical evasion course required by security regulations, which means that you yourself have been improvising the coordinates at random intervals. How could anyone plan an ambush without knowing our course?"

"I could postulate a traitor," said Harn Horva, "but I think it highly unlikely. I would guess instead that telepaths are being used." His voice became even harsher. "Narath Teyn has the pick of them on his side."

He turned to Korkhann. "Sir, I would appreciate your assistance."

"You wish to know if there are indeed ships there," Korkhann said, and nodded. "As you say, Narath Teyn has the pick, and my race is not among them. Still, I'll do my best."

He moved a little apart and stood quietly, his yellow eyes going strange and unfocused. Everyone was silent, waiting. The generators throbbed and thundered.

Vagrant blips sparked and were gone on the hot-spot screens. Gordon's mouth was dry and his chest felt tight, and the rest of him was sweating.

At last Korkhann said, "There are ships. Narath Teyn's."

"What else?" asked Lianna. "What did you hear?"

"Minds. Human, nonhuman, a babble of minds on the edge of battle." His slim clawed fingers opened in a gesture of frustration. "I could not read them clearly, but I think . . . I think. Highness, they are waiting not to capture, but to kill."

-IV-

Instantly there was an outcry in the bridge room, of anger and shock. Harn Horva quelled it with one sharp order.

"Quiet! We have no time for that." He turned again to the screens and studied them, his body taut as a drawn bow. Gordon looked at Lianna. Whatever she felt inside, she was showing nothing to the men but cool self-possession. Gordon began really to be afraid.

"Can't you message Fomalhaut for help?" he asked.

"Too far away. They couldn't possibly get here in time, and in any case our friends ahead there in the drift would attack instantly if they intercepted such a message. Which of course they would."

Harn Horva straightened, the lines deep at the corners of his mouth. "I believe our only hope is to turn and run for it. With your permission, Highness . . ."

"No," said Lianna, unexpectedly.

Gordon stared at her. So did the captain. She smiled, briefly and without humor.

"There's no need to spare me, Harn Horva, though I thank you for the intent. I know as well as you do that we might outrun their ships, but not their missiles. And the moment we change course, showing that we're aware of the ambush, we'd have a cloud of missiles after us."

Harn Horva began talking fiercely about evasive action and missile-destroyer batteries, but Lianna was already beside the communications technician.

"I will speak to the Royal ComCenter at Fomalhaut. Make it a normal transmission."

"Highness!" said the Captain desperately. "They'll intercept."

"I want them to," said Lianna, and Gordon was struck by the look in her eyes. He started to speak but Korkhann forestalled him, his feathers ruffled with emotion.

"Your plan is a bold one, Highness, and sometimes boldness pays. But I urge you to think very carefully before you commit yourself."

"And all of you as well. I understand that, Korkhann. I have thought. And I can see no other way." Looking at them all, she explained. "I will message Fomalhaut that I am going on to visit my cousin Narath Teyn at Marral, for an important conference. Then I propose to do exactly that."

For a moment there was a stunned silence. Then Gordon said, "*What?*"

Lianna continued as though she had not heard him. "You see what this will do. If it's known that I'm heading for Marral, and anything happens to me on the way, my cousin would certainly get the blame. At the very least it would rouse enough feeling against him so that his hopes of succeeding me would be pretty well ruined. Which stalemates our friends there in the drift. Narath Teyn won't dare let me be killed under circumstances that would shatter all his plans."

"That's all very fine," said Gordon, "but what happens after you get there? You know the man wants to get rid of you, and you're putting yourself squarely in his hands." He was close to Lianna now, intent only on her and quite aware of the frozen stillness around him. "No. The captain's idea is better. The chance of escaping may be small but it *is* a chance. This way . . ."

Lianna's eyes were very wide, very cool, very gray. She smiled, a small curving of the mouth. "I thank you for your concern, John Gordon. I have considered all the objections, and this is my decision." She turned to the technician. "Fomalhaut, please."

The technician looked uneasily at Harn Horva, who made a helpless gesture and said, "Do as Her Highness wishes." Neither he nor anyone else appeared to notice the coloring of Gordon's face, which was first red and then white. In fact, it was as though Gordon had suddenly become invisible.

Gordon moved forward a step, without quite realizing it. Korkhann's fingers closed tightly on his arm, and then more tightly, the sharp talons digging just a little. Gordon stiffened and then forced himself to relax and stand easily. He watched the screens while Lianna made her transmission to Fomalhaut. Nothing happened. The dark drift ahead remained quiescent, concerned with its own cold and ancient affairs which had nothing to do with humanity. The thought crossed his mind that Korkhann might have invented the lurking ships and the death-wish.

"But see here," whispered Korkhann's voice beside him. The clawed fingers pointed to the hot-spot screens and the vagrant sparks that glittered there. "Each spark is a ship's generator. The drift moves. Nothing is ever still in space. As the drift moves, so must the ships, and there scanners can see where radar is as good as blind."

"Korkhann," said Gordon softly, "my friend, you make me just the least small bit nervous."

"You'll get used to it. And don't forget . . . I *am* your friend."

Lianna finished her message, spoke briefly to the captain, and left the bridge. Gordon followed with Korkhann. Once below, Lianna said pleasantly, "Will you excuse us, Korkhann?"

Korkhann bowed and strode away down the passage on his long thin legs. Lianna flung open the door of the lounge without waiting for Gordon to do it for her. When they were inside and the door closed again, she turned and faced him.

"You must never," she said, "question my judgment or interfere with my orders in public."

Gordon looked at her. "How about in private? Or are you ruler in the bedroom, too?"

Now it was her turn to redden. "It may be hard for you to understand. You come from a different age, a different culture."

"I do indeed. And I will tell you something. I will not give up my right to say what I think." She opened her mouth, and he raised his voice, not much, but there was a note in it that held her silent. "Furthermore, when I speak as a friend, as a man who loves you and is concerned only for your safety, I will not be publicly slapped in the face for it." His eyes were as steady as hers, and as hot. "I'm beginning to wonder, Lianna. Perhaps you'd do better with someone who isn't such a lout about protocol."

"Please try to understand! I have obligations above and beyond my personal feelings. I have a kingdom I must worry about."

"I do understand," Gordon said. "I once had an empire to worry about, remember? Good night."

He left her standing. Out in the passage, in spite of his anger, he could not help smiling. He wondered how many times she'd been walked out on. Not often enough, he thought.

He went along to his own cabin and lay awake wondering if her harebrained scheme would work, if they would be allowed to pass quietly on their way to Marral, wherever that might be. He half expected every minute to feel the impact of a missile that would blow the cruiser's fragments across half this sector of space. But time went by and nothing happened, and after a while he began to think about Lianna and what might lie ahead.

When he slept at last his dreams were disturbed and sad. In all of them he lost her, sometimes in the midst of a lurid darkness where strange shapes walked, and sometimes in a vast throne room where she walked away from him, and away, and away, gliding backwards with her face toward him and her eyes on his, the cool, remote eyes of a stranger.

The cruiser skirted the edge of the drift, altered course slightly to the southwest and continued on her way unmolested.

The next "day," arbitrarily so-called in the ship's log, Korkhann met Gordon in the captain's mess, where he was toying with a gloomy breakfast all alone, having purposely waited until Harn Horva and the other officers would be finished. Lianna always took her breakfast in her private suite.

"So far," said Korkhann, "the plan seems to be working."

"Sure," said Gordon. "The victim is walking right into a trap; why shoot her on the way?"

"It might be difficult for Narath Teyn to find a way to kill her on his own world without being accused of it."

"Do you think so?"

Korkhann shook his head. "No. Knowing Narath Teyn and his world, and his people, I don't think it will be difficult at all."

They were silent for a time. Then Gordon said, "I think you'd better tell me all you can."

They went into a lounge and Korkhann opened the map panel, where the tiny suns of Fomalhaut Kingdom glittered in the dark.

"Here along the southwestern borders of the kingdom is a sort of badland, of rogue stars and uninhabited, uninhabitable worlds, with here and there a solar system capable of supporting life, like Krens, from whence I come. The peoples of these scattered systems are, like myself, nonhuman." He pointed out a tawny-yellow star that burned like a smoky cairngorm on the dark breast of drift-cloud. "That star is Marral, and its planet Teyn is where Narath keeps his court."

Gordon frowned. "It seems a strange place for an heir to a throne."

"Until recently, he was only sixth in line. He was born at Teyn. Intrigue runs somewhat in the blood, you see. His father was banished for it, some years before Lianna was born."

"And what makes Narath Teyn so much more popular with the nonhumans than Lianna?"

"He has lived his life among them. He thinks like them. He is more of them, indeed, than I am. Nonhumans are of all sorts and kinds, John Gordon, children of many different stars, products of the evolutionary conditions decreed by the environments of our separate worlds. Many are so alien as to be quite unacceptable not only to humans but to other nonhumans as well. Narath loves them all. He is a strange man, and I think not entirely sane."

Korkhann closed the map panel gently and turned away, his plumage ruffling as it did when he was deeply disturbed.

"Lianna would have done well to listen to you," he said, "and protocol be damned. But she's too brave to be sensibly fearful, and too much her father's daughter to stand for threats. She's angry now, and determined to put a stop to her cousin's activities." He shook his head. "I think she may have waited too long."

Lianna gave him no chance to try and alter her decision. In the time that followed, while the tawny star grew from a distant spark to a flaming disc in the screens, she avoided being alone with him. He caught her looking at him with a curiously speculative expression once or twice, but apart from that her manner was correct and outwardly friendly. Only Gordon knew that between them now was a wall ten feet high. He did not try to climb it. Not yet.

The cruiser went into deceleration and landed on the second of five planets that circled Marral.

Teyn.

Narath's world.

The dust and the searing heat died away. In the bridge room Lianna stood with Harn Horva and Korkhann beside the visor screens that now scanned the area outside the ship. Gordon stood a little apart, trying to calm his jumping nerves.

"They did receive your message?" Lianna said.

"Yes, Highness. We have the acknowledgement on tape."

"I'm not doubting your word, Captain. It's just that it seems strange . . ."

It did seem strange, even to Gordon. The screens showed an empty land beyond the primitive and obviously little-used port with its shuttered building and cracked pads that could only accommodate a bare handful of ships. Away from the blast area there were open gladelike forests of very thin and graceful trees that were the color of ripe wheat and not unlike it in shape. The light was strange, a heavy gold that darkened to orange in the shadows. A breeze, unheard and unfelt, swayed the tall trees. Apart from that nothing moved.

Lianna's mouth was set but her voice was silken. "If my cousin is unable to come and greet me, then I must go and greet him. I will have the land-car, Captain, and the guard. At once."

The orders were given. Lianna came and stood before Gordon. "This is a state visit. You don't need to come with me."

"I wouldn't miss it," Gordon said, and added, "Highness."

A faint color touched her cheekbones. She nodded and went on and he went with her, down to the airlock to await the unloading of the car. Korkhann, beside him, gave him one bright oblique glance. Nothing more was said, and in a short time the car appeared.

The guard formed ranks around Lianna, and incidentally around Gordon and Korkhann. The airlock opened. The standard-bearer shook out the banner of the White Sun on the strange-scented wind and marched them down the ramp to the car, where he fixed the standard in its socket and stood stiffly at attention as Lianna climbed in.

The car was a longish vehicle, unobtrusively armored and equipped with concealed firing-ports. The guard was armed. All this should have made Gordon feel more at ease. It did not. There was something about the tall swaying trees, and the way the glades led the eye along their open innocence into sudden panic of confusion and honey-colored gloom. There was something about the air, its warmth like an animal's breath, and its smell of wildness. He did not trust this world. Even the sky offended him, closing him in with a shimmering metallic curve that was almost tangible, like the roof of a trap.

The land-car sped away along a rude and unpaved track, gentling the roughness to nothing with its airfoil cushion. The land glided past, the character of it changing swiftly from flat to rolling and then to hilly, with forests thinning on the rocky knolls. The shadows seemed to deepen, as though the planet tilted toward night.

Suddenly someone, the driver or the standard-bearer who sat beside him or one of the guards, gave a yell of alarm and all the weapons in the car clacked to the firing-ports, even before Gordon could see what had caused the outcry. Korkhann pointed to a long hillslope ahead.

"See over there, among the trees..."

There were things standing in the shadowed glades, a sinuous massing of shapes completely unidentifiable to Gordon's eyes. The men in the car had fallen silent. The soft thrumbling hiss of the airfoil jets sounded very loud in the quiet, and then from the slope there came one clear cry from a silvery horn, sweet and strange, running like fox fire along the nerves.

And at that moment the host swept toward them down the hillside.

– V –

Lianna's voice sounded close to Gordon, sharp and urgent. "Do not fire!"

Gordon was about to protest. Korkhann nudged him and whispered, "Wait."

The creatures poured in a lithe and sinuous flood along the slope, spreading out and around to encircle the car, their strange shapes still made indistinct by the barred shadowings of the trees. The air rang with cries, a hooting and shrilling from inhuman throats that seemed to Gordon to be full of triumph and cruel laughter. He strained his eyes. They were large creatures. They went on four feet, but softly, not like hoofed things, springing instead like great long-legged cats, and they appeared to carry riders. . . .

No. He could see some of them now quite clearly, burnished copper and ring-spotted and smoke-colored and glossy black, and his stomach gave a lurch. Not because they were hideous. They were not, and even in that moment of shock he was struck by their outlandish beauty. But they were to improbably strange. Animal and what he had taken for rider were, centaur-like, one flesh, as though a six-legged form of life had decided to walk at least partly upright, adapting head and torso and forelimbs to a shape almost human except for the angular slenderness. Their eyes were large, slanted and glowing, cat-eyes with keen intelligence behind them. Their mouths laughed, and they moved with the joy of strength and speed, their upper bodies bending like pliant reeds.

"The Gerrn," whispered Korkhann. "The dominant race of this planet."

They were all around the car now, which had slowed almost to a standstill. Gordon caught a glimpse of Lianna's profile, cut from white stone, looking straight ahead. The tension inside the car was rapidly becoming painful, tangible as the build-up of forces just before one small spark sets off the explosion.

He whispered to Korkhann, "Can you get from their minds what their intentions are?"

"No. They're telepaths too, and far more adept at it than I am. They can guard their minds totally. I couldn't even sense that they were there, before we saw them. And I think they're shielding someone else's mind as well . . . ah!"

Gordon saw then that one of the Gerrn did in fact carry a rider.

He was a young man, only a few years older than Lianna, and as light and lithe and spare as the Gerrn themselves. He was clad in a tight-fitting suit of golden russet and his brown hair fell long around his shoulders, wind-roughened and streaked by the sun. The silver horn that had sounded the one sweet cry was slung at his side. He clung to the back of a huge black-furred male, who bore him lightly to the forefront of the host. He lifted his arms and flung them wide, smiling, a handsome young man with eyes like sapphires, and his eyes seemed to Gordon to be more strange and fey than the cat-eyes of the Gerrn.

"Welcome!" he cried. "Welcome to Teyn, cousin Lianna!"

Lianna inclined her head. The tension ebbed. Men began to breathe again, and wipe their sweaty hands and faces. Narath Teyn raised the horn to his lips and sounded it again. The Gerrn host dissolved into fluid motion, sweeping the car along in its midst.

Two hours later, Teyn Hall blazed with light and skirled with music. The hall itself stood high on the slope of a river valley, a great sprawl of native stone and timber with many windows open on the night. Wide lawns ran down to the river bank and the Gerrn village that sheltered there among the trees. Above, the night sky dripped fire from the wild auroras born of proximity to the stellar drift, and in the shaking light strange shapes fled and gamboled across the lawns, or passed in and out through the open doors, or roosted on the broad sills of the windows. Incongruous and ill at ease, six of Lianna's guardsmen stood by the car and watched, and the radioman spoke at intervals into the mike.

Inside, fires burned on huge hearths at each end of the massive hall. Chandeliers poured light from the vaulted ceiling. The air was heavy with the smells of food and wine and smoke and the mingled company. There was only one table, and Gordon sat at it with Lianna and Narath Teyn and Korkhann, who was dignifiedly able to cope with a chair. Most of the guests who filled the hall preferred the rich rugs and cushions on the floor.

In a cleared space in the center of the hall three hunched and hairy shapes made music, with a panpipe of sorts and a flat-voiced drum, while two bright red creatures with more arms and legs than anyone needed swayed around each other with mannered grace, their gestures as stylized as Kabuki dancers, their long faces and many-faceted eyes resembling red-lacquered masks. The drumbeat picked up; the pipes shrilled higher. The scarlet legs and arms moved faster and faster. The dancers swirled and swayed hypnotically, dissolving into a blur before Gordon's eyes. The heat was terrific, the dry fauve smell of the packed nonhuman bodies almost terrifying.

Narath Teyn leaned over and spoke to Lianna. Gordon could not hear what he said, but he heard Lianna's retort.

"I've come here for an understanding, cousin, and I mean to have it. All this is by the way."

Narath Teyn bowed his head, all grace and mockery. He was dressed now in green, his long hair smoothed and held with a golden circlet. His dancers reached an impossible climax, followed by an abrupt and stunning cessation of both movement and music. Narath Teyn rose, holding out flagons of wine. He shouted something in a hissing, clacking sing-song and the scarlet ones answered and came scuttering toward him, to accept their flagons with a bow. A storm of noise bust out as the guests applauded in their several ways.

Underneath the racket Gordon spoke to Korkhann. "Where does he get his ships?" he asked. "And his men?"

"There is a town and a spaceport on the other side of this world. There is much trade between these wild systems and he controls it all. In his own way he is rich and powerful. Also he . . ."

The noise in the hall died away as another sound intruded; the long whistling far-off roar of a space cruiser dropping toward a landing. Gordon saw Lianna stiffen, and his own nerves snapped even tighter.

"Well," said Narath Teyn, glancing skyward with innocent amazement, "it seems that more guests are on their way. Always a flood after a long drought!"

He dropped into a guttural tongue and pounded on the table, laughing, and the big black-furred Gerrn who had carried him sprang into the open space deserted by the dancers. He had been introduced to Gordon as Sserk, chief of the local clan of Gerrn and second under Narath Teyn. He moved around the circle now in a ritual movement, slowly, lifting each lion-clawed foot in turn. His hands were crossed above his head and each one held a knife. The rhythm of his movement was picked up by the voices of the Gerrn, becoming a sort of yowling chant that ended every so often in a deep grunted *ough!*, only to begin again when Sserk resumed his pacing. Narath Teyn, looking flushed and pleased, spoke again to Lianna.

"Also," whispered Korkhann dryly, "as I was about to say, I suspect that he has allies."

Gordon swore very quietly under his breath. "Can't you read anything in his mind?"

"The Gerrn guard him. All I can read is satisfaction, and that you may see for yourself, in his face. I'm afraid we're in for . . ."

A harsh scream cut across the chanting and a second Gerrn, a young male with spotted flanks and very powerful haunches, leaped into the circle and began a prancing counter movement, holding his two knives high. His eyes were fixed on Sserk, drunken amber, wide and shining.

The chanting took on a deeper note. Elsewhere in the room it grew quiet. Grotesque heads craned forward, strange limbs shifted and were still. The two Gerrn circled, balancing. The servitors, mostly young females of the tribe with the baby fur still fluffy on them, stopped running about and stood watching.

Sserk sprang. The knives flashed, were caught and parried, and instantly Sserk's rump dropped and his forepaws rose, one feinting with quick strokes while the other lashed. The spotted male spun lightly out of reach and reared up himself, his knives darting and clashing as Sserk parried in his turn, then leaped clear of the raking claw. They began to circle again, stamping softly, their haunches quivering.

Only Narath Teyn was not watching the fencers Gordon saw. He was waiting for something or someone and his strange fey eyes were bright with a secret triumph. Lianna sat as proud and undisturbed as though she were in her own hall at Fomalhaut, and Gordon wondered if underneath that calm she was as frightened as he.

The duel went on, it seemed, interminably. The clever hands, the murderous swift paws, the sinuous bodies darting, bounding high. The eyes alight with the pleasure of battle that was not quite to the death. After a while there was blood, and a while after that there was a lot more of it, so that the spectators close to the circle were spattered with it, and the chanting became more of a simple animal howling. In spite of himself, and ashamed of it, Gordon felt the ancient cruel excitement rise in him, found himself leaning over the table and grunting with the blows. In the end the spotted male flung down his knives and took his torn flanks dripping to the door and out of it as fast as he could go, while Sserk screamed victory and the Gerrn crowded around him with wine and praise and cloths to stop his wounds. Gordon, feeling a little sick now that the excitement was past, was reaching for his own winecup when he felt Korkhann touch him.

"Look, in the doorway..."

A tall man stood there, clad in black leather with the symbol of a jewelled mace aglitter on his breast, and a cap of black steel with a plume in it, and a cloak of somber purple to sweep to his heels.

There was someone, or something, behind him.

Gordon caught Lianna's sharp intake of breath, and then Narath Teyn sprung up and was pounding for silence, shouting a welcome to the newcome guest.

"Cyn Cryver, Count of the Marches of Outer Space! Welcome!"

The count strode into Teyn Hall and the Gerrn made way for him respectfully. And now Gordon saw that the count's companion was dressed in a cowled robe of shimmering gray that covered him, or it, completely from head to foot. The form beneath the flowing cloth seemed to be oddly stunted, and it moved with a fluid gliding motion that Gordon found distinctly unpleasant.

The count removed his cap and bent over Lianna's hand. "A most fortunate coincidence, Lady! Fortunate for me, at least. I hope you'll forgive me for choosing the same time you chose to visit your cousin."

Lianna said sweetly, "The ways of coincidence are indeed marvelous. Who shall question them?" She withdrew her hand. "Who is your companion?"

The cowled creature bobbed politely and made a thin hissing sound, then glided away to a relatively quiet corner behind the table. Cyn Cryver smiled and looked at Korkhann.

"One of the Empire's more remote allies, Lady, who out of courtesy keeps himself veiled. He occupies with me much the same position as does your minister, Korkhann, with you."

He acknowledged introduction to Gordon and sat down. The feasting went on. Gordon noticed that Korkhann seemed tense and distracted, his fingers opening and closing spasmodically around his wine-cup. The air grew hotter and noisier. In the cleared space two young Gerrn, without knives, began to circle and prance, batting at each other only half playfully. At the far end of the hall a fight broke out between two members of different species and was promptly smothered. The pipers and drummers were at it again, and a ragged-looking creature with leathery wings flapped up on to the carved balustrade of the great stair and began a rhythmic screaming that might have been song. Yet underneath all this Gordon seemed to sense an uneasiness, as though a shadow had crept across the festivities. Sserk and some of the other mature Gerrn appeared to have lost their desire for drink and jollity. One by one they began to withdraw, melting away unobtrusively through the unruly crowd.

Gordon wondered if they, like himself, felt the presence of the cowled stranger as a breath of cold wind along the spine. The corner where the creature squatted was now otherwise deserted, and the area seemed to be widening. Gordon shivered, unable to rid himself of the feeling that the damned thing was staring straight at him from behind its blank gray draperies.

Out in the circle one of the young Gerrn clipped his opponent too enthusiastically, bringing blood, and in a moment the claws and fur were flying in earnest. Lianna rose.

"I will leave you to your pleasures, cousin," she said icily. "Tomorrow we will talk."

Grabbing at the chance to escape, Gordon was at her elbow before she had finished speaking. But Narath Teyn insisted on escorting her, so that Gordon had no choice but to trail them up the great staircase, with Korkhann stalking beside him. The noise from the hall below diminished as they walked down the vaulted corridor.

"I'm sorry if my friends offended you, cousin Lianna. I forget, having lived with them all my life, that others may not. . ."

"Your friends don't offend me at all," said Lianna, "if you mean the nonhumans. You offend me. Cyn Cryver offends me."

"But, cousin. . !"

"You're a fool, Narath Teyn. And you're playing for stakes far beyond your capacity. You should have stayed content here in your forests with your Gerrn."

Gordon saw Narath Teyn's face tighten. The fey eyes shot lightning. But his composure never wavered. "It is well known that a crown conveys all wisdom to its wearer. I shall not argue."

"Your mockery seems ill-placed, cousin, since you are willing to do murder for that crown."

Narath Teyn stared at her, startled. He did not deny, nor did she give him a chance to. She pointed to the other half of her twelve guardsmen, who were posted outside her door.

"I would advise you to explain to Cyn Cryver, in case he does not understand, that I am well guarded by loyal men who cannot be drugged, bribed, or frightened from their posts. They can be killed, but in that case you must also kill their comrades below, who keep in constant touch with my cruiser. If that contact is broken, Fomalhaut will be instantly notified, and a force will come at once from the cruiser. Cyn Cryver might use his forces to stop it, but neither you nor he could gain anything by that but ultimate destruction."

Narath Teyn said, in a queer husky voice, "Have no fear, Lady."

"I have none," she said. "I bid you good night." She swept into her apartment and the guard closed the door behind her. Narath Teyn gave Gordon and Korkhann a blank glare and then turned and strode away down the corridor.

Korkhann took Gordon's arm and they walked on toward their own quarters. Gordon started to speak and Korkhann stopped him. He seemed to be listening. His urgency communicated itself to Gordon and he made no protest when Korkhann urged him on past their own doors, on faster and faster toward the far end of the corridor where it was deserted and quiet and almost dark, and there was a back stairway, winding down.

Korkhann pushed him to it with a strange desperation.

"For the moment we're not being watched. I must get down to the car, get word to Harn Horva . . ."

Gordon hesitated, his heart thundering now with alarm. "What . . ?"

"I understand now," Korkhann said. "They don't plan to kill Lianna." His yellow eyes were full of horror. "They plan something far worse!"

– VI –

Gordon started back. "I'm going to get her out of here."

"No!" Korkhann held him. "She's being watched, Gordon. There are Gerrn hidden in the room next to hers. They'd give the alarm at once. We'd never get out of the building."

"But the guards . . !"

"Gordon, listen. There is a force here that the guards can't fight. The gray stranger who came with the count . . . I tried to touch its mind and was thrown back by a shock that half stunned me. But the Gerrn are stronger. Some of them got through, a little way at least. I know, because they were so shaken that they dropped their own guard. Did you see how Sserk and the others left? They're afraid, sick-afraid of that creature, and the Gerrn are not a timid folk." He was speaking so rapidly and in such desperation that Gordon had difficulty understanding him. "Sserk looked at Lianna. As I say, his own mind was unguarded, for the moment. He was seeing her as a mindless, blasted doll, and feeling horrified, and wishing she had not come."

Now Gordon felt a cold sickness in himself. "You mean that thing has the power to . . ."

"It's like nothing I've ever felt before. I don't know what that being is or where it comes from, but its mind is more deadly than all our weapons." He started down the stairs. "Their plan still depends on secrecy. If Harn

Horva knows, and sends word to Fomalhaut, they wouldn't dare go through with it."

Probably not, Gordon thought. But Harn Horva could do more than send word to Fomalhaut. He could send men and guns, too many for even the gray stranger to handle all at once. There was a 'copter in the cruiser's hold. Help could be here in no more than thirty minutes, perhaps less. He flung himself after Korkhann.

The stairway led them winding down to a stone passage and a small door. They went through it with the sounds of revelry dim in their ears, into the warm night behind Teyn Hall, and then they ran, keeping close in the shadows. When they reached the front corner they stopped and looked cautiously around it.

The front of Teyn Hall still blazed with light, and merrymakers still swarmed in and out of the open door, though they seemed fewer now. The ground-car stood exactly as before, with six guards around it and the driver and radioman visible inside.

Gordon started forward.

Korkhann pulled him back. "It's too late. Their minds . . ."

In the instant Gordon lingered he saw what might have been the flicker of a gray robe gliding past a group of Germ and back into the hall. Then inside the car the radioman leaned forward and spoke into the mike.

"Look there," said Gordon, "they're all right, he's keeping the contact." He pulled free and ran toward the car.

He had taken perhaps five full steps when one of the guards saw him, and turned, and raised his weapon, and Gordon saw his face clearly in the window-light. He saw the others turning one by one. He set his heels in the grass and fled, back to the shelter of the corner. The guards lowered their weapons and resumed their posts, watching with glassy and uncaring eyes the shapes that leaped and scurried across the lawns and through the groves of trees.

"Next time," Korkhann said, "listen to me."

"But the radioman . . !"

"Contact will be carried on as before. Do you suppose the Gray One can't manage so simple a thing as that?" They retreated along the dark back wall. Korkhann beat his hands together softly, in anguish. "There's no hope now of getting word through. But we must do something, and quickly."

Gordon looked up at the high windows, where Lianna was. Where perhaps the gray stranger was already bobbling up the great staircase to the corridor, to strike the minds of Lianna's guards into passive jelly. Where the Gerrn lay hidden in dark rooms, watching the prey.

The Gerrn.

Suddenly Gordon turned and ran away across the wide lawns that sloped to the river and the groves of trees and the odd round roofs of the Gerrn village. Korkhann ran beside him and for once Gordon was thankful for telepathy. He did not have to waste time explaining.

They went in among the trees, into alternate shadow and bursts of shaking light from the aurora, amid intimate unfamiliar sounds of a village going about its affairs. And then there was a gathering of half-seen forms around them, the menacing soft tread of great paws. In the fire-shot gloom above him Gordon could see the narrow heads looking down at him, cat-eyes eerily catching the light.

He was fleetingly astonished to realize that he was not in the least afraid. There was no longer any time for that. He said to the Gerrn, "My mind is open to you, whether you understand my words or not. I come to see Sserk."

There was a rustling and stirring among them. A black shape drifted to the fore and a slurred harsh voice said,

"Both your minds are open to me. I know what it is you want, but I can't help you. Turn back."

"No," said Gordon "For the love you bear Narath Teyn, you will help us. Not for us, not for the Princess Lianna, but for his sake. You have touched the mind of the gray stranger . . ."

The Gerrn stirred uneasily, growling. And Korkhann said suddenly, "Cyn Cryver and the Gray One. Who truly leads, and who follows?"

"The Gray One leads," said Sserk grudgingly, "and the count follows, though he does not know it yet."

"And if Narath Teyn is king at Fomalhaut, who will lead then?"

Sserk's eyes glowed briefly in the aurora light. But he shook his head. "I can't help you."

"Sserk," said Gordon. "How long will they let Narath Teyn rule—the Gray One and Cyn Cryver and whoever is behind them? Narath Teyn wants power for the non-humans, but what do they want?"

"I could not see that far," said Sserk, very softly, "but whatever it is, it is not for us."

"Nor for Narath Teyn. They need him now because he's the legitimate heir, if the princess dies or is rendered unfit. But you know what will happen to him in the end. *You know*, Sserk."

He could feel now that Sserk was trembling. He said, "If you love him, save him." And he added, "You know that he's not altogether sane."

"But he loves us," said Sserk fiercely, and his great paw rose as though to strike Gordon. "He belongs to us."

"Then keep him here. Otherwise, he is lost."

Sserk was silent. The breeze rustled in the tall trees, and the Gerrn swayed where they stood, uneasy and disturbed. Gordon waited, his mind strangely still, occupied distantly with the last resort. If the Gerrn refused, he would find a weapon and try his best to kill the gray stranger.

"You would not live to press the firing stud," said Sserk. "Very well. For his sake . . . For his sake, we'll help."

Sweat broke out on Gordon. His knees turned weak. "Then hurry," he said, and turned to run. "We must get her out before . . ."

The Gerrn blocked his way. "Not you," Sserk said. "Stay here, where we can guard your minds, as we've done since you came." Gordon started to protest, and Sserk grabbed him roughly, shook him as an impatient father might shake a child. "Our people watch her. We may get her out, you can't. If you go back you'll give us all away and all will be lost."

"He's right," Korkhann said. "Let them go, Gordon."

They went, four of them with Sserk at their head, and Gordon watched them bitterly as they raced away along the slope of the lawn. The other Gerrn close around them, and Korkhann said, "They'll try to shield our minds. You can help them by thinking of other things."

Other things. What other things were there in the world that mattered? Still, Gordon did his best, and the minutes trickled by with the beads of icy sweat that ran on him, and suddenly there was an outcry, rather faint and confused, from Teyn Hall and then a crackle of shots. Gordon started wildly, felt the same shock run through the Gerrn, and a moment later Sserk came plunging in among the trees. He bore a struggling figure in his arms. Behind him came only three of his companions, and one of them lurched aside and sank to the ground.

"Here," Sserk said, and thrust Lianna into Gordon's arms "She does not understand. Make her, quickly, or we all die."

She fought him. "Are you behind this, John Gordon? They came through a secret door, pulled me out of bed . . ." She strained against his hands, her body warm and angry in a thin nightdress. "How dare you presume to . . ."

He slapped her, not quite dispassionately. "You can have me shot later if you want to, but right now you'll do as I tell you. Your mind depends on it, your sa . . ."

It hit him then, a hammer stroke that stunned his mind and rocked it quivering toward the edge of a dark precipice. Lianna's stricken face faded before his eyes. Someone, Korkhann he thought, let out a strangled cry and there was a deep groaning among the Gerrn. Gordon had a dim sense of forces beyond his understanding locked in terrible stuggle, and then the darkness lifted somewhat. He heard Sserk crying, "Come, quickly!"

Gerrn hands pawed and plucked at him, urging. He helped swing Lianna up onto Sserk's back, and was half lifted himself onto the furred lean withers of another big male. The village seemed to have exploded into panic. Females with their young were running wildy about. Sserk sprang away through the trees with eight or ten of the older males following. Gordon hung on with difficulty as his mount fled through belts of forest, lunging and scrambling up and down the steep places. He saw Korkhann borne more lightly on the back of another Gerrn and ahead Lianna's nightdress fluttered in the wind of Sserk's going. Overhead the aurora flamed, scarlet pink and ice green and angelic white, remote and beautiful.

Behind them there was noise and commotion, and there was something else as well. Fear. Gordon's inner being crouched and cringed, awaiting a second blow. He could picture the gray stranger, moving with that queer stunted agility, the cowled robe fluttering. . . .

And it came again. The hammer stroke. It was bearable to Gordon, but he saw Lianna reel and almost fall as the Gerrn closed around her. This time the bolt had been discharged directly at her.

Then, more quickly than before, the force weakened and fell away.

"Thank the gods," said Korkhann hoarsely, "the thing does have its limitations. The power weakens with distance."

Sserk said, "But our minds lose strength also, from weariness."

He ran faster, bounding through the glades with the girl clinging tightly to his shoulders. The others quickened their pace to match his, their bodies stretching. Yet it seemed to Gordon that they were crawling, through endless miles of golden woodland under the burning sky.

All at once he said, "Listen."

There was a new sound, far away, a soft rushing noise as though a wind blew through the trees.

Korkhann said, "Yes, the ground-car. The Gray One follows."

The Gerrn sped faster, circling farther from the roadway. But they could not lose the rushing whisper that came relentlessly closer. And Gordon knew without need of telepathy that the Gerrn were afraid, already flinching from the next blow before it fell.

A last scrambling of clawed feet up a slope and the edge of the forest was there. The shuttered building of the port, the long slim shapes of the two cruisers, one blazoned with the White Sun, the other with the Mace, stood silent in the shaking glare of the aurora. Both ships had their ports open and lighted. Gordon slid to the ground, catching Lianna as she half fell from Sserk's back.

"The Gray One is close," said the Gerrn, his flanks heaving.

Gordon could no longer hear the air-jets. The car had stopped somewhere short of the cleared space. The hair on his own neck bristled. "We're grateful," he said to the Gerrn. "The princess will not forget."

He tightened his arm around Lianna and turned with her to run. Behind him he heard Sserk's voice, saying, "What we have done, we have done. So be it." And then Korkham cried out, "Don't leave us now, or you'll have done it for nothing. I can't protect her all alone."

Gordon fled with Lianna across the cracked concrete apron, his whole mind and soul fixed on the light of the open port. He heard Korkhann's lighter footfalls pattering behind him. For a moment he thought that after all the Gray One had given up and that nothing was going to happen. And with a silent thunderclap the darkness came and beat him down floundering to his knees.

Lianna slipped away from him. He groped for her by sheer instinct, hearing her whimper. He fought, blind and squirming, across vast heaving blacknesses toward a far-off spark of light.

There were hands and voices. The spark brightened, growing dizzily. Gordon surfaced through cold ringing dimensions of dread; saw faces, uniforms, men, saw Lianna upheld in Harn Horva's arms, felt himself lifted and carried forward. Far off there was a whistling rush as of a balked and angry wind retreating. And two men carried Korkhann past him, half-conscious.

Harn Horva's voice roared out above all, "Prepare for take-off!"

Gordon was only partly aware of the clanging hatches, the warning hooters and the roaring thrust of the launch. He was in the lounge and Lianna was clinging to him, trembling like a frightened child, her face bloodless and her eyes wide.

Later, after the cruiser had leaped up into the sky and Teyn was dropping fast behind them, Gordon still held and soothed her. By then, Korkhann had come back to consciousness. His eyes were haunted but he said, with a kind of haggard pride,

"For a moment . . . for a moment I did it, all alone!"

"Korkhann, who . . . what . . . was it?" said Gordon. "The Gray One."

"I think," whispered Korkhann, "that it was not of this universe. I think an ancient evil has awakened. I . . ."

He bent his head, and for a moment would say no more. Then he said somberly, "If Narath Teyn has allies such as that, he is far more dangerous than we thought, Highness."

"I know that now," said Lianna. "We'll hold council of war when we reach Fomalhaut. And I think that on our decision, my kingdom will stand or fall."

-VII-

Outside, in the light of the flying moons, the old kings of Fomalhaut stood and dreamed in stone. All the way from the far-flung lights of the city up to this massive palace the great avenue of statues ran, eleven dynasties and more than one hundred kings, all towering up much larger than life so that the envoys who came this way would feel a sense of awe. No one came at this hour, all was silent, but in the changing light of the racing moons, the stone faces seemed to change, to smile, to glare, to brood.

In the vast darkness of the throne hall, looking out at that mighty avenue, John Gordon felt small and insignificant. From the shadowed walls other pictured faces looked down at him, the faces of further great ones in the long history of Fomalhaut Kingdom, and it seemed to him that that there was contempt in their glance.

Man of Earth, man of the old twentieth century that is now two hundred thousand years ago . . . what do you here out of your own place and time?

What indeed? And again that question came to plague him . . . reality or dream? With the question came fear, and the overwhelming desire to run for the security of Keogh's office and the calm voice explaining away all his problems. He felt a passionate homesickness for the old drab familiar world in which he had spent most of his life, and a terrifying sense of alienation took him by the throat.

He fought it, as he had had to fight it before. Sweat was on his forehead and his whole body trembled. At the same time he could jeer at himself savagely. *All the while you were in that nice familiar world, you did nothing but whine and cry to get back here.*

He was not aware that Korkhann had come into the hall, and started violently at the sound of his voice.

"It is strange, Gordon, that you tremble now, when there is no danger . . . at least for the present."

Korkhann was so vague in the shadows that he might have been human. Then his feathers rustled and his beaked face and wise eyes pushed forward into a bar of the shifting moonlight. It was hard to be angry with Korkhann, but Gordon managed it.

"I've asked you before not to read my mind."

"You do not yet understand telepathic powers," Korkhann said mildly. "I have not violated your mental privacy. But I cannot help receiving your emotions." After a moment he added, "I am to bring you to the council. Lianna sent me."

The black mood was still on Gordon, and Lianna's name brought a fresh surge of anger. "What does Lianna need of me?" After that moment of closeness, when she had been a frightened girl he could hold in his arms, she had become again the princess, remote, aloof, beautiful, and very busy with affairs of state. She seemed, in fact, to be deliberately avoiding him, as though she were ashamed of that lapse and did not wish to be reminded of it. And after all, damn it, he was still the stranger, still the primitive lout.

"In some ways," said Korkhann, this time shamelessly reading his thoughts, "you are. Lianna is a woman but she is also a reigning princess, and you must remember that your relationship is as difficult for her as it is for you."

"Oh, hell," said Gordon. "Now I get advice to the lovelorn from a . . . a . . ."

"From an overgrown myna bird?" said Korkhann. "I assume that is some creature of your own world. Well. The advice is still good."

"I'm sorry," said Gordon, and meant it. He was behaving like a petty child. He took a deep breath and straightened his shoulders. "It's just that every once in a while . . ."

"You feel lost. This is natural. You have chosen a very strange road, John Gordon. It will never be an easy one. But you knew that. Now . . . will you come?"

"Yes," said Gordon. "I'll come."

They left the vast echoing hall and went along spacious corridors. It was late and there were few people about, but Gordon had a feeling that there was tension in the silence that enwrapped the palace, a brooding sense of danger. He knew that that was in his own mind, the danger was not here, not yet. It was still in the Marches of Outer Space, the far frontier of the galaxy. Yet the fact that the council of Fomalhaut Kingdom was meeting this late at night, only hours after the cruiser had landed on the throne-world, was evidence enough of how gravely that danger was regarded.

In the small paneled room they came to, four faces looked up at Gordon with expressions between irritation and hostility. Korkhann was the oly nonhuman member of the council, and Lianna, at the head of the little table, nodded to Gordon and spoke the names of the four men.

"Is this necessary?" asked the youngest of them, a middle-aged man with burly brows. He added bluntly, "We've heard of your attachment to this Earthman, Highness, but I fail to see why . . ."

"I'm afraid," said Gordon pleasantly, "that I also fail to see why. Nevertheless, I was sent for."

Lianna said quickly, "It is necessary, Abro. Sit down, John Gordon."

He sat down at the far end of the table and bristled

inwardly until Korkhann whispered, "Must you be so fighting?" That startled Gordon into a brief smile, and he relaxed a little.

The man called Abro spoke, ignoring Gordon in a way that was a studied insult.

"It stands thus. The attempt that Narath Teyn made against you, his daring to use force against the sovereign of Fomalhaut, shows that he's dangerous. I say, hit him. Send a squadron of heavy cruisers to Teyn to teach him and his Gerrns a lesson."

Inwardly, Gordon rather agreed. Anyone who would call in an ally like the Gray One deserved destruction. But Lianna shook her pale-golden head slowly.

"My cousin Narath is not the danger. He has long conspired to replace me, but with only his wild, barbaric nonhumans to call on he could do nothing. But now, he is simply being used as a pawn by others . . . among them, Cyn Cryver, a count of the Marches of Outer Space."

"Hit the Marches, then," said Abro harshly.

Gordon began to like this blunt, tough character who had given him such a hostile greeting. But Korkhann spoke, in his hesitant, whistling voice.

"There is something hidden here, some veiled, unknown forces working behind Cyn Cryver and Narath Teyn. One such was at Teyn and would have destroyed us if the Gerrn had not changed sides. Who or what the creature was we could not tell, but it is powerful beyond belief . . . and is the true leader. Cyn Cryver is also a pawn."

"Use force against Cyn Cryver and we'll find out who or what is behind him," said one of the other councillors. "Abro is right."

"I think you are forgetting something," said Lianna. "The counts are allies of the Empire."

"So are we," said Abro, "and better and more dependable allies!"

Lianna nodded. "I agree. But all the same, we can't go

into the Marches without first taking the matter up with Throon."

They didn't like it, Gordon saw that. Like most of the citizens of the smaller star-kingdoms they had an inordinate amount of pride, and asking anyone's permission went against their grain. But all the same, the Empire was the Empire, the greatest single power in the galaxy, ruling an inconceivable vastness of suns and worlds and people from the imperial world that circled the mighty sun Canopus. Like it or not, they would ask.

Lianna succeeded in silencing them for the moment. She added, "I'm sending Korkhann to discuss it with them. John Gordon will go with him."

Gordon's heart gave a great beat of excitement. To Throon! He would see it again . . .

An angry protest had already formed on Abro's lips, but it was Hastus Nor, oldest of the councillors, who voiced the objection. He looked down the table at Gordon and then turned to Lianna.

He said, "It is no concern of ours if you have favorites, Highness. But it *is* our concern if you let them meddle in statecraft. No."

Lianna stood up, her eyes blazing. The old man did not flinch from her anger. But before she could speak, Korkhann interrupted so smoothly and swiftly that it hardly seemed like an interruption at all.

"With you permission, Highness, I would like to answer that," he said. He looked around the hostile quartet of faces. "You all know, I think, that I have certain powers and that I have not often been wrong in stating a fact."

"Get to it, Korkhann," growled the old councillor.

"Very well." Korkhann's wing unfolded and his clawed hand rested on Gordon's shoulder. "I will say this, as a fact. No one . . . I say, *no one,* in the whole galaxy, would have as much influence in the councils of the Empire than this Earthman, John Gordon."

Gordon looked up at him, astounded. "So you *have* been mind-reading?" he muttered. "Or did she tell you . . ."

Korkhann ignored him, and looked steadily at the councillors. In their faces, hostility faded into puzzlement.

"But why . . . how?" demanded Abro.

Korkhann did the odd shrugging movement that made his feathers ruffle as in a wind.

"I have given you the fact. I will not explain."

They stared, frowning and curious, at Gordon, until he was sorely tempted to shout at them, "*Because for a time I was your emperor!*" But he did not, and finally old Hastus Nor rumbled, "If Korkhann says so, it must be true, even though . . ." He stopped, then went on decisively. "Let the man Gordon go."

Gordon said softly, "Thank you. But has anyone asked me whether I *want* to go?"

He was mad clear through at being treated like a pawn, being argued over and challenged and defended, and he would have gone on to say so, but Lianna spoke very firmly.

"Gentlemen, the council is ended."

They went out with no more said, and when they had gone, Lianna came toward Gordon.

"Why did you say that?" she asked. "You want to go."

"Why should I?"

"Don't lie," she said. "I saw the eagerness in your face when it was suggested that you go to Throon."

She looked at him, and he saw the pain and doubt in her clear eyes.

"For a little while, after death had just passed us by at Teyn, I thought we had come closer," she said. "I thought it would be as it had been before with us . . ."

"So did I."

"But I was wrong. It's not I you care about."

"That," said Gordon angrily, "is a fine thing to say to a man who risked his life to get here to you. All I know is, you treat me like a . . ."

She did not let him finish. "Did you risk your life to reach *me*, John Gordon? Was it I you remembered and longed for, back in that distant age of yours, or was it the adventure, the star-ships, all that our age has that yours had not, that you really longed to return to?"

There was just enough truth in the accusation to take the anger out of Gordon, and the moment of half-guilt he felt must have shown on his face, for Lianna, looking up at him, smiled a white and bitter smile.

"I thought so," she said, and turned away. "Go to Throon, then, and be damned."

-VIII-

All the way to Canopus, Gordon spent his waking time in the bridge of the fast scout. Through the windows that were not really windows, he watched the star-groups rise up and change and fall behind. After the arid years on little Earth, he could not get enough of stars.

The titanic jumble of suns that was Hercules Cluster, the seat of power of those mighty barons who looked on star-kings as mere equals, dropped past them to the west. The vast mass of faintly glowing drift that was known as the Deneb Shoals, they skirted. They plunged on and now they were passing through the space where, that other time, the space-fleets of the Empire and its allies had fought out their final Armageddon with the League of the Dark Worlds.

Gordon looked and dreamed. Far, far off southward lay the sprawling blotch of deeper darkness that was the Cloud, from which the armadas of the Dark Worlds had poured in their prideful menace. He remembered Thallarna and he remembered Shorr Kan, the master of the League, and how he had surrendered to defeat.

"You think too much of past things and not enough of the present ones," said Korkhann, watching him shrewdly.

Gordon smiled. "If you know as much about me as I think you know, can you blame me? I was an impostor. I hardly knew what I was doing in that battle, but I was *there*, and who could forget that?"

"Power is a heady wine," said Korkhann. "You had it once, the power of a universe in your hand. Do you long for it again?"

"No," said Gordon, startled by the echo of Lianna's accusation. "I was scared to death of it when I had it."

"Were you, John Gordon?"

Before Gordon could frame an irritated answer to that, Korkhann had gone away from the bridge.

His irritation faded and was forgotten as, in the time that followed, the heart-worlds of the mighty Mid-Galactic Empire brightened far ahead.

The stunning blue-white flare of Canopus was arrogant in its hugeness and intensity. And as the scout rushed on, there came into view the planets that circled that truly royal sun. Gordon's eyes clung to one of those planets, a gray, cloud-wrapped sphere. Throon . . .

He was remembering how he had first seen it, amazed and bewildered by this future universe, playing a part for which he had no preparation, a pawn in the hands of cosmic political powers whose purposes he could not dream.

Was he anything more than right now? Wasn't he brought here to Throon so that Korkhann might exploit his supposed influence with Jhal Arn, sovereign of the Empire? Yes, he thought, it's true. But it's not just for Fomalhaut policies, it's for Lianna and against whatever mysterious, menacing things was hatching out in the Marches that threatened her most immediately.

The planet rose up to meet him, its gray-green bulk immense, the sprawling continents starred with glittering metropoli that flared in the white sunlight. Then a mighty ocean, and then, far head, what his gaze leaped to meet, the dazzling radiance that almost blinded the eye, the Glass Mountains of smooth silicates flinging back the sunset light in shaking spears and fans and banners of glory. They went over that radiance, through it, and ahead of them there loomed the cluster of airylike glass towers that was the greatest capital of the galaxy.

Over its starport, the traffic was of tremendous volume. Gordon had forgotten how many ships came and went to this center of the Empire. Clocked smoothly in by the director-computers, the bulky arrogant lines from Deneb and Aldebaran and Sol came down to the inport like a parade of giants, while the smaller craft poured like a cataract of shining midges. But their own craft, being official, skirted all this and descended toward the naval port, where the giant warships of the Empire loomed like dark thunderclouds above their docks.

An hour later, they stood in the huge building that was the seat of dynasty and the administrative center of the Empire.

Zarth Arn came to meet them, a tall figure, his dark face breaking into a smile and then becoming serious as he took Gordon's hand.

"I could wish your return to Throon had been on another occasion than this," he said. "Yes, my brother knows why you have come. You're not the first on this errand."

Korkhann asked quickly, "The others are worried about the Marches, Highness?"

Zarth Arn nodded. "They are. But that's to be talked of later. To hell with diplomacy, Gordon and I have some drinking to do!" He led Gordon to a smoothly gliding motowalk. It carried them on into another hall, a vast chamber whose glass walls were adorned with flattened reliefs of dark stars, burned-out cindery suns, ebon cosmic drift, and overpowering impression of gloom and majesty. Gordon remembered this somber magnificence, and he remembered also the equally splendid hall beyond it that seemed encompassed by the glow of a flaming nebula. The motowalk bore them upward on a smooth slant.

Everywhere, courtiers and chamberlains bowed deeply

to Zarth Arn. It seemed to Gordon that they looked a little askance at him, walking familiarly with a prince of the Empire.

"Does it seem strange to you?" he asked Zarth Arn. "To walk with me, knowing that once we inhabited each other's bodies?"

Zarth Arn smiled. "Not to me. You must remember that I crossed many times before, and dwelt in many other bodies on those occasions. But I suspect it is very strange to you, indeed."

They came to Zarth Arn's chambers, that Gordon so well remembered, high-ceilinged and austerely white except for their silken hangings. The racks of thought-spools still stood at one side of the room. He went to the tall open windows and out onto the balcony that was like a small terrace jutting from the side of the huge, oblong palace. He looked again across Throon City.

It might have been that other time all over again, he thought. For Canopus was setting, flinging a long, level radiance across the fairylike towers of the metropolis, and the heaving green ocean, and the Glass Mountains that now were a rampart of dazzling glory.

Gordon stared bemused, until Zarth Arn's voice woke him from the spell.

"Do you find it the same, Gordon?" he asked, handing him a tall glass of the brown liquor called *saqua*.

"Not quite," muttered Gordon.

Zarth Arn understood. "Lianna was here that other time, wasn't she? I hadn't meant to ask yet, but now . . . tell me, what of you two?"

"We haven't quite quarreled," Gordon answered. "But we seem to go on being strangers, and . . . she seems to think it wasn't for her I came, but for . . . this."

And his gesture took in the whole vista of the magnificence of the great city, the flashing radiance of the mountains, the majesty of the star-ships rising from the distant starport.

They were interrupted by the opening of the door. The man who entered was tall and stalwart, dressed in black with a small blazing insignia on his chest. His eyes were level and searching as he came toward Gordon.

Gordon knew him. Jhal Arn, the elder brother of Zarth Arn, and the sovereign of the Mid-Galactic Empire.

"It is strange," said Jhal Arn. "You know me, of course, from that other time. But I see you . . . the physical you . . . for the first time."

He held out his hand. "Zarth has told me that this was the gesture of greeting in your time. You are welcome in Throon, John Gordon. You are very welcome."

The words were quiet and without emphasis, but the handgrip was strong.

"But more of this later," said Jhal Arn. "You've brought a problem to Throon. And not you alone. We have important visitors from some of the Empire's strongest allies, and they too are troubled."

He went over and looked thoughtfully out at the city, whose lights were coming on as the sunset faded into dusk. Two moons shone out in the twilit sky, one of them warm golden and the other one ghostly silver in hue.

"A whisper has gone through the galaxy," said Jhal Arn. "A murmur, a breath, a sourceless rumor. And it says that in the Marches of Outer Space there is a mystery and a danger. Nothing more than that. But the very vagueness of it has disturbed some who are high in the star-kingdoms, while others scoff at it as mere fancy."

"It wasn't fancy that we encountered at Teyn," said Gordon. "Korkhann can tell you . . ."

"Korkhann has already told me," said Jhal Arn. "I sent for him, straight after you two arrived. And . . . I don't like what I heard."

He shook his head. "Later on, tonight, a decision will have to be taken. It is one that could shatter the

the political fabric of the galaxy. And yet we must make it, knowing so little . . ." He broke off, and turned to leave, and at the door he turned round and gave Gordon a crooked smile. "You sat in my place once, for a little while, John Gordon. I tell you that it is still a painful place."

When he had left, Zarth Arn said, "I'll take you to the suite assigned to you and Korkhann. I saw that it was close to this one. We have much to talk about."

He parted from Gordon at the door of the suite. Gordon went in, and was surprised by the luxury of the big room he entered. By comparison Zarth Arn's was spartan. But Zarth Arn had always been more the austere scholar-scientist than anything else.

He noticed the back of a feathered head above a metal chair, and saw that Korkhann sat by the open window looking out at the flashing panorama of lights, the brilliant lights of Throon City and the distant lights of great star-liners coming down across the star-decked sky.

Gordon walked toward the window and around the chair, saying, "I don't like what I've been hearing, Korkhann. I . . ."

Then Gordon stopped, and suddenly he shouted.

"*Korkhann!*"

The feathered one sat in unnatural immobility. And his face, the beaked face and wise yellow eyes that Gordon had first tolerated and then come to like, was strangely stony. The eyes were as opaque as cold yellow jewels, and they had not the faintest flicker of expression in them.

Gordon gripped Korkhann with his hands, feeling the astonishing slightness and fragility of the body beneath the feathers.

"Korkhann, what's happened to you? Wake up . . ."

After a moment, there was something in the eyes . . . a passing ripple of awareness. And of agony. A damned soul looking out for a split second from a place of everlasting punishment might have such an expression.

Sweat stood on Gordon's forehead. He continued to shake Korkhann, to call his name. The agony reappeared in the eyes, it was as though there was a mighty straining of the mind behind those eyes, and then it was as though something snapped and Korkhann huddled in Gordon's hands, sick and shaking, his wings quivering wildly. Inarticulate whistling sounds came from his throat.

"What was it?" cried Gordon.

It was a minute before Korkhann could look up at him, and how now his eyes were wild.

"Something that I, and you, have experienced before. But worse. You remember how the Gray One at Teyn hammered us with the power of his mind?"

Gordon shivered. He was not likely ever to forget.

"Yes," whispered Korkhann. "Whatever they are, one of them is here. Here, I think, in this palace."

-IX-

The imperial palace of Throon throbbed and glittered in the night. Out of hundreds of windows poured soft light and drifting music and the hum of many voices. The arrival of dignitaries of other star-kingdoms was occasion for a state ball, and in the great halls a brilliant throng feasted and drank. Nor was that throng all human. Scale and hide and feather brushed against silken garments. Faces humanoid but not human, eyes slitted and saucer-like and pupil-less gleamed in the light. Gargoyle shapes walked the dark gardens in which glowed great plantings of luminous flowers of Achernar.

As though in grim reminder that the Empire was not all a matter of pleasure-making, the music and hum of voices were drowned by a vast, thunderous bellowing as a full score of warships went up into the starry sky. The smaller scouts and phantoms had already screamed heavenward and now the great battle-cruisers lifted, dark bulks against the constellations, out-bound toward the Pleaiades and the big fleet-bases there.

Gordon had seen little of the festive part of the palace. He had walked with Zarth Arn behind Jhal Arn as the sovereign made an appearance there, and then they had come up here to the private chambers of Jhal Arn.

He had noted the curious gaze that the throng below had directed against himself. They were wondering, he knew, why an untitled Earthman should accompany an emperor.

He said now, "I feel I should have stayed with Korkhann. He was pretty badly shaken."

"My own guards are watching over him," said Jhal Arn. "He'll be here soon for the meeting. And there's someone else I've sent for, whom I think you'll remember, Gordon."

Presently a man entered the chambers. He wore the uniform of a captain in the imperial space-fleet, and he was a big, burly man with bristling black hair and a craggy, copper-colored face. At sight of him, Gordon leaped to his feet.

"Hull Burrel!"

The big officer looked at him puzzledly. "I can't remember that we've met . . ."

Gordon sank back into his chair. Of course Hull didn't recognize him. To both his best friend and the woman he loved he was a stranger. He felt bitterness at the impossible situation he had put himself in when he came to this age in his own physical body.

"Captain Burrel," said Jhal Arn. "Do you remember that when the League of the Dark Worlds attacked the empire, and attempted assassination had already stricken me down, so that my brother acted as ruling regent in that crisis?"

A glow came onto Hull Burrel's battered coppery face. "Am I likely to forget it, Highness? It was Prince Zarth Arn we followed when we smashed the League, in that last battle of Deneb!"

Jhal Arn went on. "When Shorr Kan sent the armadas of the League to attack us, he broadcast a galaxy-wide propaganda message. I want you to see a tape of part of that."

As Zarth Arn touched a button beside his chair, against an opposite wall appeared a sterovision picture of lifelike vividness. The picture was of a man speaking.

Gordon tensed in his chair. The man was tall and broad-shouldered, his black hair clipped short, his eyes keen and flashing. His voice cut like a sword blade, and the whole impact of that ruthless, amoral, mocking personality came through even in this reproduction.

"Shorr Kan," whispered Gordon.

He was not likely to forget the dictator of the League, the utterly cynical, utterly capable leader with whom Gordon had struggled for the fact of kingdoms.

"Listen." said Jhal Arn.

And Gordon heard it again and seemed transported back to that terrible moment. Shor Kan was saying, "The Empire's regent, Zarth Arn, is not really Zarth Arn at all . . . he is an *impostor* masquerading as Zarth Arn. Star-kings and barons, do not follow this imposter to defeat and doom!"

The sterovision scene vanished. Hull Burrel turned, looking puzzled, and said, "I remember that, Highness. His accusation was so ridiculous that no one paid any attention to it."

"The accusation was true." Jhal Arn said flatly.

Hull Burrel stared at his sovereign with incredulity written large on his face. He started to speak, then thought better of it. He looked at Zarth Arn.

Zarth Arn smiled. "Yes. Shorr Kan spoke the truth. Few know it, but in past years I used scientific means to exchange minds with men of other worlds and times. One such experiment was with the man beside you . . . John Gordon of Earth. It was Gordon, in my body, who was regent of the Empire at the moment of crisis. And Shorr Kan had found it out."

He touched a control again and said, "You'll remember that after the League fleet was smashed, the men of the Dark Worlds admitted defeat and asked for truce. This was their telestero message of surrender, which you've seen before."

Another scene flashed into existence against the wall,

one that was etched forever in Gordon's memory. In a room of Shorr Kan's palace appeared a group of wild-looking men, and one of them spoke hoarsely.

"The Dark Worlds agree to surrender on your terms, Prince Zarth! Shorr Kan's tyranny is overthrown. When he refused to surrender, we rose in rebellion against him. I can prove that by letting you see him. He is dying."

The scene switched abruptly to another room of the palace. Behind a desk sat Shorr Kan. Men around him had their weapons trained on him, and his face was marble-white as he clutched at a blackened wound in his side. His dulled eyes cleared for a moment and he grinned weakly.

"You win," he said. "Devil of a way to end up, isn't it? But I'm not complaining. I had one life and used it to the limit. You're the same way, at bottom." His voice trailed to a whisper. "Maybe I'm a throwback to your world, Gordon? Born out of my time? Maybe . . ."

And he sprawled forward across his desk and lay still, and one of the grim-faced men bent to examine him and then said, "He's dead. Better for the Dark Worlds if he'd never been born."

The reproduced scene snapped out. After a moment of stunned silece, Hull Burrel spoke in a voice that echoed his stupefaction.

"I remember that. I couldn't understand what he meant by addressing Prince Zarth as 'Gordon.' None of us could." He swung around until his dazed eyes stared into Gordon's face. "Then *you* were the one who was with me in that struggle? You . . . the one who defeated Shorr Kan?"

Zarth Arn nodded. "It is so."

Gordon drew a long breath, and then he held out his hand and said, "Hello, Hull."

The Antarian . . . for Hull Burrel was a native of a world of Antares . . . continued to stare dumbly, then seized Gordon's hand and began to babble excitedly. He was cut short by the entrance of Korkhann.

To a question from Jhal Arn, Korkhann answered, "Yes, Highness, I am quite recovered."

Gordon doubted that. The yellow eyes were haunted, and there was a fear in the beaked face he had not seen there before.

"The palace has been searched and no trace of this mysterious attacker has been found," Jhal Arn was saying. "Tell us exactly what happened."

Korkhann's voice dropped to a whisper. "There's little I can tell. It was the same sensation of overwhelming mental impact I felt at Teyn, but stronger, more irresistible. I could not fight it this time, not even for a second. I knew nothing, then, until Gordon's shouting and shaking of me brought me back to consciousness. But . . . I believe that while I was held in that grip, my mind was being examined, all my memories and knowledge ransacked, by a telepath compared to whom I am as a child."

Jhal Arn leaned forward. "Tell me, when this power seized you, was there a sensation as of mental *cold?*"

Korkhann looked astonished. "How could you guess that, Highness?"

Jhal Arn did not answer, but between him and his brother flashed a look that was grim and somber.

A chamberlain entered the room, announcing dignitaries whom Jhal Arn greeted with formal protocol. Gordon, hearing the names of some and recognizing others, felt a sharp wonder.

No fewer than three star-kings had come to this secret meeting . . . young Sath Shamar of Polaris, the aging king-regent of Cassiopeia, and the dark, crafty-looking sovereign of the Kingdom of Cepheus. There were chancellors of two other kingdoms present, and also one of the mightiest of the powerful Hercules Barons,

Jon Ollen. His domain stretched so far from the Cluster to the edge of the Marches that it was actually bigger than some of the smaller kingdoms.

He now looked like a worried man, his cadaverous face gloomy in expression. Gordon remembered his galactography well enough to realize that every realm represented here lay near the Marches of Outer Space.

Jhal Arn began without preamble. "You've all heard the rumors that certain of the counts of the Marches are preparing some mysterious and dangerous aggression. It threatens all of you but first it threatens Fomalhaut, which is why Korkhann and my friend John Gordon have come here."

Jhal Arn emphasized the word "friend," and the men who had ignored Gordon until this moment, glaced at him sharply.

Jhal Arn went on, "Tell them what happen at Teyn, Korkhann."

Korkhann told them. When he finished, there was a silence. Then young Sath Shamar said troubledly, "Of mysterious cowled strangers we have heard nothing. But lately the counts of the Marches have become high-handed with us at Polaris, and have threatened us with powers they say could destroy us."

The tight-faced ruler of Cepheus added nothing, but the old regent of Cassiopeia nodded confirmation. "There is something in the Marches . . . never have the counts been so insolent with us."

Korkhann looked at the barron and said softly, "You have something more than this, Jon Ollen? It seems to me that you are withholding something from us."

Jon Ollen's cadaverous face flushed dull red with anger and he exclaimed, "I will not have my mind read, telepath!"

"And how," asked Korkhann deprecatingly, "could I do that when you have kept a guard upon your thoughts since you entered this chamber?"

Jon Ollen said sullenly, "I don't want to hunt for trouble. My barony is colse up against the Marches, closer than any of your domains. If there is danger, I am most vulnerable to it."

Jhal Arn's voice rang decisively. "You are an ally of the Empire. If danger attacks you, we come in with you at once. If you know anything, say it."

Jon Ollen looked undecided, worried, troubled. It was a minute before he spoke.

"I know but little, really. But . . . inside the Marches, not far from our frontier, is a world known as Aar. And mysterious things have happened that seem to focus on that world."

"What kind of things?"

"A merchant ship returned to my barony from the Marches, traveling on an insane course. Our cruisers could not understand its behavior. They ran it down and boarded it. Every man aboard it was raving mad. The automatic log-recorder showed that the ship had touched down last at Aar. Then another ship that passed near Aar sent off a distress call that was suddenly smothered. And that ship was never heard from again."

"What else?"

Jon Ollen's face lengthened. "There came to my court Count Cyn Cryver of the Marches. He said that certain scientific experiments had made Aar dangerous and suggested we order all ships to avoid it. But "suggested" is hardly the word . . . he *ordered* me to do this."

"It would seem," muttered Jhal Arn thoughtfully, "that Aar is at least one focal point of the mystery."

"We could send a squadron in there to find out quickly," said Zarth Arn.

"But what if there's nothing really there?" cried Jon Ollen. "The counts would hold me responsible for the incursion. You must understand my position."

"We understand it," Jhal Arn assured him. And to his brother, "No, Zarth. The baron is right. If there's nothing there we'd have angered the counts by an invasion of their domain, to the point of starting a border war all through the Marches. We'll slip a small unmarked scout into the Marches with a few men who can investigate the place. Captain Burrel, you can lead them."

Gordon spoke up for the first time in that meeting. "I will go with Hull. Look, I'm the only one except Korkhann, who's not fitted for this kind of mission, to have *seen* one of the counts' cryptic allies. At Teyn, remember."

"Why am I not fitted for such a mission?" Korkhann demanded, his feathers seeming to ruffle up with anger.

"Because no one else is so well fitted to be Princess Lianna's right-hand man, and she mustn't lose you," said Gordon soothingly.

"It's a risky thing," muttered Jon Ollen. "I beg of you one thing . . . if you are caught, please don't implicate me in this."

"Your concern for the safety of my friends is overpowering," said Jhal Arn acidly.

The baron disregarded the sarcasm. He got to his feet. "I shall return home at once. I don't want to be mixed up in this affair too much. Your Highnesses . . . gentlemen . . . good night."

When he had gone out, Sath Shamar uttered an oath. "It's what I'd have expected of him. In the battle with the Dark Worlds, when the other barons gave the galaxy an example of space-fighting it can never forget, he held back until sure that Shorr Kan was defeated."

Jhal Arn nodded. "But the strategic position of his domain makes him valuable as an ally, so we have to put up with his selfishness."

When the star-kings and chancellors had left, Jhal Arn looked a little sadly at Gordon.

"I wish you were not set on going, my friend. Did you come back to us, only to risk your life?"

Gordon saw Korkhann looking at him, and knew what was in his mind. He remembered Lianna's bitter farewell, her accusation that it was the danger and wild beauty of this wider universe that had drawn him back here, and not love for her. He stubbornly told himself it wasn't true.

"You have said yourself," he reminded Jhal Arn, "that this danger most threatens Fomalhaut. And whatever threatens Lianna is my affair."

He was not sure that Jhal Arn believed him, and he was quite sure that Korkhann did not believe him at all.

Three days later a very small ship lay at the naval starport of Throon. It was a phantom scout, with all the insignia removed. The small crew did not wear uniforms, nor did Hull Burrell, who was to captain it.

In the palace, before he left, Gordon had a final word from Zarth Arn.

"We hope you come back with information, John Gordon. But if you don't . . . then in thirty days three full Empire squadrons will head for that world of Aar."

Gordon was surprised and a little appalled. "But that could lead to war in the Marches. Your brother admitted it."

"There are worse things than a border war," Zarth Arn said somberly. "You must remember our history that you learned before. You remember Brenn Bir?"

The name rang in Gordon's memory. "Of course. Your remote ancestor, the founder of your dynasty . . . the leader who repelled the alien invasion from the Magellanic Clouds outside the galaxy."

"And who wrecked part of the galaxy doing it," Zarth Arn nodded. "We still have his records, archives that the galaxy knows nothing about. And some detail in the description you and Korkhann gave of the cowled stranger at Teyn made us look into those archives."

Gordon felt a terrifying surmise, and it was verified by Zarth Arn's next words.

"The records of Brenn Bir described the Magellanian aliens as having a mental power so terrific that no human or nonhuman could withstand it. Only by disrupting space and hurling them out of this dimension were those invaders defeated. And now . . . it seems that after all these thousands of years, they are coming back again!"

-X-

The Marches of Outer Space had been, originally, an area only vaguely delimited. Early galactographers had defined it as that part of the galaxy which lay between the eastern and southern kingdoms, and the edge of the island universe. For when, in the twenty-second century, the three inventions of the faster-than-light sub-spectrum rays, the Mass Control, and the stasis-force that cradled men's bodies so that they remained impervious to extreme speeds and accelerations . . . when these made interstellar travel possible and the human stock poured out from Earth to colonize the galaxy, it had been toward the bigger star-systems they had gone, not the rim. Millennia later, when distant systems had broken away from Earth government and formed independent kingdoms, hardy adventurers in those kingdoms had gone into the starry wilderness of the Marches, setting up small domains that often were limited to one star and one world.

These counts of the Marches, as they called themselves, had always been a tough, insolent breed. They owed allegiance to no star-king, though they had a nominal alliance with the Empire which prevented the other kingdoms from invading their small realms. The place had long been a focus of intrigue, a refuge for outlawed men, an irritation on the body politic of the galaxy. But each jealous star-king refused to let his rivals take over the Marches, and so the situation had perpetuated itself.

"And that," thought Gordon, "is too damned bad. If this anarchic star-jungle had been celaned up, it wouldn't harbor such danger now." He wondered how many of the counts were in the conspiracy, with Cyn Cryver. There had to be others, because Cyn Cryver alone could not provide enough ships for any significant action. If a significant action was what they had in mind.

The little phantom scout was well inside the Marches now, moving on a devious course. By interstellar standards, the phantom's speed was slow. Its defensive armament was almost nonexistent and its offensive weapons were nothing more than a few missiles. But it possessed a supreme advantage for such a stealthy mission as this one . . . the ability to disappear. That was why there were phantoms in the fleet of every kingdom.

"It'd be safer to dark-out," said Hull Burrel, frownning. "But then we'd be runing blind ourselves, and I don't like doing that in this mess."

Gordon thought that if it was a mess, it was an impressive one. Scores of stars burned like great emerald and ruby and diamond lamps in the dark gloom. The radar screen showed shoals of drift between these star-systems, and here and there the Marches were rifted by great darkness, loops and lanes of cosmic dust.

He looked back the way they had come, at Hercules Cluster that blazed like bright moths swarming thick about a lamp, at the far dimmed spark of Canopus. He hoped they would live to go back there. He looked ahead and his imagination leaped beyond the stars he could see to those out on the Rim, the spiral, outflying arms of stars that fringed the wheeling galaxy, and beyond which there was nothing until the distant Magellanic Clouds.

"It's too far," he said to Hull. "Zarth Arn must be wrong; there can't really be Magellanians in the Marches.

If they had come they wouldn't have come as stealthy infiltrators, but in a great invasion."

Hull Burrel shook his head. "They came that way once before, so the histories say. And they got annihilated, when Brenn Bir used the Disruptor on them. They might try a different way, this time." The big Antarian captain added, "But I can't believe it, either. It was so long ago."

For a long time the little phantom threaded its way into the Marches, skirting great areas of drift that flowed like rivers through space, tacking and twisting its way around enormous ashen dark stars, swinging far wide of inhabited systems.

Finally there came a time when, peering at the viewer, Hull Burrel pointed out a small, bright orange star glittering far away.

"That's it. The sun of Aar."

Gordon looked. "And now?"

"Now we dark-out," grunted the Antarian. "And from here on it'll be cursed ticklish navigation."

He gave an order. An alarm rang through the ship. The big dark-out generators aft began droning loudly. At that moment all the viewer-screens and radar-screens went dark and blank.

Gordon had been in phantoms before, and had expected the phenomenon. The generators had created an aura of powerful force around the little ship, which force slightly refracted every light ray or radar beam that struck it. The phantom had become completely invisible both to eye and to radar, but by the same token those in it could see nothing outside. Navigation now must be by the special sub-spectrum radar by which the phantom could slowly feel a way forward.

In the time that followed, Gordon thought it was remarkably like a twentieth-century submarine feeling its way through ocean depths. There was the same feeling of blindness and semihelplessness, the same dread of collision, in this case with some bit of drift the straining radar might not catch, and the same half-hysterical desire to see sunlight again. And the ordeal went on and on, the sweat standing out in fine beads on Hull Burrel's forehead as he jockeyed the little ship closer toward the single planet of the orange star.

Finally, Hull gave an order and the ship hung motionless. He turned his glistening face toward Gordon.

"We should be just above the surface of Aar, but that's all I can say. I hope to God we don't come out of dark-out right over our enemies' heads!"

Gordon shrugged. "Jon Ollen said there wasn't much on this world, that it was mostly wild."

"One thing I love is an optimist who has no direct responsibility," growled the Antarian. "All right. Dark-out off!"

The droning of generators died. Instantly there poured into the bridge through the viewer screens a flood of orange sunlight. They peered out tensely, blinking in the brilliance.

"I apologize, optimist," said Hull. "It couldn't be better."

The little ship hung level with the top foliage of a golden forest. The plants . . . Gordon could not think of them as trees although they were that big . . . were thirty to forty feet high, graceful clusters of dark-green stems whose branches held masses of feathery golden-yellow leaves. They bore a remote but disquieting resemblance to the trees of Teyn and Gordon shivered, hoping it was not an omen. As far as the eye could reach, there was nothing but the roof of the forest glittering in the light of the orange sun.

"Take her down fast," ordered Hull. "We could just be ranged by radar up here."

The phantom dropped through the masses of lacy gold and landed in a grove of clustered stems, upon soft ground covered with a copper-colored brush that bore black fruits.

Gordon, peering fascinated through the viewer, suddenly shouted. "Something!"

The Antarian jumped to his side. "What?"

"It's gone now," said Gordon. "Something small, almost invisible, that darted away under the brush."

The other looked doubtful. "In the star-log, this world Aar is listed as uninhabited. An attempt was once made to colonize it but the colonists were driven away from it by dangerous conditions. This could be some formidable creature."

Gordon was doubtful. "It seemed too small."

"Nevertheless, we'd better have a look around before we go thrashing through these forests," the Antarian said decisively. He spoke to the crewmen in the bridge. "You and I will go out, Varren. Full armor."

Gordon shook his head. "I'll go with Varren. One of us has to stay to complete the mission if something happens to the other . . . and the one who stays had better be the one who can navigate the ship back out of here."

When Gordon and Varren stepped out of the ship they wore the suits that did double duty as space suits and defensive armor, complete with helmets. They carried guns.

Looking uncertainly around, Gordon began to feel a bit foolish. Nohing moved except the golden foliage high above, waving in the breeze. His helmet sound-pickup brought no sounds except the faint sounds of a forest.

"Where was this thing you saw?" asked Varren. His voice was very polite.

"Over this way," Gordon said. "I don't know . . . it could have been a leaf blowing . . ."

He suddenly stopped, looking upward. Twelve feet

above the ground, fastened solidly inside a crotch of one of the trees, was a curious structure vaguely resembling a squirrel's summer nest. Except that this was no ragged thing of twigs and leaves but a solid little box of cut wood, with a door in its side.

"It was going toward this place," said Gordon. "Look."

Varren looked. He looked up for a long time and then he remarked quietly that he would be damned.

"I'm climbing up there to take a look," said Gordon. "If it's what I *thought* I saw, it won't be too dangerous. If not . . . cover me."

The climb would not have been difficult if it had not been for the clumsy suit. But he was sweating by the time he reached a crotch on which he could stand with his face level with the little box.

Gently, Gordon pushed at the little door. A faint snapping told of a tiny catch breaking. He continued to push but it was difficult . . . something, someone, was holding the door on the inside.

Then the resistance gave way, and Gordon looked inside. At first he could see nothing but a purple gloom. But the hot orange sunlight pouring in through the open door revelaed detail as his eyes adjusted.

Those who had been trying to hold the door against him now cowered in terror at the far side of a little room. They were not much more than a foot high and they were quite human in shape. They were naked, one man, one woman, and the only strange thing about them apart from their size was the fact that their bodies were semitransparent, as translucent as plastic. He could see details of the wall-surface right through them.

They cowered. and Gordon stared, and then he heard the man speaking in a tiny voice. He could hardly hear, but it was not a language he knew.

After a long moment he slid back to the ground. He pointed upward and said to Varren, "Take a look. Maybe you can understand their language."

"Their *what?*" said Varren. He looked at Gordon as though he doubted his sanity. Then he too climbed up.

It was a long time before Varren came back down. When he did, he looked sick.

"I talked with them," he said, and then repeated that as though he didn't quite believe it. "I *talked* with them. Oh, yes, I could understand them. You see, a few thousand years ago they were our own people."

Gordon looked at him incredulously. "Those creatures? But . . ."

"The colonists," said Varren. "The ones Captain Burrel read about in the log, who were driven away from here by harmful conditions. They didn't all go away. Some had already become victims of the danger . . . a chemical constituent in either the air or the water here which, after a few generations, makes the human body evolve toward smallness."

Varren shook his head. "Poor little beggars. They couldn't tell me that but I could guess it from the few scraps of legend they did tell me. It's my guess that they mutated toward that semitransparency as a camouflage defense against other creatures here."

Gordon shivered. There was beauty and wonder in the stars, but there was also horror.

"One thing I learned." Varren added. "They're terribly afraid of something out there in the west. I got that out of them, but no more."

When they went back to the ship, it was the last statement that interested Hull Burrel the most.

"It checks," he said. "We've been making a sweep with the sub-spectrum radar and it definitely showed large metal constructions several hundred miles to the west. On this world, that can only be the place we're looking for."

The Antarian thought for a little, then said decisively, "We'd never make that distance on foot. We'll have to wait until night and move the ship closer. If we hug the treetops, it might fool their radar."

Night on Aar was a heavy darkness, for this world had no moon. The phantom purred along over foliage glistening in the light of the stars, the scattered, lonesome stars of the Marches. Hull Burrel had the controls. Gordon stood quiet and watched through the viewer-window.

He thought he saw something, finally, something far ahead that glinted a dull reflection of the starlight. He started to speak, but Hull nodded.

"I caught it. We'll go down."

Gordon waited. Instead of going down at once, the little ship slipped onward, he supposed in search for a clear opening for descent into the forest.

He put his eye to the 'scope and peered. The glint of metal ahead sprang closer, and now he could see that the vague metal bulks were the buildings of a small city. There were domes, streets, walls. But there was not a single light there, and he could see that long ago the forest had come into this city's streets, and its ways were choked with foliage. Without doubt, this would have been a center of that tragically doomed colony of many centuries ago.

But there were a few hooded lights beyond the city. He touched the 'scope adjustment. He could see little, but it appeared that the old spaceport of the dead city had lain beyond it, a dark flat surface that the forest had not yet been able to overwhelm.

Gordon could just descry the glint and shape of a few ships parked there. They were small Class Five starships, not much bigger than the phantom scout. But there was one ship that had something queer about its outlines.

He turned to say so to Hull Burrel, and as his eye left the 'scope, he saw that their craft was still gliding straight forward and had not begun to descend.

Gordon exclaimed, "What are you doing? Do you figure to land at their front door?"

The Antarian did not answer. Gordon took hold of his arm. Hull Burrel yanked it free and knocked Gordon sprawling.

But in that moment, Gordon had seen Hull's face. It was stony, immobile, the eyes vacant of all emotion or perception. In a flash, Gordon knew.

He bunched himself and launched in a desperate spring at the Antarian. He knocked Hull away from the controls, but not before the Antarian had managed to give them a hard yank in his desperate attempt to cling to them. The phantom scout stood suddenly on its head and then dived straight down through the foliage.

Gordon felt the metal wall slap him across the temple, and then there was only darkness in which he fell and fell.

–XI–

In the darkness Gordon heard the voice of a dead man speaking.

"*So that's what he looks like,*" said the voice. "*Well!*"

Whose voice was it? Gordon's pain-racked brain could not remember. Then how did he know that it was the voice of a dead man? He did not know how he knew, but he was sure that the man who spoke had died.

He must open his eyes and see who it was that spoke after death. He made an effort. And with the effort, the pain and blackness rolled back across his mind more strongly than before and he did not know anything.

When he finally awoke, he felt that it was much later. He also felt that he had one of the biggest headaches in galactic history.

He did get his eyes open this time. He was in a small metal room with a solid metal door. There was a very tiny window with bars, and orange sunlight slanting through them.

Across the room from him, Hull Burrel sprawled like one dead.

Gordon got to his feet. For a while he stood perfectly still, hoping that he was not going to fall. Then he moved painfully to the Antarian and knelt beside him.

Hull had a bruise on his chin, but no other perceptible injuries. Yet he lay like a man in deathly coma, his coppery face no longer like the side of a rough rock but gone all slack and sagging. His eyes were closed, but his mouth was open and spittle dribbled from it.

Gordon took him by the shoulders and said, "Hull," and all of a sudden the living log turned into a maddened wildcat. Hull scrambled up, thrusting Gordon away, glaring at him as if he were an attacking enemy.

Gradually Hull's eyes cleared. His muscles relaxed. He stared stupidly at Gordon and said. "What's the devil's the matter with me?"

"You were slugged," said Gordon. "Not with a club, but with mental force. You were taken under control when we were nearing this place."

"This place?" Hull Burrel looked around, at the small, dusty metal room. "I don't remember," he muttered. "This looks like a prison."

Gordon nodded. "We're in the dead town of the old colonists. And you can't have a town without a jail."

His head ached. And more than his head was hurt. His pride was severely bruised. He said, "Hull, I was a sort of hero back in that other time, when I lived in Zarth Arn's body . . . wasn't I?"

Hull stared. "You were. But what . . ."

"I was going to be a hero all over again," said Gordon bitterly. "To show that I could be good as John Gordon, too. I've done fine haven't I? Throon, Lianna . . . they'll be proud of me."

"You weren't leading this mission, I was," growled Hull Burrel. "It was I who fell on my face." He went to the little window and looked at the street choked with golden foliage. He turned around, his brows knitted. "Mental force, you said. Then there must be one of those damned Magellanians here."

Gordon shrugged. "Who else could do a thing like that? We've been taken like children. They were sitting here waiting for us.' '

Hull suddenly shouted loudly. "Varren! Kano . . . Rann . . . are you here?"

There was no answer from the crewmen whose names he had shouted.

"Wherever they are, they're not within earshot," muttered Hull, plainly worried. "What next?"

"Next, we wait," said Gordon.

They waited for more than an hour. Then the door opened without warning. Outside it stood a supercillious young man whose black uniform bore in silver the design of the Mace.

"The Count Cyn Cryver will see you now," said the young man. "You can walk, or be dragged."

"All right, we'll walk," said Gordon. "I've enough headache already."

They walked out into the hot sunlight, and along a street that had once been wide. But time and weather had cracked its pavement and seeds had lodged to grow into the feathery trees, so that now it was more like following a path in a forest.

The corroded metal fronts of buildings showed through the foiage, silent and dead. And Gordon glimpsed a statue, the figure of a man in space dress, looking proudly down from the middle of the street. It would be, he thought, the star-captain who had led the ill-fated colonists here, in the long-ago centuries.

Look and be proud, star-captain. All that you wrought died long ago, and the last descendants of your people are the furtive little hunted things in the forest. Be proud, star-captain, be happy, for your eyes are blind and cannot see. . . .

They were taken into a building that looked like a municipal center. In a shadowy big hall, Count Cyn Cryver lounged in a chair at a table, drinking a tawny-colored liquor from a tall goblet. He wore black, with his insignia arrogant on his breast, and he looked at Gordon with amused eyes.

"You kicked up quite a stir at Teyn, but it seems we

have you safe now," he said. He drank and put the goblet down. "A word of advice . . . never trust a coward. Like Jon Ollen, for instance."

A light burst upon Gordon. "Of course. That's why you were waiting for us. Jon Ollen is one of you."

Nothing else could explain it. The cadaverous baron was a traitor, and it was a safe assumption that the super-telepath who had come to Throon had been hidden in Jon Ollen's ship.

Hull Burrel demanded harshly, "Where are my men?"

Cyn Cryver smiled. "We had no need of your men or your ship, so they have been destroyed. As you will be destroyed when we no longer have any use for you."

Hull's fist clenched. He looked as though he was about to spring at Cyn Cryver, but the men with the stunners stepped forward.

"You will be examined later," Cyn Cryver said. "You are here now only because an old friend of yours wishes to see you. Tell their old friend that they are here, Bard."

One of the men went through a door at the rear of the hall. Gordon felt his skin crawl as he heard steps returning a moment later. He thought he knew what was coming.

He was wrong. It was not the cowled shape he feared that came into the hall. It was a man, broad-shouldered and tall. black-haired, tough-faced and keen-eyed, who stopped and look at them, smiling.

"By God" said Hull Burrel. "*Shorr Kan!*"

"Oh, no," said Godon. 'Can't you see, it's an impersonation they've got up . . . Lord knows why. We saw Shorr Kan die, killed by his own men."

The man who looked like Shorr Kan laughed. "You *tohught* you saw that. But you were deceived, Gordon. And if I do say so myself, it was a neat piece of deception, considering how little time we had in which to dream it up."

And it was the voice of Shorr Kan. It was also the voice of a dead man speaking in the darkness and saying, "So that's what he looks like!"

He came closer and spoke earnestly, as one explaining something to a friend. "I was in the devil of a spot, thanks to you. Your damned Disruptor had shattered our fleet, and you were coming on toward the Dark Worlds, and my faithful subjects had got wind of it and were rioting in the streets. It was my neck, if I didn't think of something pretty quick."

He grinned. "It took you all in, didn't it? I still had a few faithful officers, and when they sent out that stereovision message of surrender, they could show you poor old Shorr Kan, with a big fake wound in his side, putting on a death scene I'm really proud of."

He burst into laughter. Stupefied, because he did not want to believe this and was beginning to do so, Gordon exclaimed, "Shorr Kan's body was found in the ruins of his palace!"

The other shrugged. "A body was found. The body of a dead rioter, who was my size and wore my uniform and decorations. Of course there wasn't too much left to identify because we fired the palace before we got the devil out of there . . . which little incendiary feat was blamed on my rioting subjects."

Gordon could no longer disbelieve. He stared at Shorr Kan, at this man who had made himself master of the Dark Worlds and then, with their power, had almost shattered the star-kingdoms.

"And you've been hiding here in the Marches ever since?" he cried.

"Let me say instead that I've been making an extended visit to certain of my old friends here, among whom I number first the Count Cyn Cryver," said Shorr Kan. "When I heard you were among us, the Gordon whom I had never physically seen but whom I had known only too well . . . well, I had to give you a greeting for old time's sake."

The insolent brass of the man, his complete, mocking, light-hearted cynicism, had not changed.

Gordon said, between his teeth, "Why, I'm glad you saved your neck . . . even though it's a comedown from master of the League of the Dark Worlds, to hang onto the coattails of a Cyn Cryver. Still, it's better than dying."

Shorr Kan laughed, in honest enjoyment. "Did you hear that, Cyn? Do you wonder I admired this chap? Here, he is at the end of his rope, and he tries to slap my face in a way that'll make bad blood between you and me!"

"Look at him, Hull," said Gordon mockingly. "Isn't he the one to put a brave face on? Lord of the Cloud, master of the Dark Worlds, almost the conquerer of the Empire itself . . . and now that he's reduced to skulking in the Marches and mixing up in filthy plots with rag-tag one-world counts, he still stays cheerful."

Shorr Kan grinned, but Cyn Cryver got up and came over, looking at Gordon with livid hatred.

"I've heard enough of this," he said. "You've seen your old enemy, Shorr, and that's that. Bard, shackle them to those pillars. The Lord Susurr will come this evening and examine their minds for what they may contain of value, and after that they can be tossed on a dunghill."

"The Lord Susurr," repeated Gordon. "That would be one of your creepy little allies from Magellan, would it? Like the one we so sadly disappointed when we foxed you at Teyn?"

The rage left Cyn Cryver's face and he smiled in a deadly fashion as Gordon and Hull Burrel were shackled each to one of the slender ornamental metal pillars that ran in two rows down the hall.

"Even for you," said Cyn Cryver, "I had still a spark of pity, considering what will happen to you soon. But now it is gone." He turned his back on Gordon and told the young captain, "Guard them until the Lord Susurr comes. It will be some hours, for the lord likes not the sunlight."

Shorr Kan said brightly, "Well, lads, I fear it's goodbye now. I can see you're going to meet your end like men of courage. I've always said, 'Die like a man . . . if you can't find any way of avoiding it.' And I *don't* think you can avoid it."

Hull Burrel continued to swear, using profanity from a dozen different worlds. "That devil-born fox! All these years the whole galaxy has thought him dead, and now he bounces up here to laugh at us!"

"It's all history now," said Gordon. "Of more concern is what happens tonight, when the Lord Susurr who does not like the sunlight comes to visit us."

Hull stopped swearing and looked at him. "What's the creature going to do to us?"

"I imagine you could call it mental vivisection. I think it will take our minds and turn them inside out for every scrap of information we possess, and that it'll be only two mindless wrecks who are killed later."

Hull shivered. After a little silence he said, with an age-old hatred edging his voice, "Small wonder that Brenn Bir blasted the Magellanian invaders out of the universe, that other time."

No more was said, for there was nothing to say. Gordon stood against the pillar, with the shackles cutting his wrists behind him, and looked out through the open doorway as the long hours of afternoon crept away. The orange rays of sunlight that cut down through the interstices of the branches slanted and shifted. The breeze ruffled the leaves like autumn aspens on faraway, long-ago Earth. Beyond the trees the metal star-captain stood stiff and valiant, staring forever across his ruined city.

The guards lounged and shuffled in the doorway, glancing in now and then at the two captives. But Gordon could hear no sound of any activity from the dead city around them. What was going on here at Aar? That it was a focus for the intrigue that had hatched between the counts and Narath Teyn and the aliens from outside, he had no doubt. But it could not be a vital center of their plot, or the treacherous Jon Ollen would not have named the place and baited them to it.

Had Jon Ollen been setting a trap, not just for Hull Burrel and himself and their little ship, but for the main squadrons of the Empire? Jhal Arn had said that those squadrons would come here, if they did not return with information. If that was so, he and Hull had really messed it up. Lianna would be proud of him when she heard of it.

He thought of Lianna, and how they had parted at Fomalhaut. He did not want to think of her, and he made his mind go blank, and in a kind of stupor watched the rippling golden leaves outside. The time slipped slowly by.

The gold dulled. Gordon woke from his stupor to see that twilight had replaced the sunlight. And the guards in the doorway were now looking nervously along the street. As the dusk deepened they stepped farther away from the doorway, out into the street, as though they were doing everything possible to keep from being too near this room when the Lord Susurr came to do what he would do to the captives.

The hall was darkening, faster than the outside street. Gordon suddenly stiffened against his shackles. He heard a sound approaching.

Something was in the shadowy hall with them. something that came softly toward them from behind.

-XII-

The skin between Gordon's shoulders crawled. He heard the sound shift position as whoever had stealthily entered moved softly around in front of them.

Then, close in front of him and silhouetted against the last twilight of the open doorway, he saw the profile of Shorr Kan.

"Listen, and keep your mouths shut," whispered Shorr Kan. "You'll be dead, and worse than dead, before morning comes unless I get you out of here. There's a chance I can do it."

"And why would you do a thing like that?" asked Gordon, keeping his voice well down.

"He loves us, that's why," muttered Hull Burrel. "He's so full of loving kindness that he just can't bear to see us hurt."

"Oh, God," whispered Shorr Kan, "give me a smart enemy rather than a stupid friend. Look, I may have only minutes before the cursed H'Harn comes."

"H'Harn?"

"What you call the Magellanians. The H'Harn is the name they call themselves. The Lord Susurr is one of them and when he comes here, you're through."

Gordon did not doubt that. But all the same he asked dubiously, "If the creature is such a terrific telepath, won't he know that you're here right now?"

There was contempt in Shorr Kan's answer. "You people all think the H'Harn are omnipotent and omniscient.

They're not. In fact, they're a bit on the stupid side in some ways. They *do* have tremendous parapsychial power, but only when they concentrate it on one object. They can't spread their mental power to encompass everything, and it fades out at a certain distance."

Gordon knew that from his own experience at Teyn, but he made no comment. Shorr Kan jerked his head around to peer at the guards who waited uneasily out in the dusky street, and then continued in a hurried whisper.

"I have to be quick. Listen . . . I've been here in the Marches ever since the defeat of the Dark Worlds. I figure that sooner or later I could manipulate these popinjay counts the way I wanted to . . . set them against each other, get them to fighting, and when the smoke cleared away, Shorr Kan would be king of the Marches. And I would have done it, but for one thing.

"The agents of the H'Harn came from outside the galaxy, and made contact with Cyn Cryver and Narath Teyn and certain other counts. The H'Harn took a beating when they tried to invade long ago and it's taken them all that time to recover from it, but they're strong again and they still mean to come into our galaxy, in a different way."

"What way?" asked Gordon.

"I don't know," answered Shorr Kan. "I'm not sure that even Cyn Cryver knows. I do know that the H'Harn are preparing something big out there in the Magellanic Clouds, something against which our galaxy will be defenseless. What it is, I haven't the slightest idea."

He went on. "Those of the H'Harn who have come here so far, like Susurr and others, are agents sent ahead to make alliance with the counts and prepare the way for some kind of assault. The H'Harn have assured Cyn Cryver and the others that they'll be given half the galaxy for their aid. And the bloody fools believe it!"

"But you don't?"

"Look, Gordon, did you find me an idiot when we fought each other in the old days? The H'Harn are inhuman, so inhuman that they take good care not to show themselves bodily least they scare off their allies. Of course they'll use the counts, and of course they'll brush them aside when they've succeeded in their plans, and what will their promises be worth?"

"About as much," muttered Gordon, "as the promises of Shorr Kan."

Shorr Kan chuckled briefly. "I asked for that. But no matter. I've had to guard my thoughts carefully. The moment that damned alien gets suspicious and probes my mind I'll be through, and I can't keep my guard up forever. I've got to get out of here. But one man can't operate a ship. Three men could. That's why I need you." His whisper was emphatic. "Give me your word that you'll go where I want to go, once we get a ship, and I'll free you right now!"

"Give our word to Shorr Kan?" said Hull. "That would really be a brilliant thing to do . . ."

"Hull, listen!" said Gordon swiftly. "If Shorr Kan double-crosses us the moment we're out of this room, we'd still not be as bad off as when that alien gets through with us. Give him your word. I do."

The Antarian sullenly muttered. "All right. It's given."

Shorr Kan produced something from under his coat that glistened dully in the last light from the doorway. It was a heavy semi-circular metal hook whose inner cutting edge was serrated.

"I've no key to your shackles but this should cut them," he whispered. "Hold your hands wide, Gordon, unless you want one of them sliced off."

He slipped around behind the pillar and began sawing at the shackle. The sound seemed loud to Gordon's ears but the shadowy figures of the guards out in the street did not move.

"Almost through," muttered Shorr Kan after a few moments. "If you'll . . ."

His whisper suddenly stopped. The sawing stopped and then there was a stealthy sound of rapid withdrawal.

"What . . ." Gordon began. and then his heart throbbed painfully as he saw.

Out in the dusk-wrapped street that was still not as dark as the interior of the hall, the guardsmen were moving away, shrinking back until they met the wall of a building on the opposite side and could go no farther.

And a cowled, robed figure of shimmering gray, not quite as tall as a man, appeared in the doorway. In complete silence it moved, with that horridly fluid gliding motion that Gordon had seen once before, into the darkness of the hall toward them.

Gordon's whole body stiffened involuntarily. He heard a sharp indrawing of breath from the Antarian, who had not seen one of the H'Harn until now. There was a moment in which the shadowy figure seemed to hesitate between them, and then the choice was made and it swayed toward Gordon and he waited for the blasting mental force to burst into his brain.

A shadow skittered in the darkness, a low anguished hissing came from the H'Harn, and its body swayed unsteadily aside. And against the dim oblong of the doorway, Gordon saw Shorr Kan's silhouette as he dug the serrated hook deep, deep into the Gray One's back.

In an access of revulsion, Gordon strained violently and the almost-severed shackle snapped.

He could not see clearly the nightmare that was going on now in the dark hall. The H'Harn seemed to be tottering away, mewing and hissing, as Shorr Kan stabbed and stabbed.

"Help me kill it!" panted Shorr Kan. "Help me . . !"

There was no weapon, but Gordon grabbed up the chair beside the table. He rushed and struck. The mewing thing went down.

Pain. Pain. It shot the terrible waves though Gordon's brain, coming consciously or unconsciously from the stricken alien. He staggered, fell to his knees.

A wave of black agony swept over him and receded. He got up, shakily. He glimpsed the dark figures of the two guards in the street, running now toward the doorway of the building. There they hesitated.

"Lord Susurr?" called one, his voice high-pitched and shrill.

Shorr Kan's stunner buzzed in the dark and the two men in the doorway dropped.

"Saw Burrel's shackle, and hurry," said Shorr Kan hoarsely, handing him the hook that was now wet to the hilt.

As Gordon worked, he saw Shorr Kan stoop and tear open the robe of the huddled heap on the floor, but he could not see what the dead H'Harn looked like. He heard a sharp sound from Shorr Kan.

The shackle parted. Shorr Kan hurried them toward the rear of the hall.

"This way. I don't think we have all the time in the world."

The little spaceport beyond the dead town lay dark and silent under the stars, when they reached it. Shorr Kan led them toward one small ship that lay apart from the others. Its black bulk loomed before them, and to Gordon it seemed oddly strange in outline, with thick vanes sprouting from its sides such as he had seen on no other starship.

"It's the ship in which the four H'Harn agents came to this galaxy," said Shorr Kan, fumbling with the lock-catch. "The other three went to Teyn and other worlds, but the ship was left here with Susurr. From what I've heard, it's far faster than any ship we know of, so if we get away in it, they'll never catch us."

When they had got inside and the hooded lights in

the control-bridge were on, Hull Burrel uttered a grunt of astonishment.

"Well, don't stand there," said Shorr Kan impatiently. "You're the professional spaceman here. Get busy and take us the devil out of here."

"I never saw a control-board like this," Hull objected. "Some of those controls don't seem to mean a thing. They . . ."

"Some of the controls are familiar to you, aren't they?"

"Yes, but . . ."

"Then use the ones you know, but take off!"

Hull Burrel, his professional soul outraged by the sloppiness of such a suggestion, nevertheless took the pilot chair. It was far too small for him and his knees came almost to his chin as he poked and prodded and pulled.

The little ship went away from Aar very fast, bursting out of the darkness of the night side of the planet into the brilliant sun.

"What course?" demanded the Antarian.

Shorr Kan gave him the bearings. Hull Burrel cautiously set them up, swearing at the unfamiliarity of the calibrations.

"I'm not setting a course, I'm just making an educated guess," he grumbled. "We'll likely pile up in the drift somewhere."

Gordon watched the lonely stars ahead, as they rushed, and his shakiness left him.

"We're heading out toward the Rim of the galaxy?" he asked. and Shorr Kan nodded. "Where will we swing back in, then?"

"We won't swing back in," answered Shorr Kan calmly. "We're going right on."

Hull swung around. "What do you mean? There's nothing but intergalactic space beyond . . . nothing!"

"You forget," reminded Shorr Kan. "There are the Magellanic Clouds . . . the worlds of the H'Harn."

"For God's sake, why would we want to go *there?*"

Shorr Kan laughed. "I feared this would be a shock to you. But I have your word, remember. It stands thus: The H'Harn are preparing something out there, with which to strike at our galaxy. So . . . we go out on a reconnaissance. We find out what it is. And we bring back that knowledge so the star-kings can prepare against the H'Harn. After all . . . isn't that the mission on which you two came?"

"But why should *you* risk your neck to save the star-kingdoms?" Gordon demanded.

Shorr Kan shrugged. "The reason is simple. I couldn't stay much longer with the counts without betraying my suspicions of their H'Harn allies . . . and the moment any H'Harn saw that in my mind, I'd be dead. But I couldn't go back to the star-kingdoms . . . they'd hang me for certain when they found out I was still living."

Gordon was beginning to see the light.

"*But,*" Shorr Kan continued, "if I risk all to go to the Magellanic Clouds and come back with a warning of the H'Harn plans, the past will be forgotten. I'll be a hero, and you don't hang heroes. I gamble that I'll be on a throne again, in a year."

Hull Burrel appealed to Gordon. "Do we let him take advantage of the fact that we've given our word to do this?"

Gordon answered thoughtfully, "We do. Hull. Not just because of our word, but something else . . . he's right when he reminds us that this is our mission."

Hull Burrel uttered a loud curse. "You're a fool, John Gordon, but I'll go along with it. I've lived long enough anyway, so I might as well commit suicide going on an impossible mission with a damned fool and the biggest villain in the galaxy!"

-XIII-

The ship flew at incredible speed through the Marches of Outer Space. Everywhere about it were suns, flaming suns and ashen, dying stars and dark cindery hulks, with their planets and moons and dangerous trailing shoals of drift. A cosmic jungle, far beyond the demesne of the great star-kingdoms; a jungle not to be invaded without due caution.

Yet the men inside the ship were not worried by their demented progress.

John Gordon, at the moment, was too shaken to be worried about anything. He stared out through the after view-screen, at the wilderness in which the orange sun of Aar had already vanished, still not believing their escape. He was only faintly aware that the chair he sat in was too small for his muscular, stocky frame, or that the ceiling curve of the control-room was much too close over his head. Or that the metal surfaces around him were of a sickly and unpleasant blue, like the skin of a drowned man.

After a while he turned from the view-screen to look at Shorr Kan, who looked back at him; the dark, well-remembered face with the lean bones and sardonic eyebrows. Shorr Kan grinned.

"Yes we did," he said. "We made it. Thanks to me."

Gordon let out a long breath and passed his hand over his own face, rubbing the angles of it like a sleeper waking. "Yes," he said, "I guess we did. Hull?"

Hull Burrel looked perfectly placid and content now, even though he was perched in that ridiculously small chair. "Coping," he said. "At least, for now."

It was only then that Gordon began to get the perspective. The control-room was like the inside of a polished egg, made to hold much smaller birds than these.

"Well," said Shorr Kan, "the H'Han are a small race. No reason for them to build for our comfort."

Hull, who towered even over Shorr Kan, lifted his head, bumped it on some ovehanging equipment, and retracted it, swearing. "They didn't have to overdo it," he said. "And I wish they hadn't been quite so damned cryptic about their controls." He continued to poke and prod cautiously at the unintelligible knobs and dials, marked with alien symbols. If Hull Burrel could figure those out, Gordon thought, he was even better than the best spaceman in the galaxy.

And he had better figure them out, Gordon thought, because all our precious necks depend on it.

Shorr Kan was watching the forward view-screen now, the sub-electronic mirror that converted mass impulses from the normal space they were tearing through, literally, at FTL+, into images the eye could see. He appeared fascinated by what was pictured there.

"At a guess," he said, "what would you estimate our speed to be?"

Gordon looked at the screen. The stars, dead and living, and the banks of drift, all the tumbled splendor of the Marches, seemed to him to be almost stationary.

"We don't seem to be moving at all," he said. "Or at least, not much."

But Hull was staring at the screen as well, his copper-colored face rapt. "We're moving all right," he said. "No ship in our galaxy can move as fast as this." He answered Shorr Kan's question. "No, I couldn't guess. I'd have to have another point of reference and . . ."

Shorr Kan said, "Is it safe, in this smother?"

The Antarian turned around, his eyes just a trifle vague. "Safe? Why, I suppose . . . "

Gordon felt suddenly very nervous. If Shorr Kan, that tough and seasoned veteran, was worried about their velocity, it was something to worry about.

"Hull," he said, "why don't you slow down?" And that, he thought, must be an all-time first; back-seat driving in a starship.

"Mn," said Hull, and scowled down at the child-sized controls. "I can't read these blasted things." His voice went up a notch. "How am I going to set a course out of the galaxy and all the way to the Magellanic Clouds," he demanded, "when I can't read the instruments?"

"Set a course *where*?" said Gordon, astonished, "What are you talking about?"

Hull shook his head. "The Magellanic Clouds. Where the H'Harn come from. Weren't we going there to reconnoiter them?"

"This little ship reconnoiter a sub-galaxy?" exclaimed Gordon. He rose and went to Hull, looking at him anxiously. "Hull, are you dreaming?"

Shorr Kan joined them, stooping slightly under the ceiling. "That," he said, "is the most idiotic suggestion I ever heard."

Hull turned on him furiously, his eyes quite normal now. "Idiotic, is it? You were the one who proposed it! You said we'd go out to the Clouds and learn what the H'Harn are planning against the Empire!"

Shorr Kan's body suddenly stiffened, as though with shock. "That's ridiculous. But . . . but I *did* say that."

There were times when his dark face could get as hard and cold and keen as a sword blade. This was one of those times.

"Tell me. Hull," he said swiftly. "Why did you choose this H'Harm ship for our escape?"

Gordon said, "You chose it, Shorr Kan. You said it was faster."

"Ah," said Shorr Kan. "I did, didn't I? But how have you been able to fly the thing, Hull?"

Hull looked puzzled. "Why, I just guessed at the controls . . ."

"Guessed?" mocked Shorr Kan. "You took off like an expert, in a ship whose design is completely alien to you."

His black eyes flashed from Hull to Gordon. He dropped his voice.

"There's only one answer to the things we've been doing. We've been under alien influence. H'Harn influence."

A feeling of terrible cold swept though Gordon. "But you said the H'Harn couldn't use their mental power at any great distance!"

"And that's true," said Shorr Kan. He turned. his gaze going to a closed bulkhead door that was the way to the after part of the ship. "We haven't been back there yet, have we?"

The implication hit Gordon squarely in the center of his being. There are different sorts of fear, and many degrees of fearing, but what he felt for the H'Harn was the ultimate in sheer sickening terror. He found difficulty in pronouncing his words.

"You think there was a H'Harn in this ship? That there is one in it *now?*"

He stared at the door, seeing the creature in his mind's eye . . . the small, oddly distorted, oddly boneless thing with its limber bobbing gait, a faceless, softly-hissing enigma veiled in gray, hiding a dreadful power. . . .

"I think so," muttered Shorr Kan. "Lord knows how many of the little monsters are loose in our galaxy, although four was the number I heard. But I heard it from Cyn Cryver, and Cyn Cryver is a liar, because he told me there was only one at Aar."

Hull Burrel and Gordon looked at each other. It was still fresh in them, the horror they had felt when the H'Harn named Susurr had come toward them. Gordon said flatly, "Good God."

Then he turned to Shorr Kan to ask what they should do. And he was almost too late.

"If there's a H'Harn on this ship," Shorr Kan said, "there's only one thing to do. Find it and kill it."

With a decisive gesture, he drew the stunner from his belt.

Gordon lunged.

He brought Shorr Kan to the floor in a crashing tackle and grabbed the hand that held the stunner. He clung to it while Shorr Kan fought him like a tiger, and all the time Shorr Kan's face was blank as something carved from wood and his eyes were fixed and glazed and unseeing.

Gordon yelled, "Hull, help me!"

Hull was already leaping forward. "Then he is a traitor? I always knew we couldn't trust him . . ."

"Not that," said Gordon, panting for breath. "Look at his face. I've seen that before . . . he's under H'Harn control. Get that stunner out of his hand!"

Hull carefully peeled back Shorr Kan's fingers until he let go of the weapon, and as soon as it passed into the Antarian's hands Shorr Kan sagged and went limp. Like someone coming out of a faint he looked up at them and mumbled, "What happened? I felt . . ."

But Gordon had forgotten about him. He wrenched the stunner away from the startled Hull and disarmed it feverishly by withdrawing its charge-chamber. Then, just as quickly, he tossed the useless stunner back to Hull.

"You keep it. I'll keep the charge-chamber, and that way neither one of us can use it if the H'Harn takes control of . . . "

He never finished the sentence. A bolt as of black

lightning, the cold paralyzing force that he had felt before at Teyn, exploded with terrifying silence in his brain. There was no shield against it, no possibility of struggle. It was like death. And simply, he died.

Just as simply and suddenly, he lived again. He was on the deck and his hands were around Shorr Kan's neck, throttling him, and Hull Burrel was pulling him away with such force that he could hear the sinews cracking in the Antarian's back and shoulders.

"Let go," Hull was snarling. "Let go or I'll have to knock you out . . ."

He let go. Shorr Kan rolled over and slid away, his mouth wide and his chest heaving. "All . . . all right, now," Gordon stammered. Feeling sick and shaken, he started to get up. But instead of releasing him, Hull's grip abruptly tightened. His knee slammed into Gordon's back and Gordon fell hard forward and his skull rang on the steel deck.

The H'Harn had shifted its attention once more. Glassy-eyed and blank as a statue, the Antarian left Gordon and flung himself on Shorr Kan and tried earnestly to kill him. Shorr Kan managed to fight him off until Gordon could collect his wits and help. Together they got Hull down and held him, and then between breaths he went flaccid and lay looking at them, his eyes wild but quite sane.

"Me, too?" he said, and Gordon nodded. Hull sat up and put his head in his hands. "Why doesn't it just kill us and get it over with?"

"It can't kill us," said Shorr Kan. "Not with mental force. It could destroy our minds, one by one, but I don't think it wants to be flying through the Marches with three mindless maniacs. It seems to be trying to get two of us to eliminate each other so it'll only have one left to control. I expect it needs someone to help it fly the ship."

He stared at the closed door aft. "If we try to get back at it we'll never make it . . ."

Gordon glanced up at the view-screen, where the thronging stars and shoals of drift crept with such deceptive slowness. This was one of the most crowded regions of the Marches, and Shorr Kan had worried about their velocity. Perhaps. . . .

With desperate inspiration, so desperate that he did not pause a second to think about it, Gordon sprang to the control-board. He began at random to hit the enigmatic controls, punching, twisting, turning them this way and that.

The little ship went crazy. It flashed toward a great belt of drift, then veered wildly off toward a blue sun and its planets, then zoomed zenithward toward a double-double whose four suns yawned before them like great portals of flame. Hull Burrel and Shorr Kan were tumbled against the bulkheads, crying out their surprise.

The H'Harn hidden aft must have been startled, too startled for the moment to stop him.

Hull scrambled toward him. "You'll wreck us!" he cried. "Are you daft? Get your hand off those controls, for God's sake!"

Gordon shoved him aside. "It's our only chance to deal with that creature. Get it scared. Both of you, keep hitting the controls at random. If we all three do that, it can't stop all of us."

Hull stared at the view-screen and the dizzying whirl of suns and worlds and deadly drift. "But we'll crash. It's suicide!"

Shorr Kan had seen Gordon's point. "He's right, Hull. It's risking a crash, but it's the only way." He pushed Hull toward the control-board. "Do it!"

Dazed and only half-understanding, Hull obeyed. The three of them pushed and pulled at things like madmen. The ship corkscrewed, stood on its tail. The protective grav-stasis operating inside the ship shielded them from the worst accelerative effects, but the sheer insanity of flying in this mad fashion was terrifying.

"All right back there!" Gordon yelled. "You can read my mind, you know what I'm saying! If we crash and die, you die with us! Try to take control of any of us again and we *will* crash!"

He waited for the icy mental bolt to hit him, but it did not. And after a minute there came into his mind a telepathic feeler that was cold, alien, and . . . *fearful.*

"Stop!" thought the hidden H'Harn. "We cannot survive if you continue this. Stop it!"

-XIV-

Sweat stood out on Gordon's forehead. He saw in the view-screen that the ship was now heading with all its tremendous speed toward the irregular sprawl of a filamentary nebula. That nebula would be rotten with drift.

He took his hands off the controls. "Let be," he told the others. "But be ready to hit them again any moment."

An anxious thought came from the H'Harn. It could see quite clearly, Gordon knew, what was ahead of them, using his eyes as a viewer. "You must change course or we will perish."

"Change course to where?" said Gordon harshly. "To the Magellanic sub-galaxy? That's where you were taking us with your hypnotic suggestions."

"It is necessary for me to return there," came the sullen thought. "But we can make a bargain."

"What kind of bargain?"

"This," thought the hidden H'Harn. "Set a course toward an uninhabited world I know of that is not too distant, and land there. You may then leave the ship."

Gordon looked at the others, Hull's coppery face sweating and haggard, Shorr Kan's a mask of grim doubt.

"I got the thought." Shorr Kan nodded. "You too, Hull? Anyway, I don't think much of it for a bargain. The thing will try to trick us somehow."

"No!" came the sharp thought.

Gordon paused, undecided. He could see no other arrangement that might even possibly work. The situation was fantastic. The three of them in the racing ship, each of them vulnerable to the colossal mental power of the creature back there, but only one at a time.

A thought crossed his mind but he instantly suppressed it. It was nothing he wanted to think about even for one moment. He look at the other two and said,

"I think we've got to risk it."

"Very well," came the quick, eager thought of the H'Harn. A little too quick, a little too eager. "I will direct your companion how to fly the ship to that world."

"As you did before?" jeered Gordon. "Oh, no. You're not putting Hull under again and then using him in some underhanded fashion."

"But how then . . ?"

Gordon said, "You will explain to Hull the controls of the ship, by direct telepathic statements. He will repeat aloud to us each of your explanations. If at any moment Hull shows the slightest sign of being under your mental dominance, we'll hit the controls and keep on hitting them until we crash."

There was a long pause before any answer came. Hull was looking agonizedly at the screen, and Gordon saw in it that the filamentary nebula was terribly close, winding across space like a gigantic ragged serpent. The serpent was diamonded with points of light that came and went, bigger fragments of drift that caught the light of distant suns and then lost it.

He thought grimly that if the H'Harn did not make up its mind soon, there was not going to be any escape for any of them.

That thought pressured the H'Harn into hasty decision, as Gordon had hoped it would.

"Very well, it is agreed. But your companion must take over at once."

Hull Burrel seated himself at the controls. Gordon and Shorr Kan leaned on either side of him, watching his face for any sign of change, watching the controls, and watching each other.

"It says this is the main lateral-thrust lever," said Hull, putting his hand on a little burnished lever. "Fifty degrees east . . . seven of these little vernier marks to the left."

The gigantic snake of the nebula slid out of their view in the screen.

"Zenith and nadir thrust control," muttered Hull, touching still another of the small levers.

The star-fields changed in the screen. The ship, still running at a velocity far higher than that of any craft ever known in the galaxy, moved again with apparent sanity through the jungle of suns on a course parallel with the rim of the galaxy, arrowing slightly zenithward in the starry swarm.

Gordon felt a tension that was now unbearable. He knew that the H'Harn did not mean to let them escape, that the thing had something up its sleeve, some trap that would close directly they landed. . . .

Don't think of that, he told himself. Keep your mind on Hull and what he's saying about the controls.

After what seemed an endless time, a yellow sun very like Sol lay dead ahead, and its disc grew as the ship flew on. Presently they could see the planet that swung around it.

"Is this the world?" Gordon demanded.

"Yes," came the H'Harn's answering thought.

The creature then gave Hull further telepathic instructions, and Hull said, "Deceleration control . . . two notches," and touched another lever.

Gordon watched Hull closely. If the H'Harn meant

suddenly to seize their pilot, it was likely to be fairly soon. So far, Hull's face remained normal. But he knew how swiftly the change could come, to that inhuman stiffness. And if that happened. . . . *Don't think about it. Don't think!*

The planet rushed toward them, a green-and-gray globe, its surface hidden here and there by belts of cloud. Gordon caught the glint of a sea, far around its curve.

"Deceleration . . . two more notches, to reach stationary orbit," repeated Hull, voicing the instructions of the H'Harn.

And after a few minutes, "Needle centered on third dial . . . orbit stationary. Trim lever, four notches . . ."

He touched the trim lever and the ship rotated, then began descending tail first toward the surface of the planet. Hull Burrel said, "Descent control . . . three notches." They went down through streaming clouds, and a little muted bell rang somewhere.

"Friction alarm," said Hull. "Reduce descent velocity by two notches." He moved the lever under his hand.

They looked downward, through the aft view-screen, and saw the planet rising toward them. There was a green landscape, with forests and plains, and the silver ribbon of a river. Gordon heard the quick breathing of Shorr Kan and thought, *He's as keyed up as I am . . . think about Shorr Kan . . . think whether you can trust him. . . .*

"One-half notch less," said Hull, and moved the lever again.

They were a thousand feet above the forest when Gordon struck. He did it with the abrupt ferocity of a man who will not have a second chance and knows it. Hull Burrel's hand still held the lever. Gordon hit it and smashed it downward. The lever went wide open and there was a shrieking roar of air.

Hull shouted something and the next moment the

tail of the ship hit the ground. Gordon went flying, with the sound of the ship's collapsing fabric loud in his ears. He caromed into the control panel and the breath went out of him. There was a long falling cadence of grindings and crackings and metallic screamings. Gradually they ceased. By the time Gordon got his head cleared and his breath back, the ship was quite still, canted drunkenly over on one side.

Shorr Kan was picking himself up, streaming blood from a cut on the forehead. Hull Burrel lay on the deck, limp and motionless. In a panic, Gordon pawed at him, rolled him over and felt for the pulse in his throat.

"Dead?" asked Shorr Kan. He had opened his tunic and was tearing a strip of cloth from his undergarment.

Still gasping for breath, Gordon poked up one of Hull's eyelids and shook his head. "Unconscious. I don't think he'd badly hurt."

Shorr Kan pressed the bit of cloth over the gash on his head. It rapidly became crimson. "Lucky," he said. "We could all be dead." He glared at Gordon. "Why in the name of hell did you crash us. . . ?"

He suddenly fell silent. Shorr Kan had one of the quickest minds that Gordon had ever met. He was now looking at the after part of the alien ship.

The bulkheads back there were crumpled like tin. The tail of the descending ship had taken the full force of the impact. Shorr Kan turned again to Gordon, with an arctic light in his black eyes.

He whispered, "Do you get anything now?"

Gordon too had been listening, straining not only with his ears but with his mind.

"Nothing," he said. "Not the faintest flicker. I think the H'Harn must have died in the landing."

"It would pretty well have to be dead, the way the ship is wrecked back there," said Shorr Kan. "Of course. That's what you were trying to do, kill the H'Harn in the landing."

Gordon nodded. He felt horribly shaky, a reaction from the ordeal of mental battle.

"It was never going to let us walk away free," he said. "That was sure. I took a chance on getting it first."

Shorr Kan refolded the sopping cloth. He nodded, and the gesture made him wince. "I'll say for you, Gordon, you have the courage of your convictions. But I think you were right. I think it would have blasted our minds . . . or at least two of our minds . . . before it let any of us go free. To coin a phrase, we know too much."

"Yes," said Gordon. "I only wish we knew more."

Hull Burrel remained unconscious so long that Gordon was beginning to worry. Finally he came around, grumbling that every bone in his body was broken, then adding that it was worth it to be rid of the H'Harn. He looked at Gordon with narrowed, appraising eyes.

"I'm not sure I'd have had the nerve to risk it," he said.

"You're a spaceman," Gordon said. "You know too well what might have happened." He nodded to the crumpled hull plates. "Drag your fractures over here and give us a hand."

Hull laughed and shook his head, and came. It took them a long time to lever the plates wide enough so that they could edge through, but was no other way out . . . the lock was hopelessly jammed . . . and the impact had already done most of the work for them. They climbed out at last into warm yellow sunshine and dropped to the green-turfed ground.

Gordon looked around wonderingly. This world, or at least this portion of it, had a startling similarity to Earth. The men stood at the edge of a green forest, and not far from them the forest thinned and they had glimpses of a rolling plain. The sky was blue, the sunshine golden, the air sweet and full of the dry fragrance of leaves and grasses. It was true that the individual shrubs, trees, and plants he saw were quite unlike terrestrial ones in detail, but the overall resemblance to a scene in the temperate zone of Earth was very great.

Hull Burrel had other thoughts. He was frowning gloomily at the wreck of the ship that had brought them so far across the void.

"That one will never fly again," he said.

"Even if it was undamaged, you couldn't handle it," said Gordon. "It was only through the H'Harn that you managed."

Hull nodded. "So here we are, without a ship, on an uninhabited world."

Gordon knew what he meant. Stranded.

"But *is* it uninhabited?" said Shorr Kan. The cut had now ceased to bleed. "I know the H'Harn said it was, but those creatures are the fathers of lies. Just before we crashed I thought I saw a distant something that might be a town."

"Mm," said Gordon uneasily. 'If this world is inhabited, and the H'Harn was making for it, it's extremely likely to be one of the nonhuman worlds in this part of the Marches that follow Narath Teyn . . . and the counts."

Shorr Kan said, "I've considered that. I think we had better reconnoiter, and I think we had better be blasted careful about how we show ourselves." He pointed. "The town was off there somewhere."

They started along the edge of the forest, keeping a little way back within the trees for cover. The green plain out beyond them remained empty, rolling away to the horizon. There were a few odd birds and small animals in the forest, making small sounds, and the wind rustled the trees in a familiar way. But there was a quietness here that Gordon did not like. He handed the charge-chamber back to Hull.

"Put it back in the stunner," he said. "It isn't much, but it's something."

"What I don't understand," Hull said, while he did

that, "is the *why* of it. Why did the H'Harn direct us into his ship by mental influence and then take us back with it to the Magellanic Clouds? What use would we be to it?"

"You and I would be no use at all," said Shorr Kan. "It dawns on me that the thing didn't just want a co-pilot. I think it wanted Gordon."

"Good Lord," said Gordon, and stared at him. In the stress of the moment he had not thought that far, but he knew what Shorr Kan was driving at. He broke out in a cold sweat. "But how would it . . . of course, it's attention was aroused when we killed the other H'Harn and started to escape. It would undoubtedly have probed our minds then, even though we were not conscious of it. That's how it came to be hidden in the ship."

"So . . . it probed your mind," said Hull. "What is there about you that would make it want you so badly?"

Shorr Kan smiled ironically. "Tell him, Gordon."

"Look, Hull," Gordon said. "You learned about me so recently, at Throon, that you haven't yet realized the implications of what you learned. The Emperor himself told you how I . . . that is to say, my mind . . . was in possession of the body of Prince Zarth Arn at the time of the star-king's great war against the League."

Hull said irritably, "I'm not likely to forget that. How it was really you who led the Empire fleet, and used the . . ."

He stopped abruptly. His mouth was still open and he forgot to close it.

"Exactly," said Gordon. "It was I, and not Zarth Arn, who used the Empire's secret weapon, the Disruptor."

"The Disruptor," said Shorr Kan, sharpening the point, "which was used by the Empire thousands of years ago, to repel the H'Harn when they first tried to invade this galaxy."

Hull closed his mouth and opened his eyes wider,

looking at Gordon. "Well, of course. If the H'Harn could get their hands . . . or whatever they use in place of them . . . on anyone who knows the secret of the Disruptor, which only the Empire's royal family are supposed to know, they'd be awfully happy. Yes, I see. But . . ."

"I suggest," said Shorr Kan, "that you defer further discussion and take a look out there."

The edge of his voice cut them silent. They peered out of the trees at the great plain.

Miles out from the forest, and far away to their left, a group of specks moved across the surface of the plain. At first Gordon thought they were running game animals. But there was something wrong about their gait and pace and the way that they rose and fell a little above the ground.

The group swept along, not coming any nearer to the forest but heading in a straight line in the direction that Gordon thought of as north. As they passed by, he could see them more clearly. And he did not like what he saw.

The creatures were neither running nor flying, but doing a little of both. They were stubby-winged avian bipeds, much bigger than Korkhann's people, and lacking the civilized amenity of feathers. They had remained closer to the reptile; the equivalent, say, of the pterodactyl. Wings and body were leathery smooth, a gray or tan in color, and their heads were hideously quasi-human, with bulging skulls above long cruel beaks that seemed to have teeth in them. As with Korkhann's folk, the wings served also as arms, with powerful clawed hands.

Gordon got the impression that those hands were carrying weapons.

– X V –

The yellow sunshine poured down, and a little breeze ruffled the green foliage of the trees around them, and it was all so much like a June day on Earth that Gordon could hardly believe he stood upon the planet of a distant star.

That was what made the winged bipeds out there so frightening. It was like encountering these grotesqueries in Ohio or Iowa.

"They're Qhallas," said Shorr Kan. "When Naath Teyn came to Aar to confer with Cyn Cryver, he brought a motley lot of his nonhumans along . . . and there were two of these brutes among them."

The men crouched and watched. The nightmarish group went on, looking neither right nor left, heading straight north. They became distant dots and vanished.

Shorr Kan shaded his eyes squinting. "There . . . in the distance," he said.

They could just see another group of flying, racing specks. They too were heading north.

In the same direction the men were taking. Not, Gordon thought, a comforting idea.

"At any rate," Shorr Kan said, "it confirms my belief that I saw a town of some kind. Probably a landing field there as well." He frowned, his eyes abstracted but very keen. "I think there'll be some of the count's ships arriving here soon, and the Qhallas are going to meet them. I think that this is part of the gathering of Narath's inhuman clans."

Something tightened painfully in Gordon's belly. "Gathering . . . for what?"

"For the long-planned attack," said Shorr Kan quietly, "by the counts of the Marches and Narath's hordes, on Fomalhaut."

Gordon sprang to his feet. He set his hands around Shorr Kan's neck. He was shaking, and his eyes were ferocious.

"Attack of Fomalhaut? You knew this and you didn't tell me?"

Shorr Kan's face remained calm. So did his voice, though it was difficult enough to get it out from between Gordon's throttling hands.

"Has there been one minute since I helped you escape from Aar when we didn't have all the trouble we could handle without borrowing more?"

His gaze met Gordon's steadily, and Gordon let go. But he remained tense, gripped by a terrible fear. And with the fear came an overpowering sense of guilt. He should never have left Fomalhaut, and the Princess Lianna.

He had known, from the time when Narath trapped them on Teyn, that this attack was inevitable. He should have stayed by her, to do what he could. She had reproached him once that he loved adventure more than he did her, and had been angry with her. But perhaps she had told the truth.

"How soon?" he asked. His voice was unsteady, so that he scarcely recognized it. He was aware that Hull was talking also, and that he looked agitated, but he could not spare attention for anything but Shorr Kan's answer.

And Shorr Kan shrugged. "As soon as the combined forces are ready . . . whenever that may be. Cyn Cryver didn't tell me all his plans. But the ships of the counts will go as a fighting escort for transports carrying the hordes of Narath Teyn."

"I see," said Gordon, and clenched his hands hard and forced himself to think. Panic now was not going to help either Lianna or himself. "What part are the H'Harn going to play in this?"

Shorr Kan shook his head. "I can't answer that. Cyn Cryver was very secretive about his relations with the H'Harn." He paused, and then said soberly, "My own feeling is that the H'Harn are using Cyn Cryver and all the others as cats'-paws, in some fashion. As, of course, I had planned to do myself."

"Have you ever played straight with anyone in your whole life?" demanded Hull Burrel.

Shorr Kan nodded. "Oh, yes. Often. In fact, I never use deceit unless there's something to be gained by it."

Hull made a sound of disgust. Gordon hardly heard them. He was walking back and forth, his mind whirling.

"We've got to get back to Fomalhaut," he said.

"That," said Shorr Kan, "will not be easy. The people of this world do not have space travel. You saw them. They're a pretty squalid lot."

Gordon's face set and tightened. "You said that some of the counts' ships would likely land here soon, to take off these Qhallas for the campaign?"

"Ah," said Shorr Kan. "I think I see what's in your mind. We'll steal one of those ships when they come and take off to warn Fomalhaut. Good God, man. Be sensible!"

Hull said, "He's a blackhearted rascal, but he's right, John Gordon. Those winged devils will be swarming where the ships land."

"All right," said Gordon. "All right. The fact still remains. We need a ship. Tell me how we get it."

Hull's big coppery face reflected nothing but baffled

anger and distress. But Shorr Kan said, after a minute, "There is one way it just *might* be done."

Both Gordon and Hull kept quiet, afraid to break the tenuous thread of hope. Shorr Kan stood biting his lip and thinking. They waited. Suddenly Shorr Kan said to Gordon, "Suppose we swing it. Suppose we get to Fomalhaut. If I know the Princess Lianna, she'll want to hang me at the earliest possible moment."

Gordon answered, "I'll see to it that she doesn't."

That was a large promise. Shorr Kan smiled, with a certain unpleasant humor.

"Can you guarantee that?" he demanded. "Can you guarantee that if she doesn't, someone else . . . say the emperor . . . won't do it for her?"

It was no good lying and Gordon knew it, much as he wanted to. "No, I can't guarantee it. But I'm almost sure that, if you've earned it, I have enough influence to save your neck."

"Almost is cold comfort," said Shorr Kan. "However . . ." He studied Gordon for a moment, and Gordon knew that he was mentally going over all the alternatives, checking them swiftly once more before he committed himself. Finally he shrugged and said, "It'll have to do. Will you give me your word of honor that you'll do everything in your power to save me from execution or punishment?"

"Yes," said Gordon, "If you get us to Fomalhaut, I'll do that."

Shorr Kan considered. "I'll accept that. If I hadn't known from the past that you're a bit stupid about always keeping your word, I wouldn't trust you. As it is, I do."

Hull Burrel gave a grunt. Gordon ignored him and asked quickly, "Now . . . how do we get away from here?"

Shorr Kan's black eyes sparkled. "There's only one

possible way and that's the ships of the counts that will be coming to pick up the Qhalla warriors."

"But you said yourself we could never capture a ship. . . ."

Shorr Kan grined. "That's right. But I have a certain talent for these things. and I've thought of a way."

He talked rapidly. "Listen. I helped you escape from Aar, and together we killed the H'Harn Susurr there. But nobody on Aar, none of the counts, really knows what happened. All they know is that a H'Harn was found dead, the two prisoners—you and Hull Burrel—were missing, and that I also was missing."

"What are you getting at?" demanded Hull.

"This," said Shorr Kan. "Suppose I reappear here on the Qhalla world. Suppose I tell the counts, when they come, that it was you two who killed the H'Harn, and that when you escaped you took me along as a captive?"

"Would they believe that?" asked Gordon. "Wouldn't they want to know where we are and how you got away from us?"

"Ah, but that's the beauty of my idea," said Shorr Kan. "I'd have the two of you right with me, you see . . . your wrists bound, me covering you with the stunner. I'd tell them that when you wrecked the ship on this world, I turned the tables on you and overpowered *you*, and how could they doubt it with the proof right before their eyes? Isn't it ingenious?"

Hull Burell let out a sound that was like a roar. He jumped for Shorr Kan, got him between his hands, and started trying to break him in two.

"Hull, stop it!" Gordon cried.

The Antarian turned a flaming, raging face toward him. "Stop it? You heard the bastard, didn't you? He's the same Shorr Kan as ever!"

Shorr Kan was a strong man but the big Antarian shook him like a terrier shaking a rat. "He's got a beautiful idea, surely. He'll march us in as prisoners, and since his escape didn't work he'll claim he never tried it, and he'll throw us to the wolves!"

"Wait a minute," said Gordon, pulling at Burrel's arm. "Let him go. Too much depends on this, Hull! Let's talk about it." But the seeds of suspicion were flourishing in Gordon's own mind, and he looked very coldly at Shorr Kan, as the latter stepped quickly back and away from Hull's reluctantly opened hands.

"It does," said Gordon, "sound exactly like the kind of clever double cross you've always been good at."

"Doesn't it, though," said Shorr Kan, and smiled. "And I'll have to admit that I considered doing it just that way."

Gordon watched him narrowly. "But you changed your mind?"

"Yes, Gordon, I did." There was an odd note of patience in his voice now, as though he were explaining something to a very small child. "I've told you this before and I'll repeat it again. I could stay with the counts and deceive them all down the line, but I *cannot* deceive the H'Harn, and one stray thought would be the end of me. So I prefer to take my chances at Fomalhaut. It's simple arithmetic."

"With you, my friend," said Gordon sourly, "nothing is simple. That's why I find this difficult to believe . . . because it *is* simple."

"Then let's find something else to pitch it on," said Shorr Kan brightly. "Friendship, for example. I've always rather liked you, Gordon. I've said so in the past. Doesn't that count for anything?"

"Oh, my God," said Hull Burrel softly. "Here's the biggest scoundrel in the galaxy, and he asks you to believe in him because he *likes* you. Let me kill him, John Gordon."

"I'm tempted," Gordon said. "But wait a bit." He

paced up and down. trying to force himself to think clearly against the doubts and the agonizing apprehension that filled his mind. Finally he said, "It comes down to one thing. The only starships that will be coming to this world are the counts' ships. And this is the only possible way we could hope to get one of those ships. We have to gamble, Hull. Give him the stunner."

Hull Burrel eyed him incredulously.

Gordon said, "If you can think of another way, tell me."

Hull stood a moment with his head down like an angry buffalo. Then he swore and handed the weapon to Shorr Kan.

Instantly Shorr Kan leveled the stunner at them.

"Now you *are* my captives," he said, smiling. "Hull was absolutely right, I am going to turn you over as prisoners to the counts."

Hull's fury went quite beyond reason. He rushed forward bellowing, in the face of the stunner, his hands raised for a killing blow.

Shorr Kan stepped agilely aside and let him blunder past. Then he laughed, a laugh of pure and wicked delight.

"Look at him," he said. "Isn't he lovely?" Hull had turned around and was standing uncertainly, his big hands swinging, staring in dumb amazement as Shorr Kan laughed again. "Sorry, Hull, I had to do it. You were so *sure*. I didn't have the heart to disappoint you." He tossed the stunner in the air, caught it again expertly, and shoved it into his belt. "Come along now. Before we encounter anyone, human or Qhalla, I'll have to bind your hands, but no need for that yet."

He gave Hull a friendly clap on the back. Hull turned dusky purple, but Gordon could not help grinning a little.

They started out across the rolling plain, headed northward in the direction in which the grotesque

Qhalla bands had been hurrying. The sun sank down across the sky, and then as a rosy sunset darkened into twilight, there was a distant flashing and a rolling crack of thunder, thrice repeated in the clear evening, and they saw three shining starships come down.

Two hours later, they stood in the darkness of night and watched a scene that might have been lifted straight out of hell.

-XVI-

Red-flaring torches illuminated the crowded streets of what was less a town than a planless huddle of huts and shanties and ramshackle warehouses dumped haphazardly beside a ford of the river. The Qhallas were not civilized enough to need anything more than a meeting place and marketplace, and it was not a very big one. But it was thronged now with thousands of the winged bipeds, shuffling in the dusty lanes with such a press of bodies that the hut walls creaked at their shoulders. The shaking red light picked out their leather wings and glistening reptilian eyes. Their hoarse voices made an incessant squawking din. They made Gordon think of a horde of demons, and they stank beyond belief.

The focus of all this big crowd was the three starships that rested on the plain outside the wretched town. Two of them were big cargo ships whose gleaming sides loomed up far beyond the torchlight, into the darkness. The third ship was much smaller, a fast little cruiser. The Qhalla horde milled between the town and the two bigger ships.

"Transports," said Shorr Kan. "The smaller cruiser will be one of the counts directing his end of the operation."

Hull Burrell said contemptuously, "That mob couldn't do much against a modern star-world."

"Ah, but this is only part of it, a very small part," said Shorr Kan. "All through the Marches, on wild worlds like this, the same sort of gathering will be going on. All the nonhuman peoples will answer the call of Narath Teyn."

Remembering how the Gerrn had idolized him, Gordon had no doubt of that.

"The counts' fighting ships will take on Fomalhaut's navy," Shorr Kan added. "While they are engaged, the massed transports will go through and land these hordes for a direct assault on the capital."

The words conjured up a nightmare vision in Gordon's mind, and he felt again an agony of guilt for having left Lianna.

"The Empire is the ally of Fomalhaut," said Hull Burrel. "They'll have something to say about it."

"But this will be a surprise. By the time an Empire fleet can get there, Narath Teyn may sit on the throne of Fomalhaut. It won't be easy then to unseat him."

Shorr Kan did not go on to voice the inevitable corollary, though it was in all their minds . . . that Lianna might not then be alive to reclaim her throne, leaving Narath Teyn as the sole and rightful heir.

Gordon demanded harshly, "Are we just going to stand here and talk about it?"

Shorr Kann looked thoughtfully down from the low hill where they were hidden, above the town.

"If I take you two in as prisoners, I can convince whatever official of the counts is in charge that I'm still Cyn Cryver's ally. But there's another problem." He indicated the milling, squawking, stinking Qhallas. "The way they look, and from what I've heard of them, they'd tear us to pieces before we ever reached the ships."

"On that I believe you," said Hull. "They're a wild lot anyway, and they're worked up now to the point of madness."

Shorr Kan shrugged. "No use asking for a sticky end like that. We'll just have to wait until we see a better chance of getting through. But I'd better bind your hands now. When the chance does come, we'll have to move fast."

Gordon submitted to having his hands bound behind his back, though the prospect of being helpless among the Qhallas was not one he relished. He consoled himself with the realization that his hands wouldn't do him any good anyway. But Hull Burrel flatly refused.

"Oh, for God's sake," snarled Gordon. "What do you want to do, sit here and die?"

"I think we'll do that anyway," he muttered, looking at the Qhallas. But he put his hands behind him and let Shorr Kan tie them.

Then they sat in the grass and waited, hoping for some way to open for them to the ships.

The blazing stars of the Marches looked down from the sky. The wind brought the sound of hoarse shouting from where the torches flickered. Gordon smelled the pungent smell of the warm grasses on which they sat, and it was so familiar that it startled him.

Then he remembered. Long ago, when he was still John Gordon of New York, he had visited a friend who lived in the Ohio countryside. They had sat at night in a summer-warm meadow, and there had been fireflies, and the smell of the sun-scorched grasses had been just the same.

Gordon felt a sudden shuddering pang of disorientation. Who was he and what was he doing here, in this wild strange place? The sweet grass smell tortured him with longing to be home, on his own familiar world, where the beasts of the field did not speak with the voices of nightmare, nor form themselves into uncouth armies; where there were no H'Harn and the stars were a long way off, and life held neither splendor nor gut-wrenching, soul-destroying fear.

But then a memory came to him. A memory of Lianna. His moment of hysteria passed. He knew that only one thing mattered now; he must live long enough to get to Fomalhaut with the warning.

Shorr Kan suddenly stood up. "There!" he said, gesturing toward the Qhalla town.

Gordon and Hull also stood up. Two men—two human men—had emerged from the milling crowd of Qhallas. They stood a little apart from the throng, as though they wanted air.

"One of them wears the insignia of the Mace," said Shorr Kan. "An aide or vassal of Cyn Cryver. We'll have to take this chance. Get going!"

He gave Gordon and Hull a hard shove, and they started down the grassy slope, Shorr Kan coming behind them with the stunner leveled at ther backs.

"Hurry, damn it," snarled Shorr Kan. "Before they go back to the ship."

They staggered and stumbled down the slope. The light was bad and their bound hands made them clumsy. Now Gordon saw that the two men were turning around as though to go back through the swarming Qhallas to the ships.

Shorr Kan shouted, a loud call. The two men turned. And the uproar of the Qhallas quieted suddenly as they also turned to see.

"*Run!*" said Shorr Kan.

They ran, toward the two men. But the Qhallas had started running also, toward the strangers, their wings half-spread. They brandished weapons and their toothed beaks uttered charking noises of anger.

Shorr Kann triggered his stunner. The foremost Qhallas fell and rolled. The others held back for a moment.

The two men were staring in amazement. Now, by the torchlight, Gordon could make out their faces. One of them, who wore the emblem of the Mace, was a compact, stocky man with a dark, tight face. The other was younger, taller, and much less sure of himself.

Shorr Kan shouted at them. "Hold off your pets! I'm an ally of Cyn Cryver, bringing in prisoners."

Rather doubtfully, the older man turned and barked something at the Qhallas in their own harsh tongue. They began to gabble between themselves, confused and a little disconcerted by the stunner. The three went past them and pulled up, Gordon and Hull panting, in front of Cyn Cryver's men.

To the proud and haughty one, the man apparently in command, Shorr Kan demanded, "What is your name?"

"I am the Count Obd Doll," answered the stocky man, and stared at Shorr Kan as though he could not believe what he saw. "You . . . you are Shorr Kan. You disappeared from Aar with the Empire captives . . ."

"These same two," said Shorr Kan, "and not from choice, I assure you. They took me as a hostage. Fourtunately, they crashed their ship not far from here and in the confusion I was able to turn the tables on them."

"Why didn't you kill them?" asked Obd Doll. "Why bring them here?"

"Because Cyn Cryver wants them alive. Especially alive and able to talk. Where is he?"

Hesitantly, Obd Doll answered, "At Teyn."

Shorr Kan nodded. "Of course. The gathering place of the horde. Take us there at once."

"But," said Obd Doll, "I am on orders here." He went on with other objections, and Gordon sweated in an agony of impatience. The count appeared to be not too bright, and consequently unable to adjust to, or evaluate, a set of unexpected circumstances.

"Besides," said the count, sticking his jaw out farther in a show of strength, "how am I to know. . . ?"

Shorr Kan's face darkened and his voice sank to a kind of tigerish purring.

"Little man," he said, "these two captives may hold the key to the whole campaign. Cyn Cryver is waiting for them. Just how long do you think it wise to keep him waiting?"

Obd Doll looked shaken. "Well," he said. "Well, in that case, yes, of course. May I suggest, sir . . . call the Count Cyn Cryver from our cruiser. . . ."

So far, so good, thought Gordon . . . but it was just a little late. The Qhallas had got over their first shock and settled their confusion. They wanted the prisoners to play with, and they were closing in.

Shorr Kan had made a good try. But it was not much of an epitaph for them.

Only it seemed that Obd Doll had also made up his mind. He roared at the Qhallas, obviously ordering them to stop. Apparently they had some rudiments of discipline, for they fell back a little, and Obd Doll said hurriedly, "We had better go to the cruiser at once. These Qhallas . . . savage . . . unreliable . . . hate all humans except Narath Teyn. . . ."

It came to Gordon that the man was worried about his own skin. He didn't blame him. Narath Teyn might have calmed the Qhallas' bloodlust, but not these two men of the Marches. In fact, the younger one practically invited attack, staring with unconcealed loathing at the bird-things, and he reeked so of fear that even Gordon could smell it.

They began to move toward the cruiser. The Qhallas pressed after them, hopping, shuffling, flapping, edging a little closer with every step. They squawked among themselves, their unlovely voices edged with mounting anger. Their eyes were bright with brainless fury, watching their prey move closer to sanctuary. They had a simple desire to tear these man-creatures into small pieces and peck at them like robins at chunks of suet. Gordon thought that their shaky discipline was not going to hold out another ten paces. And now the reek of his own fear was acrid in his nostrils.

The younger of the two men had frankly given way

to panic. He drew a small gray egg out of his pocket and said in a high voice, "I'd better use the numb-gas."

"No!" said Obd Doll. "Put that thing away, you idiot. We could numb a few but the others would be on us in a minute. Just move on; we're almost there."

The men staggered, buffeted by stubby wings, grabbed at by wicked hands. Obd Doll kept up a barrage of orders and Gordon guessed that he was reminding them of their allegiance to Narath Teyn and their duty to obey, disperse, and loaded themselves into the transports. Whatever he said, it stopped their making up their minds to take the prisoners, at least until the men had reached the cruiser. The air lock door slammed shut on the horde outside, and Obd Doll mopped his brow with his hand, which was visibly shaking.

"A difficult lot to handle," he said. "Without Narath Teyn around, it's not a job I care for."

"You did well," said Shorr Kan. "Now call Teyn at once, and inform the Count Cyn Cryver that I have recovered the captives and will bring them to him there at once."

The ring of authority in his voice was such that Obd Doll all but saluted. "At once." Then he looked at Gordon and Hull Burrel, oppressed by a fresh doubt. "What'll we do with them? We have no brig . . . this is a dispatch and command cruiser. . . ."

"Put them in one of the air locks," said Shorr Kan. "Take all the spacesuits out of the lock first. Then if they want to break out into space, they're welcome."

He laughed. Obd Doll laughed. The younger man laughed. Gordon did not laugh, and neither did Hull Burrel. They looked at Shorr Kan, but Shorr Kan's back was turned and he was already on his way, a man with important matters to attend to, a man in a hurry with no time to spare for two dupes he had deceived for his own purposes. Maybe.

Hull started to curse, but smothered it. They were

shoved along by Obd Doll's men. toward an air lock on the other side of the cruiser. They were kept waiting until the helmets and suits were taken out of the lock, and then were thrust into the small coffinlike chamber. The inner door closed hermetically upon them, with a soft hissing sound that was very like mocking laughter.

Hull Burrel looked heavily at the immovable door. "Neat," he said. "They've got us nicely cooped up, and any time they decide to execute us, all they have to do is use the remote control to open the outer door of this lock." There was a manual control as well, almost suicidally handy. They carefully avoided leaning on it.

Gordon shook his head. "They won't do that. You heard Shorr Kan tell them that Cyn Cryver wants us alive."

"Yes, I heard him," said Hull. "I also know we're the only living beings who can tell the truth about how he got away from Aar. Of course, if he's really on our side, that's not important. But if he isn't . . . I don't think he'd want Cyn Cryver to hear it. Because of course the H'Harn would move in and examine him. I think he'd just blow us out into space and say we did it ourselves, two loyal Empire men choosing death before dishonor." Hull's face was set and very hard. "Do you honestly believe Shorr Kan is on your side, John Gordon?"

"Yes. Not out of nobility, but because we're his own best chance."

Hull remained standing for a time, frowning at Gordon. Then he sat down on the floor and leaned wearily against the bulkhead. "I wish," he said, "I had your simple faith."

-XVII-

The cruiser throbbed and hummed, flying through the Marches at highest speed. To Gordon, prisoned with the Antarian in the lock, it seemed to have been flying thus for interminable period. Several times the inner door had been opened and a scant ration of food and water thrust in to them by armed and careful men. But nothing else had happened, and they had not seen Shorr Kan again.

Gordon began increasingly to share Hull Burrel's skepticism about the reliability of Shorr Kan as an ally. So much so, that each time he heard the sound of a lock door opening he looked quickly at the outer one to see if this was not the moment that Hull had predicted, when they two would be catapulted on a blast of decompressed air into space and eternal silence. So far, it had always been the inner door that opened.

So far.

Agonized worry about Lianna and his own gnawing sense of guilt added to Gordon's personal torment.

"Gordon, I understand, but will you please shut *up?*" flared Hull Burrel finally. "There's not a damn thing we can do about it now, and you're getting on my nerves."

Gordon's own temper flared, but he refrained from uttering the words that came to his tongue. Instead he shut his jaw hard and went and sat with his back against the wall of the lock chamber . . . a posture that had now become practically permanent . . . and thought what the hell of a man of action he had turned out to be.

A thin, almost undetectable odor roused him from his brooding. It was pungent, unfamiliar, and it had to be coming into the lock from the air-vent connected with the main life-support system of the ship.

Gordon jumped up and approached the vent and sniffed. And that was the last thing he remembered before he fell on his face on the hard deck and never even felt the impact.

He awoke vaguely to a thin hissing noise and the sensation of being shaken. Somebody was calling his name.

"Gordon! Gordon, wake up!"

The somebody sounded urgent. There was a tickling in Gordon's nostrils. He shook his head and coughed, trying to get away from it, and the effort caused him to open his eyes.

Shorr Kan was bending over him, holding a small tube that hissed and tickled as it released gas into Gordon's mouth and nose.

"Oxygen," said Shorr Kan. "It should clear the cobwebs. You've got to come out of it, Gordon. I need you."

Gordon still felt remarkably stupid, but his mind was beginning to function again.

"Gas . . . from the air duct," he mumbled. "Knocked me out . . ."

Shorr Kan nodded. "Yes. Numb-gas. I managed to slip some canisters of it out of the ship's armory and drop them into the main air-supply of the life-support system."

Gordon stumbled up to his feet, hanging on to Shorr Kan for support. "The officers . . . the crew . . ?"

"Out like lights," said Shorr Kan, grinning. "Of course, I thoughtfully put on a spacesuit beforehand, and then vented and replaced the air supply before I took it off. Feeling better?"

"I'm all right."

"Good. The officers and crew are sleeping like babies, but they won't sleep much longer. I need your help to secure them, and I need Hull to pilot the ship while we're doing it. I've got the cruiser on automatic now, but the Marches are a risky place for that."

He went over to Hull, who was still sprawled unconscious on the deck, and held the oxygen tube under his nose. Then he looked up at Gordon and showed his teeth in a smile.

"Didn't I tell you I'd get you free?"

"You did." Gordon shook his head, which ached blindingly. "And you have. I congratulate you. The only trouble is, my head is going to fall off from being saved."

When Hull Burrel opened his eyes and saw Shorr Kan bending over him, his reaction was almost comically instinctive. He blinked once, and then put up his big hands and closed them around Shorr Kan's throat. But he was still weak as a kitten. Shorr Kan slapped his hands away and stood up.

"A grateful pair you two are," he said.

Gordon helped the Anatarian to his feet, speaking urgently as he did so, explaining. He wasn't sure how much Hull understood until he said, "The ship's on auto-pilot, and you're needed in the bridge."

First and last a spaceman, Hull pulled himself together by main force, forgetting everything else.

"On auto-pilot? Here in the Marches?" he thrust Gordon aside and went with violent, if unsteady, haste out of the lock and down the companionway to the bridge.

Shorr Kan took a roll of tough wire from stores, and then he and Gordon set to work securing the officers and men.

Obd Doll, who lay in his own small cabin, was the

last of them, and when they had him bound Shorr Kan looked thoughtfully down at him.

"I think I'll bring him round now with oxygen," he said. "He'd know the schedule that Cyn Cryver and Narath Teyn have set up for the attack on Fomalhaut, and that's something we've got to know."

"What," said Gordon, "if he won't talk?"

Shorr Kan smiled. "I think I can persuade him. You go on up to the bridge. You're the high-minded type and you'd only get in my way."

Gordon hesitated. It sounded like torture to him. But he thought of Lianna and what could be going to happen to her, and hardened his heart. He turned and went out of the cabin.

When he entered the bridge, Hull Burrel spoke without turning from the controls.

"I've laid as direct a course as possible for Fomalhaut. It'll take us too close to Teyn for comfort."

Gordon peered at the viewplate. The little cruiser was edging along the coast of a gigantic cloud of glowing dust, whose minute particles were so excited by the radiation of the stars drowned in it that it looked like a great mass of flame.

To Gordon, it seemed that the ship was merely crawling. He tried to contain his impatience. He also tried not to think of what Shorr Kan was doing.

After a while Shorr Kan came into the bridge. He took one look at Gordon's face and said seriously, "Could you hear the cries all the way up here?"

Gordon started for the door. "What did you do to him?"

Shorr Kan caught his arm. "I wouldn't go down there, Gordon. Not unless you . . ."

"Not unless I what?"

Shorr Kan's brows went up and his eyes laughed at Gordon. "Unless you want to be frightfully disappointed. Obd Doll has nothing worse the matter with him than a severe case of fright."

"You mean," said Gordon skeptically, "that he talked just because you threatened him?"

Shorr Kan nodded. "He did. You see the value of a reputation of ruthlessless. He believed I'd do exactly what I said I would, and so he told me all he knew without my having to do it. We'd soon find out if he lied, so I think he told the truth."

"When does the fleet leave Teyn?" Gordon asked.

"Obd Doll couldn't narrow that down too definitely. He said it would depend on when the last contingents of nonhumans came in . . . and they've been coming in, from all over the Marches, in answer to Narath Teyn's summons."

The words evoked in Gordon's mind a swift, ominous vision . . . of those alien hordes from worlds that had no human tradition at all, the scaled ones, the winged ones, the hairy ones, streaming through the Marches to foregather for an assault on a great star-kingdom. Yes, they would come at the call of Narath Teyn. Narath was mad. Gordon was sure of that. But there was some quality in him that had made him a leader of not-men such as the galaxy had never seen before.

"But from what Obd Doll told me of the forces that have already gathered," Shorr Kan was saying, "I'd hazard a guess that they'll leave Teyn very soon, probably in the next few days, on their way to Fomalhaut."

"What about the H'Harn," asked Hull Burrel. "Where do they come into this?"

Shorr Kan shook his head. "Obd Doll swears he doesn't know. The H'Harn have no fleet in this galaxy. He says that only Cyn Cryver and one or two others know what part, if any, the H'Harn will play."

Gordon, desperate and tense, tried to clear his mind of emotion and think calmly.

"Hull, will the communication equipment of this ship reach as far as Fomalhaut?" he asked.

Hull Burrel went into the little communications room behind the bridge. After a few minutes he came out again.

"It'll reach, but the power is so limited it would have to be audio only, not telestereo."

Shorr Kan said sharply, "You're planning to warn Fomalhaut by communicator?"

"Of course," said Gordon. "You must see it yourself . . . the time element, and the very strong possibility that we won't make it to Fomalhaut."

"Before you leap to the transmitter, think of this. Teyn and the Count's fleet are between us and Fomalhaut. They will be bound to pick up our transmission. They'll have fast cruisers after us at once. . . ."

Gordon made a brusque gesture. "We'll just have to take our chances. Fomalhaut has got to be warned."

"You didn't let me finish," said Shorr Kan. "The counts are liable to hit Fomalhaut right away, before any strong defenses can be organized. In their position, that is what I would do."

Gordon had not thought of that possibility. He was racked by doubt.

Hull said, "I'm with Gordon. Warn them, and gamble. The counts, praise be, have neither your guts nor your gall."

"I am touched," said Shorr Kan softly. "But what about us?"

"Take your chances, as Gordon said."

"What chances? They'll have us cut off within minutes after they pick up our transmission."

"I have an idea about that," said Hull.

He touched a control. On the big chartplate a sectional chart of the whole region of the Marches slid into view.

"All right," said Shorr Kan. "Look here."

Even Gordon, unused to reading the charts, could see when Shorr Kan pointed out their relative position that they could hardly hope to get past the fleet at Teyn once it was alerted. Not even by a miracle.

But Hull put his finger on a massive swarm of red flecks—a great reef, as it were, marked in the color of danger. The reef lay equally between them and Fomalhaut, one curving wing of it reaching out almost to Teyn.

"We could take a short-cut," Hull said, "through here."

Shorr Kan stared at him astonished. "Through the Broken Stars?" Then he uttered a short laugh. "I revise my opinion of you, Hull."

"What," asked Gordon, "are the Broken Stars?"

Hull said, "Did you ever stop to think why the Marches of Outer Space are such a mess of debris?"

"I haven't had very much time to consider cosmic origins."

"The scientists tell us," said the Antarian, "that long ago two fairly large star-clusters were on a collision course. When they met, of course the looser parts of the swarms simply went through each other with only a minimum of actual hits. But even those few were enough to strew debris all along the Marches.

"However, in each cluster there was a much tighter, denser core of stars, and those high-density cores collided. The result was terrific. Stars tore each other up in such a high incidence of collisions that they formed a spinning mess of half-stars, bits of stars, shattered planets, whole planets . . . you name it. Scarcely anyone ever risks going into that jungle, but at least two scientific survey ships have in the past crossed through it. If they had a chance, so do we." As a sort of afterthought he added, "I don't have to tell you how thin it is."

Gordon said, "Take it."

"Do I have a vote?" asked Shorr Kan.

With one voice, Hull and Gordon answered, "No."

Shorr Kan shrugged.

Gordon said to the Antarian, "When you send your message, tell Fomalhaut what we know about the counts and the impending attack, but *don't* mention Shorr Kan. They'd never believe that story, and they might put the whole warning down as a fake."

Hull nodded. "Since you're *persona grata* at the court of Fomalhaut, I'll send it in your name. Have you any recognition signal, so they can be sure it's you?"

Gordon thought. "Tell them it's from the man who once called Korkhann, their Minister of Nonhuman Affairs, an overgrown myna bird. Korkhann will know."

The little dispatch cruiser crawled on the chart until it was close to that ominous reef of red dots. Only then did Hull Burrel send his message.

That done, they plunged headlong into the Broken Stars.

-XVIII-

The place was like a star-captain's nightmare.

To the eye, the Broken Stars would have seemed only a region where the points of starry light were somewhat denser, through which the small ship seemed to creep.

But the radar and sensor instruments saw it differently. They saw a region where the debris of shattered suns, long, cool, and dark, whirled in small ovaloids, in spinning little maelstroms, in cones and disks and nests of wreckage. Splintered stones and dust that had once been planets lay in drifts. And the many surviving suns of the wrecked star-clusters flared out fiercely as background.

The computers that took the radar impulses and directed the cruiser's flight along the chosen course were clacking like the chattering teeth of hysterical old women. Hull Burrel, hunched over the board, listened to that uproar and watched the rapidly changing symbols, only occasionally reaching out his hand to give the computers a new course. But when he did so, it was done with all the speed of which he was capable.

Gordon and Shorr Kan, standing behind him, looked at the viewplate which showed only the swarming points of light through which they seemed barely to move. They looked then at the flashing radar screen, and were awed.

"I was in Orion Nebula once, but that was child's

play compared to this," said Gordon. "Have we got a chance at all?"

"We have," said Hull, "if we don't run into a bit of it too complicated for the radar to sense in time. But I'll tell you how you can improve our chances about a hundred percent."

"How?"

"By getting off my neck!" Hull roared, without turning. "Go and sit down. I can fly this damned suicide mission better without jawbone help."

"He's right," said Shorr Kan, and nodded to Gordon. They drew back. "There's nothing you and I can do now . . . but wait! Yes, there is one thing we can do. Back in a minute."

He went aft. Gordon sat down wearily in one of the chairs at the rear of the bridge that were intended for top-brass to sit in and harass worried pilots.

Hull had told them that radar showed no sign of pursuit at all. He had explained that when the counts saw them dive into the Broken Stars, they would write them off as finished. And, he had added, they were probably right.

Shorr Kan came back holding a couple of plastic flasks filled with a pale, slightly milky-looking liquor. He grinned sardonically at Gordon.

"I was pretty sure that Obd Doll would have something stored away. The counts of the Marches are a hard-drinking lot. Here, have one."

Gordon took the flask, but stared up at Shorr Kan in amazement. "A drink? Now? In this?" And he jerked his head toward the radar screen. "Any minute, one stray chunk of drift . . ."

Shorr Kan sat down. "Quite right. And can you think of a better time for drinking?"

Gordon shrugged. Maybe Shorr Kan made sense, at that. All Hull wanted them to do was to keep quiet and let him make his long-shot gamble for life. Very well, then. He would keep quiet. He lifted the flask and drank.

The liquor might look a little like milk and it was bland going down, but it was hellfire when it hit his insides.

"Better than anything we had in the Dark Worlds," said Shorr Kan.

"I remember," said Gordon, "when Lianna and I were your prisoners at Thallarna . . . how long ago that seems! . . . you said you'd offer us a drink but you didn't keep the stuff around because it would spoil your pose as the austere patriotic leader."

Shorr Kan smiled wryly. "And much good it did me in the end." He looked at Godon with a kind of admiration. "I had the whole galaxy in my grasp, and then you came along. By God, I have to hand it to you. You really were a spoiler."

Gordon turned and looked, startled ,toward the view-plate. Nothing there seemed to have changed but there was a new sound, a screeching and screeking along the hull.

"Relax, Gordon," said Shorr Kan. "Just tiny particles, probably no bigger than atoms. Nothing to get jumpy about." He added, "When I think about it, in spite of the remarkable things you've done, you've nearly always had the jumps."

Gordon said between his teeth, "It seems a natural reaction when one's life is in danger."

"Look at me," said Shorr Kan. "I'm in as much danger as you. More, because if we get out of this mess there's more trouble waiting for me. I'm flying for my life . . . the second time . . . me that was lord of the Dark Worlds. But do I get upset? Not a bit. If Shorr Kan has to go, he'll go with his head high."

He raised the flask with a theatrical gesture, but the smile on his dark face was mocking.

Gordon shook his head. There were times when Shorr Kan just reduced him to silence.

"So drink up and be of good heart," said Shorr Kan. "We'll get through, all will go well with you, and you'll save my neck when we get there . . . I hope!"

The computers were shuttering even more wildly, and when Gordon glanced forward he saw that the symbols were flashing in a swift stream across the radar screen. It seemed to him that Hull Burrel, hunched over the board, had his head bent in resignation, bowing to the inevitable end. Gordon turned his own head quickly away.

He thought of Lianna. It was strange how, when everything was getting unreal to him in the slow freezing terror of approaching dissolution, she remained quite real. Even if he survived, he felt that she was lost to him. But he thought of her, and was glad.

"You know, I've had an idea for a long time," Shorr Kan was saying, "that you're sort of a grain of sand in the machine, Gordon. I mean, you take someone out of his own context, his own time-frame, and hurl him into the future where he's got no business to be, and you put everything out of kilter. See how your coming, from the very first, has upset things all across the galaxy."

Gordon said dryly, "What you mean is that I upset the private plans of one Shorr Kan, that's all."

"Possibly," said Shorr Kan, with a courtly wave of his hand. "But tell me, what the devil was it like, that past time you came from? I asked you that before, but then you were lying to me and I couldn't believe a word of it."

"To tell you the truth," said Gordon, "it's getting just a little vague in my own mind." He drank and considered. "There was a man named Keogh who told me that this future I had been in before was all a dream. I just hated the Earth as it was, he said, so I made up fantasies about star-kingdoms and great wars beyond the suns. Of course at that time we didn't have anything approaching star-flight, so it must have all seemed pretty wild to him."

"We have a name for people like that," said Shorr Kan. "Planet-huggers. Hang tight to your mother-world's apron strings, because if you get away from it you might find something awfully nasty and upsetting."

Gordon glanced forward again. "Right at this moment," he said, "I'm not so sure that people who take that view are so awfully wrong."

Seen past the dark, hunched silhouette of Hull Burrel, the scene in the viewplate had slowly changed.

The points of fire that were suns seemed to be closer together. It was as though the ship was moving toward a rampart of suns, and surely they were not going to try to go that way. Hull would surely change course soon.

But time went on and he did not. Gordon drank again. The mighty blazing rampart of suns seemed closer, and still Hull did not alter course. Gordon felt a growing impulse to go and pound on Hull's arm, to make him veer off, but he fought it down. He didn't know a bloody thing about piloting a starship, and they had put the ship and themselves into Hull's hands and there was nothing to do but wait.

Shorr Kan seemed to understand how he felt. He said, "Less drift between the suns. Their attraction tends to gather up a good bit of debris. That's why he's going that way."

"Thank you for reassuring the nervous novice," said Gordon. "It's good of you."

Shorr Kan smiled. "I'm an awfully sympathetic person. Have another."

They sat, and drank, and Gordon tried not to look

at the viewplate again or listen to the computers clacking. Time seemed to run on forever and it was almost a painful shock of change when the viewplate showed that they were out of the star-swarm and into the dark, clear deeps of open space.

Hull Burrel's great paw slammed down on the automatic pilot control. The big Antarian turned to them and for the first time in that flight they saw his face.

It was wild, exalted, and his voice came to them as a kind of hoarse triumphant shout.

"By God, I did it! I ran the Broken Stars!"

And then, as he looked at them, sitting with the nearly-emptied flasks in their hands, the wildness and excitement left him. He came back and stood over them, towering.

I'll be everlastingly damned." he said. "While I did it, you two have been sitting here and drinking your heads off!"

Shorr Kan answered calmly, "You asked us not to bother you. Well, have we?"

Hull's craggy face turned scarlet. His chest heaved, and then he roared with laughter.

"Now," he said, "now I've seen everything. Get me one of those flasks. I think I want to get a little drunk myself."

They were out of the Marches, and the pure white fire of Fomalhaut gleamed like a beacon ahead.

It was many hours before Hull Burrel came back to the bridge, stretching and yawning. He started laughing again as he looked at Gordon and Shorr Kan.

"Through the Broken Stars with two topers," he said and shook his head. "Nobody will ever believe it."

"The whole fleet of Fomalhaut is on alert," he told them. "We're to land at the royal port on Hathyr."

"Any message for me?" asked Gordon.

The Antarian shook his head.

So that, Gordon thought, was that.

The radar screen showed ships far out from Fomalhaut cruising in stand-by formation.

"It's a good fleet," muttered Hull. "It's awfully good, and proved it in the fight off Deneb. But it's not very big, and the counts will eat it up."

The diamond sun swept toward them, and then the growing sphere of its largest planet. Hull brought the ship down over the far-spread towers of Hathyr City, toward the vast hexagonal mass of the royal palace. They landed in the small port behind it.

It seemed very strange to Gordon to step out and breathe natural air again, and look at a sun without a filter window in between.

A party of officers awaited them. They bowed and escorted them toward the huge bulk of the palace. Others boarded the cruiser to take charge of Obd Doll and his crew.

The old kings of Fomalhaut coldly looked down once more at Gordon, and this time he felt like snarling up at them.

"I know my place now," he wanted to tell them. "So the hell with you!"

But Shorr Kan strode along with a approving smile on his dark face, as though he were a visiting royalty who found the palace small but rather nice.

Despite his despair, Gordon had cherished a little hope. He did not know he had until suddenly it died, and that was when they three came into a small room where Lianna and Korkhann waited for them.

She was as beautiful as ever and her face was cold and hard as marble when she looked at him.

He started to say something, but before he could speak Lianna had looked beyond him and her eyes went wide with shock.

"*Shorr Kan!*"

Shorr Kan bowed magnificently to her. "Highness,"

he said, "it gladdens me to see you agin. True, you and I have had a few small bothers and fusses, but that's all in the past, and I can say that it's forgotten now."

Lianna stared at him, absolutely stunned. Gordon felt an unwilling but tremendous admiration for Shorr Kan at that moment. Raise up the armadas of the League of the Dark Worlds, smite the Empire and its allies, bring about an armageddon of the whole galaxy, and then dismiss it all lightly as a few small bothers and fusses!

"I have to state," Gordon said, "that Shorr Kan . . . who, as you can see, did not die at Thallarna but escaped to the Marches . . . was the one who rescued us and enabled us to give warning of the counts' coming attack."

He added forcefully, "I have promised Shorr Kan, because we owe him our lives, that he is safe here."

She looked at him, quite without expression. Then she said tonelessly, "If that is so, you are welcome, Shorr Kan, as our guest."

"Ah, a return of hospitality," said Shorr Kan. "It was not so long ago that you were my guest at Thallarna, Highness."

This grandly-spoken reference to the time when Gordon and Lianna had been Shorr Kan's prisoners brought a cough from Hull Burrel, who sounded as though he were choking on suppressed laughter.

Lianna turned to him. "Captain Burrel, we have been in touch with Throon. Jhal Arn has told me that elements of the Empire fleet are already on their way here."

Hull shook his head. "I'm afraid that will do no good, Highness. The counts and Narath Teyn will know that they must strike at once."

All this time Korkhann had said nothing, peering at Gordon with those wise yellow eyes that seemed to pierce straight through to the brain. Now he stepped forward, feathers rustling as his wings swept up and the delicate clawed hands at their tips caught Gordon's arm.

"But the Magellanians?" he cried.

"The H'Harn?" said Gordon startled.

"Is that what they call themselves?" Korkhann had an intensity about him that Gordon have never seen before. "Listen, John Gordon. Before I left Throon, the emperor and his brother, Zarth Arn, let me read the old records of Brenn Bir's time, when the Magellanians came to this galaxy before. *They must not come again.* What I read . . ."

He stopped, his voice quavering out into silence. When he spoke again, it was in a low, carefully controlled tone.

"You know that I am a telepath. Not one of the strongest ones, but . . . I have felt a shadow over the galaxy . . . a shadow that deepens with each hour, dark, cold. . . ."

Gordon shook his head. "We met only two of the H'Harn. One we never even saw. Shorr Kan killed the other one, to free us . . . we were in deadly danger . . ." *And I hope that guarantees your neck, Shorr Kan,* he thought. "But apparently there are only a few of them in the galaxy."

"They will come," whispered Korkhann. "They will come."

Lianna spoke. "One thing at a time. Narath and his beasts, and the counts, are enough to deal with now. Korkhann, will you see that our guests are made comfortable . . ."

She emphasized the word "guests" but Shorr Kan never turned a hair. He made another courtly bow and said to her, "Thank you, Highness, for your welcome. I've always wanted to visit Fomalhaut, for I've been told it's one of the most beautiful of the minor star-kingdoms. Until later!"

And with that truly regal wipe in the eye, he turned and went out with Hull Burrel and Korkhann.

Gordon saw Lianna turn toward him. Her face was still stone-white and there was no expression at all now in her eyes.

She came closer to him and her small hand flashed and gave him a stinging slap across the mouth.

Then her face changed. It moved like that of a nasty little girl having a tantrum. She put her head on his shoulder, and she said,

"Don't you ever leave me again, John Gordon. If you do . . ."

He felt the wetness of tears against his cheek.

Incredulous, caught by wonder, Gordon held her. Not Zarth Arn, he thought. *John Gordon.*

That long trip back across the ages had been worth it, after all.

-XIX-

The street was familiar. Gordon knew every one of the brownstone fronts. He walked on the gritty pavement toward the office building where he spent his days. In the doorway he met Keogh, who laughed at him and said, "I told you it was all a dream, that rubbish about star-kings and beautiful princesses. All a dream, and now you've awakened, you're back in the real world. *The real world . . .*"

In a panic, Gordon said, "No, no, I won't come back." And then he cried out, "*Lianna!*"

The cry seemed to echo down endless corridors, but it had an effect. Everything slid and tilted and flowed away, leaving him confused and giddy in a tumultuous nowhere. He floundered wildly, like a drowning swimmer, and called Lianna's name again, and suddenly he was looking in bewilderment around an unfamiliar room.

Through an open window he could see the vast orb of the setting sun, and the sun was Fomalhaut, not Sol. It threw a shaft of brilliant light into the room, and by it he saw Lianna sitting silently in a chair, watching him.

He sat up on the couch where he had fallen asleep, brushing beads of perspiration from his forehead. The echoes of that nightmare were strong in him, and for a moment he could not speak.

"You dreamed you were in that other time?" she said.

He nodded.

"I thought so. I was watching your face. I'm glad it was my name you called." She added after a moment, "I've talked to Captain Burrel. I have some idea what you two went through I'm not surprised you have bad dreams."

They were still, Gordon thought, just a little awkward with each other. He was sure now that she loved him, but the trouble was that they didn't quite know each other well enough yet.

"When the H'Harn touch you," he said, "it seems to leave a kind of mental scar. Twice I've dreamed that the one who held us there in the ship had actually carried us away to the Lesser Magellanic, and each time . . ."

Suddenly Gordon stopped. His mind, just aroused from sleep had abruptly perceived for the first time something that he had never thought about before.

He jumped to his feet. "There's no sign of the fleet of the counts coming out of the Marches?"

She shook her head gravely. It was not for the sovereign to Fomalhaut Kingdom to show fear, but he saw the strain in her eyes.

"Not yet," she said. "But Abro thinks that if they are going to attack they'll come soon. He agrees with Captain Burrel that they would alter their time-table in order to strike before help can get here."

Gordon said, "I think I've overlooked something that may be tremendously important. I've got to see Hull and Shorr Kan."

The softness left Lianna's eyes and little stormy lightenings gathered in them.

"Shorr Kan," she said. "The man who nearly destroyed us all . . . and yet you speak of him as though he were a friend!"

Patiently Gordon said, "He is not a friend. He is an ambitious opportunist who thinks only of his own ends. But since his only opportunities now lie with us, he threw in with us. He's going to try to use us, and we are going to try to use him, and time will tell who uses whom."

Liana aswered nothing, but he saw the set of her small chin. He ignored it and asked, "Is there some place here where we can make some galactographic computations?"

"The royal chart room," she said. "It's linked directly with all the screens in the Defense Ministry."

"Will you take me there, Lianna? And will you have Hull and Shorr Kan brought there?"

The room was deep in the palace. It had screens on every wall, all of them dark now. An officer saluted Lianna when she entered with Gordon behind her.

Presently Hull Burrel and Shorr Kan came in, and the latter swept a deep bow to Lianna, wishing Her Highness a very good evening. She regarded him with lambent eyes and an arctic smile.

"Let me say at once, Shorr Kan," she told him, "that if I had my way you'd have been executed within five minutes after you landed here. I live in hope that you will yet do something to make that possible."

Shorr Kan grinned crookedly. He looked at Gordon, and said, "Women are realists, did you know that? If you hurt one or threaten to hurt one, she'll hate you forever. Only men can make a game of it."

"Will you for God's sake quit talking about games," said Gordon. "The counts are not playing a game. Narath Teyn is not playing a game, and for certain the H'Harn are not playing a game. Or if they are, it's a game that nearly crushed the galaxy back in Brenn Bir's day."

Shorr Kan shrugged. "I'll admit that, but there's no evidence that the H'Harn are here yet in any strength."

"Are you quite sure of that?" asked Gordon.

Shorr Kan's mocking air dropped from him like a cast-off garment. "What do you mean?"

Gordon turned to Hull Burrel, who was frowning in puzzlement. "Hull, you piloted that H'Harn ship."

"You don't have to remind me," said Hull irritably. "I remember well enough."

"All right. Now, can you remember whether or not, before we realized what was happening and began to fight the creature, you were flying at top acceleration?"

Hull frowned again. "I don't see what..."

"Were you?"

"I don't know, damn it. Everything I did was put into my mind by the H'Harn, and I..."

"Yes?"

"Well, just wait a minute. I'm trying to think . . . I did seem to know that I must move a certain lever to the farthest notch. I did that, and from the way the ship responded, of course it had to be the main thrust control." Hull's face cleared. He nodded, satisfied. "Yes, we were at top acceleration."

"And what would you guess that to be?"

Hull pondered a moment, then named a figure. The officer's mouth fell open, and Lianna said instantly, "But that isn't possible!"

"I'm sorry, Highness . . . it is. The H'Harn ships are faster than anything of ours." Hull shook his head regretfully. "I'd have given a lot to bring that ship back so we could study it. Because if we do ever have to fight them in space . . ."

Gordon turned to Lianna. "Can we see a detailed chart of the portion of the Marches that contains Aar?" In a belated remembrance of protocol, he added "Highness?"

She spoke to the officer, who went to a bank of witches. Presently a great screen broke into light and life, with the bewildering complexity of star, planet, and drift markers showing in their various colors.

Gordon shrugged. "It makes no sense to me, but you can tell me, Hull. How far did we go from Aar to that point where we became aware of the H'Harn presence, and changed course?"

"Oh, look, Gordon!" Hull said. "We've got enough troubles ahead of us without rehashing the ones we've left behind."

"Answer him," said Shorr Kan, and it was the hard, cold voice of the one-time master of the Dark Worlds who spoke. His face was grim with foreboding, and Gordon thought again that he had never met anyone with the lightning awareness and comprehension of this man. Shorr Kan had already guessed what he was driving at.

Hull sweated over the chart like a sulky schoolboy, grumbling. Finally he named a distance. "It's only a rough figure . . ." he began, but Gordon cut him off.

"Using that as an average, and with that approximate velocity, how long would it have taken us to reach the Lesser Magellanic?"

Hull looked a bit startled. "So that's it. Why didn't you tell me?" He went over to the computer and started punching keys. Presently he came back with the answer.

"Between four and five months," he said. "That's Galactic Standard, of course."

Gordon and Shorr Kan looked at each other, and Lianna said with regal impatience,

"Could we perhaps be told the object of this discussion?"

"Four or five months to reach the Magellanic, and as much again to return," said Gordon slowly. "Eight to ten months before the H'Harn fleet could reach this galaxy, utilizing the information they hoped to get from us . . . It's too long. We know the H'Harn are behind the counts in this move against Fomalhaut . . . they must have had a hand in timing it. Whatever their plans are for their own strike against the galaxy, I don't believe they would include that much of a delay. Especially . . ."

"Especially," said Shorr Kan bluntly, "when their logical time to strike would be at that exact moment when the galaxy is already engaged in a massive civil war." He looked around the circle of faces. "The H'Harn have gone to a deal of trouble to foment that war. I doubt if they plan to throw away the fruits thereof."

There was a dead silence. When Gordon spoke again, he could hear his worlds dropping into it as stones drop into a cold still lake.

"I don't think the H'Harn was taking us to the Magellanic at all. I think it was taking us to somewhere a whole lot nearer. I think it was taking us to the H'Harn fleet, lying close outside our galaxy."

The silence became even deeper, as though even breathing and heartbeat had been suspended. Then Hull said almost angrily, "How could they be out there without the radar-sweeps of the Empire's warning system detecting them? Don't you realize how thoroughly we have monitored outer space ever since the time of Brenn Bir?"

"Yes," said Gordon, "but . . ."

Shorr Kan finished for him. "You've met the H'Harn, you have some idea of their powers. And you know *they* must realize how thoroughly outer space is monitored. So the first prerequisite of any large-scale invasion plan would be some means of evading radar search."

Hull Burrel thought about that, and he began to get a haunted look.

"Yes, I see that. But . . . but if they can evade radar, then the H'Harn fleet could be out there off the galaxy right now, waiting . . ."

"Waiting for the counts of Marches to launch their attack," said Gordon.

"Good God," said Hull, and turned fiercely to the communications officer. "Call Throon. The Empire must be warned."

The officer looked at Lianna, who said quietly, "Do as he asks."

"Your pardon, Highness," said Hull, and the stark look

of horror on his face was apology enough. "But when I think of those . . ."

"Yes," said Lianna. "Remember, I have had experience of them myself." She waved Hull on, to where the communications officer was busy at one of the screens.

Presently it sprang to life, and an officer in Empire uniform spoke to Hull Burrel.

His name, rank, and reputation got him switched through to the palace in record time. The aquiline face of Zarth Arn, brother to the Emperor, looked out of the screen at them.

"Captain Burrel . . . Gordon . . . you're safe, then. We were concerned. . . ."

He broke off sharply, looking beyond Gordon, with eyes that had suddenly become points of fire. He was looking at Shorr Kan.

"What kind of a masquerade is this?"

"No masquerade," said Shorr Kan. "Happily for me, the reports of my death were sheer fraud." He met Zarth Arn's bitter glare with calm amusement. "The bad penny has turned up, only this time I'm on your side. Doesn't that please you?"

Zarth Arn appeared to be too stunned to speak for the moment. Gordon seized the opportunity to make a swift explanation.

"Our lives, and quite possibly the life of the whole galaxy, may be saved because Shorr Kan got us free to bring a warning," he said. "Try and remember that, Highness."

Zarth Arn's face was perfectly white, his mouth set like a vise. He closed his eyes and took a deep breath, mastering himself. Then he looked at Lianna and said,

"Highness, my advice is to hang that man at once."

"Ah, but you must hang Gordon first," said Shorr Kan smoothly. "He gave his word to protect me."

Hull stepped closer to the screen. "Highness, with all due respect, the hell with Shorr Kan and what happens to him! The H'Harn . . . the Magellanians . . . may be at the throat of the galaxy!"

Zarth Arn's anger faded into something else. "You learned something in the Marches?"

Hull told him. Gordon watched Zarth Arn's face, saw the shadow that came there grow and deepen, and when Hull was through it seemed to Gordon that Zarth Arn had aged ten years in those few moments.

"Theory," he said. "Only theory, and yet . . . The H'Harn. Strange that we never had a name for them before." He looked at Gordon. "This is your considered opinion?"

"Yes," said Gordon, and Shorr Kan spoke up unbidden.

"Mine too. And whatever else I may be, Zarth Arn, you know that I am neither a fool nor a coward. I believe that this strike against Fomalhaut is nothing less than the spearhead of an attack by the H'Harn on the whole galaxy."

After a moment Zarth Arn said, "This must go to my brother at once, for his decision. And since this is a chance we dare not take, I think there can be only one answer. The Empire fleet must go outside the galaxy and use every possible means, either to locate the H'Harn fleet or make absolutely certain that it is not there. And I must be with it. For if we do find the H'Harn . . ."

A coldness came into Gordon's spine. "You'll take the Disruptor?" Gordon remembered how he himself had once unloosed the awful power of that weapon. He remembered how space had quaked, and how stars had trembled in their orbits; how the whole fabric of the universe had seemed to twist and tear.

Zarth Arn said, "I must." He turned his somber gaze to Lianna. "You know, of course, what this will mean to you?"

She nodded calmly. "You will need every ship to sweep the Rim . . . including those you were sending here. I understand that. But surely the H'Harn are the ultimate enemy. We'll fight our battle here alone." She even smiled. "It's no matter. Captain Burrel assures me your ships could not get here in any case until after our fate has been thoroughly settled."

The screen blanked out. They were turning to leave, Lianna silent and preoccupied, when another screen came to life. In it was a burly-browed, thickset man with scarred hands, whom Gordon had met before. Abro, Defense Minister of Fomalhaut.

Abro wasted no time on protocol. "Highness, they've come out of the Marches. The counts' fleet. They're more than twice as strong as we expected . . . and they're coming full speed toward Fomalhaut!"

-XX-

Gordon felt a chilling dismay. The counts of the Marches were throwing everything they had into this. And whether their gamble succeeded or not, in the dark background brooded the unguessable purpose and menace of the H'Harn.

"They outnumber our fleet by three to two, in heavies," Abro was saying. "Commander Engl has planned to draw back, to cover Fomalhaut and give time for the Empire squadron to arrive."

Lianna said calmly, "The plan is good. But tell him not to count on any assistance from Throon. There will be no squadron."

Abro looked stunned. "But Highness, I myself was present when . . ."

"I will not discuss this on a communicator," said Lianna. "I am summoning the council. Get to the chamber as quickly as you can, Abro."

The screen went dark. Lianna turned, her face icy and composed. But her eyes were tormented, and Gordon wanted to put his arm around her shoulders. He did not. He doubted that she wanted any of that kind of encouragement in public.

She smiled a little wanly at him and said, "I must go, John Gordon. Later."

When she had gone, Hull Burrel strode to the screens and activated those which showed the Marches and that whole region of space, studying them feverishly.

Shorr Kan shrugged. "It doesn't look good, Gordon. Other star-kingdoms will hold back when they hear that Throon isn't sending help. I'm worried."

"Nice of you to be concerned," said Gordon acidly. "About us, I mean."

Shorr Kan looked blank. "About you? Hell, I'm worried about myself! When I helped you and took that dispatch cruiser away from Obd Doll, I committed myself. No explanation will ever convince Cyn Cryver that I didn't betray him. If he wins out and gets his hands on me . . ."

He drew his fingers expressively across his throat.

Gordon admitted that this did seem to be one box that Shorr Kan couldn't talk his way out of.

"Damn right," said Shorr Kan, and added thoughtfully, "The transports will follow the counts' fleet, with Narath's army. They're the real danger. If the Fomalhaut commander—what's his name, Engl?—If Engl has sense enough to keep some of his heavies out of the battle, they can be used to hit the transports and cut them up as they try to land."

Gordon thought that made good sense, and said so. Shorr Kan grunted. "You try to propose it, Gordon. They'd never take any suggestion from me, even if it was a good one, and even though I know more strategy than any of them . . . as I once proved. They might take it from you."

"I doubt it," Gordon said. "But I'll try."

Hours later that night, when he had sat for a long time in an antechamber of the council room, the council broke up. When Lianna came out at the head of the worried-looking knot of men, she saw him and came to him.

"There was no need for you to wait all this time," she said, but he thought she was glad that he had.

"I just wanted to know what's happening. That is, if you can tell me."

Abro frowned all across his hard face, but Lianna ignored him. "You brought the warning, and you have the right to know. The main fleet of the Empire has already left Throon, on its way out of the galaxy. With it goes every possible sensory device that might enable them to locate a H'Harn fleet, including the Empire's finest telepaths."

Gordon did not think too hopefully of the chances of tracking the H'Harn by telepathy. The H'Harn were super telepaths, able to shield their minds from any probing.

Lianna continued, "We've appealed for help from the smaller star-kingdoms, but they're too far from here, most of them, to come in time. We did get a reply from the barons of Hercules . . . they're considering the matter."

Abro said brusquely, "Not for love of us. The great barons are afraid the counts of the Marches are getting too big. If they help us it will be for that reason only. And they're liable to be too late in any case."

Gordon said hesitantly, "A possibility occurred to me, but it seems out of place for me to suggest anything."

Lianna did not seem happy about it, but she said steadily, "You risked your life to help us, you have the right to speak."

Gordon outlined Shorr Kan's strategic idea of holding back a part of the fleet to hit the transports when they came.

To his surprise, Abro, who disliked him intensely, nodded thoughtful approval. "An excellent move . . . *if* we can manage to hold back any forces when we meet the counts. I'll pass it on to Engl."

When the others had gone, Lianna looked at Gordon with a faint smile.

"That was Shorr Kan's suggestion, wasn't it?"

Hours later, he sat with her on a terrace high on the vast wall of the palace. Soft darkness was about them, and the heavy scent of flowers. But there was no quiet in the great city that lay below them in the night.

The city flared with lights. Armed bodies of men were moving with swift precision, to and fro. Missile batteries were being set up in the palace grounds. In the distance, where the spaceport lay, huge, tubby space-monitors were rising up growling into the darkness to take their places in the network of defenses around the throne-world of Fomalhaut.

Gordon looked up at the starry sky. Out there two great star-fleets were drawing fatefully together, and what happened when they met would probably seal the fate of this whole star-kingdom, and possibly many more besides. There had been no further word from Hercules, and if the barons were moving to help, they were keeping it secret from everyone.

His mind reached farther out, beyond the edge of the galaxy, where the mighty Empire fleet would be searching for the H'Harn force that might or might not be hidden there. If they could find it, the Disruptor would unloose its cosmic power again and the threat from Magellan would disappear. But would they find it? Gordon felt a deep hopelessness, an almost prophetic certainty that they would not. The H'Harn would not have returned without the strongest kind of armor, offensive and defensive.

They would not have forgotten how they faced the Disruptor before.

It seemed that Lianna too was thinking of the H'Harn. She had been silent for a long time, but when she spoke it was about them.

"If Narath does invade, will he have any of those creatures with him?"

"I feel sure he will have."

"How can you be so sure?"

Heavily, Gordon explained, "The H'Harn know that I once operated the Disruptor . . . that time when my mind was in Zarth Arn's body. They think I could tell them all about it. I can't, of course. I only operated the thing by mechanically following Jhal Arn's instructions. But they think I can, so they want me."

He felt Lianna shiver, and he knew that she was remembering the stunning mental assault of the H'Harn who had nearly destroyed them at Teyn.

Gordon said somberly, "A great deal of everything that has happened in the galaxy seems to stem back to that one freakish fact—that I happened to exchange minds with Zarth Arn, one of the three men who knew the secret of the Disruptor. That was why the League of the Dark Worlds kidnapped me, and when that failed, got me . . . and you, too . . . to Thallarna."

He went on, looking out into the clamorous city. "That one fatal thing was what led the League to attack the Empire . . . they knew by then that I wasn't really Zarth Arn, and thought I couldn't use the Disruptor. And now the deadliest enemies of all—the H'Harn—they think I can tell them what they want to know about the only weapon that bars them from the galaxy. They won't stop at anything to get their hands on me."

He shook his head. "Through that one fatal coincidence, I've been a curse to this whole future time . . . as Shorr Kan said, the grain of the sand in the machine."

"No," said Lianna. She took his hands. "And even if that were so, the fault is not yours, but Zarth Arn's." She was silent a moment. Then she said softly, "I'm glad you came here, John Gordon. Very glad."

After a while she drew away from him and said, "I must go down and show myself to the defenders of my world. No, don't come with me. I have to do this alone."

After she had gone, Gordon sat for a long time looking past the moving lights and the uproar and clamorous confusions of the great city, toward the starry sky. A star-kingdom might fall, Narath might realize his ambition and sit on the throne of Fomalhaut, and he, John Gordon, and Lianna might be sent to their deaths. And that would be a world tragedy as well as a personal one.

But if the H'Harn succeeded, that would be tragedy for the whole galaxy, a catastrophe of cosmic dimensions. Thousands of years before the H'Harn had come from the outer void, bent on conquest, and only the power of the Disruptor, unloosed by Brenn Bir, had driven them back. Out there in the Magellanic Cloud they had brooded all this time, never giving up their purpose, filtering back gradually in secret, plotting with the counts, plotting wih Narath Teyn, making ready some tremendous stroke.

Doomsday had come again, after these thousands of years.

-XXI-

The starships were fighting, out between the great suns of Austrinus and the Marches of Outer Space. Two fleets of heavy cruisers, flashed side by side, and their missile broadsides seemed to light up that whole part of the galaxy with their bursting flares. On the outskirts of this mighty running battle, khostly jackals on the heels of the tigers, the phantom cruisers hung, emerging from the invisibility of dark-out to loosen their swift volleys and then retreating into invisibility again.

In the screen which Gordon watched, down in the Defense Room of the royal palace of Fomalhaut, the whole flashing struggle seemed almost incomprehensible, reduced as it was to a swarming of electronic fireflies—fluid, swirling, ever shifting. But after a time it became evident that the heavier column of the counts' fleet was pressing hard against the ships of Fomalhaut, pressing them slowly to the west and away from the star and planet they had tried to cover.

Abro's face was glistening with sweat and he muttered oaths and entreaties as he watched.

"Engl's a good man but he just doesn't have enough weight," he groaned. "Three to two . . . and their ratio is increasing. They're pushing our fleet away from Fomalhaut to make clear passage for *those!*"

And his thick finger stabbed toward the upper right-hand corner of the screen, where a new swarm of radar-dots had made its appearance and was crawling steadily down toward Fomalhaut.

The transports. And somewhere in them would be Narath Teyn, his mad and beautiful face alight with the coming triumph, and with him would be the non-human hordes that he had gathered from scores of worlds.

It gave Gordon a feeling of agonized impotence to be forced to wait here and watch the attack come toward them. But if Lianna felt that too, and had no doubt that she did, she permitted no trace of it to show in her white face.

"Still no word from the barons?" she asked, and Korkhann answered, "No," and moved his wings with a sighing sound. "No word from them, and no sign of them, Highness. It seems we must meet this attack alone."

Abro said bitterly, "If Engl had only been able to detach enough heavy cruisers, we might have had a chance to turn them back. But I don't think we can prevent a landing now."

Gordon thought that Shorr Kan had had the right strategy, and it was a pity that Engl either could not or would not follow it.

"That is out of our hands now," said Lianna, gesturing toward the tremendous battle on the screen. "We must be ready to defend our world. Come."

She spoke like a queen and she walked like one as she led the way up through the palace. Along the way, Shorr Kan stepped in beside Gordon. He had not attempted to enter the Defense Room during this crisis, knowing that he would not be allowed. Hull Burrel glared at him and went on, but Gordon paused.

"It's clear enough in all your faces," said Shorr Kan. "The Fomalhaut fleet is losing out there, isn't it?"

"It is," said Gordon, "and it's being pushed westward,

and presently this place will be absolute hell when Narath's transports land."

Shorr Kan nodded gloomily. "No doubt of that. Too bad. I've been cracking my brain trying to think of a way to get myself out of this trap. . . ."

Gordon said in mock amazement. "Why, I thought that since we're all at the end of the string, you would prefer to die nobly, fighting to the last."

Shorr Kan shrugged and said, "I've about decided I might as well die like a hero. Because to tell you the truth, I can't see a single bloody way out of this one. So what have I got to lose?"

The hours whirled by, and Gordon felt caught in a web of activities of which he knew nothing. Officials and officers streamed in and out of the palace. Lianna had no time to give him. There was nowhere to go and nothing for him to do. He had become a totally useless supernumerary.

"But I think," said a familiar voice behind him, "that you are the key person here, John Gordon."

Gordon turned and saw Korkhann regarding him with a troubled look.

"Lianna told me what you had said to her. Are you *sure* there is no information about the Disruptor which the H'Harn could extract from you?"

"Look," said Gordon, "I thought I made it clear. I know what the Disruptor force-cones look like, and how they're mounted on a ship, and how you balance six needles before you release the force, and that is *all* I know. Why do you bring this up now?"

"Because," said Korkhann bleakly, "much as I like you, it might be my duty to destroy you if you were about to be taken by the H'Harn."

Gordon was silent. Then he said, "I can see that. But there is nothing."

And he thought, *Damn the thing; will it follow me right to my death?*

"Come with me," said Korkhann. "There is nothing for you to do here, and you might as well know how we stand."

Night had fallen, and the two came out of the palace to see the flying moons race up the sky, casting their shifting glow. The palace grounds, like the city beyond, were a hive of activity. Men and vehicles moved along the great avenue where the ancient kings of Fomalhaut loomed on their pedestals. Missile batteries were evil, hulking shapes in the gracious gardens.

Shorr Kan came up to them and asked, "Where's Hull?"

"On the telestereo talking to Throon. You certainly put the fear of God into him with your notion of a H'Harn fleet ready to pounce."

Gordon said, "The fear of God is in all of us when we think of that."

"Not in this man," said Korkhann, who had been looking curiously at Shorr Kan. "Not really. He fears neither God nor man nor devil."

He added, "Your pardon for probing you just a little."

Shorr Kan waved that aside. He said to Gordon, "With my considerable military abilities . . . you'll admit that I did damn near conquer the galaxy . . . I thought my services would be welcomed in this fight. But Abro wouldn't listen to me, so I'll stick with you. You can rely on me to stand back of you in the pinch."

"I would much rather," Gordon said carefully, "that you stood anywhere else than in back of me. I'm allergic to knives."

Shorr Kan grinned. "You will have your little joke. You're the one I rely on to keep my neck out of a noose, so don't you think . . ."

Whrroosh-boom! The rushing booming sound cut sharply across the night, blotting out Shorr Kan's voice. It multiplied itself with incedible swiftness, and things visible only as streaks of light raced skyward from three different points beyond the city.

"Missiles," said Shorr Kan coolly, as soon as he could make himself heard. "If the invaders are within range, things are going to get warm in a hurry."

Now the missiles began to go out from other points, in rapid and continuous volleys. The streaks of light criss-crossed all up the heavens. Above the turmoil the moons climbed higher and higher, stately and unconcerned.

From the whole of the city came a cry. Korkhann pointed with his winged arm. High up but sweeping downward in a long slanting curve, a glowing object came.

It was, or had been, a starship. Now all its vast bulk was breaking from a red-hot glow into actual flames. It shot down toward Hathyr like a plunging comet.

With a tremendous crash, the flaming star-wreck hit the planet far beyond the city. There was a shock-wave and a blast of searing wind that knocked them staggering.

"That was close enough," said Shorr Kan. "I wish the boys would be a little more careful where they drop their birds."

"There," said Gordon. "How's that?"

Much more distant, a second comet came flaming down out of the moonlit heavens. The impact was barely noticeable. Shorr Kan nodded.

"Much better. And hope they keep them that way. A direct hit in the city . . ."

He did not finish. There was no need to. Gordon had been thinking the same thing.

Now all at once there was a new sound, a crying of voices from the city. Gordon said in alarm.

"What's that?"

"Listen," said Korkhann. "They are cheering."

The sound came nearer. Presently they could see a

great crowd surging toward them down the Avenue of the Kings, where the proud and time-stained statues seemed almost to have sprung to life, as the stroboscopic flashing of the missiles gave them a semblance of movement. In the midst of the crowd, in an open hover-car, Lianna moved slowly toward the palace. The people ran alongside, cheering her, and she raised her hand and nodded to them as calmly as though this were any ordinary peaceful procession.

In the past Gordon had resented her royal status and the protocol that surrounded her. Now he saw the other side of that, and his heart swelled with pride as she came up the steps, very erect and graceful, and turned and waved to the shouting crowd. Live or die, she seemed to be saying, you and I will go together, for we are Fomalhaut.

She left them, motioning to Gordon to follow her inside.

The missile salvos had now become unceasing, and the whole palace trembled with their vibrations. Gordon and Korkhann followed Lianna down to the Defense Room. This time Shorr Kan trailed coolly at their heels. and Gordon noted that the guards outside the room did not think to challenge him. In this hour when Fomalhaut Kingdom rocked on the brink of disaster, things were slipping a little.

Abro came through the knot of excited, sweating officers clustered by the screens. He spoke quickly to Lianna.

"No doubt about it now, Highness. The barons' fleet is headed in this direction at full speed."

Gordon felt a wave of sudden hope. The mighty Hercules barons were a match for almost any star-kingdom.

Abro must have seen a similar hope in Lianna's face, for he said grimly, "I regret to add, Highness, that their course is not toward Hathry, but toward Austrinus

Shoals, where what is left of Engl's force is still fighting the counts."

With a sinking heart, Gordon realized that from a detached point of view that was the wise, indeed the only, course. Veterans of many a campaign, the barons were not going to rush to the rescue while a hostile fleet remained in space and able to catch them flat.

"I also have reports," Abro continued, "of at least twenty-four separate landings of Narath's transports in this quadrant of Hathyr. We destroyed many of the ships but we couldn't handle them all, and now they are coming in increasing numbers, while our missile installations are being put out of action."

"We will defend the city," Lianna said. "We can hold them until the barons are free to help us."

Gordon hoped she was right. He thought that if she was not, he had come a long way to die.

Looking into her eyes, he thought that if it came to that, it was worth it.

-XXII-

A Walpurgis Night of horror held Hathyr City, as one after another of its lines of defense went down.

For a night and a day and part of another night, the starship transports had continued to land on Hathyr. A great many of them landed as fusing, flaming wrecks. But as the advance forces spread and knocked out more and more of the missile batteries, increasing numbers came down intact, and out of these poured the seemingly endless hordes.

From a hundred wild worlds in the Marches of Outer Space they came, the not-men who followed with fanatical devotion the crimson banner of Narath Teyn. The Gerrn from Teyn itself, the giant four-footed cats with their centaurlike, quite human upper bodies, their slit-pupilled eyes aglow, springing with swift joy toward the battle. The Qhallas, a rushing winged tide of alienness, their raucous battle-cries rising in squawking fury. The Torr from far across the Marches, furred, towering, four-armed. The Andaxi, like great dogs trying to be men, teeth and eyes gleaming as they came toward the kill. And others, innumerable and indescribable others —hopping, gliding, vaulting—a phantasmagoria of nightmare shapes.

They had good modern weapons, supplied by the counts. Atom-pellets exploded like a bursting wave of white fire ahead of them, burning through the streets of Hathyr City. The guns of the men of Fomalhaut answered them. Inhuman shapes were scythed down, cindered, swept away, heaped up in tattered mounds to choke the crossings. But there were always more of them, and they always pressed forward. In the battle-fury many of them threw away their weapons and reverted to the simple, satisfying use of claw and fang. They came from all sides, a ring, a noose closing slowly around the heart of the city. And in the end there were just too many of them.

Fires burned red in scores of places across the city, as though a funeral pyre for the kingdom of Fomalhaut had been lit here and was majestically, slowly growing. The stately moons looked down upon a city illuminated by the flames of its own progressive destruction, and the pressing hordes became a macabre silhouette against the fire-glow.

Gordon stood with Lianna and Korkhann and Shorr Kan on the great balcony high in the palace that looked straight down the avenue of the stone kings. The fires and the fury and the clamor of battle were creeping closer to the palace area. Against the fires they could see the hover-cars of the Fomalhaut soldiery swooping down in desperate, continuous attacks.

"Too many of them," murmured Lianna. "Narath has worked for years to win the loyalty of the non-humans, and now we see the fruit of his labors."

"How *can* a human man like Narath influence them so greatly?" Gordon gestured toward the smoke-filled, tortured streets. "They're dying, God only knows how many thousands of them, but they never even pause. They seemed to be glad to die for Narath. Why?"

"I can answer that," Korkhann. "Narath is truly human in body only. I have probed the edges of his mind, and I tell you that is an atavism, a mental throw-back to a time before the evolutionary paths diverged. Before, in short, there was any difference between human and nonhuman. That is why the beastlings love and understand him . . . because he thinks and feels as one of them, as no normal human ever can."

Gordon stared out at the panorama of destruction. "Atavism," he said. "Then we can blame all this on one infinitesimal gene?"

"Do me one favor?" said Shorr Kan sourly. "Please. Spare me the philosophical lectures."

An officer, young and a little wild-eyed, hurried onto the balcony and made a hasty salute to Lianna.

"Highness, Minister Abro begs you to leave by hover-car before the fighting comes any closer."

Lianna shook her head. "Thank the minister, and inform him that I will not leave here while men are fighting and dying for me."

Gordon started to expostulate. Then he saw her face and knew that it would be useless. He held his tongue.

Shorr Kan had no such inhibitions. "When the fighting ends you may not be able to leave. Best to go now, Highness."

Lianna said coldly, "That is the advice I would expect from the leader who ran away from Thallarna when the battle went against him."

Shorr Kan shrugged. "I'm still alive." He added, in a rueful tone, "Though that may not be for long." He had a weapon belted to his waist, as Gordon had, and he glanced down at it distastefully and said, "The closer I get to this business of dying heroically, the more dismal a prospect it seems."

Lianna ignored him, her brilliant eyes searching across the smoke and flame and uproar of the city. Gordon knew how she must feel, looking down that mighty avenue on which stood the statues of her ancestors, the embodied history of this star-kingdom, and seeing her people struggle against the tide of inhuman invasion.

She turned abruptly to Korkhann. "Tell Abro to send a message to the Barons. Say that if they do not send warships to our assistance at once, Fomalhaut may be lost."

The winged one bowed and left quickly. As Lianna turned back toward the city, a big hover-car with the insignia of Fomalhaut swept down through the drifting smoke and landed smoothly on the great balcony. The hatch doors opened.

"No!" exclaimed Lianna angrily. "I will *not* leave here! Send them away. . . ."

"Look out!" yelled Shorr Kan. "Those aren't your men!"

Gordon saw that the men who came pouring out of the open hatch wore, not the insignia of Fomalhaut but the rearing symbol of the Mace. They ran across the balcony toward the little group.

They had not drawn their weapons, apparently counting on sheer physical numbers to overwhelm the three. But Shorr Kan, dropping into a sort of gunman's crouch, drew and fired, cutting down the front rank of the attackers with exploding atom-pellets.

Gordon pulled out his own weapon, cursing the unfamiliarity of the thing as he tried to thumb off the safety. It went off in his hand. He saw that he had fired high and he triggered again more carefully and saw the pellets explode among the men of the Mace.

Those who survived kept right on coming. They were still not shooting, and it dawned on Gordon that Lianna was their target and they wanted to take no chance of killing her.

They came fast, reinforced by more men from the hover-car. They spread out in a ragged half-moon that closed rapidly into a circle, and they were so close now that neither Gordon nor Shorr Kan dared to shoot because the back-flare of the pellets would engulf them and Lianna also. Gordon shortened his grip on the weapon and used it as a club, flinging himself at the men and laying about him furiously, shouting all the while to Lianna to run back into the palace. He heard Shorr Kan roaring, "Guards! Guards!" But Shorr Kan was smothered under a press of bodies, roughed and battered, wrestled to the ground, and Gordon found himself going the same way; there were too many hands, too many boots and bony knees. He could not see whether Lianna had made her escape, but he did see that from the great hall inside the balcony a file of Lianna's guards were running desperately toward them.

The men who remained in the hover-car had no compunction at all about shooting the guards, since that did not endanger Lianna. They shot them with stunning efficiency, using heavy-calibre mounted guns that swiveled and poured crashing fire, powdering the men to nothing with spouting dust and powered glass. It got quiet again, and then the whole scene spun slowly around Gordon and flowed away into darkness, accompanied by the ringing of his skull as something struck it, hammer-like.

He woke, lying on the balcony. His head no longer rang, but simply ached. Nearby he saw Shorr Kan standing. His face was bloody. The men wearing the Mace stood around them, grim and tense.

"Lianna!" muttered Gordon, and tried to sit up.

Shorr Kan jerked his head toward the inner hall, beyond the tumbled bodies of the guards. "There. Not hurt. But the palace is theirs. That car was only the first of a fleet tricked out with the sign of Fomalhaut." One of the men struck Shorr Kan across the face, bringing more blood. Shorr Kan forebore to wince, but he stopped talking. Gordon became aware now, as his senses cleared, of a vague, inarticulate roaring, like the beating of the sea upon rocky cliffs. Then, as he was jerked to his feet, he looked out over the low rail of the balcony and saw the source of the sound.

The city had fallen. Fires still rose redly from many

points, but there was no more firing, no more sounds of battle. The whole area around the palace seemed filled with the nonhuman hordes . . . the Gerrn, the Qhallas, the Andaxi, all the grotesque, nightmarish mobs, capering in triumph smashing the gardens, howling, roaring, gesticulating.

But the loudest roar came from a solid, tremendous mass of creatures making its way down the Avenue of the Kings. They voiced their frantic joy in hissing, purring, squawking voices. And they looked ever at one human man who rode ahead of them upon the black-furred back of a giant Gerrn—Narath Teyn, with his handsome head held high as he rode to claim his kingship.

-XXIII-

The big hall, the one that opened onto the balcony, was quiet. Gordon stood, with guards behind him, and Shorr Kan stood beside him. The men who wore the Mace stood also, their weapons prominently displayed.

But Narath sat, as befitted a king.

He sat very straight, and there was a dreaming smile on his face. His brown hair fell to his shoulders, and he wore a glittering, close-fitting garment. He looked royal, and he looked mad.

Lianna sat a little distance from him. There was no expression at all on her face, except when she looked at Gordon.

"Soon," said Narath gently. "We will not have to wait much longer, cousin, for the Count Cyn Cryver and the others."

And Gordon knew who "the others" would be, and the skin crawled between his shoulders.

From the open doors that gave onto the great balcony, threads of acrid smoke drifted into the room. There came also from outside a distant, confused sound of voices, but not the roaring clamor of before. The bodies had been cleared away, both Lianna's men and Narath's. And now Gordon heard the soft hum of a hover-car descending.

Then Cyn Cryver came.

His bold, arrogant face blazed with triumph as he looked at them. He looked longest at Shorr Kan.

"It's well," he said. "I was afraid they might have killed you. And we don't want you to die too soon."

Shorr Kan made a derisive sound. "Do you have to be so damned theatrical? That was the most boring thing about my stay with you, listening all the time to your meaty, crashing statements."

Cyn Cryver's smile became deadly, but he did not answer. Narath had risen to his feet and was speaking in his gentle voice.

"You are welcome, my brother of the Marches. Very welcome. And where are our friends?"

"They are here," said Cyn Cryver. "They are coming." He looked at Lianna and his smile deepened. "You're looking well, Highness. Remarkably well, considering that your world is in our fist and your fleet is being hammered to pieces in the Shoals."

He did not, Gordon thought, seem to know yet about the Hercules barons. Not that the barons' coming would make any difference to them now. . . .

Three shapes, robed and cowled, glided silently into the hall. The H'Harn had come.

It was curious, the different reactions to them, Gordon thought. Shorr Kan looked at them with frank open disgust. Lianna paled a little, and Gordon was pretty sure he himself did the same. Even Cyn Cryver seemed a trifle ill at ease.

But Narath Teyn bent toward the cowled figures with the same dreaming smile, and said, "You come in good time, brothers. I am to be crowned."

It was only then Gordon realized the depth of alienation in Narath's mind. He, whom the not-men worshipped, who greeted the Magellanians as brothers, was less human than anyone here.

The foremost of the H'Harn spoke in a sibilant whisper. "Not yet, Narath. There is something first to be done, and it is most urgent."

The H'Harn came, with its curiously limber, bobbing

gait, to stand before Gordon. And it looked up at him from the darkness of its cowl.

"This man," it said, "possesses knowledge that we must have, at once."

"But my people are waiting," said Narath. "They must hear my cousin Lianna cede the throne to me, so that they can acclaim me king." He smiled at Lianna. "You will do that, cousin, of course. All must be right and fitting."

Cyn Cryver shook his head. "No, Narath, this must wait a little. V'ril is right. The H'Harn have helped us greatly, isn't that so? Now we must help them."

A bit sulkily, Narath sat down again. The H'Harn called V'ril continued to look up at Gordon, but Gordon could see nothing of the face that was hidden by the cowl and did not much want to see it. All he wanted was to be able to run away. With an effort he restrained himself from an hysterical attempt to do so.

"A while ago," said the H'Harn, "I went secretly to Throon in the ship of Jon Ollen, one of our allies. While I was there I probed the mind of one named Korkhann."

That was no news to Gordon, but it made him think of Korkhann for the first time since recovering consciousness. What had become of him? Dead? Probably . . . and probably Hull Burrel also, for they were not here.

"I learned," said the whispering voice, "that this man called John Gordon had in the past undergone a transfer of minds with Zarth Arn, so that for a time he dwelt in Zarth Arn's body. And during that time he operated the Disruptor."

Here it came again, Gordon thought. The damned Disruptor and the secret of it that everyone thought he knew . . . the curse that had dogged him all through both his visits to this future time, and was now about to drag him to his death.

Or worse. The H'Harn moved closer to him, a swaying of gray cloth.

"I will now," it whispered, "probe this man for the secret of the Disruptor. Be silent, everyone."

Gordon, in the clutch of ultimate terror, still tried to turn his head and give Lianna a look of reassurance, to tell her that he could not give away something he did not possess. He never finished the movement.

A bolt of mental force hit him. Compared to the mental attack of the H'Harn in the ship, this was a thunderbolt compared to an electric spark. Gordon passed into the darkness between heartbeats.

When he recovered, he was lying on the floor. Looking up dazedly, he saw Lianna's horrified face. Narath, sitting near her, looked merely bored and impatient. But Cyn Cryver and the H'Harn called V'ril seemed to be arguing.

The voice of the H'Harn had risen to a high, whistling pitch. Never before in his brief contacts with the creatures had Gordon seen one display so intense a passion.

"But," Cyn Cryver was saying, "it may be that he just doesn't know any more."

"He *must* know more!" raged V'ril. "He must, or he could not have operated the mightiest weapon in the universe. And I will tell you what I did learn from his mind. The main fleet of the Empire is outside the galaxy, searching for our fleet. Prince Zarth Arn is with them . . . and the Disruptor."

That seemed to stagger Cyn Cryver a little. Presently he said, "But you told me they could never locate your fleet . . ."

"They cannot," said the H'Harn. "But now they are forewarned, and when we attack Throon and the key worlds, then they will know where we are! And they may use the Disruptor, even though in doing so they sacrifice some of their people. So now it is more important than ever that we know the range and working principles of that weapon before we move!"

Narath stood up and said firmly, "I have had enough of this. Settle this matter later. My people are waiting out there to acclaim me king . . ."

V'ril's cowled head turned toward Narath. Narath went gray, and suddenly sat down and was silent.

"An expert telepath could have hidden the key knowledge deep in this man's mind," said V'ril, looking at Gordon. "So deeply, so subtly, that he would not be consciously aware of it even though he used the knowledge . . . so deeply that even a powerful mental probe would not reveal it. But there is one way to search it out."

Gordon, not understanding, saw that for the first time, when they heard this, the other two H'Harn moved and wavered and tittered a little, as though in sudden mirth. Somehow that mirthfulness chilled him with a horror deeper than anything before.

"The Fusion," whispered V'ril. "The merging of two minds, so that nothing in either mind can be hidden from the other when they are twinned. No mental trickery can hide a secret from that."

The creature hissed a command to the guards, "Force him to his knees."

The men grabbed Gordon's arms from behind and forced him down. From their quick breathing, Gordon thought that even though they were men of the Mace and allies of the H'Harn, they did not like this.

The robed creature now stood with his head a little higher than Gordon's.

Then V'ril began to unwind his robes, and they came away, and also there came away the cowl which was part of them, and the H'Harn stood naked.

Glistening, moist-looking, like a small skinned man with gray-green flesh, and a boneless fluidity in the arms and legs. The damp gristly flesh seemed to writhe and flow of its own accord. And the face . . .

Gordon wanted to shut his eyes but could not. The head was small and spheroid and the face was blank and most horrible in its blankness. A tiny mouth, nauseatingly pretty, two holes for breathing, and big eyes that were filmed over, dull, obscurely opalescent.

The blank face came toward Gordon, bending slightly. It was as though the H'Harn bent to kiss him, and that completed the horrifying abnormality of the moment. Gordon struggled, strained, but was held firmly. He heard Lianna cry out.

The eyes were close to his, the cool forehead touched his forehead.

Then the eyes that had become his whole visible universe seemed to change, the dull opalescence in them deepened into a glow. Brighter and brighter became the glow until it was as though he looked into a fiery nebula.

Gordon felt himself falling through.

-XXIV-

He was John Gordon of old Earth.

He was also V'ril of Amamabarane.

He remembered all the details of Gordon's life, on Earth and then in this future universe.

But he also remembered every detail of his life as one of the people of Amamabarane, the great hive of stars which the humans called the Lesser Magellanic.

Utterly bewildering, was this double set of memories, to the part of him that was Gordon. But the part of him that was V'ril was accustomed to it.

The memories came easily. Memories of his native world deep in the star-cloud Amamabarane. The cherished planet where the mighty and all-conquering H'Harn had first evolved.

But they had not always been mighty. There had been a time when the H'Harn had been only one of many species, and by no means the cleverest or the strongest. There were other races which had used them contemptuously, had called them stupid, and weak.

But where are those races now? Gone, dead, wiped out by the little H'Harn . . . a great and satisfactory vengeance.

For the H'Harn had found that deep in their minds they had the seed of a power. A power of telepathic force, of mental compulsion. They had not understood it and they had used it at first in petty ways, to influence others stronger and quicker than themselves, to protect themselves from predators.

But in time, they realized that the power could achieve much more if they could strengthen it. There began a secret, earnest attempt to bring about that goal. Those of them who had more of the power were allowed to mate only with those of a similar grade. Time went by, and their power grew and grew, but they kept it secret from others.

Until they were sure.

And then a great day came. A day when the despised H'Harn revealed their mastery of mental compulsion, using it on those they hated. Breaking them, mastering them, driving them mad, hurting and hurting them until they died.

The triumph of the H'Harn, the golden legend of our race! How good it was to see them writhe and scream die!

Not all of them. Some were spared to be the servants of the H'Harn. And among these were the clever ones who had built cities and starships.

They were used now, these clever ones and their starships, to take the H'Harn to other worlds. And so began the glorious saga of H'Harn conquest, that did not stop until all the desirable worlds of Amamabarane were under the H'Harn yoke.

But there were still other worlds, far off, in the great galaxy which was like a continent of stars, to which Amamabarane was merely an off-shore island. There were countless worlds there, where countless peoples lived who did not serve the H'Harn. This was intolerable to contemplate, so vast had become the H'Harn appetite for power. So the preparations for conquest were begun.

The subject peoples of Amamabarane were forced by the H'Harn to labor until they died, preparing an armada of ships. And after a time, that armada departed, to bring many H'Harn to the galaxy which was to be taught to accept its masters.

But then . . . the one great catastrophe, the dark and ugly scar that marred the glory of H'Harn history. The peoples of that galaxy, with incredible impudence, resisted the H'Harn. And with a weapon that disrupted the space-time continuum itself, they annihilated the H'Harn armada.

That had been long ago, but no H'Harn had ever forgotten it. The wickedness of men who dared to resist the H'Harn, who dared even to *destroy* them, must be punished. The black scar of defeat must be healed with their blood.

Through thousands on thousands of years, the subjects and servants of the H'Harn, in all Amamabarane, were driven to toil on this project. Their cleverest minds were set to devise new weapons, new ships of a swiftness hitherto unknown. But the project lagged. The servant peoples often preferred to die rather than to serve the H'Harn longer. They did not realize that they were mere tools which the masters used, and that it mattered not at all if the tool were broken.

But when thousands of years had passed, the time time came when the H'Harn were ready again. Its mighty fleet of invasion had weapons and speeds and devices hitherto undreamed-of, including a shield of cunning force that hid the ships, and which no detection device could penetrate. Secret, unseen, the fleet approached the galaxy.

And secretly, unsuspected, it waited now outside the galaxy, beyond the end of what the humans called the Vela Spur. For the moment had not yet come.

Agents had gone ahead from Amamabarane, to foment war and trouble in the galaxy. War would bring the main forces of the Empire and the star-kings far from their capitals.

And when that happened, the H'Harn would strike.

Secret, unseen, unsuspected, their ships would land upon the greatest worlds of the star kings, upon Throon where the Disruptor was still kept against a day of adversity. Taken unaware and more or less defenseless, the people of Throon would fall an easy prey, and the Disruptor would be in the hands of the H'Harn. The Emperor could hardly use it in his own defense, since it would mean the destruction of Throon itself, with its sister planets and its sun.

Only now the picture had changed. This contemptible human had given a warning, and the Disruptor was in space, once more a threat of destruction to the H'Harn. It was vital to know the range and nature of the Disruptor's force, so that means could be found to neutralize or combat it.

But . . .

But . . .

Astonishment and anger and a sudden ripping apart of the mental fusion, and John Gordon, again quite alone within himself, looked dazedly into the raging eyes of the H'Harn.

"It is true," hissed V'ril. "This man used the Disruptor without knowing anything of its nature. It is incredible. . . ."

Into Gordon's whirling mind came a remembrance of a time when Shorr Kan had said contemptuously that the H'Harn, for all their powers, were stupid.

He knew now, from sharing the mind of a H'Harn, that it was true. The race that sought to conquer galaxies was a low, stupid, detestable species which in the ordinary course of events would have come to nothing. But the possession of one key power, the telepathic power of mental probing, mental compulsion, had given these creatures dominance over races far superior to them.

Gordon had always feared the H'Harn. He began now to hate them with a bitter hatred. They were leechlike, unclean, intolerable. He knew now why long ago Brenn Bir of the Empire had taken the chance of riving space itself to destroy these creatures.

As his mind cleared, Gordon found that the guards had pulled him back to his feet. V'ril had put on the robe and cowl again and Gordon thanked God for that. He did not want to see that ghastly body. He felt defiled to the soul by the sharing of that creature's mind and memories.

V'ril raised a shrouded arm and pointed at Gordon. "This man must die at once," he said. "Because of the Fusion, he now knows where our fleet is hidden. Kill him!"

Cyn Cryver nodded and the guards stepped back and raised their weapons. Still hardly able to take it in, Gordon flashed at last a look at Lianna.

Lianna had sprung to her feet. "No!" she exclaimed. She swung around to Narath. "If this man is killed, I will not cede the throne to you, Narath Teyn!"

Cyn Cryver laughed harshly. "A lot of difference that will make! Narath will be king in any case."

But the dreaming smile left Narath's face and it became troubled. He raised a hand to the guards who were aiming their weapons at Gordon, and said, "Wait!" He spoke then to Cyn Cryver. "My cousin *must* formally cede the throne to me, before the people, or all will not be lawful. I must have this submission from her. I have waited so long for it. I must!"

His handsome face was quivering now, and storm clouds gathered in his eyes. Cyn Cryver looked at him narrowly, and then said to V'ril, "The ceremony is important to our brother Narath. We had better let the man live."

Looking at Cyn Cryver's flinty expression as he stared fixedly at V'ril, Gordon was absolutely sure that he was adding, in thought, "*Until the ceremony is over. Then we'll kill him at once.*"

For V'ril made no objection. He whispered, "Very well. But there are messages that must be sent to our brothers in the fleet."

V'ril looked toward the other two H'Harn. Gordon thought he could guess what the message would be. "*Warn the fleet that the Empire armada is searching for them! Tell them to strike now at Throon!*" The two H'Harn bobbed and glided away out of the hall.

Narath took Lianna by the hand, in as courtly a fashion as though he were leading her to a ball.

"Come, cousin. My people are waiting."

Lianna's face was stony, expressionless. She walked with Narath, out onto the great balcony.

The others followed, the four guards keeping their weapons trained upon Gordon and Shorr Kan. But when they were out on the balcony, Narath turned and spoke with sharp annoyance.

"Not beside me, Cyn Cryver . . . this is *my* triumph. Stay back."

A crooked smile crossed Cyn Cryver's face but he nodded. He and V'ril and the guardsmen remained at the back of the balcony.

Shorr Kan made as though to join them but Cyn Cryver shook his head. "Oh, no," he said. "Keep your distance, so that we can shoot you down without danger to ourselves."

Shorr Kann shrugged and fell back. And now Narath had led Lianna to the front of the balcony, and the white sun of Fomalhaut blazed down on his glittering figure. He raised his hand.

A tremendous roar went up. From where he stood at the back of the balcony, Gordon could see that the palace grounds were crammed with the grotesque hordes of the not-men, a heaving sea of them that lapped against the walls and swirled up onto the columns of the stone kings, where leather-winged creatures perched and screamed. Mingled with them were the lesser number of humans who wore the uniforms of the counts of the Marches.

He wondered what Lianna was thinking as she looked out on that roaring crowd. None of her own people were there; the people of Hathyr city were dispersed, hiding or slain. And the human and inhuman conquerors shouted and cheered, and the old kings of Fomalhaut looked down with calm faces upon the end of all that they had wrought.

Again Narath raised his hand, and the roaring acclaim swelled up in a greater cry than before. He had reached the summit of his life, and the not-men whose fanatical devotion he had won were hailing him, and his whole bearing expressed his joy and his pride, and his great love for these his people.

The wave of sound died down, and Narath said, "Now, cousin."

Lianna, her figure rigidly erect, spoke in a clear, cold voice that Gordon could hardly recognize.

"I, Lianna, Princess Regent of Fomalhaut, do now cede my sovereignty, and recognize and affirm that sovereignty to have passed from me to . . ."

The thin whistling of small missiles interrupted her, and then Gordon saw Cyn Cryver and his guardsmen reel and fall as tiny atomic pellets drove into their bodies and flared there, blackening flesh and garments.

Gordon swung around. In the otherwise empty hall behind the balcony stood Hull Burrel and Korkhann, and they held the weapons that had just been fired, cutting down all but the H'Harn. V'ril, warned by some telepathic flash at the last moment, had darted aside in time to escape.

Narath turned around angrily. "What. . . ?"

Korkhann fired, his yellowbird-eyes clear and merciless. The tiny missile went deep into Narath's side.

Narath swayed, but did not fall. It seemed that he

refused to fall, refused to admit death and defeat. He turned with a strangely regal movement to face the crowd below . . . a crowd unable to see what was happening above them. He tried to raise his arm, and then fell forward across the balcony rail and hung there. A silence began to spread across the gardens and down the Avenue of Kings.

Hull Burrel cried abruptly, "*No!*"

Korkhann, his eyes now glazed and strange, was swinging his weapon around to point at the Antarian.

Gordon saw V'ril, and knew instantly what was happening. He rushed forward over the smoking bodies of the Mace-men. He grasped the robed H'Harn in his arms . . . and he ran forward and hurled it out over the rail, swiftly, before it could think to stop him. In the brief seconds of its fall, mental force, not directed this time, merely projected as an instinctive reflex. It was cut short with shocking finality, and Gordon smiled. The H'Harn, it seemed, feared most dreadfully to die.

Korkhann lowered his weapon, unfired.

Down below the silence had become complete, as though every throat held breath, and the crowd stared up at the glittering figure of Narath Teyn doubled over the low rail, his bright hair streaming, his arms outspread as though he reached down to them in an appeal for help.

In that frozen moment, Shorr Kan acted with a lightning swiftness that Gordon was never to forget.

Shorr Kan rushed to the front of the balcony. He threw his arms skyward in a wild gesture, and he shouted to that stunned crowd in the lingua-franca of the not-men of the Marches.

"The counts have killed Narath Heyn! *Vengeance!*"

Gerrn and Andaxi and Qhalla, all the nameless others, the inhuman faces, looked up toward him. And then it sank in.

Narath was dead. Narath of Teyn, he whom they worshipped, whose banner they had followed, had been slain. A heart-stopping cry of rage and sorrow went up fom them the comming led cry of all those thousands of inhuman throats, growling, hissing, screeching.

"Vengeance for Narath! Kill the counts!"

The crowd exploded into violence. The not-men fell, with fang and talon, beak and claw, upon the men of the Marches who a moment before had stood beside them as allies.

The cry of sorrow and of vengeance went out from the palace, spreading until it seemed that from the whole city of Hathyr there came a great inhuman baying.

Hull Burrel had run forward, while Korkhann still stood a little dazed by the H'Harn assault that had almost made him kill his comrade.

"This way," cried Hull. "Quickly! They'll be up here in minutes. Korkhann knew all the secret passages in the palace and that's how we saved ourselves when the palace fell. Hurry!"

Gordon took Lianna by the hand and ran with her. Shorr Kan delayed long enough to pick up weapons from the dead guards, one of which he tossed to Gordon. He was chuckling.

"That set them going, didn't it? They're not too bright, those nonhumans . . . begging your pardon, Korkhann . . . and they reacted beautifully."

A seemingly solid section of the wall at the side of the great hall had been swung open, revealing a passageway. They crowded through and Shorr Kan slammed shut the panel behind them.

Lianna was sobbing, but Gordon paid no attention to her. He cried to Korkhann.

"Can you take us to a communications center. I must send a message. . . ."

Korkhann, unused to violence, seemed still a little dazed. "A message to the . . . the barons . . ?"

"A message to Zarth Arn and the Empire fleet!" snapped Gordon. "I know where the H'Harn armada is, and I must get that word through!"

-XXV-

Korkhann led them down by narrow, twisting ways buried within the walls of the palace, illuminated dimly by an occasional bulb. He brought them at last through another concealed door, into a long corridor.

"The palace Communications Center," said Korkhann. "The fourth door ahead."

There was no one in the hallway, and they went down it rapidly, Gordon and Shorr Kan in the lead. And now, even through the massive partitions of the palace, they could hear a growing uproar above them.

"The horde is inside the palace," said Korkhann. "They will be killing all the counts' men . . ."

"And us too, if they find us," said Hull Burrel.

They flung open the fourth door. Beyond it was the large room filled with the instruments of galactic communication. They went in very fast. A man who wore the uniform of the Mace sat at the bank of controls, which he touched with a curious uncertainty. Behind him stood two robed H'Harn, the ones V'ril had sent with the message for the H'Harn fleet. The man froze with his hands in mid air. The H'Harn turned swiftly, and died with the motion uncompleted.

Gordon aimed his weapon at the frightened operator. "Did you send that message for the H'Harn?"

The man's face was greasy with sweat. He looked down at the small gray crumpled mounds and shivered. "I was trying to. But they use different frequencies . . . modulations . . . all different from ours, and that takes time. They told me they'd take me over and hurt my mind if I didn't hurry, but I couldn't. . . ."

The stupid H'Harn running true to form, thought Gordon. Use all other peoples simply as tools, and break them if they do not instantly perform.

He turned to Hull Burrel. "You were in touch with Zarth Arn's fleet until the attack came. Reach them now."

Hull threw the operator out of the chair and began punching buttons and turning vernier controls.

The uproar in the palace above them was penetrating more loudly to this level. Shorr Kan closed the door of the Communications Center and locked it.

"They'll get down here eventually," he said. "But it may hold them for a while."

Gordon watched the door, sweating, until Hull established contact with the fleet. Telestereo was not possible at such distances, but Gordon could hear the voices of the fleet communications officers as they acknowledged and cut through channels to the top, and presently the voice of Zarth Arn was speaking to him.

"Just beyond the end of the Vela Spur," said Gordon. "That's where the H'Harn fleet is lying. They've got some new form of radar-concealment." He went on to give every scrap his memory recalled, from the time his mind was twinned with V'ril's. "I don't know," he finished, "if even this will help you to pin them down, but at least it's something."

"I'll tell you, Gordon," said Zarth Arn, "we'll give it a damned good try!"

The contact was instantly broken.

So that was done. Everything was done that they could do. They looked at each other, not saying anything, and Gordon went over and took Lianna in his arms.

The uproar in the palace was louder and closer. They could hear doors being smashed in. There were screeching and yowling and barking voices, the flap of wings and the clatter of running hooves, always coming closer.

"It looks to me," said Shorr Kan, "as though we're getting near to all this heroic dying you've been dwelling on in such a morbid fashion." He shrugged. "Oh, well. At least Cyn Cryver got his. I could have forgiven the man his rascalities, but oh God, what a bore he was!"

Suddenly a new sound penetrated the palace. It was less a sound than a deep bass vibration, growing rapidly stronger, shaking the whole fabric of the great building, then passing overhead and away.

Shorr Kan's eyes flashed. "That was a heavy battle-cruiser! Now I wonder. . . ."

A second mighty ship went over the palace, shaking it till it trembled, and then a third.

Then, upon the telestereo plate, there appeared the image of a man . . . an elderly man, hard-faced and cold-eyed, wearing on his cloak the flaring emblem of the Hercules Cluster.

"The Baron Zu Rizal speaking," he began, and then saw Lianna and said, "Highness, I rejoice that you are safe!"

Shorr Kan had instantly turned his back to the telestereo, an action that did not surprise Gordon in the least.

"We smashed the counts' fleet in the Austrinus Shoals," Zu Rizal was saying, "and we are now over Hathyr with our ful lforces and what is left of the Fomalhaut Navy. Your city is obviously occupied by Narath's hordes . . . shall we blast them?"

"No, wait," said Lianna. "Narath Teyn and Cyn Cryver are dead, and I think . . ."

Korkhann stepped forward and spoke to her in a low voice. She nodded, and then spoke again to Zu Rizal.

"With Narath dead, I think the horde will return to

its own worlds, if they know that destruction is their alternative. Korkhann has said that he will offer them the terms."

"Very well," said Zu Rizal. "We will cruise on stand-by until further word from you."

The image disappeared, and only then did Shorr Kan turn around again.

A sudden silence had fallen on the palace. The great warships were still thundering by overhead, but the screech and yowl and crying of the horde had faded away. It seemed that the coming of the ships had sent them scurrying outside, as though they felt that the palace had become a possible trap. They wanted running room.

"I think," said Korkhann, "that they will listen to me, because I am not human either." He pointed to the communicator panel. "Get word to the officers of the counts' transports, to be ready to receive these peoples and take them back to the Marches."

He started away and then stopped for a moment and said, "One more thing, Highness. I regret to say that Abro was killed in the attack on the palace."

Gordon felt a sense of loss. Abro had disliked him thoroughly, but he had respected the man even so.

Hull Burrel remained with his ear to the instrument on whose wave-length he had communcated with the faraway Empire fleet. His face was gray and lined with strain.

"Nothing yet," he said. "There may be nothing for a long time."

If ever, thought Gordon. The H'Harn were powerful. If they should strike first, from their refuge of invisibility, and destroy the ship that carried Zarth Arn and the Disruptor . . .

He forced himself not to think of that.

The hours went by, and the great ships thundered

past above, and Gordon and Lianna and Hull Burrel waited. At one point, Gordon realized that Shorr Kan had quietly disappeared.

Long later, Gordon would learn the story of what happened beyond the rim of the galaxy. Of the Empire fleet, with Zarth Arn's flagship in its van, racing toward the Vela Spur. And of how Zarth Arn had unloosed the terrible force of the Disruptor, time after time, bracketing with cold precision an area of space where there was nothing to be seen, until the continuum itself was bent and twisted and torn and all the stars along the rim quaked in their orbits, and the force that had concealed the H'Harn fleet was shattered. And still the Disruptor struck its vast invisible bolt, now aimed unerringly at the fleeing ships, until the H'Harn fleet had vanished forever from the universe.

All Gordon knew now was that these were the longest hours of his life, until the shaken voice of Zarth Arn came through.

"It's done. The H'Harn are smashed, and what's left of them are in flight, back to the Lesser Magellanic."

For a moment, none of them could speak. Then Gordon, remembering the foulness of the life he had briefly fused with, muttered a heartfelt, "Thank God!"

"They will not come again." Zarth Arn's voice, thready with distance, held an iron resolve. "We shall gather a force from all the star-kingdoms, to go after them and smash them on every world where they rule."

He added, "Gordon?"

"Yes?"

"I know now what you meant when you told me how using the Disruptor shook you. I've known about the thing all my life, but I never *used* it till now. I hope I never have to again."

When the contact was broken, they looked at each other, too exhausted to drained of emotion to feel much of anything. The relief, the joy, the triumph . . .

all that would come later. In the meantime, it was enough to be alive and know that hope lived too.

Lianna led the way out of the room, up the ways of the palace, all empty now.

They came out onto the great balcony and in their faces was the diamond flare of Fomalhaut, setting toward the horizon. Across the ravaged city its brilliant rays struck down into the streets, and everywhere the hordes were moving out, out across the plain to where the transports waited.

Down the great Avenue of the Kings, away from the palace, went a little troop of the Gerrn, not running now but walking slowly. They went apart from the others, as a guard of honor, and across the back of their giant leader lay the body of a man in glittering garments. Narath of Teyn was going home.

Down from the sky rolled the massive thunder, as the barons continued their grim patrol. And, as she looked out over the scarred city with the forlorn smokes still rising from it, Lianna's fingers tightened on Gordon's.

"It will live again," she said. "The people will come back, and you and I will help them to rebuild. And . . . it's a small price to pay for the defeat of the H'Harn."

There was a discreet cough behind them. They turned and found Shorr Kan standing there, ignoring Hull Burrel's frown.

"Highness, I'm glad that all came well," said Shorr Kan blandly. "You will admit that I was of some help."

"I'll admit that your quick thinking about Narath's death saved us, yes," said Lianna, as though the words were wrenched from unwilling lips.

"Good. Now I have a small favor to ask." Shorr Kan came closer, speaking in a confidential voice. "It's the damned barons I'm thinking about. They're a tough lot, not like you and Gordon. No sense of humor at all. If they catch me, they'll hang me in a minute."

He added, "And there's Jhal Arn to think about as well.

He must still believe that I was concerned in the assassination of his father, although I wasn't . . . that was all Corbulo's idea, and stupid as Corbulo's ideas always were. But I shouldn't care to fall into his hands, either."

Lianna looked at him coldly. "I quite see your point. Now what is this favor?"

"Well," said Shorr Kan, "you'll remember that I overpowered Obd Doll and the rest of the crew of that little cruiser and we brought them here? Yes. Obd Doll and his men are down in the palace dungeons . . . luckily for them, since the Horde couldn't get to them. The cruiser is still in the royal spaceport, and I have ascertained that it's undamaged."

"Go on."

"I've been talking to Obd Doll and his men. They're pretty disgusted at the mess Cyn Cryver led them into with his plotting. They'd like to go back home and start their world going again under new leadership . . . sane, conservative leadership."

"In other words," said Gordon ironically, "Shorr Kan's leadership."

He nodded. "It does so happen, that not only do they not hold it against me that I captured them, but they think I'd be just the man to bring things to order on their world. They think they can convince their people."

"Go on," said Lianna.

"The favor I ask, Highness, is simply that you let me take Obd Doll and his men with me in that cruiser, and send word to the barons . . . without mentioning me, of course . . . to let the ship through."

"So that you can start new trouble in the Marches?" cried Lianna. "You . . !"

"Please, Highness!" said Shorr Kan, looking pained. "I'm all through with that now, an older and wiser man. All I want is a little planet where I can live at peace, nothing more."

"Oh, Lord!" said Gordon. "You ought to put that to music."

"I think," said Lianna, "that you will raise a racket in times to come, all through the Marches, and I will live to regret this day. But I am a queen, and a debt is a debt. Take your people and go."

Shorr Kan gallantly kissed her hand. He shook Gordon's, and turned away. He stopped when he saw Hull Burrel glaring at him. He went up to the Antarian and took him by the hand.

"It's hard to part this way, old friend," he said. "We've been through a lot together, and I know how you must feel to see me go."

Hull's coppery face flushed scarlet and he began to make inarticulate growling noises. But Shorr Kan wrung his unwilling hand and said,

"Don't try to express your sorrow at my leaving, Hull. No tears, old friend, no weakness! Farewell."

He went away with a jaunty stride, heels clicking on the marble floor. Gordon, turning to Lianna, was amazed to see a half-smile on her face.

"At last I see what it is in that devil that attracts you," she said. "One hardly ever meets a man who is perfect at anything . . . but Shorr Kan is the perfect rogue."

In a short while, a small dispatch cruiser went skyward from the royal spaceport, and they watched it streak away across the flaring heavens.

And the white sun went down.